$\mathcal{V}$OICES OF THE $\mathcal{S}$OUTH

# BAND OF ANGELS

# ROBERT

# PENN

# WARREN

# BAND

# OF

# ANGELS

LOUISIANA STATE UNIVERSITY PRESS
BATON ROUGE

Published by Louisiana State University Press
Copyright © 1955, 1983 by Robert Penn Warren
Originally published by Random House
LSU Press edition published 1994 by arrangement with the Estate of
   Robert Penn Warren
All rights reserved
Manufactured in the United States of America
ISBN-13: 978-0-8071-1946-4 (pbk. : alk. paper)


Library of Congress Catalog Card No. 55-5814

The paper in this book meets the guidelines for permanence and durability of
the Committee on Production Guidelines for Book Longevity of the Council
on Library Resources. ∞

*To Eleanor*

# BAND OF ANGELS

*When shall I be dead and rid*
*Of the wrong my father did?*

A. E. HOUSMAN

# I

OH, WHO AM I? FOR SO LONG THAT WAS, YOU MIGHT SAY, THE CRY of my heart. There were times when I would say to myself my own name—my name is Amantha Starr—over and over again, trying, somehow, to make myself come true. But then, even the name might fade away in the air, in the bigness of the world. The world is big, and you feel lost in it, as though the bigness recedes forever, in all directions, like a desert of sand, and distance flees glimmering from you in all directions. Or the world is big, and the bigness grows tall and close, like walls coming together with a great weight and you will be crushed to nothingness. Nothingness—there are two kinds, the kind which is being only yourself, lonely as the distance withdraws forever, and the kind when the walls of the world come together to crush you.

*If I could only be free,* I used to think, free from the lonely nothingness of being only yourself when the world flees away, and free from the closing walls that would crush you to nothingness.

And then, sometimes, there would come into my head the picture of a grassy place, a place with sun, maybe water running and sparkling, or just still and bright, and myself sitting there. I can never describe this place too clearly, even to myself, the way you can't describe a dream. When you try to tell somebody about a dream, you find in the telling that you are simply having another dream, and different, and even the feeling of the old one changes.

But the feeling I have in this dream—if you can call it a dream—is of being light and free, a feeling of suddenly lifting up my arms as though I were discovering myself, waking up, saying: *Why, I'm Amantha Starr!*

But there was, in sober fact, a grassy place, no dream, with cedars in the background, a line of willows to one side dipping into the branch that runs down to join the river, and to the other side, the grave, just a sunken, trenchlike spot, not awfully long, in the soft Kentucky grass that the sheep have cropped down as neat as can be. At the head of the grave there is a little stone, and on the stone folded wings carved, and the word *Renie*, and the dates *1820-1844.*

I am a child, and I am playing there, playing house with dolls and dishes. It is a pleasant place to play, with the sound of water, with sunlight and dappling shade, and a joree is flitting in the dusk of cedars and saying his name, over and over, in a most sweetly melancholy iteration.

The grave is the grave of my mother.

Sometimes this real spot and the spot of my imagination, of my dream of freedom and delight, seem to become the same spot. But how can that be, when the place in my dream is a place of beginnings and the place in my true recollection has a grave, the mark of endings? When the dream place is a place of freedom, the real place a place of immobility and constriction? Why, then, do the two images, with such poignant excitement, sometimes merge in my heart?

I see myself, a child, rise from play and go and lie down, very carefully and neatly, in the grassy trench, on my back, looking up at the sky beyond the cedar boughs. Then I feel that I am being held by arms reaching over in love and tenderness. I cannot remember the face of my mother.

It would seem from this episode—of true or false memory, I cannot say—that I, a motherless child, was unloved. That is not true. I was well loved, and greatly indulged. Spoiled, I should think, is the word. Aunt Sukie, who was my black mammy, spoiled me because she loved me, for women like Aunt Sukie can live only by loving some small creature that they, in the accepted and sad irony of their lot and nature, know will soon grow up and withdraw, indifferent or contemptuous, even in affection. And my father, he indulged me, too.

My father's name was Aaron Pendleton Starr. His father, Rodney Pendleton Starr, had come to Kentucky in the 1790's, bringing with him the marks of his rank and privilege, the silver and china, the linen and damask, the portraits in peeling gold frames. I do not wish to make these items of household plunder sound too grand. The silver teapot was dented, the linen was thriftily mended, and since not every ancestral likeness had been limned by the brush of a maestro, dignity, despite scarlet coat, and foamy lace at stalwart throat, sometimes seemed merely bovine, and beauty, despite the sheen of silk and the glitter of diamond, sometimes seemed merely a simper. I have seen far grander things since, in Louisiana, where ostentation indulged a pitch that old Virginia people, like my father, might have considered vulgar—as people are accustomed to regard anything as vulgar that overreaches their own attempts at self-justification. But when I was a child, it all seemed grand enough to my limited perspective.

The house which old Rodney Starr had built in the country south of Lexington, near Danville, was of brick, two stories, a chimney at each end of the main bulk, with an *L.* running back, and there was a portico with pillars, not very high or imposing. There were, however, some fine trees about the place, for trees grow well in that part of Kentucky, and these had been left from the time before the white men came over the mountains. I sometimes see in my mind's eye those towering masses of green that characterized *Starrwood* —beech and white oak and maple and tulip tree rising in sun-gilded steeps and terraces of boughs and shade-dark grottos giving into the inwardness of the tree. The upper leaves move in some cool visitation of air, not enough to be named a breeze but enough to refresh your cheek, and the shade lies blue-dark on the cropped grass under the trees. Then coming back to the reality of things, I remember that the house may have been burned long since, burned by carelessness, violence of soldiery, or stroke of lightning, and the trees may be fire-blasted or have bowed to axe or age.

From the happy time before I was nine and left *Starrwood*, I remember things only in starts and patches, for from childhood you remember things only in portentous disconnection, each in a kind of mystic isolation.

I remember my dolls. I remember Jessie, a beautiful doll with a china head and real hair glued on so delicately it seemed to grow, with big blue eyes, and with a most elaborate dress, all bows and in-

sertions and sashes. I cannot say that I loved Jessie. I knew her too
fleetingly, and you love a doll only if it gets banged and bruised in
daily intercourse with you and your infantile ineptitudes.

I was in the attic one spring day with Aunt Sukie, who was there
to put away some winter things. She looked up from rummaging in
a chest, and said: "Look-ee—look heah, Chile!" And she was holding
up the doll. It was, as I have said, very splendid, too splendid, I
have since decided, to have ever been part of the life of a little girl,
my life or that of any other little girl.

"Ain't doin nobody no good layin up heah," Aunt Sukie was saying, and she gave me the doll. I remember the reverence with which
I inspected the perfections. Then I cradled it in my arms and jog-
gled it a little from side to side, but I was all but overcome by a
sense of my own unworthiness. I felt that, somehow, it would fly to
pieces, or evaporate instantly, from my crude reality. Aunt Sukie
had scolded me often enough for my carelessness or blundering energy—"ought a-bin a mule-colt, you—come bustin crost my clean
kitchen lak you do"—and now I felt that all my sins would descend
upon me at once.

But Jessie did not fly in pieces, or evaporate, and when Aunt
Sukie went downstairs, I followed, still holding intact the miraculous
creation. Reverence was beginning to admit an intermixture of curiosity. By the time we had got back to the kitchen, I asked her what
the doll's name was.

"Call hit Jessie, call hit Jansie," she said. "Call it whap-doodle fer
all of me."

I said I would call it Jessie. Then I asked whose doll it was.

"Yore'n," she said, "yore'n now, and nobody keer."

I asked whose doll it used to be.

"Miss Eye-leen," she said, clattering pots, or making some other
constructive racket, as was her custom when I embarked on one of
my interrogations, when, as she put it, I had done got bad bit by the
pester-bug.

I asked who Miss Eileen was.

"Her," Aunt Sukie said, in a tone that admitted exactly nothing,
that seemed to rob that Miss Eileen of whatever existence she had
once had, for Aunt Sukie could bleach out the world, could disinte-
grate it, with a tone.

Who was "her"?

"Her," Aunt Sukie repeated. Then she made a grudging restoration of the reality of *her*. "Her," she said, "Miss Eye-leen, dat lady yore pappy long back married and brung home."

Was this her doll she used to play with?

"Bet she never played wid no doll. Bet she jes kep hit to be a-keepin."

Did she keep it for her little girl?

"Gal—little gal"—Aunt Sukie shrugged with a heaving contemptuousness that flowed down from the shoulders to undulate the ample expanse of her bosom—"what she do wid a little gal? Warn't the kind of woman kin git one. Did'n have no juice."

Where was she now?

"Whar she?" Aunt Sukie echoed. Then answered: "Whar she doan keer if hit rain ner shine, sleet ner snow, and the cawn crop doan make."

Where was that?

"Down in the graveyard. Under de ground. She daid."

That evening after my supper—when the days got long, if I behaved myself, my father let me sup with him—I showed the doll to my father. He admired it with, at first, no recognition, and then, as recognition came, I was already embarked on telling him how I knew all about Miss Eileen, how Aunt Sukie bet she never played with a doll, how she had no little girl because she had no juice, how she was dead and didn't care, nor rain nor shine, and was down in the graveyard, under the ground.

Suddenly, though not ungently, he set me off his knee. Once on his feet, he stood there with an air of bewilderment, as though he had forgotten his intention, as though he had risen only from some obscure inner surge of discomfort.

My father was a man of middle height, or some over, a trifle burly. He had dark hair, with a trace of gray beginning, and his face, though lined a little, was fresh and well complected, of a reddish cast, from full blood and weather. Despite his prosperity and station, he affected, as did the old Virginians, and many old-fashioned Kentuckians of that stock, somewhat shabby clothes worn with a telling negligence. That is the figure I see standing before me, a man in strong life, wearing an old dark coat, his faintly grizzled hair unkempt, his ruddy face disturbed as he looks down, first at the little girl before him, then at the elegant doll grasped in his big hand. I see his hand, red and strong-veined, with crisp black hairs sprouting from the flesh, and I feel the old fear of that instant that such a hand would crush the doll, would close unwittingly on it, and that would be the end.

Then he inclined slightly toward me, and demanded: "Who told you?"

Aunt Sukie, I said, and launched into an elaboration of my knowledge, how he had married her and brought her here, and how she was dead. Did she die because she didn't have any juice, and couldn't get a little girl?

He seemed not to hear.

What made my own mother die? I asked. She must have had juice, because she got a little girl, she got me, and therefore, I asked, why did she die?

With a heaviness of effort, as though he forced himself to listen to me at all, my father said: "She just died. Of a fever."

I pondered that. Then I said: "Why isn't she buried down in the graveyard? With Miss Eileen, and those other folks?"

For a moment I was sure he hadn't heard me, even though he was looking directly at me with a disturbing intentness. Then he twitched his head, like a man trying to avoid the annoyance of a gnat, and said, very quietly: "I wanted your mother up closer to the house. Where she'd be closer to me. And to you."

After a pause, still somewhat infected by his gravity and intentness, for he kept staring at me, I asked: "My mother—did she have a doll?"

"I reckon so," he said.

"Was it like this?" And I pointed to Jessie in his fist, concerned, in the practicality and egotism of infancy, to locate another doll if such lay hidden about the house, doing nobody any good.

"No," he said abruptly, "it wouldn't be like that."

I made a move to take Jessie from him, but, as though with an unconscious motion, he lifted it beyond my reach. "It's time for you to go to bed," he said. "Tell Marthy to put you to bed."

I reached for the doll.

"Didn't you hear me?" he demanded.

It wasn't the words that suddenly froze me. He often used those very words to me, with a kind of mock ferocity, when I teased him by disobedience. He would say those words, scowling awesomely, and I would flee with delicious terror, and he would chase me, growling and muttering, down dark halls, into plunder rooms and bedrooms and dining room and parlor, behind couches and doors, making prodigious blunders of calculation, as he tiptoed about, snorting savagely, ignoring me as I shivered behind a curtain with my hands pressed over my mouth to stifle the sound of my breathing—but always finding me in the end, seizing me, throwing me high in the air, my small, white, bare heels kicking and my nightdress swirling. For this game usually came after Marthy had made me ready for bed, and I crept down for a last good night, the pursuit, the last terror and squealing ecstasy.

But now the terror—terror is too strong a word, the shock—was real. He meant what he said. But I had courage, barely, to reach once more for the doll.

"Get to bed," he burst out, and as I retreated rapidly toward the door, he added, apologetically, in something like his old voice, "Take Bu-Bula to bed with you."

"No!" I cried, as loud as I could, and rushed out of the room, and up the stairs, my heart flooded with confusion and anger. I could hear my father moving back toward the kitchen. Then I heard him calling Aunt Sukie.

That was the last time I ever saw the doll Jessie. I never knew what my father did with it, and over the many years I often wondered. I never had the courage to ask him.

Later on, the next time my father went to Lexington, he brought me another doll—I already had a half-dozen or so—this time a doll of such gorgeousness that even Jessie would have seemed drab in comparison. I called her Melinda, a name my father and I decided upon only after councils and conferences of the utmost gravity. But, somehow, I could never love Melinda with a whole heart. Something had poisoned the springs of my affection. I remember that when my father was by, I often pretended to more concern for Melinda than I really felt, all this to be nice and grateful to him. But I also remember that once or twice, from some obscure impulse, I studiedly ignored Melinda in his presence, or pushed her aside with some gesture shaded with contempt or disprisement.

In any case, it was Bu-Bula I truly loved. Even that night when, at my father's suggestion that I take Bu-Bula instead of Jessie, I had screamed denial, I had, in the end, gone to sleep with Bu-Bula in my arms. Marthy had put me to bed; she had given me Bu-Bula, whom I promptly flung to the floor; she had, after some perfunctory gestures of comfort, left me alone with my tears. When I had cried myself out, long after the last restless robins had quieted down and the spring twilight was extinguished, I picked up Bu-Bula from the floor, and went to sleep. But before I went to sleep, I thought of my mother, and wondered what she had been like. She had had juice. She had had a little girl. The little girl was me.

Bu-Bula and twilight and myself in bed—all that stirs another recollection. It is, again, a spring or summer twilight—the same year, the next year, the year before, I do not know. I have been put to bed and Marthy has promised to get Bu-Bula, forgotten down at my play-spot near the cedars, and bring her to me. I am lying in my bed, waiting, watching the twilight fade, noticing idly the faint shimmer of heat lightning in the dusk beyond my window, and how the shimmer is reflected on the wall of my room like moiré silk. Then I hear the thunder, not loud, and I see the leaves beyond my window suddenly lift and stir, and I know that it is coming up a rain. I know that Marthy has forgotten Bu-Bula. Bu-Bula lies off yonder in the grass, in the dark soon, and it will rain on poor Bu-Bula.

By the time I have run downstairs and out into the yard, it is almost dark. The wind is strong now. It whips my nightdress, and all the upper branches of *Starrwood* are moaning. When the lightning comes now, I can see, astonishingly, the shapes of the heaving, piled-up masses of black cloud, and catch a bright, flickering impression of the infinite arcades of sky beyond, before they collapse in sudden darkness. But the thunder is not near yet, and no rain. I remember, however, how cold the grass felt to my bare feet as I ran down toward the cedars.

It was dark when I got there. And I couldn't find Bu-Bula, not anywhere, not anywhere in the dark, and I began to call her name, over and over, and my eyes filled with tears. The feeling for poor Bu-Bula, alone in the dark and rain, underwent some strange transmutation, even as I called her name. I had begun calling that I might find and protect her, and then, suddenly, I was calling that she might protect me, for I was suddenly alone in the dark. Then the rain struck. It struck with a driving, icy impact. Just at that moment my groping hand found Bu-Bula.

Without Bu-Bula to cling to, I don't know how I might have survived. The lightning shivered the very earth under my feet, and in its blaze the trees seemed to dance uprooted, the leaves pale with an incandescent and flickering green, the boughs heaving. The thunder is incessant and, actually, engulfing. I know that I screamed, and even now I can recall the tension of my face as I stretch my mouth for the scream, and I feel the drive of the hail-hard drops of rain into my mouth and very throat, and terror redoubles when I can't hear my own voice.

There is the peak of distress when in a lightning flare I see, suddenly above me, a moving shape, and in the instant of ensuing blackness and immediate thunder-peal, I am seized and swung up by a great force. But in the terror and astonishing racket, I hear a voice, and it is saying my baby-name: "Manty—poor Manty, Manty-Darling."

It is my father, and he has found me, and is holding me under his coat, and murmuring my name.

In the house there is a great to-do over me. I am still shaking like a chill, and am torn by dry sobs that won't stop. They bring hot water, they bathe me, they dry my hair, they put on flannels, like winter, and rub my chest with a scented grease, but all the time my father is holding me and murmuring to me. Then I am safe in my own bed, with one hand clutching Bu-Bula—poor Bu-Bula still damp and chilly despite the ministrations that she, too, had received—and with the other hand clinging to the strong forefinger of my father's left hand. With his right hand he is stroking my forehead, and hair, very gently, still murmuring to me: "Little Manty—brave little Manty."

To an eye not squinted askew by affection, Bu-Bula could scarcely have seemed to warrant my discomfort of that night. Bu-Bula was not, by any stretch of imagination, a pretty doll. Her face had been whittled by a jackknife out of a chunk of soft pine, and her features were, to say the least, of an uninspired order. The fact that I had broken off the tip of her once rather pointed pine nose did not help her appearance, nor—to be honest—impair it overmuch. Her carved lips were too generous, and the creator's attempt to insert as teeth tiny fragments of mussel shells found in the river had been a snaggly failure no dentist might repair. The lips had been stained with pokeberry juice, and each cheek bore, too, a circle of the same bright dye to simulate the flush of health. Her eyes were black buttons held in place by a little tack—a cobbler's sprig, to be exact, for in those days all the footgear of the "people," that is, of the slaves, was made on the place. At *Starrwood,* old Shaddy was a very good cobbler. At least, there was a minimum of complaint about blisters and bleedings induced by his brogans and russets.

But to come back to Bu-Bula. Her golden locks were a hank of tow, tacked on. Her body was wood, with wood arms and legs attached by strings drawn through burned-through holes, burned through with a red-hot awl. As for clothing, the waist was a strip of white cloth, with a hole cut for the head, pulled down back and front, and tacked to poor Bu-Bula's tummy and backsides, with absolute disregard for her sensibilities, and a piece of red gingham had been wrapped around her middle, tacked on and faced with a strip of squirrel skin, like a broad belt. Such was Bu-Bula, whom I loved so dear, far beyond her deserts.

But I don't know, in the end, what deserts, charms, achievements, virtues and beauties have to do with love. We can love for so many different, and paradoxical, qualities in the object of our love—for strength or for weakness, for beauty or for ugliness, for gaiety or for sadness, for sweetness or for bitterness, for goodness or for wickedness, for need or for imperious independence. Then, if we wonder from what secret springs in ourselves gushes our love, our poor brain goes giddy from speculation, and we wonder what is all meaning and worth. Is it our own need that makes us lean toward and wish to succor need, or is it our strength? What way would our strength, if we had it, incline our heart? Do we give love in order to receive love, and even in the transport or endearment carry the usurer's tight-lipped and secret calculation, unacknowledged even by ourselves? Or do we give with an arrogance after all, a passion for self-definition? Or do we simply want a hand, any hand, a human object, to clutch in the dark on the blanket, and fear lies behind everything? Do we want happiness, or is it pain, pain as the index of reality, that we, in the chamber of the heart, want?

Oh, if I knew the answer, perhaps then I could feel free.

So we are back where I started.

We had come, however, to Bu-Bula, uncharming Bu-Bula, whom I loved, for whatever reasons. But perhaps one reason I loved her was that I had seen her come into existence. She had been a chunk of white pine, the hank of tow, the snippets of cloth, and I had seen these things take shape, grow together, and suddenly glow with her being. Shaddy—his real name was Shadrach—had sat on a stool in the kitchen, before the big fireplace where the pots hung on the crane and simmered, and the evening meat dripped grease from the spit to flare sweetly on the embers, and his dark hands had moved deftly about the task of creation. The glint of the knife, the curl of the shavings, the tap of the hammer, the snip of the shears—all was delight and enthrallment.

I had always been enthralled by Shaddy's skills, and for hours I had sat beside him in his cubbyhole of a workshop, down at the barn. I suppose that I loved him about as much as I loved Aunt Sukie, even if a little differently. Aunt Sukie grumbled and scolded, and pretended to be greatly outdone with me. Then she would seize me and envelope me in the great, soft, spicy tide of her affection. But Shaddy never scolded, and he would listen to me talk, no matter how long the pester-bug bit me. Often, however, I just wanted to hear him talk, when the notion hit him and he started on some rambling tale of what he had done long ago, how the young 'uns did when he was a sprout, the people he had known, the wicked and the good, or tales about animals and snakes and bugaboos and Raw-Head-and-Bloody-Bones and Jack-muh-Lantum.

He was a grizzled old Negro, with a seamed, cunning, gnomish face, brown and not real black, and he knew everything and could put it into a tale, and he had time to give me, for nobody supervised his work, he did it his own way and his own gait. Sometimes, on the hot summer afternoons, when the world was breathless and the workshop would be the only cool place you could think about, he would lay aside his knife or hammer, and take the sprigs out of his mouth, if it was brogans and not a horse-collar or something like harness he was working on, and would pick me up, on his lap, and coddle me and talk to me. If it was the time after he had made me Bu-Bula, I would be holding her, and he would be holding me, and his voice would go on and on, unwinding the tale of sweet recollection, or dire pains and punishments, or thrilling strangenesses. Now and then he would joggle me and Bu-Bula, the way you joggle a baby, and in the breathless world with only the single glare of sun beyond the door of his shadowy cubby, everything would become his voice with its mixture of lulling comfort and secret excitement.

Or Shaddy would play with me in the kitchen, where he was privileged to come, first as an expert above the level of field hand, and second, as some sort of cousin of Aunt Sukie. He did not depend for his nourishment on the Saturday issue of rations the driver

laid out, but had in addition to pot-licker and side-meat and hominy, such delicacies as fried ham and chicken-back and coffee and
chunks of devil-cake and an occasional dash of sillabub, left in the
bowl.

In the quick evenings of winter, after dark, that is the time I remember Shaddy in the kitchen, by the cook-hearth, with the firelight on him, making Bu-Bula with his blunt fingers that were so
peculiarly deft, or with myself on his lap, or being held high in his
grip until I yelped, or being tickled and jounced, or held quiet and
told a tale. "Come heah—come heah, and give Ole Shaddy a big
hug and a big ole kiss, and Shaddy, he'll tell you sumpin," he would
promise.

What would he tell me, I would demand, making a pretense of
bargaining.

"Gonna tell how ole Mr. Carter-wright, how he live right down
this-heah pike, how mean he wuz, how he open up little gals and et
they liver-and-lights lak you eat apple-dumplins—"

"You Shaddy, you stop talkin that foolishness," Aunt Sukie would
say. "Ole-man Carter-wright never done no sich. You gonna git
frailed, a-scarin my Baby-Chile."

But I wanted to be scared. By this time I was near Shadrach's
knee. And his voice was going on: "—yeah, and he scrape out they
haid and et they little brains lak you eat cawn-mush, and gonna tell
you how Jack-muh-Lantum got him, got him in the swump."

"Yeah," Aunt Sukie said, and whanged a pot, "and Jack-muh-
Lantum gonna git you and git you with a cowhide with fish-hooks
tied on the end fer a cracker."

I was on Shaddy's lap now, and he was saying, "Give Shaddy that
big ole hug, and he tell you." So I hugged him, and he said give
him the big ole kiss and he would tell me how Mr. Cartwright ate
the liver-and-lights out of little gals, and he made like he was going
to eat me so, baring his old yellow teeth, and grabbing my stomach
with all five fingers of one hand, while with the other hand he held
my back. I screamed in delight.

It was an old game, with a thousand variations, but one night it
was, all at once, different. The first difference was in the quiet way
Aunt Sukie laid aside her great spoon. The second difference was in
the quietness of her voice, no hint of the familiar railing or scolding.
She just looked quiet at Shaddy, and said: "That chile gittin too big,
you to fool her up that a-way."

"She lak hit," he said, not really noticing, "she lak me to tell how Ole-man Carter-wright et they insides and—"

"Tell me, tell me!" I screamed.

"Me—I ain't talkin bout that foolishness," Aunt Sukie said, still quieter.

The quietness now seemed to make an impression on Shaddy, for there was a hint of guilefulness, of falseness—of something, of something that sticks in my mind now—when he replied: "What you talkin bout, den?" And he gave me another grab and jounce to make me scream and demonstrate my willingness for the pleasure.

"You know what I'm talkin bout," she said.

"Talkin foolishness, den," he said.

She came quite close, almost upon us, and put her hands on her hips. "Think I doan know," she said.

"Know what?" he demanded.

"Know you."

"Know me—" he half echoed. "Me—Ole Shaddy, jes Ole Shaddy." All at once he addressed me earnestly: "Doan Ole Shaddy be good to his Baby-Gal?"

"Yeah," Aunt Sukie was saying, ignoring his by-play, "I knows you. And doan you reckin I doan know yore goins-on down yander."

"Down yander whar?"

"In yore little ole work-place, down the barn-shed. I knows, and I says dat chile gittin too big fer foolin up, I says you ain't keerful you gonna git cowhide and cat-o-nine and buck-paddle laid on till you cain't yell, I says you gonna git brine-water and vinegar and kay-yen laid on till you kin yell agin, I says you get pepper-tea and—"

I felt Shadrach's body go tense, and felt his hands gripping me, and he was saying: "Ain't gonna whup me, ain't nobody ever gonna whup me! Ain't ne'er gonna tote no scabby back, not fer no man!"

"Marse A-ren—he find out, and whuppen won't be nuthin but the first hem-and-haw—"

"Marse A-ren, him"—I felt Shadrach's whole body shaking, and me in his grasp—"him, he ain't nuthin—them muck-a-mucks, so high and mighty—ain't nuthin—pull off they pants and ain't nuthin but buckra—"

I must have been wincing in Shaddy's grasp, for suddenly Aunt Sukie pointed at me and said: "You hurt that chile and I'll 'fore-Gawd muck-a-muck you."

Shadrach looked at me as though he had not previously known

I was there. "Her!" he exclaimed. Then he shoved me off, in a gesture charged with rejection and revulsion. Then he, too, was standing, saying: "Yeah, what she?—ain't nuthin, no better'n nuthin—yeah, what she?"

I remember the way, that instant, the light from the cook-hearth fell on his face, and how it was now slick and glistening, as though sweat had just popped out, and how the lips contorted to show the yellow teeth, how the grimace of mock ferocity about eating my liver-and-lights was, suddenly, real. What I felt, as I well remember, was a kind of incredulity, but at the same time I knew that it was a terrible game coming true.

I simply felt that the stability of things had gone, that the floor under my feet might rock, was in fact rocking, and that all the objects of my solid world might suddenly dance with the giddy insubstantiality of the shadows flung on the kitchen walls by the flickering flames of the cook-hearth, and in my head the words kept echoing, as if they might go on forever: "Yeah, what she, what she?"

That part is all very clear. What is not clear is what came directly afterward. I don't remember what Aunt Sukie did, how I got fed and put to bed, whether or not I saw my father then—not anything. But I do know that I told my father something about the episode. I know that fact, because of its consequences, not because I remember the circumstance of telling him, or what I actually said. I do not even know whether I did it that night, or a week later, or a month.

But one morning there came a racket down at the quarters. My father entered the room where I was having my breakfast, and ordered me to stay in the house, and his voice was curt and impersonal. Then, a little later, out the window, in the sun-bright, frosty morning, I saw a gig go bowling past, on our drive, a strange man, with black whiskers and black hat and coat, holding the reins and a whip, a cheroot clenched in his jaws, smoke and frost-steamed breath making a trailing cloud behind his rapid head. Beside him was Shadrach. I could see a big bandage about Shadrach's head, like an untidy turban. Handcuffs were on his wrists. I caught the glint of metal at his ankles.

Shadrach had not been whipped. This was not because Shadrach was the not uncommon kind of slave that, never having been whipped, developed a pride in the fact and a potentiality for murderous violence if that pride was affronted by the cowhide. Such a slave could kill. But my father wasn't, I'm sure, afraid. It was, simply, that he didn't believe in whipping. He took the view that, if you had to whip a nigger, the nigger wasn't worth keeping anyway. Also my father was a humane man, and in the years of my recollection he had never had to sell off a soul. In fact, selling your people was against his principles. But with Shadrach he presumably felt that he had no choice, even if he knew that being sold off was, in the minds of many slaves, a worse fate than all the cowhiding and pickling possible.

As I pieced the story together from bits of gossip and dire whispers among the people, my father had not told Shadrach that he was to be sold. He had simply sent a message into Danville to summon a trader. Upon the trader's arrival, he had conducted him to the quarters, pointed out Shadrach, and ordered Shadrach to go with the man. Shadrach had attempted to run, but had been seized by a couple of the buck field-hands. Shadrach had resisted ferociously, had struck one of the field-hands with a stone, but had been clubbed into submission.

I imagine that the field-hands were none too gentle with Shadrach, and maybe laid on a lick or two with a premium of enthusiasm. For Shadrach was a sort of pet, Shadrach didn't really have to work, Shadrach was gorged with chicken-back and devil-cake, Shadrach had carried himself high among the lowly. "Yeah—yeah—" one of the black children said, telling the thing over to me with a thrill of horror, "Shaddy whop Big Jake wid a rock, and Big Jake, he whop Shaddy on de haid, and a hickory wagin-spoke—whop, Lawd, he whop him!—whop Ole Shaddy, Shaddy ole Fat-ass settin by the fire, Shady ole Grease-gut settin by the fire—yeah, Lawd, he whop him!" The mighty had fallen.

I cannot remember, as I said, how much time had elapsed between the scene in the kitchen and my last sight of Shaddy, with his turban, being taken away by the speculator, or flesh-merchant, or soul-driver, or whatever you wish to call the man who made his living in the trade. I can't be certain that I even saw Shaddy in between those two occasions. But there is the vision before my eyes of myself and Shaddy, Shaddy pleading with me, saying: "Shaddy, he did 'n mean nothin—Ole Shaddy, he love his Baby-Gal—Shaddy made Bu-Bula fer his Manty-Baby—Shaddy would'n hurt his Baby-Gal—come give Shaddy his big ole hug—"

Was the scene real? Had Shaddy, fearing my revelation, come to me to beg and wheedle? Or did I dream the scene long after? Real or dreamed, I remember, and to a degree even now, relive, the feelings that accompanied the scene, my guilt at telling on him (the fact accomplished or contemplated, or perhaps put into my head by his pleading), my resentment for that moment when he had shaken my world to shadow, my mysterious attraction toward him and his terrible tales and lulling voice, my gratitude for Bu-Bula, my natural and childish desire to enjoy the love he proffered me, a desire not quite canceled by the present revulsion.

For, I am sure, Shaddy did love me, in his own sad, confused, bitter, lonesome, evil, and kindly way. Even the moment when the force of his deepest rage and lifelong resentment was untriggered that night in the kitchen, and he flung me aside in repudiation, even that had something to do with his loving me, with some meaning I held for him. And I am sure that he went to his grave, wherever that was, off among strangers, feeling that I, his Manty-Baby, had rejected his love, had spat upon the niggerness in him.

But Shadrach left me Bu-Bula. He also left me something more enduring, the image of his face, with the glare of the cook-hearth on it, when he turned to me and said: "Yeah, what she?—what she?"

After Shaddy had gone, there was a change in Aunt Sukie. For days, whenever I tried to talk to her, she would grunt and sulk, or slam a pot, or enter into some dire, dark, inward muttering below the threshold of my comprehension. I was hurt to the heart, for I loved her. But I was hurt, too, because of the injustice. It was Aunt Sukie who had, in the first place, made the trouble that night by the cook-hearth, and yet, somehow, now I was to blame. In the end, of course, she took me back to her bosom. But there was some lurking reservation.

Or was the reservation, rather, in me, since I had now had some experience of the insubstantiality of things?

Except for Aunt Sukie, the world did seem the same. Or perhaps, in one way, nicer, for I am now inclined to think that after that time my father saw more of me. He had, however, always been a most attentive parent, as though he had to make up a little for the death of my mother. He dandled me and played with me, and brought me presents, and with his own hands, big and clumsy, tried to tie ribbons and button up shoes, and count toes, and with unruly voice and uncertain ear sang to me when he sat on the veranda in the gloaming, with me on his lap, or by the fire in his room. He sang the song about little boys being made of toads and snails and puppy-dog tails and little girls being made of sugar and spice and everything nice. Then he would ask me: "What are little boys made of?"

And I would sing the toads and snails and puppy-dog tails, and he would make a comically horrid face of disgust, and say something like *ug-ug*, and I would emulate his dramatic expression and retching noise. Then he would ask: "And what are little girls made of?"

Smugly, I would sing the right answer, and he would smack his lips, and say: "Um-um, um!" And I would do likewise, feeling flushed with virtue and value, all full of sugar and spice and niceness. Then smacking his lips, he would hug me tight and kiss me, and tousel my hair with affection, and say, "Dear little Miss Sugar-and-Spice."

Or he took me riding. He had, in fact, given me instruction from the time I could remember, walking beside fat little Pet, with one hand propping me on the saddle, with the other leading the pony, moving decorously under the shade of the trees, then out into the sunlit lawn, making the one lazy, droopy old peacock move out of our way, which he did with sulky and offended regality, fixing us with beady, unforgiving eyes. But now I was a big girl, and he let me ride a real horse, on a real sidesaddle, like a lady, and he taught me to jump. It is true that the real horse was a gentle little mare, named Pearlie, nothing at all like the flashing, powerful roan beast, Marmion, that my father favored, and that could gather and lift over the big gate with such imperious suddenness that you thought you had heard the clap of great pinions. And it is true that the jumps I took were merely inches off the turf. But, oh the beauty and delight of that motion, and its moment of freedom off the earth, and the satisfaction of my father's face as he said, "Oh, that's my Manty! That's my brave little Manty!"

Or there would be the hours he sat with me, teaching me to read, pointing at the letters with his big forefinger, listening to me with infinite patience, teaching me to spell, teaching me little rhymes, then later real poems, teaching me how to write, holding my hand to guide it. But all things must find their natural end, and it was, partly at least, the necessity of my education that brought the end to this period of my life.

My father went away for two weeks on a trip. He kissed me, told me to be good and mind Aunt Sukie, and got into the carriage, and Jacob, who doubled as butler and coachman, picked up the reins. I wept as the carriage rolled off.

During this absence, however, there was one little compensation. I had forgotten to remark that one of the changes in my life after the departure of Shadrach was the sharp dwindling of my intercourse with the children from the quarters. But in the last year or so, when the children, my late playmates, came up, Marthy, Aunt Sukie's lieutenant, would order them off. They might stand at some distance, staring at me, fixing me with a wide, nonplused gaze, even calling out, in a moment of boldness, "Manty—doan you wanna play? Doan you play no more, Manty?"

Marthy would yell: "Done tole you, git on way!"

But now with my father gone, they began to drift back to my play-place, the first day standing off at a distance, in the sunshine, the larger ones pretending to be engrossed with their own concerns but stealing sidewise glances at me, the little ones standing with their popped-out bellies glistening below the level of the abbreviated singlet, their only garment, standing with the thumb of one hand stuck in the mouth, and with the other scratching, in lofty indifference, the little black belly or private parts.

Now within one day we had resumed the old companionship.

Then my father came back. In the morning of that day, Jacob had gone into Danville with the carriage, and now, at mid-afternoon, as we played down by the cedars, one of the middle-sized children lifted his head, stared, and said: "Dar he!"

Then, in one motion, big and little, they were all up, up and away, the big ones fast and skittering, like grease spilled on a hot stove, suddenly gone from sight like millet seed in a blast of wind, the last and least one with bare backsides and chunky little unsteady black legs, chunky as sausage, pumping soberly along, a thumb still in his mouth. But he, too, was gone, gone back to the quarters or hiding in the canes on the branch below the lawn or skulking down at the barn, long before the carriage was there and my father's arms engulfed me.

A week later—this was late August of 1852—my father took me away. I was going away to school, he explained, where I was going to be a big girl and learn a lot and have other children to play with and study with, and where I was going to be very good and make him proud of me. I had never before been off the land of *Starrwood*.

We went by carriage to Danville, then by stage to Lexington, then to Louisville, then by steamboat to Cincinnati. The great brilliant, opening, coruscating happy confusion of the world held me, and when my nerves simply gave out, and could throb and tingle no more with excitement, I dropped my head on my father's shoulder, or crumpled entire against his side, and slept.

We stopped some days in Cincinnati, at a great hotel, and in all the glitter and strangeness, I was pampered beyond belief. For one thing, I had to have new clothes. The Lord knows what kind of clothes I had had in the country, a mixture of my father's unformed taste and Aunt Sukie's ingenuity. But now everything was to be new. My father, I quickly sensed, knew as little as possible on the topic, and in the stores he seemed as awkward and heavy-handed as a bear, prodding some piece of muslin or dimity, dangling a length of silk ribbon, looking bewildered and severe. But there was Miss Idell.

Miss Idell, as she asked me to call her, was really Mrs. Muller, the wife of Mr. Herman Muller, who was a lawyer in Cincinnati and did some work for my father. Mr. Muller was about the age of my father, or a little younger, had a curly reddish-gold beard and an impressive expanse of shirt-front and plaid waistcoat, and wore a diamond stickpin, but he treated my father, despite his country shabbiness, with gratifying respect. They were, in fact, friends, or friends of a sort, as much friends as, with their differences, they might be expected to be, the old-fashioned planter, or farmer, born and raised in Kentucky, but still feeling himself half in Virginia, the Virginia of the century before, and the new-fashioned lawyer and speculator, with his gleaming cuffs and stickpin, his German heartiness, one jump, I should guess, off a Bavarian cheese-farm, but now with a finger in every pie, westward lands, steamboats, railroads, banks, and with a conversation always coming back to money, much money, as he earnestly leaned forward, shifting his bulk with some inward relish, toying with the crisp gold curls of his beard, saying to my father: "Ah, Aaron—my friend—there's money in it!"

Before this point in the conversation, Miss Idell's attention might

have wandered, she might have been smoothing with excessive so-
licitude the cloth that sheathed her fine thighs, or have been idly
trying to catch a reflection of herself in a mirror on the restaurant
wall, but now, as the conversation rose to the climactic pitch of
money, much money, she would again rejoin us in spirit, lean forward a little, too, and her bright blue eyes would achieve the last
glitter.

I greatly admired Miss Idell. Nothing, nothing, I was sure, had
ever been as beautiful as she, with her small blue shovel bonnet,
discreetly ornamented with the tiniest roses, her tight blue bodice
defining the high richness of her bosom and the elegance of her
waist, the tight sleeves of the upper arm flaring out with ruffles just
a little below the elbow, to reveal the false undersleeves of lace that
came down to be gathered about the exquisite wrist. From the
sheathed stem of the waist, the skirt flared out, to near fill the carriage, or dominate the sidewalk, and down the middle of the skirt
flowed a great concourse of ruffles, gathered at the waist, and
widening downward, and downward, like a delicate cascade. Miss
Idell carried a pink-and-blue parasol, with a silver handle.

In the carriage, I would secretly touch the silver handle of the
parasol, or, with elaborate carelessness, let my hand touch the
spread skirt, and pinch a tiny twist of the fabric between thumb and
forefinger, with desperate, continuous pressure, as though I might
squeeze out and possess some of the mystic virtue that infused all
things honored by Miss Idell's contact.

I would treasure, though despairingly, a compliment she had
given me, trying to twist it into a promise, a guarantee, made by
fate that I, too, should be beautiful. It was on one of the shopping
expeditions with my father. Awkwardly, with some hemming and
hawing, my father managed to indicate that the garment—I forget
what it was—that Miss Idell was recommending to be made for me,
was probably a little out of keeping with the tone of the school
where I was to be.

Miss Idell turned her bland blue gaze upon him, and said, "Oh,
my dear Mr. Starr, just put Manty in another school and keep the
delicious ruffles."

My father, I imagine, was not notable for his humor, and certainly
now he failed to respond to Miss Idell's teasing. He began to explain, soberly, that the arrangements had been made already, that
he thought it would be a good place for me, and so forth.

But she cut him short, with an imperious flick of the furled parasol. "Oh, fudge," she said, with some real asperity in her tone, "that silly place! I just don't understand you. Hermann and I were just talking about it. There's a nice seminary right here. And if Manty were here, then I could keep an eye on her, and—"

My father mustered his forces, and even more soberly explained that he wanted me to have a good education, that I was a bookish little girl and already could puzzle out some Latin—and that he didn't think a serious view of the world, such as he hoped I would get where I was going, ever hurt anybody.

At this Miss Idell shifted her parasol to her left hand, leaned toward me, and took my chin in her right hand, and lifted my face for exhibition. "Look!" she commanded my father. "Look, she's going to be beautiful. Can't you see it coming on? Look at those eyes, those beautiful, big, wide, trusting brown eyes—oh, how I wish—" And here, with the natural instinct of an expert to let slip no chance of parading gift and skill, she turned her blue gaze full on my father, and repeated: "Oh, how I wish I had such brown eyes, and not these common blue ones."

But she was a true expert, and did not linger on that note. The words might not even have been said, the transition was so swift, for she was again lifting up my face and saying, "Look—look at the cut of her mouth—it will be a sweet, full mouth—none of your sort of unworked buttonhole, slit mouths for little Manty—and you, you monster—" She turned in mock anger back to my father: "—you would send this darling up among those whey-faces and knob-heads of Oberlin!"

With distress, and yet with a surge of vanity, I saw myself surrounded by whey-faces and knob-heads, whatever such things were, all unworthy of my beauty. But my father was saying something, something else placatory. Then Miss Idell cut in again, and said how at Oberlin they ate nothing but Graham bread and water, and maybe some boiled cabbage with no pork, and that I would peak and pine away, and be thin as a beanpole with no figure, if I didn't die of galloping consumption. Then she tapped her parasol on the floor, to make a final point. "Besides," she said, "up there they're all Abolitionists."

My father, somewhat taken aback, allowed that they might be a kind of Abolitionists, he had looked into it, but they weren't the worst kind.

"What will all your friends think, down in Kentucky," she demanded, "and you flirting with Abolitionists?"

My father said he guessed he didn't see much of his friends, somehow. He just lived quiet with me on his place.

"Yes," Miss Idell said, "on a place full of niggers."

My father said that he was just doing the best he knew how.

That night, after my father had kissed me good night in my bed, in the room connecting with his at the hotel, I got up, and by the light from the window, inspected myself in the mirror. I even lifted up my nightgown to make the inspection more scrupulous, holding it up high, high as my neck. Yes, I was thin as a beanpole, not a bit like Miss Idell. I puc my hands on my skinniness, and was filled with despair. Why, oh why, would my father send me to a place where I would die of galloping consumption, or at least, be a beanpole? And perhaps a whey-face to boot.

We went to Oberlin. We went to the house of a Mrs. Turpin, who was certainly no beanpole or whey-face. She erred, in fact, on the side of amplitude, and her face was well weathered, far beyond the color of whey. It was a severe, motherly face, admitting no nonsense, but ready to give comfort. Mr. Turpin, who was something of a beanpole and a whey-face, taught Latin in the college. He led us, too, in evening and morning prayers, with an accomplished professional air, and made some references, not too covert even for my childish ear, to a brother who might be brought to see the light of justice and the commonality of the human soul. I knew that he was meaning my father.

My father was kneeling with us all, and when I squinched through my fingers to see him, he had his own eyes tight shut. He was on his knees, and to see him that way, when I had never seen him that way, and knew he was so strong, was very peculiar. It was all very peculiar, for at *Starrwood* the only prayers we had were my prayers, which my father, rather haltingly, had taught me. I said them, in my nightdress, kneeling by my bed, with my father staying to hear me.

In two days my father left. As he prepared to go, I saw, in a whirling commotion of spirit, all the things that were, on the instant, fading from me, the play-place and the trees of *Starrwood*— *Starrwood* and all my life there, the tootle of tumble-out horn at first light, the faint *pot-rack, pot-rack,* at twilight, of the guineas that roosted in the trees behind the house, and the warm, live, cinnamon smell of Aunt Sukie's bosom and armpits when she held me to her. It was all whirling away in some gray mist of distance.

My father leaned over to kiss me good-bye. He told me to be a good girl and make him proud of me. I nodded dumbly.

Then he whispered: "But I'm always proud of my little Manty."

Then more secretly, into my very ear: "Dear little Miss Sugar-and-Spice."

I didn't cry till long after he was gone.

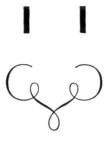

IF IN CINCINNATI, UNDER THE GLITTERING INFECTION OF MISS IDELL, I had made my first acquaintance with beauty and vanity, in Oberlin, in the house of Turpin, I learned to disprize the former and rebuke the latter, and learned that my garments, created under the aegis of Miss Idell, were not suitable for a child of God, particularly a child of God of nine and a half years. Not that Mrs. Turpin descended on my little wardrobe with power and denunciation in one blast. No, she merely drew out a ribbon here and whacked off a ruffle there, explaining, between snips of the scissors, the vanity of beauty in this, our perishing world.

A child wants the approbation of its world, perishing or not, and I wanted the severe approbation of Mrs. Turpin. But at the same time, my heart bled for some poor ribbon and I yearned toward the brightness of Miss Idell and the promise of my own beauty she had made me.

Later on, as my religious sense ripened—and paradoxically enough, when my body began to ripen, too—I strove in prayer against my yearning to be beautiful. I sometimes worked myself to weeping over the incorrigible vanity, and then took some satisfaction that my eyes got red from the contrite tears. I couldn't keep my eyes red all the time, but I could comb back my hair as tight as possible to correct its crisp curliness, and could pull down the corners of my mouth in a fixed grimace of self-critical meditation.

Then the time would come for me to go to Cincinnati, and see my father, and Miss Idell, and I would know again on what shifting sands stood my mansion of salvation.

The only time I felt secure from temptation was just at the end of my stay at Oberlin when I fell in love with Seth Parton—poor Seth, with his big, fumbling, farm-boy hands, and beautiful dark eyes, afire with the compelling poetry of spirit and sanctification. Dear Seth—who stood beside me in the winter woods of Lorain County, Ohio, and promised me the assimilation of body and soul in the gleaming vision of reality.

Yes, Seth had something of the blazing faith and saintly vigor of the little band of founders, who, some fifteen years earlier, lamenting the degeneracy of the Church and the ruined world, had come here to establish their ideal commonwealth. They were, in brief, old-fashioned reformers, a breed gone out of our country now with the tide of success and money-madness, with Mr. Astor and Mr. Vanderbilt running things, with railroads across the continent, and people filling up the plains and extracting rich ores from every mountain, and only those who have failed in the scramble are now given to reform and criticism, or are willing to speak well of the time past.

When the old founders came to Lorain County, they were so obsessed with the deplorable condition of the ruined world, that they lighted on one of the more ruinous spots of that world. It was flat, swampish, and unwholesome.

But strong backs and cunning hands sometimes supplemented the obsessed eyes, and many a student who came here in patched pantaloons, to swap sweat for Euclid and the tongue of the Prophets, brought with him, already, the wisdom of the barnyard or the sleights of the sawmill.

So by the time I came, Oberlin was a comely town, with a pretty square in the middle, Tappan Square, old Tappan Hall and College Chapel, and near by the other college buildings, square-jawed, too, and handsome, and the elms along the streets. Inside the tidy houses, there were comfortable beds and, in season, crackling fires, and if there was a good deal more of Scripture-reading and prayer than the childish heart thought edifying or the childish knee-bones found good, there was also motherly affection from even the grimmer female countenances, and Mr. Turpin himself could make his thin, whey-faced jokes for the very young.

The bread-and-water days were over by my time. Those days, in fact, had never been dictated merely by the early poverty. The old reformers had seen the body and the soul as one, and if the Oberlinites were to give the model for the purification of the soul of the world, they had to give the model for healthy bodies, too. So, with ferocious conviction, they ate Dr. Graham's bread and drank cold water, and avoided all salt and pepper that might inflame the blood and all animal foods that might make sodden the mind. But many a farm boy who came here for Hebrew and philosophy, kept an unregenerate hankering for beef stew and pippin pie and now commons were not too short.

No, I never rose hungry from the Turpin table, but I did yearn, now and then, for the fiery tingle of the smoked sausage of my old diet and the libidinous richness of Aunt Sukie's cobblers. In houses dominated by the Aunt Sukies of the world, either from the old barbarous simplicity and deprivation of the race, or from example of the master's indulgence, food is not a mere means to an end. It is an absolute, gorging good.

My father, too, shared something of this philosophy, and he must have recognized my yearning, for when I made my visits to Cincinnati to meet him, he would stuff me with all the rich foods in sight, and would pinch my arm, or cheek, and say, "Got to plump my baby up. We don't want any beanpole, do we, Miss Idell?" And Mr. Muller, Miss Idell's husband, would laugh with his deep *ho-ho,* as if he were gargling some rich beverage, and pull the gold curls of his beard, and Miss Idell would critically inspect me, and say: "I do believe, maybe she'll make it." And at that I would flush with astonishing pleasure, and with hope.

Then back to Oberlin, where, after all, I found life had its sweetness. For one thing, I enjoyed a peculiar attention and status, not unlike that enjoyed there by visiting Red Indian converts, Abolition speakers who had been rotten-egged in Southern, or Northern, towns, runaway slaves dropping off at this way station of the Underground Railroad, or returned missionaries still shaking with tropical fevers and crammed with tales of the savage obscenities of the Gold Coast. Only, my status was, you might say, a status by ambiguity.

I was among neither the saved nor the saviors who appeared so dramatically before us. If I was saved, I was still a carrier of the fascinating evil from below the Ohio River, for slavery, in Oberlin, implied all the other sins in its train, romantic and mysterious.

I was in an ambiguous position, somewhat like the reformed cannibal who may be suspected to retire to his chamber, divest himself of Christian pants and shirt, paint his hide, squat on the floor, and indulge in a few last, secret tidbits. How could my salvation be complete if my father still held slaves? As a friend succinctly put it, I lived on black sweat.

For a while, after this was pointed out to me, my dinners actually sat heavy on my stomach, and one night I vomited. I must confess that this last was caused less by moral horror than by the sudden image of myself spooning happily into a steaming cauldron of black sweat. After the vomiting, the restoring thought came to me that perhaps my situation was one of sublime opportunity. I saw myself— a picture I call up before me now—as a little girl clothed in flowing white, face downcast in meekness but shining with a light of mission, pleading with my father, convicting him of error, saving his soul, amid the rejoicing of a choir of black-faced figures, blacker than life and clad, too, strangely enough, in white robes like my own— strangely, I say, for the faces were the faces of Aunt Sukie, old Jacob, Marthy, and the rest and they, certainly, had never worn white robes at *Starrwood*.

I confided my hopeful project to my best friend, Ellie Pettigrew, an apple-cheeked, bouncing girl whose good health and animal spirits were not notably mortified by a notably rigorous program of watching and prayer. She thought my notion was wonderful. She was, I could see, a trifle envious of my opportunity. Her own father was most drearily saved already.

When I did next see my father, it was Christmastime, the Christmas of my third year at Oberlin. In those days at Oberlin Christmas celebration was abjured as pagan, and on my way to Cincinnati I resolved to hold myself aloof from the druidical taint while waiting for the moment to touch on my father's salvation. But when I felt my father's big hug, and he blew in my ear, I quite forgot my duty. The glitter of the grand restaurant, the beauty of Miss Idell, the aromatic evergreens and festive candles, the presents for me—including a big chocolate cake sent by Aunt Sukie—completed my ruination. I was too happy in the gauds of the perishing world. For one thing, I stayed part of the time at the Muller house, instead of at a hotel with my father. Mr. Muller, they told me, was ill and had gone away to the South for his health. I would be company for her, Miss Idell said. I was allowed to inspect her entire wardrobe. I even tried things on. I was totally beguiled.

Only toward the time of my departure did guilt set in, and did I steel myself to my resolve. I was to leave the next morning. That I might be abed early, my father and I had an early dinner. We were sitting in the dining room of his hotel, still at table, while he drank a glass of some liquor to aid, he said, digestion. All at once, the urgency of the occasion overwhelmed me.

With the brutality of awkwardness, I plunged into the topic, like a surgeon doing an operation with a meat-ax. I told my father that he was damned. I told him that he jeopardized my soul by making me live on black sweat. I told him he ought to get rid of his slaves. This was all in a rush of words.

"Gre't God!" he ejaculated, at my first spate, and I was so caught up in myself that I did not flinch at his blasphemy. His eyes were about to pop out of his head.

"Gre't God," he said again, "you want me to get shed of Aunt Sukie—of Marthy? I always thought you liked them."

I explained that I loved them, but they ought to be free.

"Where would they go?" he demanded.

They could stay right where they were, I said.

"Yes, and then what's the difference?" he retorted.

"The difference," I cried, "the difference—it's just the salvation of your immortal soul!" The great phrase came rolling forth with a terrifying, denunciatory ease that astonished even me.

There was a party of people, early diners like ourselves, at a table near by, two gentlemen and two ladies, young persons of fashion. Now in the general silence following my utterance, one of those gentlemen snickered.

It was too much. I was already aware that things were going badly, and now this mean snicker of the unredeemed world sealed my failure. Tears of embarrassment and despair flooded my eyes.

At my utterance my father's face had manifested a mixture of puzzlement, and distress, perhaps irritation, too. As I now think back, I realize that he had been touched in some confusing and painful way, that he was irritated because here was a situation he didn't know how to deal with except by some kind of patronizing and dishonest evasion.

But the laugh, that was different. His face went hard, as though an iron shutter had suddenly been pulled down on a window. That snicker—oh, he knew, in his simple, old-fashioned way, and with what must have been a sudden gush of relief, how to deal with that.

He rose, laid down his napkin and, without haste, took a couple of strides to the other table. Standing there in his countrified clothes, with a voice and pronunciation that, I suddenly noticed, were not what my ear had lately become accustomed to, he said: "Your laughing, sir, has caused pain to"—he seemed to be undecided about a word, and half turned his head, as though to inspect me and determine exactly what I was. Then, quite soberly, he continued—"to this young lady."

I was, as a matter of fact, nothing but a teary little girl of thirteen, lost and embarrassed, but that definition suddenly made some amends for his failure to take me seriously, and a flicker of hope came into my heart.

My father was going on: "And I indulge myself by saying that I hold your breeding in utmost contempt."

The man flushed, and seemed about to rise, but my father said: "And furthermore I don't believe that you dare to resent my remarks. If you do, you will regret it."

That instant, as my father was about to turn away, one of the ladies said, "Listen, he's threatening you, John—call the police, John!"

"The police—" my father said, meditatively, looking at the man named John. Then he shook his head and addressed the lady: "No, madam, he won't even call the police."

This time my father did turn away. He saw me from my chair, and walked decorously by my side toward the hall.

Just as we reached the door, I caught the rising voice of one of the ladies. All I caught was "—ought not to laugh at a child like that."

That was worse than the laughter. Now to be called a child. Everything I had done and said, and what my father had done seemed, all at once, silly. I felt an awful embarrassment, as though blasts of laughter were ringing out of the room behind us, to strip me naked, to define us forever. I tried to draw back from my father, to disassociate myself from him, as though I now sensed the strain of impurity, the impulse to escape, in his rising to my defense, as though, too, I found fatuous his proffered amends in calling me a young lady.

At the door of my room my father kissed me an awkward good night. He knew something was wrong between us. He said he hoped I would sleep well. Then he was gone, and I burst into tears.

I lay past the period of weeping, while the tears dried on my cheeks, and all my life to come seemed a blankness, like the dark above me. At last the door from my father's room opened a trifle, an uncertain pencil of light fell into my room, and my father's voice said: "You asleep, Manty-Darling?"

I wasn't asleep, I said.

He came in, tiptoeing anyway, and set the little bed-lamp he carried on a table far from my bed, as though he preferred to be in shadow for whatever transaction he intended. He placed a chair by my bed, and sat down, stiffly, with his hands on his knees. Being between me and the little lamp, he was only a dark bulk to me, and his shadow fell across me on the bed.

For some time, he said nothing. My own feelings turned round and round tiredly inside me. The anger and the spite were there in me, but they were tired now—like trapped mice, in a box, and I was the box, and they had been scampering desperately back and forth, and beating themselves at the walls, and squeaking in fear and outrage, and now they were tired and quivery, and had to rest just a minute before they flung themselves once more against the restraining walls.

Yes, I was tired. And somehow, despite everything, the presence of my father made me feel that now I could go to sleep.

"Manty," he said, finally, and the voice surprised me from the verge of sleep. "Manty," he repeated, "I'm sorry."

With that, in abrupt wakefulness, there came to me some hard sense of an advantage just gained, not to be exploited yet but held in reserve, some possibility of self-justification and of revenge. So I made no reply.

"Manty," he said, "I reckon I didn't treat you right, Honey."

I didn't reply, lying still, on my back, with my arms crossed tight across my chest, and with the sense that by not replying I would not diminish, or squander, that secret, precious advantage I hugged.

"You know," he was saying from his shadowy bulk, where I just made out the gleam of his eyes, "I didn't mean to hurt your feelings."

"Oh, it wasn't *my* feelings," I said, underscoring bitterly, but ever so little, the word *my*, exploiting, ever so little, the advantage. "It was for you I said it."

"I know," he said, gravely. "It was just it all sort of surprised me. It was just I hadn't thought about—" He stopped, then began again. "No," he said, "that's not telling the truth. I had thought about it. A man does, even if he knows it doesn't do any good."

"You could set them free," I said.

"Baby," he said, "I'd have to take care of 'em, anyway. And Manty-Baby, I just haven't got that much money."

I retorted learnedly that in the end you made money by paying wages. That was what at Oberlin they called the argument of self-interest. It wasn't as good as the argument from righteousness, but it was an argument. So I offered it. But my father gave a sad little laugh, and said that for him that end would be too long a time coming. He didn't have that much money, he repeated, and what he had he wanted to keep. For me, he added. So that I would never need, and could live wherever I wanted.

"I don't want to live on black sweat," I said. "That way, I wouldn't want to live at all!" And I felt high and pure, and filled with a sudden excitement, at the violence of my words, at the thought of dying, dying so beautifully.

But my father was saying that sometimes you just had to live the way you could. Even if he had been born on *Starrwood*, he sometimes wished he lived somewhere else. He had even tried to invest a little money somewhere else, just sort of feeling his way, he said. He might even have sold out long back, he said, except he didn't believe in selling your people.

"But you sold Shaddy," I said, and I knew I had him there.

He hesitated a moment, and then said, heavily: "That was different."

But I scarcely heard him, for some feeling was in me, powerful and new, but I didn't know what it was. Then, all at once, I sat up in bed and leaned at my father, with a sense of terrible urgency. "Oh, why did you sell him?" I cried. And in my inner tumult, I felt I had to know the answer.

He could not give me an answer. He shifted his weight in the chair, his eyes gleaming in the shadow. All he could say was: "Sometimes—sometimes, Honey—you have to do things."

"Oh, why did you do it?" I demanded again, caught up in my own question.

"Sometimes you have to do things you don't want to," he said.

I leaned at him. I felt, as if a great hand were at the back of my neck, thrusting me forward. "Oh, but you did want to!" I cried.

I leaned there at him, on the bed-edge, in that attitude of accusation, and felt as though the shadow had rolled away from his face, and I truly saw it, myself dazzled by the truth of my own words, whatever that truth was. Then quite calmly I said: "You were jealous of him."

Then I lay back down. I felt quiet and pure.

My father didn't say a word. He kept on sitting there until I had gone to sleep.

Next morning we parted with some restraint, and I was glad to go back to Oberlin, to get back to a world that, I now felt, I understood better than I understood him. I let letters from him lie unopened for days. I prayed a great deal. All during the following months, even when I saw my father, I held my distance, and lived in some dreary corner of my heart, like somebody who has come into reduced circumstances, and huddles in a corner of the now ruinous mansion, amid cobwebs and dust, gnawing crusts of bread, drinking stale water. My sad case became known to all. I was the girl whose father had rejected her and rejected salvation, but who prayed for him still. The more devout of my contemporaries were tender with me, and I stood high in esteem. Some of the faculty offered tactful sympathy.

It was fall, beyond the next harvest, before a change came in my feeling for my father.

Not infrequently the students would give their services for a cornhusking at Oberlin, either as an offering to the cause of Oberlin, or as charity for some poor family, preferably that of a widow. A certain sociability rewarded us, we sang appropriate songs, told stories, and being young, enjoyed the mere fact of the gregarious activity. On this particular occasion I had greatly enjoyed myself.

Afterward, we were walking home across the fields, a thin crust of snow underfoot and a brilliant moon overhead, some sort of residual gaiety in the heart mixed with the melancholy sweetness of the

night scene. Somehow, I didn't quite know why, I began to tell
about cornhuskings at *Starrwood*, talking to Ellie and a couple of
other students. I told how in that section, at corn-time, the people—
the slaves, that is—from several farms would gather on a place to do
the husking. I had seen the huskings on our place—two or three
times—for my father would let me stay awake to see the jubilation
and dancing and hear the music.

It was all very gay. The lanterns hung from the barn beams and
over at one side the musicians, fiddlers, a real fiddle maybe, and a
gourd fiddle with horsehair strings to give a strange, ghostly note to
tickle the silence when it came in by itself, the man who beat on an
overturned tub, the man with the clap-bones, lengths of beef-rib
held between the fingers to snap and rattle with the music. In the
middle of the barn the people sat in a big circle, and over at the
other side, balancing on the heap of unshucked corn, was a big,
fine-looking old Negro, blue-black and shining in the face, with a
long black coat and a red neck-scarf, and a voice like a melodious
bull, and he tossed down the corn to be shucked, and yelled out the
songs to be sung, and made his big voice ride over all the voices and
the music, filling the barn till the boards bulged. He was the "corn-
general." And all the time the big jug of whisky went round and
round, for the master whose corn was being shucked provided the
entertainment.

Then the last ear was shucked, and the corn-general let out a
whoop, and they rolled out two barrels, and across the tops, between them, placed a springy board, on which a man and woman
got up, facing each other, and began to dance at some clattering, in-
credible pace, while the board jounced, and the crowd yelled and
sang:

> *Step it, Jabby, step it higher!*
> *Old Virginny never tire!*
> *Heel and toe, ketch a-fire!*

I remembered it all very vividly, my own excitement, recaptured
now as I told it, bemusing me again, I suppose, with the long-lost
past.

But most of all the old feeling came back as I recalled the moment when, later, in the midst of the general dancing, the corn-
general let out one of his whoops, and all the people ran at my father, and grabbed him, lifting him high above me, above the crowd,

jubilating and yelling. I was frozen with terror. Then I saw that my father was laughing. They bounced him and jounced him, and he kept on laughing. And they sang:

> Ride Ole Massa,
> Ride him high,
> If he give me the whisky, I be drunk till I die!

I was telling about all this, as best I could, and I suppose that in the bemusement of memory, my account took on some tone of romantic nostalgia. I even sort of sang the song about Ride Ole Massa. It was Ellie who broke in upon my feeling. "Do you mean"—she said, pausing in horror—"do you mean that he—" and she emphasized the he, as though she were too tactful to nominate the he as my father. Then she finished: "—that he gave whiskey to those poor slaves to make them work at night!"

I burst out that they didn't have to come to the husking if they didn't want, that it was a kind of party, that we ourselves had just that night been to a husking and had enjoyed it. But Ellie retorted that we hadn't done it for pleasure, we had done it for good. And the other girl, somewhat older than Ellie and I, said: "Yes, which proves that we aren't slaves—slaves that he—that he can bribe with strong drink!"

And added, immediately, with an inward, falling inflection of pity: "At night, after the day's hard task is done."

"But he's not bribing them," I cried out. "He just wants them to have a good time, he just wants—"

Then Seth Parton's voice, so clear and cold, as though from the very depth of the beautiful, glittering northern night, fell on my ear. It said: "We must never be deceived by incidental virtue."

I swung to the voice. I had forgotten that he was there. He had been a companion to the older girl. He was, I knew, in the last year of the college and would begin his theology the next year. I had heard that he was brilliant and devout. But until that instant I had never heard him utter a word, for the throttled noise he had made along with his rigid bow upon being introduced that evening could scarcely be called a word.

Now, over my left shoulder, I saw him, a tall, gangling figure, with arms long and loose from shoulders narrow but strong-looking, the shoulders draped in a threadbare coat, a wisp of scarf about the long, erect neck, the bare head, with rumpled hair, held high and severe, the long, big-nosed, hungry profile, with its cast of arrogance and noble pain, sharp against the winter-starred enormous night. For one moment his words struck some chord of devout vigilance in my heart, and I thrilled to the tone of high truth, but then I thought: *he is talking about my father.* So I cried out: "But he's good!"

"Good," Seth Parton said, just saying the word, without meaning, as though it were a word in a foreign language. Then: "Goodness, it may be the mask for evil."

"But he *is* good," I repeated.

"I am not concerned with your father as a person," Seth Parton said. "What is the small and foolish goodness of a person? May not the Adversary use best our small personal goodness for the greatness of Evil?"

Then I heard the voice of Ellie saying, "Yes, yes, and he gave them whiskey to fool them." And the voice of the older girl, "Yes, and he rode on their shoulders—on the shoulders of men—" And the voices, after the terrible utterance of Seth Parton, were like the mean little yipping of fice dogs.

So I turned to him, suddenly, as though to take refuge in the terribleness.

His face, way up there, was saying: "No, we must not be concerned with persons. Only with Truth!" And he whipped out his long angular right arm against the sky, and I saw how big his hand was. The hand opened, all at once, at the end of his gesture, as though it released something, and flung that thing away. I had the distinct image that the hand flung my father away, my father so little and shriveled and pitiful that he was crumpled in the palm of that hand, like a wad of paper, to be flung away, to whirl across the snow, forever.

I couldn't stand it. I felt that I had done it, that I myself had crushed him to nothing and flung him away. Tears were starting down my face. I turned and ran across the snow toward the lights of the town, not so far off now. Once or twice Ellie, or the other girl, called after me. But I only ran harder.

The next day Ellie approached me as usual, apple-cheeked and assured. I listened to her indifferently, to the arguments and justifications. How well I knew them, already! And how fully I believed them. But even my own conviction could not make her words seem more than a jostling of the air. At last, in a blend of magnanimity and conquest she suggested that, then and there, we offer up a prayer for my father's salvation. And she promptly dropped to her round knees, arranged her hands, and lifted her face at the appropriate angle.

She waited, then turned to me. "What are you waiting for?" she demanded.

"I just don't feel like praying," I said.

That was it, I just didn't feel like praying. I had lost the picture of myself as the young girl clothed in white robes, with face shining in meekness and mission, and I didn't have any other picture to take its place. I felt forlorn, and listless, and even as I repudiated Ellie, and the old image of myself, I felt a sneaking sense of loss and alienation. The future, suddenly, seemed nothing but a vista of grayness.

It was late that afternoon that Mrs. Turpin knocked on my door. There was a visitor for me, she said, eying me with respectful curiosity. At the stairhead, she could stand it no longer. In ill-concealed awe, she whispered: "It's that Mr. Parton—that Seth Parton!"

Her expression clearly indicated that the world was unhinged, and I unhinged in the middle of it: Seth Parton was coming to see me—me, an unsteady, outlander young girl whose soul, if saved at all, was saved by the barest—and I wasn't aware of the improbability and honor.

"Don't you even know what he wants?" she asked.

I shook my head, again, and passed down the stairs and into the rigor of the parlor.

He stood in the midst of the horsehair furniture, head high and suffering, his left arm hanging straight down, with the wisp of his scarf in turn hanging from the fingers as from a hook, the right arm down, but slightly crooked to allow the big, red hand, with its cold-cracked knuckles and splay-jointed fingers, to rest on the monumental family Bible conveniently placed on the marble-topped, walnut center table. His poor, cracked boots were planted side by side, solid as doom, on the patch of Turpin red carpet.

Upon entering the room, after the first flickering impression of him standing there, I had looked shyly down at the floor, and found his boots. Now I slowly lifted my gaze, and saw his face. I saw that some moisture was running down it, and at first I thought that he was sweating, even in the chill of the unused room. Then I saw that a little snow yet clung on his threadbare shoulders, and realized that the moisture was from the melting of snow that yet lay on his hair. I stole a look out the window. Yes, it was snowing now.

I had known of Seth Parton's hardihood in virtue. I had known that every penny he earned over the cost of his grim diet went to spreading the Gospel. I had known that he patched his own clothes, by firelight to save candle, long after midnight, when his study and devotion were done. I had known that, summer and winter, he never wore a hat, exposing that high, taut, challenging head to whatever distress the elements might afford, and that only in the severity of a blizzard did he use special protection for his body, beyond that wisp of scarf, and then only a hacked-off piece of old drugget, rigged like a cape for his shoulders and held in place by laces and lappets of his own contriving.

Now as I looked at his hair, made darker than nature by the wetness of melted snow, I felt a kind of awe, and then, as I noticed how a few strands of hair, soaked more than the rest to lose resilience, had got plastered down on his forehead like a spit-curl, in an effect of ill-considered vanity and absurdity, my awe suddenly melted, like snow itself, into a flowing softness that suffused me utterly.

Bemused by this feeling, by its novelty, almost forgetting his presence, I asked myself: *what is it, what is it?* Then I knew I was feeling sorry for him. In the past I had felt sorry for people, or rather, had thought I had. But this was different. I was experiencing for the first, terrible, never-to-return time, the soft, sweet, destructive joy of pity.

I discovered that I, without shame, was staring fixedly into his face. I saw his lips twitch, and the spasmodic working of his Adam's apple.

The time from my entry into the parlor until this instant must have been no time at all, really. But it had seemed long, full of the shades and scruples of my developing sensations. Now, suddenly, the Adam's apple stopped its spasmodic working, and there was his voice, as cold and detached as when I had heard it, not many hours earlier, as the very expression of the glittering, icebound night.

It was saying: "I do not come to you to apologize, or retract."

"No, sir," I said, hearing my voice very meek and thin and seeing my exhaled breath go white in the chill of the room. But I didn't feel meek. I felt, instead, suddenly old and wise, and felt like reaching out to straighten the plastered absurdity of the spit-curl on his forehead.

"If your father," he said, "is what is called a good master, he is the more dangerous."

"He means to be good," I said.

He ignored me, saying: "The good master is the worst enemy of justice. Indulgence rivets the shackle. Affection corrupts the heart. Kindness seduces the—" His gaze had lifted from me, beyond me, and his voice had assumed a more vibrant timbre. But he suddenly stopped, and looked down at me. "I need not tell you what you already know," he said. "I come to tell you that if I caused you pain last night, it is not because I would rejoice in pain. I myself suffered distress, and upon returning to my lodgings I paced in perturbation of spirit."

"Oh, that's all right," I said. And it really did seem all right. My father seemed very far away, and I felt that he could live out his own kind of goodness, and badness, and had nothing to do with the strangeness of this moment.

"But I knew that my perturbation was a weakness. I prayed to be delivered. And my prayer was granted. What I knew in my intellectual part, came again into the certitude of spirit. I could again declare that the person was nothing—that you, a person, a young female, Miss Amantha Starr, were nothing—and that Truth was all. If you suffered from the declaration of Truth, it was because you were ensnared in error, it was because—"

"I reckon it was because I love my father," I said.

"Love must scourge, in the name of Truth," he retorted, taking as stubborn defense what I had meant as apology. "But if I speak Truth," he continued, "if last night I spoke Truth and gave pain, it did not mean that I lacked regard for—" He stopped, abruptly, and the Adam's apple again twitched, and the strong spots of cold-inflamed red that marked his cheekbones spilled over the general pallor of his face.

"What I mean is—" he again began, with decision, "—is that I did not lack personal regard for the person whom I accidentally happened to be addressing. But by personal regard, I mean only such regard as is appropriate to—" He again stopped, and again, doggedly, went on: "—appropriate to the hope of brotherhood in Christ. But, as I have said, the person is nothing and—" The splay-jointed fingers of the big hand on the family Bible of the Turpins were spreading and unspreading in a slow, desperate rhythm.

Suddenly, he jerked his hand off, as though he had touched a hot stove. He studied the hand with enormous curiosity. Then fortified, he returned to me, leaning at me a little from the height of his high, constricted shoulders, addressing me with the asperity of a pedagogue, saying: "I hope I have made myself clear."

I nodded. "Yes, sir," I said.

"In that case," he affirmed, "I shall take my leave."

"Yes, sir," I said.

For a moment he did not move. I felt a sudden shyness and shame in looking into his face. I couldn't look any more at the pallor, the symmetrical red spots on the cheekbones, the rather large, slightly protruding, but colorless lower lip, the deep-set dark eyes that seemed to peer pitilessly into me but, at the same time, seemed to beseech pity. I was ashamed, as though I had surprised nakedness. So I looked down.

I saw a boot move. Then the other, moving toward the door. Each large boot set itself softly on the floor, as on uncertain ice, and at each step water squished audibly from the poor, broken seams. I didn't move my head, and the boots passed from my field of vision. Then I heard the outer door of the hall as it shut.

I ran into the hall, to the door, then to the window beyond. I looked out. I saw him marching off into the light snowfall, the boots leaving their regular marks behind him, his head high amid the descending flakes.

I was standing there, although he had passed from my sight, when Mrs. Turpin came into the hall. Then she was standing beside me, and I could feel her curiosity like a gentle suction. A deep stubbornness, a sense of my identity in the face of all the insidious pulls of the world, made me hold my posture, my eyes fixed through the pane. Then she said: "What did he want?"

The words released me. I swung to her, crying out in sudden, imploring anguish, "Oh, he'll catch cold, he'll catch cold!"

Her face, in the instant, was not the face I had known those years. It was as though another face shone through the old folds and weathered flesh and the competent maternalism, a face of gentle, quizzical softness, a face that was old with all her years but old without having suffered age. "Shucks, child," she said, "shucks!" And I realized that never before, in my hearing at least, had she allowed herself even that most innocent expletive.

"Shucks!" she repeated, with an air of almost gay defiance, "You'll be the one to catch cold. Froze to death in that parlor."

She reached out and felt my hands. "Go warm your hands before you catch cold," she said.

"Oh, I'm not cold," I said, and added, with a quick, crazy gush of joy out of my heart, "Oh, I'll never be cold again!"

And without meaning to, just because her face was the way it was, and I was, in that instant, the way I was in my insides, I jumped to her, and kissed her left cheek, with a poorly aimed, desperate smack, and turned, and fled up the stairs to my room.

Shortly after this event just recounted, I went to Cincinnati to see my father. He was as usual with me, the affectionate parent, showing me off, now and then covertly ruffling my hair to give its natural curl some play, asking me a thousand questions and, with excellent courtesy, enduring my answers.

But I noted, without quite putting my observation into words, a certain excess in his attention to me. No, there was no more attention to me than before. There was, rather, a difference in tone. Punctiliousness—that was the new quality, as though he were being very careful to fulfill a bond.

I took this to be some new attempt on his part to make amends for his failure with me more than a year before, when I had tried to save his soul. I had, of course, seen him in the meantime, and he had made various efforts to indicate to me that he longed for our old clarity of feeling. Now, sitting in a restaurant to pamper my spendid appetite, taking tea by the fireside of Miss Idell—Mr. Muller was still ill, now in a nursing establishment in Cincinnati, they said—walking with me in the street that I might admire the vanity of the shops, my father made his new effort, so resolute, systematic, and unflinching that something touched my heart. I wanted to tell him not to bother, that it was all right now, that he was he and I was I.

Then came the day when I was to stay with Miss Idell, at her house, while my father transacted business in the city. She treated me with her gay-attentiveness, making me feel very grown-up while she took tea with me in female intimacy by the fireside. Then, at the door of the little drawing room, escorted by the soft-footed maid, my father appeared.

For one instant, I did not believe it was my father. It was my father's face, even if a face very uncharacteristically sheepish and blushing, but something was most definitely wrong, something denied his very identity. Then I knew. He was wearing new clothes, clothes the like of which I had, certainly, seen on the streets and in the hotels of Cincinnati, but clothes which on him outraged all probability. He wore a dark wool coat, cut shorter than his old one, a waistcoat with some sort of design on it, and plaid trousers, cut very close to the calf of the leg and spreading just enough at the bottom to accommodate snugly the tops of the glistening boots.

Just as I became aware of all, Miss Idell conquered her own paralysis and, swaying back and forth in her chair, surrendered like a willow to gales of laughter. Then she leaped up, one hand lifting to dab at her eyes with a floating bit of lace handkerchief, the other stretching out to my father in graceful, despairing appeal, and ran toward him, exclaiming, "Oh, Arey—oh, Arey—I'll just die, Arey—"

Arey—that word meant nothing to me, and on the first utterance, I thought, in my confusion, that she was addressing, was running toward, someone in the hall beyond my father. Then the maid shut the door, and there was nobody, nobody else, only my father, and he was that Arey to whom she cried in such gaily outraged voice. His name was, I remembered quite coldly, Aaron Pendleton Starr. She had always called him Mr. Starr.

Just as she reached him, with the arm still outstretched as though to touch him, I caught his eyes looking beyond her, at me, and his voice said sharply, "Miss Idell!"

She froze in her tracks. But she was equal to the occasion, or almost, and within a second, her voice—I couldn't see her face—was saying, "Oh, you must forgive me—you must forgive me, Mr. Starr —for laughing. The new clothes, they are very handsome, really. I do admire them, Mr. Starr. And forgive the familiar address. But we have known each other so long, haven't we, Mr. Starr?"

She conducted him to the fireside, she poured his tea, and they both devoted themselves to me, with that punctiliousness which I had earlier observed on the part of my father, and into which she now entered with conspiratorial intentness. And all at once I saw so clearly, at last.

I saw it all. Mr. Muller was dead. He must have been dead some time, and they just didn't tell me, telling me a lie instead, but a white lie for which I could forgive them. My father was going to marry Miss Idell, and they didn't dare tell me yet. They wanted to make sure that I would be happy. Couldn't they see that I was no longer a child?

I really felt sorry for their innocence. I was aware that if this revelation had come to me not many months earlier I should have felt the whole matter as a desertion by my father, as a betrayal, and by Miss Idell, too, I suppose. But now, in my new certainty of self, and of life, I felt indulgent, and kindly. Even my first resentment that they thought I was young enough to be fooled, and needed to be fooled, passed away. I did not even feel resentment, or not much, when after I was abed, he leaned to kiss me good night, and whispered into my ear, "Good night, Miss Sugar-and-Spice," and I detected some haste, and some faint note of placation, in his words. I still forgave all. Or rather, I felt no need to forgive.

As I fell asleep I wondered how life would be back at *Starrwood*, with my father and Miss Idell. I sank into a floating dream of happiness there, gaiety and peace there with them. But all at once, I was sharp awake. With profound clarity, I knew my life lay elsewhere. I saw the high, hieratic head of Seth Parton moving off through falling snow.

I returned to Oberlin, without regret. But always, even on my earlier returns, I had found that life there had its sweetness, even if a sweetness that now, from my new sense of age, I could look condescendingly back on. With the other little girls of the primary division I had run squealing down the elm-shaded streets, that is, if no grownup was coming our way, or had pensively walked in the spring meadow hunting four-leaf clovers. Later, at the age of secret-telling, we paired off, two by two, arms draped over each other's shoulders, or daintily holding each other by the waist, tightening the hold only to emphasize a final revelation, or imply the dire deepness of our trust. Secret-telling throve more in the autumn woods, with the excuse of gathering hickory nuts, than it did in the summer fields, or throve more still in winter, at night in our rooms, when we sat sacked up to the neck in the voluminous flannel nightdress, swathed in the wool wrapper, hunching in chairs drawn close together, clasped hands between knees, and the brow furrowed with the seriousness of the communication.

We had had so much to communicate. Whom did we like? Miss Stiles, she was nice, she understood the seriousness of your problem about sanctification. She also let you cry on her shoulder if you were homesick, or had had your first period, or were struck by a strange, wild despair of your own life. Miss Hopewell, she was mean. No, you had to say that she failed by an excess of spiritual pride, and you would remember her in your prayers. Had Delsie Dawson really reached an understanding with that theology student? Would she go West with him on a mission to the Crows or Blackfeet, or whatever they were? Or Africa. Yes, Africa! Oh, how you yearned to make your own life sublime. And was it right to wear broad ruffles? Or a bit of lace at the collar, if the collar was fairly high?

In the old days nobody had even showed any neck at Oberlin. Old Mrs. Zilpah Grant had laid it down that to expose a neck makes a strong appeal to the sensual feelings of the other sex, and she had rigorously maintained that no good woman would wish to excite impurity in the mind of even her husband. But by my day necks did get exposed in Oberlin, and half moons of some very pretty shoulders, too, and some of our secret talk was about exactly how much was required to excite impurity. We didn't want to excite it. We simply wanted to know where lay the terrible line.

So in our whispered confabulations, we passed on, year by year, the terrible secret stories from the days before our time, like the story of poor Horace Norton who had fallen in love with some young lady and had written her letters pleading for a meeting in the woods. The postmaster, a Mr. Taylor, a godly man, had suspected the nature of the missives, and had begun to open them. The letters, tradition had it, were obscene, and years later, as we whispered the story, we shuddered, our heads together in communal horror and reprobation.

I wanted desperately, in those days, to know what was in Horace's letters, and even now I should like to know, as I see him sitting, late at night in a cold room, hunched over the sheet of paper, his big farmerish hand making the marks that were the sweetness of his dream or the barnyard health and brutality of his lust.

Anyway, justice was done on Horace. Mr. Taylor forged a reply from the young lady, agreeing to the woodland tryst. When Horace arrived, Mr. Taylor and some students of theology seized him, gave him an hour of lecture on the cupidity of the flesh, and then spread-eagled him on a log for the blood-flogging. Later, the college expelled Horace, and the question of the justification of the lynching was a favorite topic in the local debating societies. The Supreme shine of Ohio, and to be on the verge, if I could only attend more closely, only strain a litttle more my intellectual ear, on the verge of knowing the inwardness of that grand, infatuate gabble.

In the months that followed I worked unremittingly at the book he had specified, but when he came to hear my lesson, what I thought I knew always fled from me. I sat beside Seth Parton, at the pine table, and yearned to touch, even with the most fleeting touch of a finger, the cold-reddened, rawboned wrist that extended before me on the board, and the under-music of that desire was pitiless even as my mind strove to grasp the thorns of the holy language.

I thought of the time to come when I should grasp that thorniness and it should be soft as a flower, of the time when I should understand the high words uttered in the street, when he should turn at me with a smile cleansing his face of all severities. I had never seen him smile. But I knew that he, at the moment of my comprehension, would smile, and I tried to dream what that smile would be like.

Then the time came for his sermon. For ten days before the occasion, he suspended my lessons. He had to wrestle for a truth in prayer, he said, and his frailty could not endure distraction. This was in February. The sermon was to be on the twenty-sixth.

Seth preached in the late afternoon. That morning Dr. Finney, old now but yet with the jut-nosed grandeur of an old eagle, had preached on "Blood, the Price of Salvation," and to speak in the afternoon to hearts yet shaken by that morning's apocalyptic ferocity, would have been a test for any man. And Seth began bumblingly enough, sad and confused in black coat and unaccustomed cravat.

Sick, I sat and heard the uneasy movement of bodies, saw the heads shift in wandering attention. I myself scarcely heard what Seth was saying. It was, as best I could determine, a dreary history of the abandoned doctrine of sanctification at Oberlin, and arguments pro and con. But there is one last argument, he was saying in his flat voice, staring out over the heads of the people. "It is—" he said, and his right arm shot up above his head, his eyes lifted and flashed, and with a distinct thump, like a smitten board, his left fist struck his chest. "It is," he said, "the voice of God in the heart. Let not the world, nor the world's racket confound! Let not the sluggishness of blood, nor the horror of darkness, deceive! God were not God to deny possibility. And I affirm the possibility of the last joy. Who has not felt the possibility? For all joy is of God. Look in your heart, look in your heart—"

Then, with a sudden lifting of both arms, as though to lift us on high, he chanted,

> Oh, let me be the flame upon the brand!
> Oh, let me be the song upon the tongue!
> Oh, let me be the wind that walks the land,
> And in God's youth, let us be forever young!

He had stepped around the pulpit. As the last word still echoed in the chapel, he dropped to his knees, his arms and face still uplifted. "Oh, God," he said, in a vibrant voice of prayer, "there are no words with which to pray for joy. We offer the heart."

In the ensuing silence, I heard the sound of weeping. A woman near me was weeping, but when I looked at her, I saw that her face was transfigured. Others wept. Then old Dr. Finney rose, and there were tears on his gaunt cheeks. "On this day," he said, "we weep for joys forgone and forfeit. But, oh, God! in Thy goodness, we weep in joy!"

Then he turned toward the platform, where Seth yet knelt. He stretched out his arm toward him. "My son, my son," he said.

I waited in the back of the chapel, while the people crowded around Seth. I was not waiting for him. My timidity in this moment of his greatness would have forbidden such a thought. But I wanted to fill my eyes with him. I saw his head above the heads of ordinary stature. His face was very pale now, and sunken. When, finally, still surrounded, he began to move toward the door, his steps had a retarded, somnambulistic motion. As the group approached the door, I sank back into a pew, nearly concealed from sight.

But Seth's glance was upon me. I saw him lift his arms from the elbows, and make a motion to part the group from before him, to pass through. The motion he made was like that a man makes in a canebrake, to part the canes for his passage. The eyes of all followed him as he made his way to me.

He stopped a litttle before me. "I would speak with you," he said.

I nodded, dumbly.

"Come," he commanded, and I came out of the pew, and made my painful way toward the door, as he indicated, through the silence. He followed me, without further communication with those who waited.

He said nothing to me, but moved down the street by Tappan Square, in the decaying light of late afternoon, in winter. We proceeded to the point where the town raveled into the openness of the fields, where the sidewalk gave way to a few boards flung down here and there for the worst of the mud. We passed the last house, and saw the snow smooth on the fields, except where streaked brown by the lines of corn stobs showing through.

Some five hundred paces down the road, Seth halted, stepped over the rail fence to the left-hand field, and wordlessly turned to give me a hand for help. Then he released my hand and moved on, across the field, toward the woods, which looked black against the western light.

Upon entering the woods, I could detect no proper path, but there was little undergrowth, and Seth moved forward with certainty, as though he trod a foreordained track. When some dry stalk of alder or a loop of denuded grapevine impeded, he did not swerve, he simply thrust it aside, as he had thrust aside the people about him inside the door of the chapel. Our feet rustled on dry leaves, for there was less snow here than in the field.

Without warning, Seth stopped just at the edge of a small open spot, cast his glance about as though to assure himself, then moved a little forward away from the trees. Then he bent his gaze upon me. "I must say something to you," he said.

I nodded, waiting.

"First," he began, with hint of dry, scholastic system, "I would say that you have led me to a great truth. In humbleness I say that without you, and what I take to be the purged significance of your being, I should not have discovered the truth. Though you may be but the ignorant vessel of truth. That truth is the possibility of sanctified joy. You have heard my public discourse. Do you grasp my private meaning?"

I nodded again, but all I felt was some sad befuddlement and falling away of heart. Why, oh, why, had he brought me here?

As if to answer my inward question, he resumed: "Second, I would say why I have brought you here. Look about you."

I looked about me.

"Memorize the spot," he commanded. "Mark all."

I saw a small opening, or glade, set amid the bare oaks and hickories and ironwoods. I saw a little growth here and there about the

edge, blackberry or haw or such, with tattered leaves clinging. I
saw a great fallen tree trunk, old, long since rotting into earth, a few
stubs of roots sticking in air. I saw the undisturbed snow over the
earth in the glade.

"Do you know what this spot is?" he demanded.

I shook my head.

"You stand on the spot," he said, "to which, years ago, that lustful
boy Norton would have lured a young female. Do you know that
history?"

I nodded.

"Yes," he said with asperity, "yes, all know it. Even after these
years, and meanwhile what good deeds have perished! But this is
known in whisper, and recounted in shadow. Do you know why they
tell it, and tell it again?"

Did I or did I not know why? And his question froze me inwardly
with guilt and fear.

"This is why," he said. "For in every telling there is complicity.
There's guilty spying on the deed that might have defiled this spot.
There is entrance into the deed, and teller and listener enact all,
and their breath comes short in the whisper and in the darkness of
mind. They enter upon the defiled spot." Abruptly he leaned at me.
"Do you know why I have brought you here?" he demanded.

All I knew was a kind of dizziness, and a hollow beating of my
blood.

"I will tell you," he said. "I have brought you here that we may
redeem this spot." He reached down and, with his right hand,
seized my left wrist. He stared down into my eyes. "To redeem this
spot," he repeated, almost in a whisper, and his grip tightened, to
the point of pain. He leaned over, pressing on my wrist so that my
body was forced to sag. The tumult in my bosom was, all at once,
more than I could bear, and with it a suffocation, which was, also, a
joy. I felt my knees go to nothing, and my thighs flow from me. Then
I realized that I was kneeling, that I had dropped down, my knees in
the snow. Seth leaned over me, still gripping my wrist, peering down
into my face.

"Yes," he said, the whisper now almost breathless to nothing, "to
redeem it." Then more strongly: "Listen—this is the test. I said to
myself, I will discover that spot the lustful boy defiled. This is it.
I said to myself, if I can conduct her there, if there I can put behind

dry-eyed haste, made ready for the trip to Kentucky. As I turned toward the door, my glance fell upon poor Bu-Bula, propped stoically on my bureau. I ran to her and picked her up, and kissed her, over and over.

Poor Bu-Bula, she was all I had in the world.

When I got off the stage at Danville, it was early afternoon of a wintry day. At the inn I asked how I might get to *Starrwood*. The man whom I asked looked curiously at me, and volunteered that Mr. Starr was dead. But how was I to get there, I repeated. "Mam," he said, "you might try the livery stable." Then he added: "But you gonna be late. They gonna bury this afternoon."

In the office of the livery stable, a dirty hole heated by an iron stove enameled and crazed over by toasted tobacco ambeer and spit, I found an old man who seemed to be the proprietor, a colored hostler squatting by the stove, and another man who, from his appearance, I took to be a prosperous citizen, elderly too. I stated my need.

Without replying, the proprietor consulted his big watch, lashed to his person by a leather thong. He shook his head. "If they ain't throwed in the first clod, hit's nigh," he said.

But I had to go, I had to go, I cried out, beseeching him.

The prosperous, elderly citizen, who had been scrutinizing me, leaned a little forward and said: "Miss, I think a young lady in your need deserves our best help. I'm sure Mr. Sawyer here—I'm sure he'll send you out."

"Hit'll be a dollar," Mr. Sawyer said.

"And, Miss," the prosperous citizen, now politely on his feet, was saying, "if you don't mind telling, and don't take as just idle curiosity what I mean in human sympathy—Miss, why are you anxious to get to the burying?"

"He's my father," I said, "and, oh, please, please take me!"

"Hit'll be a dollar," Mr. Sawyer said.

I jerked open my purse. I thrust money at him, saying, "Please, please."

"Hitch up Pompey," the owner ordered the Negro.

With awful deliberation the Negro uncoiled his body from the squatting position by the stove, rose to his tottering and improbable height, and sloped toward the inner door.

"Move!" ejaculated the prosperous citizen, and with his stick struck the swaying, tenuous behind of the hostler.

"Oh, hurry, hurry!" I was saying, to nobody in particular.

"Pompey is a right nice-steppin gelding, Miss," the proprietor comforted. Then, as with a scruple for accuracy, added: "Once you git him in the shafts."

The prosperous citizen came and stood in front of me. "I'm right happy to make your acquaintance, Miss"—he seemed to hesitate for an instant, then continued—"Miss Starr." He bowed. "Even if 'tis a sad occasion," he amended.

With my urging, and a dollar for himself, the Negro made Pompey do his reasonable best to *Starrwood.* Under the gray sky, the scene unrolled, the rows of leafless trees, the swelling pastures with some unseasonable green showing, the stone walls and hedgerows. After all my years away—seven years now—it all came to me with a combination of heart-wrenching nostalgia and a sense of rejection. Home —I was. coming home. *Starrwood* was mine now, but was I *Starrwood's?*

When we reached the turn in the drive, beyond the house, I leaned to look down to my old play-place, by the cedars. But nobody was there, nobody. My first thought was that the funeral was over, everybody had gone. I could see quite clearly now the little depression of my mother's grave, the gray patch of the stone, and the unmarked turf all about, and with that recognition there came a surge of relief. There had been, and was to be, no funeral. It was all a crazy, evil joke, or dream.

Then I saw the group of dark-clad figures, under the gray sky, down at the graveyard. My first awareness was not the renewal of grief, it was an impulse to cry out, "No—no—that's the wrong place —come over here—over here to the cedars!" For that was where my mother lay. She lay there because there she would be closer to the house, and to him, my father had said, and he should be buried there with her.

I jumped from the vehicle, and rushed across the grass toward the group. Then I saw that the mound of raw earth had been rounded off, and that the people, those strangers over there who had made this hideous mistake, all stood with heads bowed in the final prayer. All but one.

Despite the prayer, a hunched old Negro woman was approaching me from the fringe of the group. I did not know who it was, not even when she was close, and I saw the face, just the face of another very old Negro woman, the skin shrunken, losing its gloss, sagging off the bone, the toothless mouth fallen. Then the voice said, "Manty—Manty-Chile."

And I knew it was Aunt Sukie, and knew all the years that had passed. When she put her arms around me, I felt the sad slackness now of her bosom, the shrunkenness, and with my own arms about her, I knew how frail and small, as though to break in your hands, were the bones that supported her being. That knowledge was, somehow, the last accent of grief.

We stood there for a moment in the embrace. Then I felt her stiffen and her head lift. "Who dat?" she demanded, staring over my shoulder.

I turned to look. From the direction of the drive, with the background of the house and the tall, leafless trees of *Starrwood*, under the gray sky, a man was approaching. I saw another rig on the drive beyond the one that had brought me and a second man waiting in it.

"Who dat?" Aunt Sukie demanded again, querulously. "Who dat, and him comin?"

THE MAN CAME TOWARD ME, A MAN NOT TALL, BULKY BUT NOT FAT, a squarish-built man filling his clothes, the kind of man who makes you feel the perilous tightening of the seams when his body moves under the clothes, that makes you think of the animal creak of leather in boots or belt, as he sits at his heavy ease. Oh, his image is clear enough to me! I see the black unshaven stubble of his jaw, the peculiar wideness of his eyes, staring eyes, gray and protruding, committed only outward, implying no human life inward, inside the gray iron screen of his stare.

But perhaps his appearance did him wrong, for after he had stopped before me and fixed his stare upon me, what he said came like words from another face. "Lady—" he said, then stopped, and seemed to reflect on what he had said. "Lady," he said, "I can't say as I like what I'm gonna do. But, lady—" and he paused again. Then he said quite flatly: "I'm the Sheriff of this-here county."

Several people from the graveside had come near us. Now the Sheriff turned to them. "I call all you all to witness," he announced, in an official tone. Then back to me: "Do you state and affirm that your name is Amantha?"

"Yes, sir," I said, and felt a terrible prickle of blood.

"Do you state and affirm that you go by the name of Amantha Starr?"

"But it *is* my name!" I cried out. "That's my father—my father over there—" And I swung toward the raw grave.

The right arm of the square-built man flicked out, and his hand snapped shut on my upper arm like some mechanism of metal. "Amantha Starr," he said in that official voice, "if that's what you go by, it is sworn and affirmed that you are the issue of the body of one Renie, who was a chattel of Aaron Pendleton Starr, deceased, and—"

And I knew it was true. I knew it as truly as though I had known it all my life, and with some unformulated surge of emotion, a hope, a despair, a yearning, I swung toward the other grave, the old grave over yonder by the cedars, and in the timeless flicker of my consciousness I felt myself a child again, lying on my back in that little embracing trough, safe, under the sunny sky and cedars, safe—

But the voice was going on: "—and as her issue you are declared by the law of this here Commonwealth, to be a chattel of the estate of Aaron Pendleton Starr, deceased, and subject to such claims, whatsoever, as may—"

"Look here, Sheriff—" said one of the standers-by, one of the gentlemen mourners, "maybe this lady—this girl—maybe she's got papers."

"Huh," the Sheriff grunted. Then to me: "You got papers?"

"Papers?" I echoed, in question.

"Yeah, papers!" The Sheriff said. "Papers yore pappy give you. Didn't he ever give you papers? Spent all that money and sent you up North and all, and he's bound to give you papers." A trace of outrage was coming into his tone. "Think hard," he said, the tone of outrage mounting. "You don't find them papers and I gotta do something I won't like, and you won't neither." And he shook my arm irritably, as though he would, by God, make me remember.

But there was nothing for me to remember.

"But a will," somebody else was saying, "maybe in the will—"

"I got to go by my warrant," the Sheriff said.

"But if there's a will—"

"Yes, sir, there's a will all right," a voice said behind me, and I turned, toward a flicker of hope in the midst of nightmare. The speaker was the prosperous, elderly citizen who had sat in the office of the livery stable and so courteously had there taken my part.

"Yes, there's a will," he was repeating, "and you gentlemen know how a will begins—you all being the kind of gentlemen having estates to set in order before taking out for the Beulah shore." The prosperous elderly citizen seemed to relish the ensuing moment of silence while the mourners stared. Then he resumed: "I mean, gentlemen, that part about paying the just debts." Again he relished the silence. "Well, gentlemen," he resumed, "if it's Mr. Aaron Pendleton Starr's will you have in mind, you needn't bother to go any further. For if you read the paper you know that the Court of Fayette County, Commonwealth of Kentucky, has just foreclosed on him for every penny he's got, and every clod of dirt, and every—"

"Mr. Marmaduke," the first mourner interrupted coldly, "are we to understand that it is you who have sworn this claim against this—" He nodded at me, pausing.

Mr. Marmaduke shrugged. "The Court has awarded me," he said, "for I am the man the money was owed to. Owed to, so a fine gentleman could go whoring after his pleasure, and what I loaned him was more than all this is worth, too!" And he swung his arm in an all-embracing gesture, toward the fields, the graves, the house of *Starrwood*, and me.

"—you'd take her here—right now—right from the side of the grave—"

"By God!" another mourner broke in, "right from the grave of—"

But something was happening to Mr. Marmaduke's face, something terrible was happening to it. It wasn't the face of the nice old gentleman in the livery stable office. Something was twisting it, inside. And the face said: "I'll settle my claim for this female property for $1200. To anybody. Right here and now."

Suddenly I saw the lady in the black manteau and heavy veils, the lady who had stood apart from the group, and who had had for me the strange familiarity—I saw her moving rapidly toward the house where various carriages attended. Then as she got into a carriage, some flowing movement of the body told me who it was. It was Miss Idell—no, it couldn't be, but it was—oh, it was—and I called out, "Miss Idell—oh, Miss Idell!" crying out in my anguish, jerking against the grip of the square-built man.

But the carriage fled down the drive.

I heard Mr. Marmaduke saying: "Yes, I'll take the I.O.U. of any of you gentlemen. Then you all can set her free."

He shrugged again: "Me—I can't afford that luxury."

And the twisted delight was growing on his face.

"Oh, it's monstrous!" a woman's voice cried out.

Mr. Marmaduke seemed to meditate, very gravely, the burden of the cry. Then he looked at the woman. "Mam," he said, "you know who I am?"

"Yes," she said, "yes, you're Cy Marmaduke!"

"Yes'm," he agreed, "I'm Cy Marmaduke." His voice, which had been like the voices of the other men, those lawyers and planters, was all at once different. It had taken on a sly parody of servility, a parody of the nasal intonation of the pore white trash.

"Yes'm, Cy Marmaduke. And I ne'er chose this spot to come to light in, burn, and expire. No, mam, but I'm heah now. Born up yander in Poverty Hollow, weaned in Buttermilk Cove, in the shadow of Starvation Mountain, and reared with the wild pigs, and my pa, when a carriage come down the big road with a high muck-a-muck ridin, he jes stepped in the ditch. Yes'm, me too, and I walked this-heah country, rain ner shine, totin a little budget on my back, and sold thimbles and notions and nutmegs out-a my budget to them as would buy, but mam, you ain't the kind as e'er bought, pore folks bought, and then I got me a little ole spavin mule and a little ole coach-dray fer my totin and I put my dime and my two-bits out to loan, and mam, I jes got rich, mighty rich, mam, and it didn't take no time a-tall, mam, jes forty years and all my sweat and pain and road-walkin, and mam, it is shore now a pleasure to put big money out to loan to a fine gentleman like Mr. Starr, fer more'n he's worth, so he kin go whorin crost the river, and it'd shore be a pleasure to set his nigger free."

"Nigger!" one of the mourners exclaimed. "Look at that girl, Marmaduke, she's not a—"

"A nigger is what you kin sell," Mr. Marmaduke said. "Fer I don't want to keep no niggers. It wasn't my kind brung 'em here. Fer me, I'd a-put 'em all in a sling and slung 'em to hell on a Sunday. And I aim to sell this 'un a-fore she kin swallow her own spit."

But the same lady broke in, saying: "Oh, wait, Mr. Marmaduke! We'll get up an offering—an offering of mercy—at the church, at St. Thomas', and Mr. Marmaduke, you'll hold her, won't you, till we do it?"

"Mam," he said, "if you Pisscopers are gonna free ever nigger gal gets sold out-a Kentucky you better cut Mr. Astor in on yore bread and wine. And madam," his voice dramatically changed its quality, back to the voice I had first heard, the voice of cultivation and courtesy, "madam, with your kind permission I offer my regards and take my leave."

He lifted his hat most decorously, and bowed.

Then said to the Sheriff: "I suggest you serve your paper, and we be gone."

"Come on, gal," the Sheriff said to me, and drew me forward.

I twisted in his grasp and flung a glance, a wild despairing appeal, back over the group of mourners, stretching my free arm to them, crying out, "My father—oh, he was your friend—your friend!"

I saw them there, the gentlemen in black coats, the ladies in black, the prescribed decorum of grief, all the faces white and staring at me.

It was Aunt Sukie who leaped forward. With some last flash of force in the old bones, she leaped at the Sheriff, clawing at him, crying, "My baby—my baby—oh, ain't gonna sell my chile!"

The Sheriff kept pushing her off, backing away from her, just trying to keep clear.

Then Mr. Marmaduke said: "If she won't quit, Sheriff, slap her down."

The Sheriff shoved her, hard enough to bring her down to one knee.

"You old black toot," Mr. Marmaduke said, calmly, "I'm going to sell you off, you the first one." Then he looked up at the group of blacks, who had come to the funeral and stood yonder at the edge of the graveyard. "Yeah, you niggers," Mr. Marmaduke yelled to them across the distance of lawn. "I aim to sell all of you, ever one—ever last one, you hear!—vendue or dicker—vendue or dicker—cry-off or jew-down—ever last one!"

Then he turned and moved toward the drive, where his rig waited. When we approached the rig, he turned to the Sheriff. "If she's got a valise or bag or something, get it. Get it before the niggers steal it. It goes with the gal."

"All right," the Sheriff said.

Who had I, Amantha Starr, been before that moment? I had been defined by the world around me, by the high trees and glowing cook-hearth of *Starrwood*, and the bare classrooms and soaring hymns of Oberlin, by the faces bent on me in their warmth and concern, the faces of Aunt Sukie, Shaddy, Miss Idell, Mrs. Turpin, my father, Seth

Parton. But now all had fled away from me, into the deserts of distance, and I was, therefore, nothing.

For in and of myself, or so it seemed, I had been nothing. I had been nothing except their continuing creation. Therefore, though I remember much of that earlier time, my own feelings, my desires, my own story, I do not know who I was. Or do we ever come to know more? Oh, are we nothing more than the events of our own story, the beads on the string, the little nodes of fear and hope, love and terror, lust and despair, appetite and calculation, and the innermost sensation of blood and dream? No, I put it badly, for by that comparison what would the string be but that self, and that is the very thing it is so hard to know the existence of.

And there come into my head the words of one of my teachers at Oberlin, saying, "And if this philosopher has showed that all we have is the flow of sensations and recollections, then what is man? But we must say to this philosopher that there must be a soul to have the sensations and recollections." I wrote down the words in my book.

But that soul, it seemed, was slain at the graveside of my father, was slain there by his betrayal. I did not then put it thus. My hatred had not yet reached its formulation. Now, there was only the numbness, the muffling of all things, the period in which I was a being without being, as though my inner experience reflected the abstract definition of the law, which called me a chattel, a non-person, the thing without soul, and I was suspended in that vacuum of no identity, in the numbness somehow aware of the pain that was being awaited.

Can I convey this to one who has not felt it? Or have all, in one way or another, felt it, too?

And so, sitting in the rig, between the square, animal bulk of the man who had given me my legal definition, and the bitter old bones of Mr. Marmaduke, who had, we might say, given me my economic one, I was whirled away, under the declining light, past the winter-gone pastures and the darkening, raddled woods, distantly haunted by the call of crows, across the landscape of Kentucky, that land which is so celebrated in song and story as a spot of romance and the natural habitat of beauty and delight.

Now we fled through that landscape, and the last vision of *Starrwood* was in my head, the vision seized in my last backward glance, as our rig wheeled off down the drive: the great trees, the white gleam of the house beyond, as in shadow, the group of people under the trees in the foreground, a gentleman kindly assisting Aunt Sukie to rise, one lady with head bowed and hand pressed to her face as though weeping, or as though she could not bear the sight before her, another gentleman forward from the group of black-clad mourners, his right hand lifted after us in a gesture of command, his mouth open to utter a call.

But if he uttered that call we did not hear it, and so I see him there, frozen in that posture, all of them frozen forever there in my anguish—no, frozen in their own anguish—and we fled away through twilight thickening to night, toward the sparse lamps of Danville, where I was lodged in an attic of Mr. Marmaduke's large, scarcely furnished, hollow house, and locked in the attic.

Later Mr. Marmaduke brought me some food, food that, quite obviously, he had himself prepared, and I now have some vision of him puttering in dawn-light, or late evening, in the vast, abandoned kitchen of the servantless house, frying an egg, frying a hunk of sow-belly, frying some hominy, brewing some penurious coffee, assembling the same sort of meal for himself now that he had once wolfed down, in the hill shanty of his birth, or hungry, had longed for.

Now I stared at the chunk of meat congealing in its grease, at the mottled egg, and could not eat. I looked around at the dirty boxes and rubbish of the attic, the shadow-hung and cobweb-hung beams, and I was sure that nothing was real. I touched my face, I prodded my body, and I was sure that this was not myself, it was somebody else, yes, somebody I should feel very, very sorry for.

And with that thought a horrible question dawned. Was I here—oh, no, it wasn't I—but was I here because I hadn't felt sorry enough for somebody? Back in Oberlin I had heard the tales, and I had felt sorry. But sorry enough, sorry enough? Had I really believed the tales about what it was like to be a poor black man, a poor slave? Was that the trouble? That I had never had belief and sympathy in my heart?

In the midst of that thought I heard a movement at the door, and it swung inward, and I took that almost for a sign. I leaped up and ran to Mr. Marmaduke and seized his sleeve, compelling him, saying, "Listen—you've got to listen, for I do believe it, I swear I believe it, and I feel sorry—and you see, it's all a mistake—it isn't right—and it can't be true, it can't happen to me, not to me, to me—for I'm Amantha Starr—I'm Amantha Starr!"

He was looking down at me, peering painfully down. Then he said: "Yeah, you're Amantha Starr, all right. And that's why you are here, because you are you, gal."

With that, as I stood there absolutely paralyzed with the notion he had voiced, he turned and picked up the tray, and swung toward the door.

After he had gone, I still stood in that paralysis of horror. But what was the horror? Then I thought: *It's because I am I.*

And I thought: *It's because life is coming true: I am I.*

In the end I slept, though fitfully. Once or twice I thought I heard footsteps on the ladder-stair leading to the attic, and once, I was almost sure, I heard a hand laid to the latch.

Mr. Marmaduke did not dispose of me in Danville. He took me to Lexington, where traders and speculators came for stock, choice and common, to be shipped down-river. He sold me, not by vendue, but by a private dicker, to a Mr. Calloway, a big man in the trade, who was making up a coffle for Louisiana.

But before we left for Lexington the afternoon after my arrest, there had been, Mr. Marmaduke told me, some effort on my behalf. Some ladies from St. Thomas' Church did call on him and beg him to hold me until they could try to raise money by a mercy offering, or perhaps a bazaar. "But they'd be piddling around forever," Mr. Marmaduke said, "and then try to jew me down. Oh, yeah, I know their kind. Every one of 'em has a house full of niggers, and try to jew me down to set you free." Then he burst out: "But for me—I don't want any niggers, now or never, nor you."

He added, too, that there would be a piece in the paper about me. The longer I stayed around the more trouble would get stirred up, he said. "Yeah," he said, sourly, "and trouble for me."

Mr. Marmaduke bade me farewell in the office of Robards' Slave Market on West Short Street. He ordered a colored boy to fetch my valise. "This goes with you," he said, glumly. Then he stared into my face. "Listen," he said to me, "don't you be blaming me."

In my numbness, I stared back at him. Suddenly, he burst out.

"Durn it, I can't help it. If I set you free, every nigger in the place starts yowling to get free. I didn't make niggers and I didn't make 'em slaves."

I wanted to cry out that I wasn't a nigger, I wasn't a slave, I was Amantha Starr— Oh, I was Amantha—Little Manty—Little Miss Sugar-and-Spice. I could feel the pain of wanting to cry out.

But he had taken a step to me, leaning, shaking his old head, where now I saw the dandruff scurfing to the baby-pink scalp under the sparse gray hair, leaning his old tallow-white face down with an expression of sadness, saying: "Maybe it won't be so bad. A pretty gal like you are, maybe some young buck down in Louisiana'll buy you—one of those Frenchy fellers down there—and you know what he'll do?—do you know now?"

He leaned closer, and I wasn't hearing his words, I was simply regarding, with extraordinary concentration and precision, the most minute details of his face, the veining of the eyeballs, the tiny silken folds of flesh at the corners of the mouth, the gray splotch on a tooth. Then, in a whisper, awful, confidential, he said: "He'll —— you."

He had used a word that, to my conscious recollection, I had never heard spoken, the vile word, but it rang like a bell with all the clarity of knowledge, or rather, with the clarity of nightmare knowledge, for with the clarity was a swirl of mysterious darkness, and even as the word echoed in what seemed the enormous hollowness of my head, I felt another sort of echo, apparently unrelated, even in the outlying provinces of my body, a tingling of the fingers, a sudden coldness in my legs, then a prickling of the spine, not terror, not desire, but a sensation without a name. And at the same time, I felt peculiarly disembodied, out of myself, almost floating, with some far-off sense of pitifulness for the body which Amantha Starr had left behind.

"Yeah—yeah," he was saying.

It was the nasal, pore-white-trash voice, the voice of his sad youth, saying, "Yeah, and then you git old, and it don't matter. Not if you done had it. You kin git old, but they can't take hit away, if you done had it. Yeah, nigger or no, hit is yourn."

He paused again. "But me—" he began, and his face twisted into the bitterness that was almost delight. "But me—I never had it. Not much to speak on, not more'n a nigger two-bits worth. All them years and me trampin the roads and hankerin and I seen them fine ladies ride by—yeah, soft-hand and sweet-titty—yeah, and I stepped in the ditch. Yeah—" he paused heavily. "Yeah, and then—"

Suddenly, he spat on the floor. "Then I got rich," he said, "but everthing, it always comes too late."

He collected himself. "I nigh come in to you last night," he said. "I put my hand on the door. Did'n you hear me?"

And he leaned for the question, as though the answer meant all to him.

He seemed about to turn away. But he did not. He fumbled in his pocket, and brought out something which he held concealed in his hand.

"Maybe hit won't be so bad," he said. "Maybe you'll git somethin you like out-a hit, and hell"—he paused—"if you don't, ain't nuthin lasts ferever."

He thrust out his hand at me. "Here," he ordered, "take it."

Automatically, I put out my hand, and he dropped something into it. The thing was a silver dollar.

He looked into my face as though expecting something—pleasure, gratitude, what?—but not finding it, shook his head impatiently, and said: "Now don't you go blamin me."

Then he was gone out of the office, and I held the dollar in my hand.

I was ashamed that I had not flung the coin in his face, that tallowy, moist-eyed, old, sad face. What forbade me, I don't know. But now as I think back, I am glad that, for whatever reason, I did not reject the gift.

But I did get rid of the dollar afterward, when I was put with the other slaves of Mr. Calloway's coffle. I gave the dollar to a middle-aged Negro woman, simply because she was the one nearest me. At that the others began to importune me. They made such a racket that Mr. Calloway's driver, a strong, slick-faced, smart-looking mulatto, waded into the fracas, and confiscated the dollar.

It was the night of the day when Mr. Marmaduke left me, and I had given the dollar to the old slave woman, that I made the attempt to get free. It was done without premeditation, simply as a reflex, as impersonal as doom. It was the middle of the night. I lay on the cot in one of the decent little rooms of Mr. Robards' market, the rooms provided for the choice stock in contrast to the barracoon shed for the common.

I was not asleep, but in the state of blankness with some sort of consciousness flickering along the edges of that darkness, like flames nibbling in darkness at the last dry grass about the edge of a black swamp where fire cannot go. In that flickering consciousness, I was aware of what I did. No, I cannot say that *I* did anything. My body made certain motions leading to a certain end, and *I*, with complete detachment and no surprise, was aware of the process.

My body rose stealthily from the bed. The hands opened the valise and found a small pair of scissors, ordinarily used to dress the nails. With this instrument the hands cut a long strip of the coarse linen with which the bed was covered. In this process the breath of the body came short and shallow. Then my body went to the one window, and looked down. There, in the starlight, was the little alley, and beyond it, the barracoon and sheds. Some last embers smoldered in the darkness of one of the sheds, where bodies would be lying at random like cast-off garments.

The hands felt the iron of the bars on the window, vertical bars, and seemed to puzzle slowly, slowly in a kind of sad, stupid animalness, over that verticality, rubbing the fingers up and down on the metal in an uncertain motion. Then, with one foot on the ledge of the window, the body rose flat against the bars, and the hands, at the highest point they could reach, managed to tie both ends of the strip to a bar. In this process, the throat began to emit, in perfect rhythm, a muted, sweet, anxious, yearning whimpering, somewhat like the whimper of a puppy when it strains against a leash toward its food tray.

With great caution, so as not to slip off the window ledge, the body turned around, to face into the room, and the hands dropped the loop of linen about the neck. Again, with caution, and in perfect silence, without even a breath, the body, still on the ledge, leaned forward to put the first, probationary pressure on the throat. Inside the body, the heart was making a great thumping, a sound of great hollow resonance, a sound bespeaking terror—or joy?

Whatever that heart meant, it was not mine, merely belonging to that body, which now, with the increased pressure, could not breathe, and felt the blood pounding in the neck veins. This, though the body had not yet stepped from the ledge. Meanwhile, in detachment, the *I* felt sorry for that poor body—poor thing, poor little thing, would it hurt? Then, clear as day, I saw Mr. Marmaduke's face and heard his voice saying, "Maybe you'll git somethin you like out-a hit, and hell, if you don't, ain't nuthin lasts ferever."

With that, even as the body teetered on the ledge, *I* thought how strange that the last face to be seen, the last voice to be heard, were those of Mr. Marmaduke—not of people loved, Miss Idell, Seth Parton, my father. Then, in a flash, like a loud cry inside me, I knew it: *but it's them, it's them—they did this to me! It's they who are making me do this!*

And in that burst of rage and outrage, the *I* and the body became, again, one thing. And I was I. I had stepped from the ledge.

It would have been too innocent to suppose, as I in my innocence had supposed, that a man of business as experienced as Mr. Calloway would leave a considerable investment subject to any casual whim of pride or idle gust of despair. He had not.

Precaution had been taken, all right, but the mulatto driver, or whatever he was, must have been drowsing at his post in the hall, for he didn't come bursting into my room until I was swinging free of the ledge, swinging free, an ignominious, disheveled parcel in a white chemise, bare heels kicking for the lost ledge, hands clawing hopelessly for a grip on the bars above my shoulders, an ignoble jouncing and clawing which annulled any nobility of purpose I might have had.

I have since told myself that the kicking and clawing was automatic, the mere reflex of the brute life threatened by my human resolve, and that the reflex of brute life does not impugn the sincerity of the resolve, but even so, I have sometimes blushed with shame, seeing myself in these desperate contortions, the hung-up cat, the bulge-eyed failure.

For I was a failure. With a whish of a great knife, the mulatto slashed through the linen strip, grabbed me in one arm as I fell and righted me, dropped the knife and with the free hand whacked me diligently on the back. Breath came pouring back into me, like fire.

All at once, Mr. Calloway was charging into the room, holding a candle high and askew in one hand, with the other trying to tuck the long tentlike tails of a nightshirt into his trousers, flopping his bare feet on the boards, yelling, "God-durn you, Jack, you let that gal hang herself and I'll buck-paddle you—I'll sell you down-river—I'll—"

Somehow, he had managed to deposit the candlestick on a chair, had managed to hitch his trousers up, all the while in motion, flopping his feet, yelling direly; and with the last incompleted threat, he fetched the mulatto a sweeping backhand blow across the face, and as the victim staggered back, himself grabbed me, all the while saying, "Durn you, you slut—God-durn you—me buy you and you go and cheat me—and I—I'll—I'll—" His words came to an apoplectic conclusion, and all he could do was suck in great hanks of his black mustaches and grind them in his yellow teeth, and drop into a chair and snatch me across his knees and spank my backsides while I cried, and the candle-flame from the candle set on the other chair sputtered and swayed to make the shadows dance.

I can't say that I was crying from pain. The spanking might almost have been done in a kind of fun, a sinister horseplay. No, I was crying from indignity, outrage and failure. Anyway, in a moment, Mr. Calloway leaped from the chair, dumping me to the floor, flung his gaze wildly around, and then, as though some force had gone out of him, sat right back down. He must have realized, all at once, that his investment actually was safe, that it lay there on the floor in considerable untidiness but full value, and the relief of that realization just took the starch out of him.

For the moment he simply sat there, and recovered himself. Then he got up, hauled me up by an arm, and looked into my face. Then he said: "Look heah, gal, you done tried it now." Then, after further studious inspection which seemed to assure him of something: "Yeah, and I reckin you ain't gonna try it again. You just ain't the kind, gal."

With that pronouncement, which with its sad, sardonic wisdom cut some fiber in my nature, Mr. Calloway gave me a thrust, not a very hard thrust but enough to tumble me sidewise to the bed, to sprawl there watching him, my eyes dry now, while he assembled himself, picked up the candle, ordered the mulatto, durn him, to come on, took one half-hearted swipe at his head as he dodged past like a shadow toward the door, and then, himself, followed out, still precariously hitching at his trousers, as when he had entered, and setting his bare feet on the boards.

The next thing I really remember is a couple of days later, at Louisville, as we boarded the *Kentucky Queen*, a packet of 590 tons, bound for New Orleans. We were crossing the plank to the main deck, that is, the lowest deck, the mulatto and I, he watchful at my side, ready to grab me if I made to heave myself over the side. Just as we got aboard, Mr. Calloway emerged from among the piles of cargo. He was looking very much the dandy now, fine plaid trousers cut close, glistening boots that complained elegantly at every motion, red waistcoat with gold chain stout enough for logging operations, opulent linen, black coat and black tie and black hat, a black cheroot set at an authoritative angle and the black mustaches curled and oiled to a patent-leather glister. Mr. Calloway was arrayed for the moment of his greatness, the trip down-river.

Mr. Calloway planted himself firmly in our path. He pointed the cheroot at me, like a weapon. "Gal," he said, "I am putting you in a cabin upstairs. Like you was a lady, mind you. And you gonna stay in there except when you git out fer a promenade—" he lingered on the word with relish, defining himself as a man of the world and travel, "and you ain't gonna complain to nobody, or say nuthin, if you understand what I mean."

He turned and stabbed with his cheroot toward the depth of the over-hung, shadowy vistas of the main deck. "Look there," he commanded.

In the recesses of the main deck, back of the engines, in the open shed roofed by the boiler deck, I saw the mountainous piles of hemp bales and bacon flitches and whisky barrels and tobacco hogsheads, and the pens of merino sheep and swine, all the famous produce of Kentucky bulging from the shadows to the very guards.

Then I saw the human figures in that tumbled shadowy landscape, some thirty figures I should estimate, figures with black or brown faces, men, women, children, propped vacantly against the bales and staring at the shore, lounging on the floor, talking and laughing or snoring, a man smoking a cob pipe, a mother solicitously picking the nits from the head of a girl-child. Two of the men were manacled, a leg and a wrist of each chained to one of the uprights supporting the boiler deck. They were Mr. Calloway's coffle, they, too, famous produce of Kentucky.

"Look there," he said, "any shenanigans out-a you, and you git chained to a post. Back in there where it's dark and cozy. And see them niggers chained up?" He paused again for effect. "Wal, they is rough niggers. Folks up here in Kentucky don't understand about breaking niggers like down-river. Wal, what I'm saying is, some of these niggers ain't good broke yet, and is sort of hot-natured. If'n you do shenanigans and I got to put you down here, and it come night, ain't no tellin what'll happen, and durn, I don't care, so long as they don't bruise you bad. Now, come on."

With that, to the accompanying creak of his varnished boots, he stalked off toward the stairs, or companionway, or what you may call it, that led to the boiler deck where the salon and cabins were. I followed him up there, through the white-and-gold grandeur of the salon into the ladies' section. Mr. Calloway flung open the door to a cabin, and stalked on in. I followed.

"I got money tied up in you," he said, "but I ruther put you downstairs and let them bucks wear down a couple hundred dollars off you, then git a lot of worriment." This with the expansive air of a man accustomed to large operations, before he stepped out, shut the door, and locked it, and strode off to the moment of his greatness, to lounge on the red plush under the gilded jimcrackery of the salon, the leering cupidons with the expression of an infantile victim of mumps, the carved cornucopias spilling plaster apples of horrendous red; to spread the napkin over his stomach and confidently order the steward to bring him some of that-there French fricasseed calf-kidney and some pickled pig-head à la viennoise, and, nigger, rush that claret.

The Kentucky Queen had been grand once, but long before this. Now her engines lurched and heaved on their bed-bolts, and when some sleeker, more prideful craft boomed for free-way and swept past under the imperial black streamers of smoke, her captain now never rose to the challenge and flung pitch-pine and flitches of bacon like ten-dollar bills into the furnace till the boiler plates bulged and the rivets groaned, and now the French fricasseed calf-kidney resembled nothing so much as what might remain after a flash-fire in a cattle barn, and the claret, but for its color, was an indifferent vinegar. No, as she humped and clanked down the river, the Kentucky Queen was just trying to hang on to the old dream of herself, but she was adequate for Mr. Calloway's dream of himself, at least when that resplendent nigger-merchant would prop his elbow on the mahogany, steal a comforting glance of himself in the bar mirror, and lift his glass of planter's punch, with the old, solacing words, "Here's to your health, gentlemen!" Yes, gentlemen!

Meanwhile, I lay on my back, on one of those two berths in the little cabin, probably the smallest and the dingiest of cabins, and stared at the ceiling, and the whistle blew till the little window rat-

tled, and a bell clanged irritably, and at the first thrash of the paddles in the water, a shudder took the whole structure of the vessel
and my body on the bed, too, and the *Kentucky Queen* yawed to the
deep inner swag of the river.

And in that moment I knew again, as vividly as life, the moment
when I had first lain in the cabin of a steamboat, when I had first
heard that preliminary agitation, when I had first been left alone in
such a cubicle to feel the vibration. That remembered moment was
the time when, so many years before, on my first trip north from
*Starrwood,* on the way from Louisville to Cincinnati, my father had
laid me in our cabin to rest, and had left me there and gone out to
his own world.

With the fusion of that old moment and the present one, the recollection of his leaving me, which had actually been a moment of
drowsy contentment for the nine-year-old child, became now a
moment of irremediable anguish at abandonment, and my father's
act of closing the door upon me became all the later acts, the act of
dropping me at Oberlin among the whey-faces that he might pursue
his pleasure, of deserting me for Miss Idell, of leaving me to the
clutches of money-lenders, of binding me to slavery, of setting me
forth, boxed in this little room, on the dark heave of the river. For
darkness was now settling down.

Oh, he had always betrayed me, in every act, from the act of my
begetting to the act of his death. Oh, he had always lied to me. And
I remembered how he had said that my mother's grave was apart
from the others because he wanted her nearer the house, to him and
to me, and that lie, somehow, summed up all the other lies, and with
that recollection came an access of hatred. It came with a surging
exhilaration. With that hatred something seemed to be settled, something relieved. What, I could not say, but I fell quickly asleep, not
into the drugged stupor of the past week but into what seemed to be
a deep, natural sleep of exhaustion.

I was awakened by a minor chunking in the ribs, and opened my
eyes to see Mr. Calloway prodding me with a forefinger, and beyond
him in the dim cabin, two other figures, one of them indistinguish-
able, the other an old colored woman holding up a lighted lucifer to
a gas fixture on the wall, the rays streaking down across the seamed,
severe old face that squinted upward at the task. For an instant, in
the confusion of waking, despite Mr. Calloway, the strangeness, the
heave of the engines, I felt the joyful relief of coming out of the bad

dream, and almost called out her name, "Aunt Sukie, Aunt Sukie!"

But it wasn't Aunt Sukie. The flare of the ignited gas showed me that much, and reaffirmed the reality of Mr. Calloway, who stood there gently hiccuping, picking his teeth with a gold toothpick with one hand, and with the other indicating the third person, a young mulatto woman, who held a tray with some covered dishes. "Here's your grub," he declared, "and bet you never et better."

I sat up in the berth, and the young woman put the tray on my lap. I sat there looking at the covered dishes.

Mr. Calloway jerked his thumb at the old woman. "This here is Aunt Budge," he said. "She's gonna sleep in here, and you better do like she says. You don't do right, and she'll snatch you bald-headed, and that don't work, and hit's main deck and nigger-bait fer you. Now eat."

Mechanically, I lifted the lid from one of the dishes and took a bite, of what I can't remember. Mr. Calloway watched the action, then went out of the cabin. With a long backward look, the young mulatto woman, who had been covertly inspecting me all the while, followed him. The old woman shut the door, bolted it, sat down in a chair, folded her arms, and regarded me.

I got down what few bites I could. Then I simply couldn't put another morsel to my mouth. I sat there, under the old, baneful gaze of the black mammy, with a fork in my hand, some scrap on the fork, and simply couldn't lift my hand.

I could not lift the fork, even though I saw her rise from her chair, settling her heavy flesh to her bones like somebody hitching a heavy coat down on the shoulders, and move across the few feet of cabin toward me.

"I can't," I said, almost wailing, "I just can't." And I let the fork drop, and saw it lie there among the cold gobbets.

I saw her hand come down into my range of vision, and for an instant I did not know its intention. Then the hand seized the edge of the tray and lifted it. So I looked up. She stood there, now holding the tray with both hands, looking down at me. "Mought as well have et," she said. "Ain't nuthin gonna change nuthin." And her gaze remained uncompromising.

Then she said: "Chile, doan you know that?"

I could not believe that I had heard those last words, and that last voice. They did not belong to the face that now stared down at me. But she had said it. "Chile," she had said, and a warm gush flooded

my heart, and I reached out to lay hand on a fold of her dress, saying, "Listen—listen—let me tell you—I'm Amantha, Amantha Starr
—and it's like this—it happened like this—and—"

But she moved away from me. The fold of her dress stretched taut
to the point where my fingers gripped it. I was leaning out of the
berth, desperately gripping the cloth, hanging on to something. Then
she moved farther, and it was drawn from my grasp.

"Ain't listenin to nuthin," she said, in the former voice, and moved
farther away, as to remove from the locus of infection. "Whut I doan
know doan hurt. You is you, and me is me and I ain't hearin nuthin."

She turned her back, set down the tray, and went to the other
berth. She sat down on it, removed her shoes, shoes with high lace
tops of soft kid, once the property of some lady, now down at heel
and slashed open in the forepart for comfort. Then she lay back on
the berth, heaved up her legs, grimly disposed her hands crossed on
her bosom, closing herself in upon herself, and slept.

I lay there with some sense of the last betrayal. It was as though
Aunt Sukie, Aunt Sukie herself, had, at last, drawn away from me,
leaving me to emptiness. I lay there and wished that I were dead,
and free. With that wish, there came some sense of a lifting flicker
of wings, over bright water. And I remembered that, back at Oberlin, we had been told how slaves on slave ships, manacled and
packed spoon-fashion, tight beyond motion on the shelf-decks in the
stinking holds, would dream of a bright flight back home, and would
hold the breath for suffocation, or swallow the tongue, that they
might fly away, back home, over the ocean, over the bright line of
booming surf and excellently white shore, over the jungle, to the
sweet village where flowers brilliantly bloomed and beloved faces
lifted to greet them from the shadow of tidy beehive-shaped grass
huts. And I remembered how my imagination had swelled to the
throttling horror and heroism of the act.

So now, remembering, I tried, experimentally, to draw my tongue
back upon my palate. Would I fly away, be free and fly away?

But where, oh where, would I fly?

The question, however, did not matter. I merely had a fit of coughing. Then I heard Aunt Budge stir and moan in her sleep.

Oh, who would save me?

For an instant, for the first time in a long time, I thought of my
mother, and the never-seen face, calm and beautiful, leaned over my
imagination, and my heart gushed with joy: *oh, she loved me!*

Then, suddenly, I thought: *but she was a nigger.*
The face was gone.

Before I went to sleep, lying in my dullness of heart, I thought of those huddled down on the lower deck, and wondered why none of them leaped into the water, to escape or die, why none of the manacled ones held the breath or swallowed the tongue. The thought of their own infirmity of spirit was, as I began to fall asleep, some comfort, some comfort at least. They were no better than I.

But with that came, somewhere deep in me, a flash of refusal. No, no, I was not to be compared with them, I was not one of them, I was no nigger, I was I, I was Amantha.

And I began to tell myself, with calmness and rationality, that my name was Amantha Starr. I told myself that everything was simply an absurd mistake, a mistake and not in the true nature of things, and a mere mistake, no matter how absurd, can always be rectified. Of course, it would be rectified, for I was I, I was not somebody else, somebody without value, unloved. Yes, I was loved.

Miss Idell—why, she would come for me—she had merely rushed away for money. Yes, she would seek me, for she had loved me, had promised that I would be beautiful.

And Seth—oh, Seth, he would hear and come. He would come and take my hand and raise me up in freedom and joy. For he had promised me the perfect joy.

Yes, I was I, and I fell asleep in that certainty, and Seth, with a dawning smile, reached out his hand to me.

With a start of alarm I awoke from that sleep. The motion of the steamboat had stopped.

There was some rattle and bang outside, and muffled shouting. I jumped from the berth.

"Git down, you," the old woman's voice said from the darkness. "Git down, ain't nuthin but takin on firewood."

By that day the finest steamboats, the thousand-ton palaces like the *Eclipse* carried their fuel in large supply, but older ones, like the *Kentucky Queen*, still hitched their way along the river from woodstop to wood-stop, the woodpile flung down on a mud-shelf by some flea-bit farmer or sow-belly planter, or the woodpile at the edge of deep forest where bearded, malarial, likker-soaked ruffians of every hue and blood-mix, with red neck-rags and ax-blades glinting in sunlight or campfire, stared over the water with ultimate disdain, spat, and faded back into the shadow of the trees.

But I saw nothing that night of the wooding. It was two or three days later before I saw the process, a rainy afternoon, late, the light dying in gray deliquescence over the uneasy corn-clearings and leafless woods of Missouri. High on the mud-bank was a shack precariously clinging to the viscous slippage of earth, a sort of groggery and store, with two or three men huddled on its porch, eating something, drinking from a bottle, staring down at the *Kentucky Queen.*

Below the groggery was the woodpile. Lines from the steamboat ran up the bank to be snubbed around fire-black stumps, to hold her unsteadily in, and the plank, canted at an improbable upward angle toward the woodpile, stabbed into and sucked from the mud-bank, with the unremitting slew and drag of the river. Up one side of the plank to the shore, in single file, cat-stepping and precarious on the wet board, the Negroes went, then clawing up the mud-bank toward the pile, then returning with the wood-length, down the slick bank, mud-slimed and streaked, down the other side of the plank, into the shadow of the main deck where my vision could not follow. Near the woodpile, maintained on that slick surface by some miracle of balance, waving a knobbed stick, a pistol stuck in his broad belt, drizzle plastering his wild, uncovered red hair, hovered the bellowing mate.

Watching the process, I became aware that not all of the wooders were deck hands. Some vague familiarity in one or two of the figures told me, at last, that among them were the male slaves of Mr. Calloway's coffle. Yes, as was common, he had them thriftily working their own passage to Louisiana.

It was one of Mr. Calloway's slaves that went over.

The wood-length went spinning so high and gay, and the fellow's plunge over was so decisive, that my first thought was that he was making a break, was risking death in the river for this chance to escape. My heart lifted with a joyous surge.

But even as my heart leaped, and my eyes fixed on the swirling spot of brown water where the form had disappeared, even as I heard Mr. Calloway's outraged yell, "Git that nigger! Ten dollars to git that nigger!"—even as I was aware of all that, the man's head broke water, I saw the wild, bulging whiteness of his flung gaze, saw his mouth spread open to some horrendous dimension as though to drink all the river, and heard him cry out. He cried: "Save me!—Oh, massa, save me!"

It had been nothing but mud on the plank, after all.

It was only luck that saved him. As he again started under, his hand struck the spinning chunk, and he grabbed it. Then chunk and man swerved from the suck toward the main current into a little eddy in the lee of the steamboat.

They threw him a rope with a loop, yelling to him to take it. For quite a while he couldn't bring himself to let go of the revolving chunk. Then he managed, and they drew him aboard. It took some prying to get his hands off the rope.

"Well, sir," a gentleman with an upriver accent offered, "he's lucky to be a nigger. Been an Irishman and gone over, nobody would have offered ten dollars to fetch him out. They'd just let him go yelling on down-river to Mexico, and saved what they owed him for wages."

At that moment Mr. Calloway, down on the main deck, was engaged in a discussion with the Irish deck hand who had heaved the slave the rope. The Irishman seemed to expect the ten dollars. Mr. Calloway's position, as his voice affirmed loud enough to instruct us all, was that the mick hadn't gone in after the nigger, had just tossed him a line, and anybody could have done that. They compromised on four dollars.

By this time the plank had been hauled in, the whistle had tooted, the paddle wheel had thrashed the water to a caramel froth and shaken the steamboat like an accordion in the hands of a maniac, and Aunt Budge and I were alone by the rail now, staring westward toward evening, a faint wash of saffron over one spot of the universal gray.

I had been robbed of something. I had been robbed of some deep confidence.

Ordinarily, Aunt Budge was my guardian, on deck for my airing or in the cabin, wrapped in her somber silence, leaning on the rail, or sitting in a chair in the cabin, arms folded upon herself. But the mulatto girl, who occasionally relieved Aunt Budge in the cabin, was anything but silent. She would stare at me with picklock intensity, question after question.

I simply couldn't answer the questions, not even when the unflickering yellow eyes abased themselves, and in a histrionic whine, she identified herself with me, her hard lot with my own, her hopes with mine, murmuring, "Yeah, yeah, us pore niggers. No matter how white we git, we got dem long heels—got nigger heels—" And she would thrust out her foot for my inspection. "—Yeah, pore niggers lak us, ain't nothin fer us—jes to love one-nuther, lak Jesus say."

What did she want? Whatever it was, it chilled my blood.

Once, after such a conversation, after she had gone I leaped up and drew up my skirt and inspected my heels. Then I remembered how my father, back when he held me on his lap and played patty-cake, had looked at my hands and then had kissed each finger. Had he been secretly looking all the time for the tell-tale blue half moons on my fingernails—the sure mark, they said, of black blood, even if only a spoonful?

Now in the cabin, I looked at my fingers. They told me nothing I could be sure of.

It had been early March—March, 1859—when we left Louisville, with the rawness of the season in that section. But now we were moving into another season. The air that moved to us from the shore might now bear, in tantalizing uncertainty, the odor of new earth, the sweetness of bursting buds. Willows on the mud-shelves, visible above the high water, showed the tracery of green, and higher, maples were coming to the goldness of bud, oaks to redness. Toward evening the swallows came over the river. They would dart downward at the water, brush it with a lightning delicacy, and flare upward in the sunset. Once, I saw a single drop of water fall flashing from an ascending bird.

Off Arkansas, again toward evening, a great flight of duck rose from the margin of the flooded woodlands westward, wheeling over the river. A gentleman stood on the deck and behind him a Negro, a body servant. The gentleman would fire a fowling piece into the midst of the flight, would hand the discharged weapon back to the Negro and receive another, ready and primed, and would fire again, almost all in one motion. Another gentleman, watching this for a bit, went away and returned with a pistol. Amid the incredulous chafing of the company, he lifted that instrument, laying the barrel across the left wrist, and fired. The duck that his ball hit seemed to hang motionless for an astonishing moment, then slithered crazily sidewise down the air.

"Bravo, bravo!" someone cried, and the marksman laughed in amiable modesty, and lounged on the rail. The wounded duck, still struggling in the water, fell astern.

Out of the western light, against the color of evening, inexhaustibly, the flight of duck came streaming. The first gentleman, he with the two fowling pieces and the black squire-at-arms, though now ignored by the company, continued, methodically and dourly, to fire. On the high bluffs, near Memphis, a horseman reined at the very verge. High above us, motionless, he was sharp and hieratic against the morning sky. He was like a statue of dire and beautiful meaning, but a meaning not fathomable. Or like a heroic creature of air.

Farther south, where the levees were built along the river to guard against flood, we rode so high on the full current that we saw over the embankments, and beyond, over the fields, to groves and houses and flowering orchards. Now and then, someone on the levee, lost and landbound, waved to us. Once, out of a sudden yearning, I waved in return.

Once, on the westward shore, against black forest, under the pink light of evening, I saw a deer stand on a spit of land, drinking. As I looked at it, my heart, as though untouched by my condition, swelled with every beautiful hope I had ever cherished, the hope of having life be meaningful, the pity I had felt for Seth Parton in the Turpin parlor with snow melting on his hair, the recollection of a little rabbit with beating heart I had once held in my hand, long ago at *Starrwood*—and oh, poor Bu-Bula lost, and forgotten, blaming me, far off in Oberlin.

I became aware that Aunt Budge, standing by my side, was shivering in the evening chill. "Oh," I cried, "you are cold!" And before she could answer, I had run to the cabin for a shawl for her. I came back with it, joyful, somehow expecting the world to be different now, purged of all pain.

But the world was not different.

Toward Vicksburg, I saw the blooming tree. It was a peach tree, in full bloom, it had stood in some yard or scrub garden, along a creek or bayou, and the flood had come and snatched it up by the roots, and whirled it away. Now it rode the brown current, the pink blossoms yet unshattered, and in the bright sunshine I saw a circular dance of little white butterflies, among and over the blossoms. I wracked my head to try to remember if there could be such butterflies—I think they call them cabbage-butterflies, poor sober name for such a thing—this early in the season. I told myself that, after all, it might be a trick of light, and distance.

That night, as usual, Mr. Calloway came by the cabin for his inspection, followed by the yellow girl bearing my tray of supper.

I was not hungry. I toyed with a mouthful or two, while Mr. Calloway watched me, and near him, the girl. "Eat, eat up," Mr. Calloway said, expansively, then with his gold toothpick took a stab at some recalcitrant remnant of his own dinner. "Eat up," he repeated. "Got to put some meat on yore bones. I don't sell niggers by the pound, I sell 'em by the lump, but a juicy lump shore fetches more'n a scrawny one. Ain't that so, Jillie?"

With that he gave a commendatory whack to the young mulatto woman's near rump, at which attention she grinned and gave a slight upward hitch of the flattered part of the lump that was herself.

"Yeah," he continued, "Jillie cost me plenty. But I wouldn't take nigh double right now. But you"—and he leaned over me, "you better eat the grub and git some meat on. Yeah"—and he leaned closer, looking me more nearly in the face, into my very eyes—"yeah, you git some meat on and you'll fetch somethin." And for a moment, with an air of discovery, he was rapt in his inspection.

That is, until the girl Jillie interrupted. "Mr. Call-way," she said in honeyed tone, "did'n that nice Tenn-see gennel-man, did'n he say somethin bout you takin a hand of cards?"

"Damn if he didn't," Mr. Calloway agreed, straightened up, established his toothpick in the left corner of his mouth, jauntily under the mustache, and marched out of the cabin.

Jillie shut the door after him, then turned decisively back to me. She took the tray off my lap. "Starve, and be damned to you," she said.

She set the tray down and leaned over me. "Git some meat on," she mimicked, "yeah, but you won't have nuthin lak this!" And she slapped herself on the rump, jiggling herself. "Yeah," she was saying, "he lak what I got—" And she slapped and jiggled, "Yeah, he laks somethin to really wrap round him, yeah—and ain't no good rollin them big eyes at him—yeah, I seen you roll 'em—but listen!" And she leaned menacingly over me, whispering: "White ner no, I cut yore thote."

I was cringing back on the berth, making some inarticulate protest, saying I had not done anything, I did not know what she meant.

"Oh, yeah," she cried, "I'll tell you what you done. You try to make him take a shine on you and not sell you. But he sell you. Yeah, you think you whiter'n me, but you ain't, you jes nigger too. Yeah, and he gonna sell you, and some feller buy you, and what he do, what he den do?"

She leaned at me, and asked quite calmly: "You know what he do to you, some feller?"

She waited, as though politely for an answer. Then she straightened up, away from the berth, saying, "Yeah, and I show you—nigger, and think you so white, yeah, and I show you."

There she stood, swaying in her obscene pantomime, hands clutching and weaving the air, her red *tignon* slipping off her head to the floor, her hair coming loose, her face slick and damp in the rays of the gas jet.

Then the old woman, who had been sitting motionless in the chair, spoke. She said: "I'se gonna break yore back, you doan git out-*a* here."

Instantly the yellow girl stopped. She looked at the old woman. The old woman said nothing, but under that implacable regard, the girl left the room.

As soon as the door had closed behind her, I gave a kind of sob, a gasping sob, for, as I discovered, I had been holding my breath. I leaped from the berth and ran to the old woman and flung myself on her bosom. Saying nothing, she received me, her arms around me. After a moment, one of her hands began to pat my shoulder, and then, a moment later, when my sobs continued, she began to rock her body a little and to croon something, something quite wordless and sad. I began to relax to her comfort, to the comfort, too, of blurred recollection, and my childhood.

How long I lay there in that condition, I don't know. But all at once, my body was stiff again, I was pushing against her, trying to get away, away from her embrace, and in the silence after her crooning had stopped, I was gasping, "Let me go, let me go."

I got away from her, shoving her off, and went to my berth. I flung myself down there, face down.

What had happened was simply this. The odor of her body, the warm, spicy smell that had been at first part of the comfort of the moment, part of my recollection and peace, the smell of old Aunt Sukie, long ago, was suddenly horrible to me. I simply could not stand it.

Some time in the night, lying there on the berth still fully dressed, I dreamed a confused dream. It had something to do with my being manacled, down on the main deck, and all the slaves being manacled too, and somehow I was trying to tell them if we could all hold our breath we would be free, but they knew I was trying to hold my breath so I would not smell them, and so they laughed wickedly. But somehow Seth Parton was involved in the dream, standing high above us and saying that in sanctification all should be free, and he smiled down at me, the smile I once had hoped to see, had dreamed of seeing, and all at once, under his smile, the manacles fell off, off me and the others, and I expected to feel lifted up, and expected to see all the others lifted up in effortless flight to whirl away.

But my father was there, and he seized my hand, gently as though to caress it, murmuring how I was Little Miss Sugar-and-Spice. This until he noticed the nails. Whereupon he looked curiously at them, then flung my hand aside, and sang in a falsetto voice, "Long heels, Long heels," in the tune of "Greensleeves," and broke into wild laughter, and his feet tapped and snapped on the deck, and he leaped in a most improbable buck-and-wing dance and was, in a clap, like a wizard, gone.

The slaves crowded around me, squatting on their hams like apes, Old Shaddy and Aunt Sukie strangely among them, all gabbling and leering, scratching themselves and laughing at me and pointing at me, and so I cried out for Seth, but he wasn't there. So I awoke, ready to call for him.

After a reasonable while, I slept again, and the *Kentucky Queen,* with the clumping rhythm of its engines, moved on the broad bosom of the river, southward, leaving behind all I had been, all I had felt and seen, *Starrwood,* and Mr. Marmaduke, the horseman high on the bluff, and the person who had waved to me from the levee, a deer that had stood by the river's edge in the pink light of evening, and the last melancholy half-horse, half-alligator ruffians who had glared, red-eyed, at us from a wooding stage before fading back into the shadow of their trees, the peach tree floating seaward with the flittering coronal of butterflies snared in its bloom.

Night after night it had been like this, the question there, if not in my mind, in my very blood: *oh, what will happen to me?* My mind might begin the question, but then before the answer could appear, it would go numb. But the answer would be in the cold tingling of my spine, in the constriction of breath, the terror of dreams, the terror, the lyric moment dissolving in terror, the degradation, the power of hands without names, the flash of bodies, the laughter of mouths, and in all the terror there was the most terrible fact, a kind of complicity that would make me wake sweating with shame and guilt.

And once I woke to the aged râles of Aunt Budge's nocturnal breath, and knew that everything, my being snatched away to darkness and abuse, was only a punishment for this guilty complicity. But how—oh, how—could that be, when the crime had not come until after the punishment, and was, in itself, part of the punishment? But the logic of that human protest seemed, suddenly, trivial, for the guilt was there and I was sweating in it, and the order of guilt and punishment in time was meaningless, for there was a deeper logic, not of time, and thus in the clarity of waking nightmare, the old sermons of Oberlin came alive in their very language, but their language became my flesh.

So in the recognition of the justice of my punishment, I was somehow justified in embracing the sweetness of terror, to affirm justice— and to again compound my guilt. Was there no way to break out of that desperate circle?

The night was charged with the scent of blooming. Now and then an unseasonable heat lightning played over the horizon, flickering into my cabin and, no doubt, brushing the broad water with reflected light to make the shores, over yonder, leap up darker and more solid. And with that constant clumping vibration of the engines, the jimcrack gilt joinery of the great salon creaked sadly in the darkness, like a barn door when the wind shifts, and tiny particles of gold and red and white flaked off the rich ceiling and sifted downward into the uninhabited vacancy.

# I V

THE MORNING OF THE SALE IN NEW ORLEANS, WE WERE ASSEMBLED, the whole coffle, in a back room of the slave-house, or jail, which Mr. Calloway patronized. I sat on a bench by the wall, waiting. I saw the mulatto driver call out the oldest man in our coffle, sturdy but with grizzled poll. His head got a treatment. A woman had the task of tweezering out the offending hairs, and then working a little ordinary bootblacking discreetly in. What remained was for Mr. Calloway to threaten not to sell the fellow at all but send him to his own plantation, if he did not learn, letter-perfect, his new age: "Yassuh, massa, yassuh—forty-three come corn-pulling time, and my mammy say frost late dat year."

He repeated, the slave I mean, the lesson with studious attention, and tears of anger and despair flooded my eyes. Then, all at once, my eyes were dry. I said to myself that I would never have done that.

The Kentucky stock that Mr. Calloway had assembled was slick and well fed—he would have bought no other kind for the long trip down—but at Memphis he had picked up bargains, all three with a good dose of plantation scurf, their skin gray-scaly and their hair with the dusty lackluster and reddish tint at the root that are the sign in the black man of bad nourishment. On the short way down from Memphis, Mr. Calloway had, of course, prescribed special feeding for these members of his train, treating them with something of the sinister benevolence practiced by the Strassburger on a goose.

Now down at the other end of the room, Mr. Calloway was supervising the filling of a great wood tub with scalding water, and suddenly, at an order from him, one of the Memphis bargains pulled off his shirt, let his trousers drop, and with a sharp prod from Mr. Calloway's stick, stepped into the tub. It all was happening so fast I didn't believe it. I saw the black man standing there stark naked, the vapor wreathing up whitely around his black skinniness, and I was staring at him, and it all seemed an obscene dream, a vision I had conjured up, and what I felt, as soon as I felt anything after the first coldness of perception, was a guiltiness, a fear and a guiltiness that I had summoned up the obscenity.

Then I was aware of all the eyes on me, the faces grinning at me.

So I simply closed my eyes. If I closed them tight, nothing would be real. But I heard the snickers.

Then I was ashamed of myself for that weakness. At least, I would not be a coward. At least, I would open my eyes.

Yonder at the tub they were scrubbing the fellow down with a broom. Next they rubbed him with sacking, and next, to supplement the forced diet of sow-belly and lard-soaked cornbread, they wiped the fellow with a little bacon grease and soot, worked well into the hide and brought to a gloss. To conclude, he got new pants of Georgia stripe, calico shirt, campeachy hat and russet brogans, and was ready to impose on credulity.

As for me, Mr. Calloway seemed to find a certain lack of gaiety in me, and sent out for some lengths of red ribbon. He told me to tie one around my waist, in a bow. I honestly tried to tie a bow. But I couldn't. My fingers, suddenly, felt so big, like summer squash for size, but light and inflated, like the hog-bladders that, at hog-killing time on *Starrwood*, for me as a child with the colored children, Old Shaddy had blown up to make toy balloons.

"Durn," Mr. Calloway said, and seized the ribbon. With a struggle and wheezing, he managed to get some kind of a bow—oh, how gay!

The mulatto driver marshaled out some ten of the gang, lined them up and led them into the street. Mr. Calloway turned to me. "Come on, gal," he ordered, "and no shenanigans!"

Perhaps it was his words, perhaps the sight of people, ordinary people, moving casually in an ordinary street, perhaps merely the brightness of the air and the extravagant pink of a great camellia tree flaring above the scaling beige stucco of a courtyard wall. Anyway, it was not by decision or plan. The act surprised even me. I started to run.

I could not have taken more than two steps before Mr. Calloway's grip was on my shoulder. As he swung me around to face him, I cried out, but the people passing only looked curiously at us—at least, till this day, I see the face of a gentleman passing who stared at us and I thought of the gentlemen at my father's grave, the last one I had seen as I looked back, standing there forever with upraised arm. But Mr. Calloway swung me around and his face came close to mine, the lips drawn angrily back under the black mustaches to show the yellow teeth. "Fool," he was saying, "you durn little Kentucky fool! You ruin my sale, and you wish you hadn't. They ain't nothing I can't break, and I'll break you if you ain't worth five dollars when I'm through."

The little troop of the mulatto driver was well ahead now, the men moving in the slow, sloping gait of the field hand, setting their brogans down strangely on the smooth surface, their heads hanging a little forward and swinging in a narrow angle from side to side, the way the heads of cattle do in the sauntering rhythm of the forequarters.

"Now, march," Mr. Calloway commanded. I followed up the *banquette*—that's what they used to call the sidewalk in New Orleans— close to the stucco walls, walls so beautiful in the light with their discreet hints of many colors in the gray, or buff, under the iron balconies that spilled bloom and vine in arabesques to match their own intricacy, past an old yellow woman with a great black skirt and red turban who sat on a stool offering little cakes for sale, rice cakes I would learn later—offering them to me, "M'selle, m'selle, cala, cala!"—past the cathedral where, through the open doors, in the depth of inner dimness, I caught a flicker of candles. And Mr. Calloway's expensive boots creaked rhythmically at my side.

We came to a large and handsome building at an intersection of streets, Royal and Saint Louis Streets to be exact, and entered by a small door toward the rear. Thence down passages, to a point where the driver ahead stopped and all the gang bunched together, in the dimness, bodies touching, waiting, and in that instant of silence I could hear the sound of their breathing.

Then Mr. Calloway led us into a great hall, nobly proportioned,

with columns and frescoes, the pavement of black and white marble
—all in all, the finest interior I had ever seen. In the hall were
ladies and gentlemen, sunlight falling over all from the high windows. As we bunched together in the sudden light, the gaze of all
turned upon us. Under that communal gaze, with a hitch and sway
of self-proclamation in the shoulders, and his seegar at a more
declarative angle, Mr. Calloway moved forward, to the vicinity of
a little dais, on which was a table. We followed.

The building, I had forgotten to mention, was the Saint Louis
Hotel.

The auction proceeded, like any auction, I suppose, except that
in these elegant surroundings, the crier-off modified the usual exuber-
ance. He would call up the property being offered, enumerate the
subject's points, and invite any interested gentlemen to make a personal inspection. Then the inspection, examination of teeth, the delicate lifting up of eyelids, the working of joints for clean articulation,
the hoisting of trousers, or skirt, to see the make of leg, the opening
of shirt to see if there were marks of the rawhide (a marked back
meant a bad nigger), the measurement of hands (if the buyer was
a cotton planter, for a strong hand, with shrewd fingers, was the
picker-hand). And through it all, the creature in question stood
dumb and indifferent, or grinned with a slack amiability, saying
"Yassuh, yassuh, forty-three years ole, come corn-pulling time"—yes,
the grizzle-poll of fifty told his lie—"Yassuh," and I hated them all.

I stood, and saw it, and did not believe that I could endure it. No,
I would spit in the face that came close to peer under my lifted
eyelid, I would sink my teeth into the finger that would lift my lip,
and I would not let go.

Then my turn came. I was the last. I mounted the platform, and
under command slowly revolved my person.

When the crier-off issued his invitation to inspect, there was
usually a moment before anyone came forward, a moment of mutual
courtesy among prospective buyers. But now, immediately, a man
moved forward, shouldering his way, lifting his right forefinger to
the crier-off. I saw the hand lifted, the flash of a diamond, then the
forefinger lifted separate from the other fingers—ah, that was the
finger!—and I felt my teeth come together, edge to edge.

At the same time I had some impression of the man, a youngish
man, a dandy, too much of a dandy, rawness showing through the
veneer, too much elbow in the swagger, toes turned out too much—

all the marks of the back-country, somewhere-in-Mississippi, two-jumps-and-a-spit-from-the-canebrake, fifth-crop cotton-snob, complete with shirt-frills, diamond ring, and a mortgage on every nigger. In approaching the platform he had just elbowed another man, elbowed him without apology.

That other man withdrew his bulk slightly from the contact, flicked a glance at the young man and his lifted finger, and then, with deliberation, raised his own right hand, in which was clutched, about midway, a heavy blackthorn stick with a great silver knob, the knob uppermost. "Sir," he said in a strong voice, "I bid you two thousand dollars."

In the silence, the young man turned and gaped. As for the speaker, a man of middle years, not much taller than average, thick of body, black-coated, squarish face very ruddy, jaws square, eyes gray, wide-set, and slightly bulged, hair thick and iron-gray and combed straight back on top of the large head as though it might end in a tie-ribbon behind—as for him, he stood there with his stick lifted in command and seemed oblivious of the company.

The young man recovered himself, said, "Hey, just a minute, I reckon I'll look at the gal," and took another stride toward the platform.

"I suggest," the older man said, in his strong voice, "that the gentleman refrain from his inspection unless he is prepared to top my bid."

The young man turned. "Look here," he said, "you ain't stopping me."

A sudden flurry of whispered conversation at the side of the platform caught me. "Him, you mean?" someone was saying, apparently in answer to a question, nodding across toward the older man with the blackthorn. And added, in a tone that implied much, but what I could not guess: "That—why, that's Hamish Bond."

Meanwhile, that subject, with the blackthorn lowered a little now, spoke again: "I would not stop the gentleman, but—"

"You're tooting, you won't stop me," the youngish man retorted, and leaped upon the platform, to me. He laid hand on my shoulder, turned me to face him, said: "Now, gal, you—"

"I suggest," Hamish Bond said very coolly to the master of the auction, "that if inspection of the property now proceeds, I withdraw my bid. And the other bid may not be as good—if, indeed, there is really a bid at all from that—from that person."

"What's that?" the youngish man said, and leaped off the platform toward Hamish Bond.

Hamish Bond ignored him. Addressing the master of the auction, he continued: "And I suggest that the ladies and gentlemen here be not detained while someone diverts himself in a manner more fitting to Gallatin Street than to the Rue Royale."

The youngish man was upon Hamish Bond now, demanding, "Just say it plain that's me you're talking about!"

Hamish Bond set his heavy, bulging gaze upon him, as though he had just discovered his presence. "Yes," he said slowly, almost sadly, "yes, you'd be happier down on Gallatin."

With the first *yes*, the right hand of the youngish man had slipped into the ruffles of his shirt, and lingered there, and with the last syllable of Hamish Bond's utterance, the blade—bowie, Spanish dirk, whatever it was—flashed out as precise as punctuation.

A woman cried out.

Then the episode was over. I saw the glint of the silver knob of the blackthorn. I did not see the instant of contact, but I did hear the yelp of pain, and as the group fell back, I saw the youngish man bent over from the waist, jerking his head in pain, holding with his left hand his broken right wrist.

I could see, too, that Hamish Bond stood now propped heavily on the blackthorn, his right foot a trifle out-thrust to pin the knife to the floor, his large head somewhat down and forward that he might inspect the moaning victim, his face now flushing dark and wearing an expression of heavy, brooding satisfaction. And I remember that with my thrill of gratitude, hope, or whatever it was that sprang up in me at the act undertaken—as I thought—in my protection, ran a tiny tremor of fear. Of fear, and unformulated excitement.

With his right foot, Hamish Bond spurned the knife aside, then approached the platform. I saw that he had some kind of a limp, a stiffness of the right knee, and that in walking he set the blackthorn down with deliberation for each step. At the platform, he leaned on his stick, ignoring me, and held out a bank note to the crier-off.

"Send to my house this afternoon for the difference," he said, "and send the girl's papers."

Even as the crier-off reached out for the bank note, he said, "Well —you know, Mr. Bond—the whole thing—the whole affair—that fellow wanting to inspect—what you did—now I don't want to criticize—but—irregular—"

The words were trailing off, but Hamish Bond did not deliver the bank note. "If you are not satisfied with the transaction," he said, "I humbly withdraw."

And my heart sank to lostness.

The crier-off had, however, grasped the note. "Oh, no," he assured Hamish Bond, "no offense, Mr. Bond—no, sir, Mr. Bond—it's just—it's just—"

Under Hamish Bond's stare the words were fading like water poured on sand.

When the silence was complete, Hamish Bond turned to me. "Come on, gal," he said.

But he moved ahead, looking to neither right nor left, swaying to the stiffness of the lame right leg, setting his blackthorn down with a distinct click on the marble, with metronomic precision, his square, black-coated back receding over the distance of black and white marble, under the pillars and the color of frescoes.

Suddenly, he seemed very far away. I felt that I was being abandoned. I felt the impulse to cry out, to run after.

My master was already out the grand door, in the street, before I caught up.

All the way down the river, I had lived in apprehension of my fate and, as I have said, in an anguish of complicity. But how different from what I had dreamed and feared was the event to come! There had been, of course, the frilled and toes-turned-out dandy, with pomaded hair and slick face and strong, hairy hand laid on my shoulder—he was directly out of the terror. But the voice of Hamish Bond had fallen across that terror. Only to give me the new terror of abandonment.

I overtook him, however, and followed along the brilliant street, close behind him on the *banquette*, as though he were a talisman to guide me through the air that was full of the odor of blossoming, of offal in the street, of coffee being roasted beyond some courtyard wall, of the exciting effluvium of the river. Then not more than a couple of blocks from the Saint Louis Hotel, he stopped before the gate of a courtyard, pushed open the great iron grill, and entered. He proceeded across the courtyard, past the stone well flanked by benches, past the great stone urns in which clipped orange trees grew, past all the strange vines and brilliant blossoms that clambered the walls or hung in garlands from the inner balconies, setting his blackthorn down deliberately on the clean, fitted stone of the court-yard. Then we entered the darkness of the house, dark, that is, after the brilliant sun.

For a moment I stood blinking in the dimness, then a woman appeared, a tallish figure, face of light color, severe under the pale blue *tignon*, and spoke French to Hamish Bond. " 'Sieur 'Amsh," she called him, or something like that, and looked curiously at me. He replied in French, but my ear was so unused to the spoken language despite my long study of it, that I caught little. Clearly, however, he was defining me and my condition; I caught the secret surprise on the woman's face, and the new sharpness of her glance at me.

She turned away, and the master said, "Follow her, gal." With that he turned and went deeper into the house, the diminishing tap of the blackthorn marking his distance, and I followed the woman up a winding stair to one level, then down a hall, up another stair, into a wide, bright room, sparsely but well furnished. I stood in the middle of the room still holding my valise.

Now, more clearly, I saw the woman. She was about forty-five, probably a quadroon, well made and tallish and, as I have said, rather severe of face, but the severity was without meanness, a clean straight thrust of nose and wide spacing of eyes. Under level brows and the pale blue *tignon* with its artfully sculptured folds, the eyes were a brown amber, deep-set and large and very steady in their gaze upon me.

Suddenly, she reached out and took the valise from my hand and set it on top of a carved chest beside the door. "My name is Michele," she said in French. "What is yours?"

I told her.

"*Américaine*," she said, and I nodded.

"Of what part?" she asked, in tolerable English.

I told her Kentucky.

"You have come a long way," she said. Then she gave a quick, dismissing gesture with her right hand, dismissing what, I did not know, and said: "But it is folly!"

I almost spoke up, to say that it was no folly of mine, but she spoke again, scarcely addressing me, saying: "But much of life is folly and—" She hesitated, then lapsed into her natural language, like an afterthought: "*Et pas toujours la part la plus mauvaise.*"

With that she left me, not closing the door behind her. Slowly, I turned to look out the window, wide and reaching from floor to ceiling, that gave on a little balcony. In that bright space, framed by the back-flung jalousies and the vines and iron lace of the balcony, were the sun-drenched roofs of red and umber and yellow and blue tiles, the receding roofs making a tumbled geometric landscape beyond which rose the tall central spire of the cathedral, surmounted by the gold cross.

I thought how, in the midst of my trouble, I had not once prayed. In Oberlin I had prayed much, and had yearned for obedience to God's will. Now all I carried from that old time was, I suppose, my sense of nameless guilt.

Oh, why hadn't I been able to pray?

And I couldn't pray now, for how can you pray when your very heart feels dry as an old raisin, and the world seems to stretch away from you in all directions, like endless sand?

So I flung myself down on the big tester bed, on my back, and stared at the gray ceiling.

And so I had come to live in the house of Hamish Bond.

The sunlight fell across my balcony, and the festooned vines looked like black fretwork against the blaze of light. I heard faintly the sounds of the city, and somewhere, deep in the house, the clank of a pot or pan. A fly buzzed in the room, then came and settled on my forehead, but I did not move. I felt, somehow, that I had to endure it, that small irritation, as though that small suffering might forfend a great suffering. The past and future, it seemed, fell away from me, all joys and angers and apprehension sinking to nothingness, or to the pitiful shadows of themselves. My eyes fixed again on the gray ceiling, and I felt now the small beads of sweat gathering at my armpits, and sliding down with a delicate, tickling sensation, and felt the dampness growing at the back of my knees.

Meanwhile, as more and more the past and the future, joy and sorrow, and all the items of the objective world fell away, I became aware of the inwardness of my body, of the blood moving in darkness, the heart expanding and contracting in its appalling regularity, and as though one could mysteriously see into the total inward darkness, I had an actual vision of the heart's slick, wet, muscular movement, ruby-red and glistening despite darkness, a vision of the intricate loops and swollen bulgings of inwardness, the grayness, the lymphic whiteness, blood-redness, sweet flabbiness, softness, dark-ness. It was as though, there in the bright daylight, I were falling inward, were flowing inward, as though myself were some dark, delicious pit into which I fell inexhaustibly, like sleep, like dying, but I didn't want to stop the falling, the flowing, the dying.

Then, all at once, I popped up to a sitting position, crying out— or I thought I cried out, "I've got to stop—oh, I've got to stop!" I scrambled off the bed, in awkward, headlong desperation, really tumbling off the bed with one knee and hand on the floor to break my fall.

As I looked up, I saw far yonder, over the roofs, the gold cross of the cathedral again, and in my wild moment of disorientation, I felt myself in the position of prayer, my knee on the floor by a bedside, and it suddenly seemed a sign. So I dropped my other knee to the floor and pressed my forehead against the bed's edge, and murmured God's name, over and over, trying to pray.

I suppose that I did begin to pray, but all at once all that was in my head, no matter what words of desperate appeal were coming from my lips, was the image of Seth Parton, that day in the winter woods, standing in the snowy glade, his head high against the sky, his arm lifted triumphantly, crying out: "There shall be joy!"

And I couldn't pray. I knew that I could not pray now—now when I most needed prayer, forlorn, forgotten, enslaved, lost in a foreign land—because that night long back, after the scene in the snowy woods, after I had got back to my room, I had tried to pray, to pray to be worthy of the joy Seth promised, but had only been able to weep, in desolation of spirit, in mysterious despair.

So it was all my fault. If I had then had the strength to pray, all would have been different, I would not be here now, in the house of the oppressor.

But if it was all my fault, why, all at once, did I hate Seth Parton?

I leaped to my feet. I found myself busily reciting the multiplica-tion table, out loud, very precisely and rapidly, like a bright little girl doing her lesson. I had got halfway through the *three's* before I realized what I was doing. But if you can't pray, I suppose you have to hang on to something.

Not long afterwards, by the time I felt my normal self again, normal except for a peculiar apathy, a serving girl brought up a tray of food. She was a brown girl, wearing an osnaburg frock with a clean white apron and headcloth. Her name, she said, was Dollie. She asked mine. She studied me with overt curiosity. More subtly, I examined her, as though I might read there some indication of the establishment. But her smooth brown face told me nothing, nothing except, perhaps, that Dollie was inclined to sullenness and wore her air of stupidity like a mask. I did not like Dollie.

She left me to eat my food alone. I ate it with appetite, despite the strange flavors. Afterward I felt terribly sleepy. I lay down, and when I awoke, the dusk was coming on. And as the dusk deepened, heat lightning, far off on the southern and eastern horizon, flickered on and off, defining off there on the horizon the low striations of cloud, and near at hand defining, for an instant, some line of roof or cluster of chimney pots. I sat in a chair by the window, and watched the night come on.

It was long after full dark when the tall amber-eyed woman, carrying a lamp and accompanied now by Dollie bearing another tray, appeared. I noticed that as she came into the room she did not at first locate me, sitting as I was at the edge of the window with my head leaned against the jamb of the jalousie. I noticed, too, her quick darting inspection of the room and, perhaps, an air of apprehension for the instant before she discovered my presence. Then her eyes found me.

"*Voilà,*" she said, and set down the lamp.

Coming to stand directly in front of me, she asked: "Why did you not light a lamp?" And gestured to a lamp on the table by the bed.

"Why?" I returned, listlessly. "Why should I?" Then, as I heard my own words, a surge of emotion welled up in me, and I flung out an arm in a violent gesture of repudiation, and cried out: "Yes, why should I? For me, it's all the same! Light or dark!"

She shrugged slightly, then said, "Nothing is always the same. There is always some difference."

"But not for me," I retorted.

She continued to regard me with her detached composure, and all at once I could not bear that look upon me, and burst out: "I know why you look that way—yes, I know—it's because you think you can control me—" As I spoke, I saw no change in her face, so I started up from my chair and seized her arm, shaking it, saying: "But you can't—you can't control me. I could jump out the window. I'd be dead but I'd prove you can't control me." And I leaned close at her now, almost whispering: "Then what would you do?"

With that golden calmness of face, she looked down at my hand clutching her arm, then into my eyes. "What would I do?" she spoke, in meditation. Then, answering herself: "I should probably weep."

"Yes," I rejoined bitterly, "weep because you'd be afraid of *him*. Oh, I saw your face when you first came in and thought I wasn't here. You were afraid. Afraid of what he might do."

"Do you know what he would do?" she asked me, calmly.

"Beat you!" I answered, and felt a sudden elation at the flicker of an image of Hamish Bond striking her, striking her with some whip, or his blackthorn, and of her composed face shattered into pain.

"No," she said, "he would try to comfort me. For he, too, would be sorry."

"Sorry for his two thousand dollars," I said.

"He has many thousands of dollars," she said, evenly, lifted her arm from my now enfeebled grasp, and turned toward the door.

Halfway there, she looked back, and said: "Do not forget to arrange the net against the mosquitoes. The season is upon us." And she turned away again.

"Listen!" I called after her, and she faced me.

"Listen," I said, "you're a slave of his, aren't you?"

She looked at me across the distance of the room, over the lighted lamp on the table between us. "*Une esclave*," she repeated. Then: "Yes—yes, that is one way it might be said."

And she disappeared into the shadows of the hall.

Dollie had been standing back by the wall. I had forgotten her. Now she came forward and picked up the tray with the dirty dishes. Standing there with the tray held sloping in her hands, as though the wrists were too weak for the burden, she looked at me over the dirty dishes, and said: "Me—I'm a slave, too."

She came closer. The tray sloped more perilously, the wrists seemed weaker, the dishes slid toward the outer edge of the tray, and I almost said for her to watch what she was doing. But her face stopped me, some slyness, some gratification, some glint of the secret life beneath that brown, masklike sullenness. Then, leaning nearer, she said: "Yeah, but you—you find out—you one, too!"

With those words still in the air to hold me bemused, she slipped to the door, and as she disappeared down the dark hall, I thought I heard a giggle.

As soon as the last sound of Dollie's descent had died, I went to the door and examined it. It was a heavy door with an iron lock. A key was in the lock, on the outside. I put the key on the inside, closed and locked the door. There was a heavy latch bolt. I put that in place, too. Then I ate a little of the supper from the new tray Dollie had brought. I crouched in the chair by the table, by the lamp, now and then looking across at the door. Now and then insects came out of the night to whirl about the bright globe of the lamp.

After a while, I rose, took off only my dress and shoes, then lay down on the bed. I arranged the *baire*. But I had no intention of going to sleep. And if I did slip off to sleep—well, there was the door, locked. To break it would wake the dead. I left the lamp burning.

I lay there a long time, wide-eyed. I heard laughter in the street, far away. When the air stirred the *baire* above me, I smelled the odor of the river. Once I heard the hoot of a steamboat. And all the time I was straining for some sound within the house. The sound would be that metronomic tap.

Well, I had steeled myself. I knew what to do. If that man came through that door, I would fling myself from the balcony, and die on the stones. Ah, I would be quick, quick enough for that, quicker than he. For he had a crippled leg. Yes, I would do it, and my breath, at the thought, came quick and shallow. Somehow, I almost longed for that wild, vindictive, vindicatory leap.

I came suddenly, coldly, awake, awake in the dark, for the lamp had burned out. I came awake thinking on the instant that I was waking from a nightmare, then thinking, no, no, I was waking to the nightmare, for now I knew what had waked me. I heard now the measured tap of the blackthorn in the hall below.

I sat up in the bed. I heard it tap out the shriveling of time, of distance, with a torturer's deliberation. I held my breath. Then the blackthorn stopped, and I couldn't stand it, not to breathe.

Then from the floor below I heard the faint sound of a door closing.

Even after I had brought myself to lie back down, I was shaking as though with a chill. I lay there and stared at the dark ceiling, and a cloud must have drawn off the moon, for the strange pinkish moonlight of that country and season flooded into my room. Far off, in the street, I heard a cry, rage or pain or joy, I could not tell.

Later, I went to sleep.

In broad daylight, to the blaze of sun, I snapped awake to that same sound, the sound that I had tuned my sleep to, the tap of the blackthorn, now in the hall below. I sat up in bed, rigid. But the sound was moving away, diminishing down the stairs, was lost, came again, but now from the patio, from the stones of the courtyard. I rushed to the window, and stood screened by the bougainvillaea of my balcony, my fingers twined in the tangle of vine, my face almost sunk in the leaves and violent blossoms, bees murmuring in the blossoms about my head, and I peered down at him through the leaf-jagged interstices.

He had reached the middle of the court when the great brown-maned beast of a dog sprang up from the shadows by one of the urns in which grew the orange trees, and came to him, in three heavy, lunging bounds. At each bound I heard the dry click and rasp of the nails as the beast's big paws came down on the stone.

The dog came at Hamish Bond, paused an instant, then reared on hind legs and put its forepaws on the man's shoulders, standing higher than the man. The great squarish head with the red tongue flapping heavily forth from the open jaws, between the whiteness of the tushes, thrust forward and downward to the level of the man's face.

When the dog leaped on him Hamish Bond did not stagger. He did not even move, as though his bulk were of some preternatural weight that fixed it to the spot. He stood there for a moment, then switched his blackthorn from the right hand to the left, and placed his right hand under the throat of the dog, grasping the heavy spiked collar, thrusting the weight of the dog from him, holding the dog there, at arm's length. The dog let its forepaws slip from the man's shoulders and hang with limp wrists there in the air, with the ridiculous simulation, ridiculous for that murderous-looking brute, of some spaniel or lap dog sitting up to do the trick of begging.

Meanwhile, the man and the dog stared steadily into each other's eyes, the dog with the great jaws spread in that tush-studded grin and uttering a heavy, throaty sound. Then the man imitated the sound, the same, heavy, rasping expulsion of breath, with the same rhythmic interval. This three or four times, then after each expulsion, but with the same timbre, he said the word, "Boy!" He said: "Ha-a-a, Boy—ha-a-a, Boy!"

They stood there, in the morning brightness, in that peculiar communion, then Hamish Bond's right hand released its grip on the collar, and the beast, with an astonishing quietness, an astonishing softness, like a kitten, dropped the forequarters to earth, and stood motionless. Hamish Bond patted the dog's head, then moved off toward the outer gate. The dog stood there looking after him in that new quietness.

I, too, watched Hamish Bond move toward the gate. He moved forward and away, swinging the right leg somewhat stiffly but with certainty. I was not even sure that I did not detect some bend in the knee, after all. He was only a little lame, just a little.

I looked back at the dog, still in the middle of the court, staring at the empty gateway. That, I decided, was the kind of dog I had heard about at Oberlin. It was what planters, they said, called a nigger-dog. I had learned about them, from books, from pamphlets, from the mouths of slaves who had fled, who had been pursued by that terror, who had finally reached Oberlin on their way to the North Star. I had seen the scarce-healed mark of those great white tushes, the raw, jagged-out scar on black flesh. They usually bred the nigger-dog, I remembered, from mastiff and bloodhound, sometimes with a strain of bulldog.

That was what now waited in the courtyard.

But as I stared down at that threat, at that great brute, I suddenly felt a thrill, a crazy joy: *I would be free.* That challenge had given me, as it were, the will to be free, will and power and joy, as I stared down.

The brute, with lowered head and slow, gliding, humping movement of the musculature of the shoulders, had meanwhile moved back into the shade by the stone urn from which spread an orange tree.

I turned from the balcony, back into the room. The exaltation that had come from the challenge faded. I faced the emptiness of the room, of the day to come, of my life. My soul felt dry.

There was a knock at the door. I opened it. Michele entered, greeted me with her characteristic gravity. But I did not reply to her greeting. I took a step toward her, and without thought, as though her presence had touched off the charge of an unsuspected desperation, burst out: "Look—I can't stand it!"

"*Ma petite,*" she began, "but what—"

But I myself did not know what it was I couldn't stand, what made me say, again, "No, I can't stand it. I'll go mad. I can't sit here, locked in this room and—"

"*Mais, ma petite,*" she said, "you locked the door yourself."

"Just let me come downstairs," I was saying.

"Why didn't you come downstairs?"

"I'll work—oh, I promise—just let me come down—" I was saying.

"Work," she echoed, and a faint smile touched her face. "There are many hands here for the work." She reached out and lifted my right hand and inspected it. "And that is just as well," she added, "for this little hand—it has never done much work, has it?"

I jerked my hand back. "But you'll make me go mad," I said.

"I am embroidering the initials on some napkins," she said. "If you like, you may sit with me. And embroider, if you like."

So we sat by the window in a pleasant shady room facing on a back courtyard, where sunlight washed the brick pavement on one side, and on the other dappled it through vines, and where the clatter and tinkle of kitchen work came to us across the opening. I plied my needle, trying to imitate Michele's meticulous art, tracing out, thread by thread, the boldly designed letter *B* at the corner of the napkin, set above some sort of wavy pattern.

A bird was in the vine outside the window, chirping away. Then I heard the scrape of wood and metal, and looked up to see a big door flung open on the wall across the court and a colored man lead out a fine bay horse. The man began to curry the horse, which stood nobly there in the sun, now and then tossing the head and arching the neck, now and then stamping the brick, once letting two or three great golden apples of manure drop with solid ripeness to the brick.

At that moment I was looking at the creature, seeing the powerful, somnolent bulge of the just-curried flank toward me glisten silkily in the sun, gold glinting from the rich brown; and when the creature performed the act I have just named, it seemed, all at once, part of that hypnotic beauty of the scene, somehow the fulfillment, for as it happened I felt a flash of happiness, of excitement, as at discovery and release. Now, looking back from my present age at that moment, I suppose that, after my period of pain and loneliness, this shady room and the white linen in my hand and the peaceful scene beyond the window must have signified some restoration to life, however illusory, and that the natural act of the animal spoke to me of some deep, redeeming unity in life that makes beauty out of disgust.

Then I felt a burst of shame at my own feeling, as though I had been detected in evil. I know that my face flushed, and I hung my head, pretending a new absorption in my task.

I was so preoccupied that when I heard a strange voice there immediately before me, I almost jumped out of my skin. I looked up to see the colored man, the groom or whatever he was, leaning inward on the window sill, smiling at Michele from his brown, aging face. Then he spoke again, in a slow, slurring voice, the voice of the darkies back home, saying, "Mee-chele—howdy, Mishy-Honey."

The man was, I should judge, about fifty, rather grizzled, dark brown in the rather blunt wrinkled face, the wrinkles giving a quizzical expression, quizzicality mixed with a slow, amiable shrewdness. He was not tall, as I could tell from his posture at the sill, and though broad-shouldered, was sinewy and dry rather than bulky. His shirt sleeves were hacked off high up so that I could see the bare arms, lightly but strongly muscled, like a strong young boy's, but with big veins standing out over the biceps. The hands, which hung into the room over the sill, looked extraordinarily large and coarse in comparison with the wrist bones. They seemed, in fact, to belong to another body, or better, to have some cunning independent life of their own, to be ready to stir, in a flash, from their present passivity into a strong action.

He had addressed Michele as "Mishy-Honey," and he simply did not seem to be the person to use that familiarity. Even as he spoke I expected some stinging rebuke.

"Jimmee," she replied calmly.

"Mishy," he said, "git me sumpum, some meat and bread or sumpum. I'm hongry. I got de ole fam-fam, and ain't no lie."

"If you have *faim*," she said, with a not unkind gravity, "why don't you get food from the kitchen?"

He shook his head, grinning at her. "Aw, Honey," he said wheedling, "you git it. Doan taste so good, you doan git it."

She thrust her needle into the linen, rose and laid the work on the chair. I stole a look at her face, but could tell nothing from it. Then she went from the room, quick-footed and straight-backed.

For the first time now the man turned his gaze on me, with a kind of indolent, friendly curiosity.

"Done heared bout ye," he announced. "Kantuck," he said. Then:

"Me—I'm Tenn-see. But long back when they brung me down. But I reck-lict Tenn-see. Reck-lict me some them gals, high-juiced and sweet-smellin. I lak 'em bright-skinned, and Honey, I doan mind one monstous bit lookin at ye."

He was leaning in over the sill, the cunning, boyish, conniving grin on his wrinkled face. Then Michele's voice called "Jimmee!"

She stood in the middle of the court, near the horse, a plate in one hand, a glass of milk in the other. Indolently, with a backward grin, the man went to her, stopped deliberately in front of her, squared himself, and while she stood there defenseless, the plate in one hand, the milk in the other, placed his right hand on the back of her neck, drew her face down to the level of his, for she must have been an inch taller than he, and kissed her a single big smack on the mouth.

Then he stepped back, took the milk and the plate, and grinned at her. At the distance, I could see her flushing. Then fleetingly, she smiled at him, an indulgent, affectionate smile, and turned away.

The smile was the most incongruous thing of all, the last thing I should have expected. As I puzzled over it, bending again at my needle, I was aware of some unease, some nagging discomfort, some sense of isolation. Why had the scene disturbed me? I had the impulse to put it arbitrarily from my mind.

But I was not permitted to do so. Michele had, meanwhile, returned to her seat. And now she asked, in a casual, quiet voice, not even looking up at me: "What did he say to you?"

I started guiltily, so confused by what seemed her clairvoyant detection that I stammered, "What—what did who—who?"

"Him," she said, with a shade of impatience that I took to be at my own disingenuousness.

Beyond the window, beyond the patch of sun in which the horse yet stood, in the shade by the stable wall, the man was hunkered down on his heels, eating his sandwich, the glass of milk on the bricks before him.

"What did he say?" she repeated.

"Oh, nothing," I replied. "Just that he'd heard of me being from Kentucky." But I was sure I was flushing at my lie.

"But you must not let him bother you," she said. "He is just that way, and you can ignore him. Be kind, but ignore him."

What was she telling? I asked myself that, even as the anger grew in me. Anger at being caught in my lie? Anger because I did

not know why I had told the lie? Then another anger: *She tells me
this because she thinks I am a Negro. And that man—*

That man, too, had taken me for a Negro, no better than himself.
He had leered at me, had said what he said, *high-juiced and sweet-
smellin, high-juiced and sweet-smellin,* and I saw again the wrinkled
face as it had been when he leaned in, framed by the vines at the
window, leering, old, old and Negro, and I was overwhelmed by
my anger and revulsion.

And then, in the same instant, as his image was vivid before me,
in my mind, I saw his bare brown arms, the thin, strong muscles
plaited over the boy-bone, and the big veins standing over the
biceps under the slick skin, and where the shirt sleeve was hacked
off, the slick brown curve of the shoulder, bright-filmed with sweat.
And I was aware in a cold, fascinated awareness that I had the
impulse to reach out my hand and touch that shoulder.

But was it in me only now, at the recollected image, or had it
been in me earlier, in reality, and I had not known it? Had it been
then, and that man, that Jimmee, had known it in his conniving
grin?

I felt like leaping up and running from the room.

But the woman's voice was going on: "—is my husband."

The preposterousness of that announcement struck across my own
feelings. I managed an incredulous question: "Him?" And it flashed
into my mind, with a sudden vindictive satisfaction, that she was
jealous, that was it, jealous.

But as though she could read my heart, she was saying: "I tell
you this that you may not think I am jealous. It is just the way he is.
He has done things that he cannot help. It may be he is the father
of Dollie's baby and—"

"She has a baby?"

"Yes, and he may be the father, but he denies it. And she says
that the father is Rau-Ru, but she—"

"Who is Rau-Ru?"

"You will see, in time. He calls himself the *k'la* of the master. You
will see, and Dollie may say he is the father because she wants him.
But she has lied before. She has lied about the master, I know. And
the father may be Jimmee. Or who? But if it is Jimmee—" she
paused, lifted her needle from the task, and shrugged.

"In any case," she continued, "Jimmee and I, we understand each
other. And he needs me. And"—she paused again, and now looked

straight at me as though mustering strength for a confession, then continued—"and I need him. And that, in life, is something. Not all, but something."

Without knowing why, I was embarrassed by her gaze, by the very air of confession. No, there was something more, as I should read it now. I had not clearly stated to myself my hopes for life, my yearning for love and fullness, but I was young, and in youth those things do not need to be stated. They are in your very breath. Even in my condition in the strange land and strange house, that must have been so. Now to hear that woman admit to the dwindling of life, the willingness to accept the little for the large, struck me with a frightening inner confusion. I feared, you might say, that some contagion in her eyes would seize me and I should be robbed of hope. So I dropped my gaze from her, and stared at my needle.

But hope of what? What could I, a slave, hope for?

I had finished the embroidery of the letter B and now pretended to be about to begin work on the design below it, the wavy line looping between the three peaks. I must have stared at it a long time, taking refuge in it.

Then I heard the woman's voice, again. "Do you know what that is?" she asked.

"What what is?"

Her forefinger touched the wavy line under the B on my napkin. "It is the sea," she said.

"The sea?" And I looked up, with some sense, I suppose, of the openness and release in that word, some flicker of that image of the sea.

"It represents the sea," she said. "For he"—and her forefinger now moved to the big B of the napkin on my knee—"he was long on the sea."

I looked down at the bold initial, as though it might divulge something.

"He traded on the sea," she said. "He has been in many countries. He has much to remember." With that last statement, she touched her forefinger to her brow as though to indicate that the far life of Hamish Bond had been distilled and stored behind his heavy-boned, ruddy, square forehead, above the straight black eyebrows and bulging gray eyes.

In my mind I saw him on a ship, on the bridge I guess, on some high part, and the ship was heaving in a wind-wracked sea, and spume was flying before his face, but he seemed, somehow, motionless and fixed in the middle of the great commotion. His mouth was open, and that strong voice was coming out against the wind, conquering the wind. It was saying: "I bid two thousand dollars—I bid two thousand dollars!"

Then, in the instant of its appearance, the fantasy was gone. There I was in the ordinary, pleasant room, and the woman had risen and laid her embroidery down, and was saying something about having to see how work was going on upstairs, and then she was gone.

I said, out loud to the empty room: "I've got to get out—I've got to get out of this house!"

But I did not. Instead, I found my way down shadowy corridors, back toward the kitchen. I was going back there to see that baby of Dollie's.

I was leaning over the basket, a basket set on a chair, staring at the little brown creature so sound asleep that a fly crawling over the bare chest did not disturb it.

I was leaning thus, when Dollie's voice broke in: "What you doin down heah?"

"The baby—" I began, by way of explanation, then stopped. Then I said: "It's an awful pretty baby."

"You think hit's so durn pretty," she said, sourly, "hit is shore one thing hit doan cost no money to git."

At that I heard an unrestrained giggle from the shadows of the hall beyond the kitchen.

"Doan tetch hit," Dollie was saying to me. "All the botheration gittin hit down, and you wake hit up, I cut somebody's thote."

Just after sunset I heard the stick in the patio, on the stairs, in the hall, approaching. Then Hamish Bond was standing on my door sill, filling the space.

"May I come in?" he asked, and at my nod, entered. He stood in the middle of the room, by the table where a lamp already burned. He carried a packet in his left hand, extended toward me.

"It's just something," he said in his strong voice, then hesitated. "Just something I thought you might like," he finished.

I reached out and took the packet. "Thank you," I said.

He waited as though for me to investigate the contents, but I made no move to do so, sensing, somehow, a victory in my restraint. He shifted his weight, then found his voice. "I'm going away," he said, "in a couple of days. While I'm away, if you want anything, just ask Michele."

"Thank you," I said, "but I don't want anything." That, too, gave me a sense of victory.

"Good night," he said, and moved toward the door. Halfway there, he stopped, and looked back. "What do you want me to call you?" he asked.

Before thinking, I had answered my familiar name, the name of childhood: "Manty—they call me Manty."

He seemed to reflect on that, then resumed his movement toward the door. At the sill, he looked back. He thrust his blackthorn in the direction of the packet in my hand. "That," he said, "that's nothing—just something I thought you might like." His voice had some note of apology in it.

Then turning away, he said: "Good night." Then concluded, with a tinge of experimental uncertainty in his strong voice: "—Manty."

He was, at the next instant, beyond the jamb, out of my vision

But the word, the sound of my name, had touched off a gush of sweetness in my heart.

Then immediately I was overwhelmed with shame, shame at that sweetness, sweetness at that word from the mouth of the person who was most clearly my oppressor, the person to whom I was chattel, two thousand dollars' worth of human flesh to be used at pleasure and discarded at will. It seemed shameful that in the depth of my being I had so longed for my name spoken that hearing it might dissolve my anger, dissolve all logic, dissolve my very being into the sweet impotence of childhood.

But I suppose my response was only natural. I was, after all, not much more than a child. I had been snatched from my old world and dropped into a new one burgeoning with confused shadow and nameless terror. I had, in a way, lost my very identity. And in the lamplit room, my name, heard from the lips of that mysterious looming creature at the threshold where the lamplight scarcely penetrated, that creature who was the source of all power and the disposer of fate, gave me back my identity.

But now in my shame at my response, I angrily flung aside the parcel my master had given me, a bright parcel with ribbons.

Later, when Dollie came in, I pointed it out to her. "Take it," I said indifferently, "whatever it is."

It was sweetmeats, what you give a child, and seeing that, my anger flared up again, as Dollie popped one of the things into her mouth, and stood there chewing it with mouth open, her face rapt in innocent inwardness—innocent and brutal, so it seemed to me in that moment of my disgust.

She swallowed the last of the piece, and picked up the box. Then said: "You kin hole my baby sometime, you want."

"Thank you," I said, feeling, suddenly, that I never wanted to see that small creature again, and I was sure that I caught, mysteriously, the faint scent of urine and sour milk and stale pot likker that had hung over the basket in the kitchen.

Dollie went to the door. Just as she reached it, with a flash of cold, inspired, calculated cruelty, I said: "Who is Rau-Ru?"

She turned. "Him?" she said. "Rau-Ru?" Then: "Ain't no common nigger—naw, Lawd, naw, Lawd!" And sniggered, sniggering off down the hall.


So that was the first day I ventured down into the house of Hamish Bond. That night, as I lay abed, the images of the day came and went in my head, but I could not find their meaning, their continuity. Then idly, among the flowing recapitulation of images, the image of Jimmee came to me, leaning in the window with his quizzical, wrinkled face. And all at once, it was the face of Shaddy, Old Shaddy, back at *Starrwood*.

I rose up in bed, on my elbow, as at a cry in the night, filled with some excitement. But the excitement gave way to apprehension, to guilt, to fear. Then I thought: *I told on Shadrach and they sold him away, and that is why I, too, have been sold away, into slavery.*

If that was true, then I would never be able to escape. How crazy my hope had been!

Then a sense of injustice came over me. Why should I suffer because of Shadrach, one of thousands, tens of thousands, sold away, another common old nigger, sold away?

Why should I suffer for that?

*Ain't no common nigger—naw, Lawd, naw, Lawd!:* but that was not about Shadrach, that was about Rau-Ru, what Dollie had said about Rau-Ru, sniggering off down the hall.

But next morning came, and I said to Michele: "Who is Rau-Ru?"

"He ran the master's plantation, one of them, upriver," she said, "the one at *Pointe du Loup*."

"Where does he get such a funny name?" I asked.

"Funny?" echoed Michele, and added that the name was like any name.

"But where does it come from?" I insisted.

"From his own country," she said.

"But where—where is that?"

"I don't know," she said.

"You mean he is not from America?"

"No."

"But where?"

"I don't know, not precisely," she said. "When he first came to the island, he—"

"Island—what island?"

"The island—a little island near Cuba. 'Sieur 'Amsh, he brought him."

"And then Mr. Bond brought him here?" I demanded.

"Yes."

"Ah," I said, and leaned forward peremptorily, like a prosecutor, like a teacher, "and so Mr. Bond broke the law"—oh, yes, I knew that law, we all knew it at Oberlin. "He broke the law forbidding the importation of slaves, and he, Rau-Ru, could have denounced Mr. Bond for holding him a slave, and—"

"A slave—" Michele interrupted. "Rau-Ru would think it queer to hear himself called a slave."

"Well," I demanded, hearing my voice edged with the dry, thin, triumphant irony of pedagogy, "what is he then?"

"He is the *k'la*," she said, and rose abruptly, and left me.

What was the *k'la*?

And as I turned the question over in my mind, I suddenly remembered that Michele, too, had come from another country, from that island, she had just said, whatever that island was, and Hamish Bond had brought her in as a slave.

And so, inflamed by my thought, I ran down the hall and up the stairs, to the door of the room occupied by Hamish Bond, for I had heard the tap of her heels in that direction.

The door was open. I stopped at the threshold, looking, for the

first time, into that room, a big, bare, sun-swept room, with tre-
mendous bed, armoire and bureau, grand and expensive, gilded and
festooned, and masculine apparel flung here and there with imperial
carelessness. Michele had already looped back the net and was
stripping the bed to remake it.

I had come down the hall at top speed, ready to dash up and
confront Michele with my dazzling idea. But now, all at once, I
stopped at the threshold, as though the sill were a mystic line I
might not cross. Michele, holding a bolster in her hand, looked up
at me in surprise. I was speaking, jumbling my words forth, as
though the spoken words but continued, without interruption, the
discourse in my head: "—yes, you're a slave—you said you were—
*esclave,* you said—and Hamish Bond brought you in, and it's against
the law—and you, you can denounce him now, even now—"

I concluded in breathless triumph.

She was looking soberly at me over the bolster forgotten in her
hands.

"Why didn't you denounce him?" I demanded angrily, leaning
over the sill.

"Because," she said, "there was no reason to do so."

"But you were a slave," I urged, my anger mounting, "*une esclave,
une esclave,* that's what you said yourself, and—"

"Oh, go away!" she burst out at me, and I saw her fingers clench
the bolster.

I was frozen by surprise, surprise and, I suppose, terror at seeing
the ice of her calm crack, the mask of her calm dropped.

"Oh, go away!" she cried again. And cried out: "Why—why did
you ever come to this house?" And she flung the bolster down on
the bed.

That action released me. I fled up the hall, to the floor above, to
my room, and shut the door.

Later, she found me there, huddled on my bed, in fear and sense
of betrayal, huddling away from her touch as she tried to reach me
to lay a hand on my shoulder.

She was sorry, she said. She had come to apologize, she said. And
said: "Oh, everything was so long ago. Things are so long ago,
and you think they are gone, but then, all at once, for just a moment,
they are not gone."

She touched my shoulder. "*Ma petite,*" she said, "forgive me."

Two days later, Michele came to my room and announced that 'Sieur 'Amsh had gone upriver, to *Pointe du Loup*, for a few days, but had left orders for her to take me into town. For what, I asked. To buy material for clothes. I told her I wanted nothing. What were clothes for me?

"If you do not go," she said, "I cannot make you. But it would be a distress for me. And besides, you are beautiful."

So we went. I was tense with excitement. All the possibilities of flight, of freedom crowded my head. This was the beginning. I would observe everything. I would learn the city. I would be ready when the time came.

In the shops they called me "Miss" or "Mademoiselle," and gave the deference due to a young lady of breeding, with money to spend. And Michele stood at my elbow, like the faithful nurse. Yes, once I was past that great beast of a dog, and out the iron gate of Hamish Bond's house, freedom would be easy. I would be lost in a world of white faces.

Meanwhile, I hugged the irony: the *Miss*, the *Mademoiselle*, addressed to me, the slave. How that knowledge would have pinched their pride, those counter-jumpers!

But there was another irony to come, as the days drifted past, and the dressmaker came and made me the dresses, and they were beautiful, and one moment their beauty was a flash of joy, but the next it was the last irony: beautiful dresses for me, the slave. I stared at them with a sick lassitude. I sat with Michele and embroidered the napkins, the bold *B* over the looped symbol of sea waves. I went into the kitchen and leaned over the brown baby. I held it in my arms, and tested a painful division in my emotion. I found the kitten in the back patio, and took it to my room and fed it and loved it. I wandered over the house, the shadowy rooms with the gilt and brass of the garnishings of the furniture, massive Empire it was, glinting in the dimness, the office or study of Hamish Bond, where a great brass binnacle sat on a table like an altar, and books and papers were flung about in disorder, and strange weapons, all shapes of blades, straight or curved or wavy, thick or thin, long or short, swords and scimitars and krisses, glimmered wickedly on the walls. I stood in the rooms and wondered what would become of me, and my heart pounded in the silence.

"What will become of me?" I cried out to Michele, and she laid her embroidery down and looked at me.

"*Ma petite*," she said, calmly, "you will live." And there was no irony in her voice.

But that was no answer. So I demanded: "What did he do it for?"

"Who?" she asked.

"He," I said, and jabbed my needle at the big *B* on my napkin.

"Do what?" she said.

"Buy me," I replied. "Why did he buy me?" And as I pronounced the word *buy,* and repeated it, a strange sensation came over me, something like anger, then a faint sickness coupled with a nameless agitation, this succeeded by a slight sensation just below, and at, the nipples on my breasts, a sensation both of being bruised and of tingling.

"Why did he do it?" I repeated.

"I don't know," she said. "There could be so many reasons, and I don't know which. For that matter," she continued, "he himself may not know."

"But why did he do it?"

"I don't know," she said, patiently. "But he is a kind man, and you are fortunate. But it is a strange kindness. It is not like the kindness of people ordinarily, for you can understand that sort of kindness. But he—" She paused, reflecting. Then: "You might say that his kindness is like a disease. He has it as a man might have a long disease."

# V

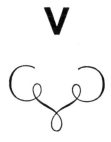

"IT IS A VERY BEAUTIFUL DRESS," HAMISH BOND SAID GRAVELY, AND reached out the blackthorn to touch with its tip the hem of the skirt as I stood there, just inside the door of the dining room, for his inspection.

It was a beautiful dress. I bowed my head before him, and let my fingers lightly caress the pink bouffant skirt, slashed with chocolate color. I saw the tip of the blackthorn still touching the hem.

Then I heard his voice: "I told Michele to ask you to let me see one of your new dresses just because—" He hesitated, and I heard the slight sound of his shift of weight.

"Because," he resumed, "I thought you might eat dinner with me." I did not look up.

"Of course," he was saying, "if you prefer eating with Michele, as you have been doing, then—"

He hesitated again. Then: "Would you mind?"

"No, sir, I don't mind," I said, and still did not look up. What else was there for me to say?

So he sat at one end of the big table, in front of the silver candelabra, and I at one side, a little to his right, and Jimmee, no longer wearing the torn shirt that exposed his sweat-bright and boy-muscled shoulders, but stiff in a buttoned-up black coat, poured claret, and

Hamish Bond tried to talk with me, talking of indifferent things, the weather, his trip to his plantation upriver, the culture of cane, and I lifted my eyes from my plate only to say yes, sir, or no, sir.

Then, at last there was a period of silence. I did not look up to see his face, but I could see against the whiteness of the tablecloth, his right hand reach out for his wineglass, a strong hand, heavy-jointed, browned by weather, sparsely sprigged by strong black hairs. Then, with a start, I saw what I had never noticed before: the second finger of the hand was cut off just below the first joint. There was just the stub left, blunt and healed over with a painful twist of tissue.

I saw the fingers slowly revolve the wineglass, then stop.

Then in a voice that filled the room with its authority, and a hint of suppressed violence, he said: "This is foolishness!"

I looked sharply up at him. But his face showed nothing except, perhaps, a more than usual glitter of the eyes.

"This is foolishness," he repeated, in a more moderate voice. "You don't have to eat here. And I don't have to listen to myself talking this damned nonsense. I just reckoned it wouldn't be so lonesome, if you ate here."

He stopped, then all at once leaned at me, and with a flicker of ferocity in his tone, asked: "Don't you want some dessert?"

I shook my head.

"Dollie can bring it right now."

"No thanks," I said.

"You don't have to ever eat here," he said.

I slipped from my chair, and stood there, my hands hanging at my sides. "Excuse me," I said.

He said nothing, and I began to move toward the door. By the time I got there I was almost running. At the top of the stairs, in the dark hall, I stopped and heard my heart's preternatural beating. What was it beating for? The effort of scrambling up the stairs, fear, excitement? All of those things, but also from a sense of victory, of power, and crazily, there floating in the dark, I saw the image of his hand on the white, candle-lit tablecloth, the strong flesh, browned by weather, sprigged by black hairs, the fingers turning the stem of the wineglass, the stub of the amputated second finger sticking out to exhibit the painful twist of tissue.

The next night, at the hour of his dinner, I came down. He was already seated. A quick glance told me that my place was laid.

He straightened up, and gave me what I took to be a stern forbidding look. Then he smiled. I had never seen him smile before,
and a smile on that heavy, square-jawed, bulge-eyed face was the
strangest thing. It was like light suddenly breaking through on
a gray day to make a land of wet rock look gilded and bright. The
flesh crinkled up around the eyes and the heavy lips pulled back and
up and the smile was really a kind of grin, a grin of boyishness, of
shamefaced ferocious boyishness.

"Well, Manty—Manty," he was saying, "so you decided to give
the old fellow's damned nonsense one more try, huh?"

I found myself smiling back at him. For no reason, just because
his grin caught me into that. But when I detected the smile on my
face, I quickly recomposed my expression.

"Be damned, gal," he was saying, "you *can* smile. I caught you
right red-handed at it, gal. I never reckoned you could."

Later that night, as I lay abed, I thought about finding my place
at the table already laid. Had he been sure I would come? I felt
a flicker of anger at him for being sure. Then, coming right with
the anger, I felt a kind of warm, comforting peace at the thought
that somebody did know, or care, what you were going to do. Knew
even better than you yourself. It was like an arm being put around
your shoulders.

But suppose the place had not been laid, and waiting? That
thought struck me with a frightful chill. Could I have borne that
coldness, that rejection? I felt lonesome and forlorn, lying there in
the dark.

*Oh, that's silly, just silly,* I said to myself, for I knew now that I
could, in the end, escape. I knew my power.

The season, with its strange somnambulistic, submarine muffling
and muting, moved on into summer. The heat and dampness hung
like gauze in the afternoon brilliance. The shadows in the courtyard lay on the sun-glittering stone like black tin, the straight-edged
black shadow of the wall, the jag-edged shadow of vine, the ovoidal
shadows of the orange trees. Sometimes, lying in my room for the
siesta, seeing the bougainvillaea leaves in the black jags against the
brilliance of sky, I wanted to scream out to break the silence. But
a sound would then come, the creak of a cart, a call far off, the hoot
of a steamboat. There was the sense of time being wound tighter

and tighter, like thread on a bobbin, of your nerves being wound. And the heat was worse, day by day.

"We should have left before now," Michele said one morning.

"To go where?" I asked.

"*Pointe du Loup,*" she said. "Only once have we stayed in the city so late. In '53. And that was folly. It was *la saison de la fièvre.*"

"*La fièvre?*" I echoed.

"*La fièvre jaune,*" she said. "Bronze John. Ten thousand died. But he stayed."

"Who stayed?"

"Who do you think?" she queried in mild surprise, laying aside the embroidery. And answered herself: "'Sieur 'Amsh, of course, and it was folly, for he might have gone and been safe. But *une folie noble.* It was the disease of his kindness."

"Did he make you stay and be noble, too?" I asked, ironically. "You and the others?"

"No," she said. "'Sieur 'Amsh, he told those who wished to go to the country that they might go. Some went. Dollie went. Jimmee would have gone, for he is a man natural, but I said that if he went, I would never again lie down beside him and I would spit on his food as I set it before him. So he stayed, and once he had stayed and there was the great dying, he behaved well, and laughed a great deal, for, as I said, he is *un homme naturel,* and does the best he can when there is no help for it."

My hands moved, folding cloth, adjusting it, and her voice went on: "This house was full of the sick and dying. 'Sieur 'Amsh had them brought here. We worked the best we could; he, too, the best he could with his infirm leg. At noon in the city the air was always black with smoke, for barrels of tar were burning in the streets to kill infection. Cannon were everywhere in the street and they fired all day to drive off the impurity of air. The sound of cannon that would not stop made the sick ones have convulsions, some of them. Birds did not fly across the sky.

"People died in the street and lay there. They could not bury the dead, there were so many. They piled them like cord wood and burned them, and everything did not burn well, and when all was cooled the dogs came. They shot dogs in the street and they lay there.

"Many people died in our house, for all we could do. We heard the cries of men with the carts who gathered the dead like garbage.

They were always drunk, and who could blame them? They stopped at the gate and rang the bell loud, and shouted, 'Des morts—avez-vous des morts!' Then there came the Black Day at the end of August when more died than ever, and all seemed doomed. But the storms came, and the dying stopped.

"We went to *Pointe du Loup*, at last. Then it all seemed a bad dream, even the times when you yourself had wanted to die, for there was no reason to live.

"The corn-pulling time was over when we came."

But now was now, in New Orleans, summer, but no fever.

When night came, darkness would be sudden, like a knife-edge.

Often in the evenings, after our dinner, we walked into the back courtyard, where a light barouche waited, the matched bays now and then clinking their shoes on the stone in discreet impatience. Their coats glistened with muted richness in the light of the big lantern suspended on a beam above the stable entrance. A swarm of insects revolved about the lantern, some great heavy, horny things that clanged like metal against the glass, and made a click then when they fell to the stone, some small as midges, glittering like gold dust, spinning in the orb of light of which the lantern was center.

Hamish Bond handed me up into the vehicle, then braced himself on his stick, lifted his left foot to set it on the edge of the floor of the vehicle, cramping his thigh upward for the unnatural posture, and heaved up with a strange swooping, athletic motion.

It was astonishing. It was as though, at that moment, you saw two persons, the burly man of middle years, with the lame leg and clumsy power, and somehow, trapped in that bulk but shining through it like light behind dingy glass, the form of a youth, supple, thin-hipped, long-armed, high-headed, leaping into the air, suspended in the air like a bird, beyond reason and gravity.

It was, as I said, astonishing. The vehicle would lurch dangerously as his left leg drove down to heave up his weight, lurch like a small boat when a wave hits broadside. The first time it happened, feeling that plunge and seeing that shocking apparition heave above me, I screamed. It wasn't a loud scream, but nevertheless, a scream.

"Manty, Manty!" he exclaimed, standing there in the swaying barouche, swinging his right arm wide to maintain his balance, the blackthorn in that hand like a cutlass, laughing with some strain of wild, unexpected gaiety, saying, "Ha, ha! Manty—did I skeer you, Manty? Did I skeer you, little Manty?"

Then he sat down, suddenly his burly, decorous self. "Out the shell road," Hamish Bond ordered Jimmee, and we passed over the uneasy streets, where people moved in the flickering light of the street lamps, fathers with their large families, moving ceremoniously forward like a flock grazing in formation, young lovers, groups of young blades with black mustaches, starched linen glittering, and thin gold-headed canes, young men already edged by their evening arrogance and wine. Somewhere, far off, would be the sound of music.

Then we would pass the outlying districts, huts precariously hung together of junk, old boards and palmetto leaves, a smudge-fire glowing before each one, and around the fire crouched human forms, the firelight touching the faces with a strange intensity in the general darkness. But the night was hot, and those romantic fires were smudges, just smudges to drive off mosquitoes. Along part of our way, the fires were reflected in the water and gilt scum of a big ditch or bayou.

Jimmee's matched bays would slip into their long, easy stride, and our wheels would hiss over the crushed shell. If there was moonlight it would have the pinkish glow. If no moon, the stars would seem very steady and bright in the blackness. Often there was heat lightning. That far-off, uneasy flickering made the whole dark land seem to rock and sway a little as though it floated, unmoored, on a great secret water. At Lake Pontchartrain the water stretched mysteriously away northward, under the moonlight, starlight, or uneasiness of lightning. I had never seen that much water. It was like the ocean, I thought.

We ate an ice, and I looked across the water. Once I said to Hamish Bond that it was beautiful. "A pond," he replied, "a cow-pond full of mud-turtles." Then added: "You ought to see Genoa. At night, I mean. When you're laying off, hove to, and the lights show way up yonder on the mountain."

I replied politely that I should like to see it.

He did not seem to hear me. Then said, with some grimness: "I've seen it. I've laid out there, beyond the roadstead, and seen it. All night long. You see the lights go out, one by one, up there on the mountain, only the last ones left." He waited a full minute. Then resumed. "I've seen a lot of things. A man sees a lot in his time, but

I don't know what good it does him." He waited again. Then: "I've laid off Teneriffe, too, and seen the lights."

Some nights, not often however, guests came to the house of Hamish Bond. On those nights I had my dinner with Michele, as before. Sitting in our little room we might catch the sound of laughter, or a voice raised in argument. They were always male voices, for no ladies came to this house.

"There was a time when they came," Michele told me. "*Grandes dames*, even Madame Gouvier, she came—the aunt of 'Sieur Prieur-Denis—with her hair white and piled up this high—" And she indicated with her long flexible golden hand the height above her own head. "And the diamonds," she continued, and touched her breast where a brooch might have been. "But that," she said, and hesitated, "was *une autre époque*."

"When?" I asked.

"Long ago," she said.

"When?"

"Twelve, fifteen years ago. It was the time when—when it seemed that he was to marry. He was betrothed, in the end." She had just finished the wavy loops beneath the big *B*. Now she spread the napkin on her knee and inspected the perfection of her work.

"Who was she?"

"She had very black eyes. You cannot imagine how black, in her paleness. And her hair was black. They said she was beautiful."

"Was she?" I asked.

Michele looked at me, suddenly with the old distant, assessing look of the first days of my arrival in the house of Hamish Bond. "How do I know?" she demanded.

But Hamish Bond had not married the beautiful young woman, who was named, I learned, Mathilde. Why?

"How do I know?" Michele demanded.

The lady whose name was Mathilde had gone into a convent. Where, according to Michele's suddenly acid comment, she had probably belonged.

So now the voices in the other room were always voices of men, the voice of a Mr. De Bow, who had a magazine, the voice of Monsieur Charles de Marigny Prieur-Denis, who was rich, a dandy and gallant, a cousin of Hamish Bond, the voice—one evening only—of Mr. Judah Benjamin, who, they said, was a Senator from Washington, the voices of other men talking about politics, about cotton, about sugar, about slaves, about money, about tariff.

And later, when they had all gone, and all that was left was the smeared glasses and the empty port decanter over which a last wakeful fly buzzed fretfully, Hamish Bond would come back, and tap the floor with his stick, and say, "God-a-Mighty, Manty, the world is full of fools!" And once, having uttered that dictum, he looked sharply at me, looked for a full half-minute until I squirmed with embarrassment, and lowered my eyes. Then, dourly, he said: "Fools, yeah. And I'm the biggest."

Then I heard his voice: "You don't have to sit up all night and hear tell of all the fools in the world."

Then: "Off to bed with you, little Manty!"

Then Rau-Ru came.

As I came down to the study one June evening, I encountered Dollie in the hall. She leaned at me, whispering: "The *k'la*—he done come!"

But what was the *k'la?*

And a half-minute later, when I had entered the room where the big ship's compass glittered, and the metals of the barbarous display on the walls, the krisses and cutlasses and scimitars, and had greeted Hamish, Dollie burst in, forgetting manners, and said to her master: "He done heah!"

And Hamish said: "Send him in."

I don't know what I had expected, certainly not the lithe figure of glittering white except for the red sash, that all at once, but without haste, was there before us, the face of preternatural blackness, like enameled steel, against the white of the loose blouse.

For an instant he stood there, and I saw that his eyes were wide, large, and deep-set, his nose wide but not flattened, the under-lip full, if not to the comic fullness favored in the make-up of minstrel shows of our day, and the corners of the mouth were drawn back so that the effect of that mouth was one of arrogant reserve and not blubbering docility. A mustache of a few hairs hung wispily down below the corners of the mouth, in a kind of ambitious boyishness.

*How funny,* I thought, looking at that mustache, *how funny!*

But at the same time I found myself smiling with a kind of indulgence as though that strong figure were younger than I. Actually, he was a lot older than I, about twenty-five.

The duration of Rau-Ru's pause there in the middle of the study floor was the flicker of an eye, nothing, but it was the moment of my first impression, and is therefore fixed forever, balanced there, and beyond the white-clad figure, yonder in the hall, is Dollie peering secretly in.

I had remembered that, according to Michele, Dollie boasted Rau-Ru the father of her child. *The little liar,* I now thought.

All this in the fixed instant of his pause. Then he had stepped toward Hamish Bond, had seized his right hand, bowed over it, and to my astonishment, had kissed it. No, that wasn't what he did, I suddenly realized. He had touched his brow to the back of the hand. He straightened up, and Hamish Bond grabbed him by the right shoulder—this with Hamish Bond's left hand—and with his right hand slapped Rau-Ru's left shoulder in the immemorial gesture of fatherly affection.

"Rau-Ru, Rau-Ru," he said, grinning, and then uttered a spate of outlandish gabble, much like the racket of the provoked master of a turkey flock.

Rau-Ru replied in kind, standing happily under the friendly slaps.

And all at once I felt cut off, outside, displaced. I was not, after all, the favorite. I did not ask myself: *the favorite what?* And so did not have to reply: *the favorite slave.*

As matters stood, my jealousy had scarcely time to be converted into a contempt for that barbarous communal gabble, before Hamish Bond turned suddenly to me, with the air of a host apologetic at an oversight, and with his left hand still on Rau-Ru's shoulder, said: "This is Rau-Ru."

Even as I somewhat coldly inclined my head to acknowledge the introduction, I was thinking: *How is he going to introduce me? Like one slave to another?* And was aware, in that split second, of the blackness of the fellow, for all his nigger finery. And aware of the whiteness of my small hands laid decorously together at my waist.

For that same split second Hamish Bond seemed to hesitate, as though he, too, were debating the delicate question. If he was debating the question, he solved it by ignoring it. He did not identify me. "You've heard of Rau-Ru," was all he said.

I had heard of him, yes, but had probably heard less than anybody else in Louisiana. Old Man Bond's free nigger, that high-muck-a-muck of Bond's free niggers (for all the slaves of any master who inclined to more than the minimum of decency might get that

name), Bond's high-stepper, Big Bond's boss driver, Big Bond's
Fancy-Pants—yes, Rau-Ru was famous. No constable or paddy-roll
ever stopped him. No steamboat captain ever asked to see his pass.
No snag-toothed dirt-farmer or swamp-rat ever let the pent-up
outrage of his own deprivation flare in word or blow at the sight of
Rau-Ru's slick finery. He was Old Man Bond's nigger.

I had heard of him, but not yet those things, and the other things.
All I knew now was that he practically ran Hamish Bond's big upriver place, that he was—no, was *not*—the father of that child of
Dollie's that I had dandled in the kitchen, that his presence and the
secret gabble with Hamish Bond made me feel rejected and cut off.

That summer he would go and come in the house. He would dis-
appear upriver, and return. He would sit long hours with Hamish
Bond in the study at some business. (Unlike Jimmee, or the other
slaves, when he appeared before his master, he was always invited
to sit. And I recall now that they used to say that Jefferson Davis, at
his place up in Mississippi, had his Isaiah Montgomery sit with him.)

But when Rau-Ru was not with the master he might be lounging
in the patio, by an orange tree, in delicious idleness, slowly, whisper-
ingly, whetting the blade of his knife on the big stone urn in which
the tree grew, spitting delicately now and then on the stone to lubri-
cate the fastidious motion. Or he would lounge there and read from
a book which he had drawn from his pocket. Or sometimes he would
meet me in the house and startle me, for he moved without noise,
on a cat-stride, setting the foot down, the patent-leather boot down,
as though weightless in a dream.

How white, in the shadowy hall, his eyeballs shone against the
enameled blackness of his face!

But I also met Charles de Marigny Prieur-Denis in that hall. He
was, as Michele had told me, a kinsman of Hamish Bond, by the
American mother of Prieur-Denis. He was the only one of those
gentlemen who gathered for the evenings of wine and conversation
with Hamish who ever came by daylight, and the only one, I was
about to say, who was to have any significance for my life.

But that last would have been a lie, for how much of my life had
been, and was to be, defined by men like those men whom I heard
only behind the door of the dining room, men sitting around a table,
after the duck or venison or beef, after the fruit and ice, after the
coffee, after the walnuts, men fingering slowly the port glass, the

brandy glass? Men at their after-dinner ease, heavy with food and opinion, off in Virginia, in Kentucky, in Massachusetts, in New York? Men sitting at dinner long before my birth?

As for Charles I saw him first in the hall of the house of Hamish Bond, in the middle of a summer afternoon. I was just coming down to the foot of the stairs, after my siesta, and there he was, a figure in white trousers and black coat of a silky sheen, and loose black tie, leaning lightly on a gold-headed cane, looking up the stair at me. He was a youngish-looking man. His face was oval but strong-featured, with a black mustache, the skin an even olive tone, and large brown eyes of melancholy beauty.

When I looked up and discovered him there, I uttered a little cry of surprise. For a moment, he stood there regarding me, not speaking, standing with a peculiar immobility, an immobility, I was to learn, that was not of heaviness but of litheness, an immobility in which you felt latent the untriggered swiftness and grace. He stood there in his silence, which was a gift of his, too. But a sort of smile was growing on his face, and watching that smile, which seemed to have a soft sweetness insinuated with its confident amusement, I found myself beginning to smile, as an apology, I reckon, for my little scream.

"You came," he said then, "soft as—" He hesitated, as though searching the precise and inevitable comparison, lifting his right hand, with thumb and forefinger just touching at the tips, in a gesture of histrionic grace, then said: "—as the dew of dawn. *Doucement comme la rosée de l'aube.*"

"I am sorry I screamed," I said, in French.

"You'll have to let me improve your French," he said with a pedagogical severity.

But he suddenly brightened, saying: "And there is no time like the moment. I shall give you a lesson, now. Say after me, please: *Je viens doucement comme la rosée de l'aube.*"

In my embarrassment, I couldn't reply.

"Say it," he commanded severely, and began again: *Je viens doucement—*"

Then, with relief, I heard the tap of Hamish Bond's stick, back in the gloom of the house, approaching.

Later that summer, I encountered Monsieur Prieur-Denis at various times. He was free of the house, and might be found at any moment, in the hall or patio, or sitting at ease in the study. Whenever I saw him, he would not greet me, but would lift his forefinger severely, and command: "*Répète, ma petite, je viens doucement—*"

And always I flushed with embarrassment, and wanted to run away, away from that sudden smile with its sweetness, its gay irony, its confidence.

Then one day it was different. It was late in the summer, about the first of August. I came out of the back of the house, into the hall, and there he was, as on the first day, standing at ease, waiting. He lifted his finger at me, in his joke, his lips parted to speak, and I saw the even, very white teeth under the precise black mustache, the gleam of the damp lower lip.

I don't know what got into me, what caused it. It wasn't a decision, I felt a tingle of boldness, I felt my head go up as at a dare, and before Monsieur Prieur-Denis could utter a word of that joke, which suddenly seemed to me silly and childish, I heard my voice saying, firmly: "*Je viens doucement comme la rosée de l'aube.*"

I stared him straight in the eye, and heard my heart pounding with triumph.

"Ah," Monsieur Prieur-Denis said, "so you have learned your lesson, and—"

But I never heard the end of the sentence, for I had turned, and scampered away like a child, dodging past him, across the hall, up the stairs, carrying my beating heart and my triumph into the quiet upper reaches of the house.

That triumph was but part of the great triumph I now confidently awaited, that new confidence but part of my confidence in freedom. I lay in my bed at night and saw the great white steamboat churning up the brown river, away, away, and I would be on it, leaving the house of Hamish Bond far behind me. Now every time I smiled, and saw his face soften, I would think: *that smile is oil on the lock, it will open.* For the time, I knew, was coming on.

One by one the difficulties I had earlier envisaged seemed to solve themselves. I had known that I had to learn the city to escape. I had feared the great brute of a nigger-dog that waited in the patio. I had wondered how I would get money.

But at Hamish Bond's own order, Michele had taken me into the city, often. And she gave me money, this too, at Hamish Bond's command. When I was out with her, on the early expeditions, I spent money with childish carelessness, to deceive her, to make her think I put no store by it. Then, when I should be able to go alone she would not wonder about what became of my money—the money I would be hoarding.

But for a long time there had been no chance of going out alone. I was afraid of the dog.

I was, however, very clever about that. I congratulated myself on my cleverness.

I didn't thank Hamish Bond immediately for the money. I waited for some days, and for two or three trips into the city with Michele, before mentioning it. Then, one evening I thanked him. It was nice to have money, I said, to spend for my fancy. But, I added with calculated girlish wistfulness, it was somewhat hard on Michele to have to go with me so often. I said I would try to be more considerate in the future.

"Huh," he said, "why don't you go by yourself?"

I hesitated, gauging the moment. Then said: "The dog."

"The dog?" he echoed, in question. Then he laughed. He laughed fit to kill. In the middle of laughing, he managed to say: "You mean old Rob Roy? You mean that old cow?"

He rose from the table and I heard him go out into the hall and open the front door. Then I heard the tap of his returning blackthorn, and between those taps, the click of the nails of the beast on the polished floor, approaching.

Then the dog came into the room, ahead of the master, into the circle of candlelight, and stared at me from the great, blank, gold-colored eyes.

"Pat him," Hamish Bond's voice commanded, "pat the pore ole booger."

I looked at the dog, the gold eyes, the black, brutal jowls slackly hanging, in that very slackness an obscene bestiality, the red, wet tongue hanging out of the jaws between white tushes.

"Pat him," the voice said.

I put out my hand and touched the beast's head. My first sensation was of the massiveness of bone beneath my fingers. Then, with shocking suddenness, the beast dropped from beneath my fingers, dropped as though it had been shot, right to the floor. As my hand yet hung in the air, the beast rolled over on its back, with an awkward, heaving motion, the parody of a puppy's playfulness, and lay there with white belly and throat exposed, tongue lolling foolishly out one side of the dangerous jaws, big, black forepaws flopping idly in the air.

"See," Hamish Bond was saying, "see the pore old booger, he wouldn't hurt a fly."

"Yes, sir," I said, looking down at the thing, the thin powerful pinch-in of the back belly and hind-quarters, the black bulge of the scrotum, the big bulge of the chest, all that dangerousness ridiculously negated by the silly waving paws and flopping tongue.

"So pore little Manty was afraid of you, you booger," Hamish Bond was saying, leaning over to scratch the under-throat of the beast. "Pore little Manty was afraid of you—silly little Manty."

Silly little Manty, indeed! And suddenly I felt contempt for Hamish Bond. He was a fool. I'd walk past his silly brute and be gone, and then—then he'd wish—he'd wish what?

He would wish that he had had a real nigger-dog, a great beast of a dog. And into my mind the great beast of fable leaped, with the throaty exhalation and thud a great beast makes at the end of the leap, a killer of a beast, eyes wide and burning, tushes a-gleam.

Contemptuously, with my patent-leather toe, I prodded the disorganized comic hulk on the floor.

But on the instant with my flush of victory, with the disappearance of the fear, came a sense of loss.

Why had the fear been precious to me? Was it that the fear itself defined me, and the challenge of the feared thing was my own chance to know myself real? Why did I feel ridiculously diminished? And suddenly, as I stood there, I was envious, in recollection, of that Negro who had long back escaped to Oberlin to show to a bevy of gaping, prissy, pious-tongued girls the scarce-healed cicatrice on his flesh where the terrible fangs of reality had slashed.

Then, in recollection, I felt hatred for that Negro sitting under the lamp, exposing his precious arm. Who was he, ignorant, stupid, unwashed, wall-eyed, afraid? In recollection I caught the sour smell of his rags. Who was he to be so grand because dog-bit?

You didn't have to be dog-bit to be free.

I had about decided to get aboard a steamboat just at the moment of departure, risk getting a cabin on short notice, buy a ticket for some point well upriver but disembark at the first stop where the general movement of passengers ashore would give me some cover, say Vicksburg, and then, with the safe mask of my white face and gentility, make my way overland, north.

The time came. Everything was working perfectly. I had money in my purse. I had pushed open the iron grill of Hamish Bond's patio, for the last time, and gone out. The *Pride of Cincinnati* was to lift plank at four that afternoon, and already the black smoke of her stacks feathered high over the city. Since there was some apprehension about an outbreak of yellow fever, even this late in the season, in August, my last-minute appearance on the boat would not seem remarkable. Old Bronze John always encouraged sudden travel.

I walked down the street, decorously under my parasol, and my heart beat strongly and calmly in my bosom. I would stop twice on the way to the levee, once to buy a valise of some sort and a few oddments of toilet, and once to pick up two dresses I had ordered from the seamstress, and had left for this occasion, since clearly I couldn't leave the house equipped for a journey.

Now I was looking for some little colored boy who could be hired to carry my valise, once I had got it. Not that I couldn't carry it, but the fact would have excited notice. I had to gamble on finding a boy, but that was an easy gamble on a summer afternoon, when any patch of shade might show a solitary specimen snoozing like a puppy, or a group huddled over a game of mumble-peg. I found my boy, struck a bargain for two coppers, and proceeded. All was well.

All was well except for the one unpredictable thing.

Years ago, if I had been asked what that unpredictable thing had turned out to be, I should have said that it was Rau-Ru—Rau-Ru suddenly there on the *banquette*. But now, if asked, I should reply, in candor, that the unpredictable thing was myself. I suppose that that is always, in any calculation, the one factor unpredictable, the one thing unknowable: the self.

That afternoon in August, after I had been to the seamstress, with the little colored boy trailing me with my valise, I proceeded toward the levee, whence rose, like the pillar of smoke for the wanderers of the Bible story, the smoke from the stacks of the *Pride of Cincinnati*. I was walking fast—I had to restrain myself to keep from running, excitement mounting in my breast now—and once, fearful that I had outpaced my little attendant and valise, I looked back. There he was, all right, dawdling a little, yes, but coming along on his short legs, the valise bumping in the neighborhood of his nigh shin.

I saw the urchin, paused for an instant to let him catch up, and was about to call back, "Hurry, hurry!" when I saw, some forty feet away, coming up the *banquette* on the other side of the street, in the shadow of the wall there, a white-clad figure, but a figure vague because of my preoccupation. Then, on a stroke, it was not vague, there was the red sash, the flat straw hat like a sailor's, there was the enameled black face, and the eyes were fixed, over the distance, directly into mine.

And my heart was ice.

Oh, how foolish I had been! All this time lulled in my foolishness—deceived by money in my purse, the unlocked gate of the patio, my unaccompanied expeditions, the flop-pawed silliness of the dog, the indulgence of the master. All was a lie, for all the time eyes had been upon me. And I had the vision of Hamish Bond's face, big there against the sky and the tiles of roofs and the colored stucco, the face with the indulgent smile wiped out, a cold and bulge-eyed brutishness. It was as though all my little stratagems had been enacted under his powerful, hair-sprigged, finger-maimed hand, gigantically poised above me, and now at his sardonic pleasure, it would drop, and I would be snatched back to whatever nightmare thing was in store for me.

I stood there on the *banquette,* and the nightmare was coiling around me to blot out the sun-dazzle. Or to be sensible, it was merely the rush of blood to my head, the dizziness, the blacking of my vision.

But it passed, and there was my last cunning of desperation. "Oh, Rau-Ru!" I called.

Promptly, the white-clad figure detached itself from the shadow of walls, the whiteness of the costume flashed to a new intensity in the blaze of sunlight, and Rau-Ru advanced toward me, opening his reserved smile to show the glinting whiteness of teeth, moving toward me in his inimitable cat-ease of stride, setting the glint of patent-leather boots punctiliously into the street-dust. He carried his hat in his hand.

"M'selle," he said.

He yet stood below the level of the *banquette,* in the dust, and waited. This meant that, despite his stature, he was now lower than I. I looked, curiously, down into his face. I say *curiously,* but perhaps another word would do better. I was finding something there in his face, and was bemused by it. Rather, I was finding something in the situation, merely in the fact that his face was a few inches lower than mine. I was finding something in myself, a sense of power, and in my bemusement my apprehension fled away, my fear that I would not be able to brazen out the moment, that he would drag me disgracefully home.

He said again: "M'selle."

That jerked me out of myself. "Rau-Ru," I said, and heard the new authority in my tone, "this little nigger"—and I indicated the valiant little valise-toter—"this little nigger"—and I heard my voice give the delicate flick to the word, affirming what my deep need needed to affirm—"this little nigger is so plum lazy I'll never get home. Not in this world. Won't you carry my bag, Rau-Ru?"

He looked at the boy, and the little fellow ducked his head a trifle as though to dodge a swipe, but kept his pop-eyed gaze canted warily sidewise and up, to assess the magnificent apparition of Rau-Ru. Then Rau-Ru, wordlessly, put out his hand toward the boy.

Slowly, in disgrace, the boy hung the handle of the valise on the outstretched forefinger of Rau-Ru's hand, as though on a peg. He stood there, hope on the ebb in him, his eyes on me now, his small toes working a little on the board of the *banquette*.

Pore little nigger, he just wanted his coppers.

I reached into my purse, took a coin, and laid it in his palm. He looked down at it, a big, silver-shiny two-bit piece on the gray-pink of the palm. He couldn't believe it. He lifted up his gaze to my face to read me. Then—so much like the cork of a popgun that you almost heard the *pop!*—was gone. Way up the street now, off the *banquette*, his heels flashed in their extending plume of dust.

Without a word to Rau-Ru, I moved on, and turned left at the next corner, veering away from the direction of the levee. But I wouldn't head directly home. I was too clever for that. I took a wandering and circuitous route, thinking that by this aimless peregrination I should lull any suspicion which Rau-Ru, the spy, the master's informer, might have had at finding me, in the first place, so far off the accustomed track.

Then, with a sudden recollection of the moment when I had stood above him and looked down into his face, I thought: *Who is he to question which way I choose to go? What is he but another nigger carrying my valise?*

And I walked up the street, never looking back but bearing in my mind the hard gratification of that image of the white-clad figure cat-stepping behind me, at the humble distance.

When I entered the portal of Hamish Bond's patio, the big dog stirred by the orange tree, then dropped his head. I saw the vines ruffling grayish on the balcony of my own room, high up. I entered the house, and Rau-Ru followed obediently.

"You can set it down," I said to him, and he put down the valise. "Thank you," I said.

"*A votre service,*" he said, and disappeared down the hall.

Dollie, previously undetected, regarded me from the shadow of the stairs.

"What are you looking at?" I demanded sharply of her.

"You," she said, "you. Next thing you be gittin Ole Man Bond a-totin atter you."

And she moved across the hall, carrying in one hand an imaginary valise, moving in a swaying, comic burlesque of Rau-Ru's not-to-be-imitated stride.

When I first got up to my room, after the fiasco, all seemed void. I lay on the bed and saw the sky, beyond the gold cross of the Cathedral spire, grow more purplish, but a purple flecked and veined with a sulphurous light. Then I closed my eyes and heard the wind in my vines.

But this blackness began to fill out again, not clearly, just with the faintest shadows of new hopes, new plans. Well, I had faced down Rau-Ru. There was no proof that I had tried to flee. Just the suspicion. I would face down Old Bond, too. I would face him down. I would make him withdraw his spies. I didn't know how I would do it, but I knew I could.

With a sudden sense of power, I rose from the bed. I carefully prepared my toilet. I put on the most beautiful of my dresses, the one Old Bond liked best, too—the pink with the chocolate slashing in the skirt. Then I went down to dinner. I gave my master a most cold good evening.

When he tried to make conversation I did not even look at him, and if I deigned to answer, I made merely the most irrelevant monosyllable, while he lunged and blundered on, like a man trying to get through a thicket on a dark night.

Finally, he fell silent. He stopped right in the middle of some sentence, just stopped. I knew he was looking at me.

Then he said: "Pore little Manty, what's the matter?"

"Nothing," I said, shortly.

"But something is the matter," he said. And added: "I don't want anything to be the matter, Manty."

"Well," I said, feeling the flush of the moment, "in that case don't set your spies on me. Do you hear? Just lock my door and be done, will you?"

I rose from the table, stared straight into his stunned face, intoxicated with victory. "And further," I said, "in the future I shall dine with your other—your other slaves—" and ran toward the door, stopping at the door to turn back, to say with a mincing, grimacing parody of servility, "Massa."

Then I fled up the stairs, to my room, and flung myself across the foot of the bed. I had carefully refrained from locking my door. I expected him to follow. Well, when he did, I would finish it off. I didn't know how, but I was sure.

And he came. After a little, up from the hall, up the stairs, two flights, the stick making its regular sound.

He knocked on my door. "Come in," I called, and plunged my head deeper into the coverlet in an excess of despair. He came to stand at the foot of the bed. I heard the stick, then his breathing.

"Are you sick, Manty?" he asked, then.

"No," I said.

"You got a fever, Manty?"

"I haven't got a fever," I said.

He picked up my wrist, as though to count my pulse.

"Don't!" I cried, and sat up, and jerked away from him. "Don't you ever touch me!"

"But, Manty—" and he was staring at me in grievous confusion.

"Don't *but* me any *buts*," I said, "after what you've done." And I plunged on: "After you've set your spies on me, after you've set that —that fancy nigger of yours to following me!"

"But, Manty—" he repeated, and took a step to come around the bed toward me, and stumbled on something, and might have fallen had he not grasped the bedpost. Then he leaned to remove the offending object, and I knew immediately what it was.

It was my new valise.

I suppose one valise more or less meant nothing to Hamish Bond, who in a way always seemed oblivious to the objects around him, that is, to objects with which he was not immediately dealing, and it is very probable that he would have laid it to one side without a thought. But when he picked it up, I assumed—wrongly I am certain

—that I was now fully discovered. So I burst out: "All right, there it is. Yes, there is the valise. Yes, I was running away." I plunged on, in a rapturous abandon, a savage glee that grew as I watched distress grow on his face.

"Yes, I was getting on the steamboat, and if it hadn't been for that Rau-Ru of yours—but he made me come back here—and oh! I'll die."

I stopped, breathless, trying to know, in a way, the meaning of what I had said.

"Manty," Hamish Bond was saying, and all at once the defenselessness of his face stirred a last cold, calculating anger in me.

"I wish," I said quite coldly, quite calmly, "I wish that I had been taken to any other house in the world. And not yours. Do you understand?"

Then, as I watched his face, an unpremeditated cry sprang to my lips. "Oh, why did you bring me here?" I cried.

Whatever confusion and distress had been struggling on Hamish Bond's face, were then, on the stroke, gone. There was nothing in his face now, the emptiness of shock. Then his eyes blinked once or twice, slowly, as though he were reorienting himself in consciousness. I saw his tongue tip come out and wet his lips, as though in preparation for speech. But he said nothing.

Then he managed the words: "Why—" he slowly repeated the question, "why did I do it?"

He shook his head almost imperceptibly, as though some small insect were annoying him. Then he said: "I just don't know. I just don't know, Manty."

"Don't call me Manty," I snapped at him.

But he ignored that. He retreated from the bed, toward the perimeter of the candlelight, setting the ferrule of the blackthorn to the bare floor. He leaned on his stick and stared heavily back at me. "A man lives a long time," he said, "and it looks like there's always something else he don't know—"

He didn't finish the sentence. Over there at the edge of the light I could see the faint gleam of the candle flame in his eyes. He twitched his head, a couple of times. Then he spoke with his strong, accustomed voice. "Listen," he said, "you don't have to stay here if you don't want to. I am sending you away."

"Yes," I retorted sarcastically, "selling me. I hope you get back your two thousand dollars."

But he had lifted his stick to cut me short, and said: "There is a steamboat tomorrow to Cincinnati, *The Golden Fleece.* You'll be on it. I have a business correspondent in Cincinnati. He'll take charge for you there. He will arrange for—"

He stopped. Then: "There's no use to discuss it now. Everything will be arranged for you."

He pointed with his stick over to my valise, where he had dropped it. He grinned at me with a certain wryness—at least that was the expression as well as I could make out over there in the shadow. "And I reckon you'll need more luggage than that," he said.

Then he went out, and down the hall.

So that was the way it would end, I thought, and felt nothing but a drained lassitude. So that was the way: they would put you on a boat, and all day you would see the water slide beneath you, slick as oil, and you would lie in your berth and hear the engines heave and clump all night, and then, at the end of a certain time, you would be free.

The wind had stopped just before I went to bed. It had stopped suddenly, and the suddenness of the silence had been palpable, filling the night, and in that silence I had slept.

I had left a candle burning, under its hurricane glass, just because I was too lazy to get up and blow it out.

What woke me, I don't know. Perhaps the first stroke of wind on the house. Anyway, I was, all at once, awake, and in the maniacal middle of that preposterous tropical racket, I could identify nothing, not time nor place nor self. In that first instant, the candle was still burning, but the flame, even under the hurricane glass, was dancing in a vertiginous blur of light and shadow. Then the candleholder itself, globe and all, lifted and went crashing against the wall, and in the first smack of darkness of that identifiable event, I knew where, and what, I was.

Somewhere a chimney or something, something big, fell horrendously. A voice somewhere was screaming, a woman's voice. A covey of roof tiles—though at the moment I had no notion what—ended flight in a crash on my balcony, like a massive destruction of crockery. The wind uttered perpetually a sound like a million cats in the rut-yowl. The lightning was probing the city with great jags and thrusts, probing for me, grabbing for me in the disorder of the city like a hand grabbing for something in a box of straw.

A sudden gust drenched me, even there on the bed.

I leaped from the bed and tried to shove one wing of the window shut. I stood there shoving against the wind, and the wind was nearly snatching me naked. I heaved my weight against the frame. An upper pane of glass blew out. It shattered in all directions. I must have screamed, but I am sure that the scream was not audible, for on the same instant lightning struck a chimney across the street. I saw the ragged blaze of the bolt, and felt the rolling wash of the concussion. Then I was on the floor, shaking with cold terror, and the rain was lashing me to the bone.

What I next knew was hands on me, big hands dragging me from the window into the lee of the wall, picking me up, and I opened my eyes to catch, in a flash of lightning, the face of Hamish Bond leaning over, his soaked hair whipped down over his brow, his face running with rain, glistening in the lightning flash, his mouth saying something, something not audible in the competing din. Then it was dark—or had I simply closed my eyes?—and it wasn't now, it was years back and I was out in the storm, out in the dark, lost, where I had gone to save poor Bu-Bula, poor Bu-Bula, the doll Old Shaddy had made me, and the thunder was scaring me to death, and I clutched the thin-soaked fabric of the shirt that stuck to Hamish Bond's chest, clinging there, quivering in his arms, my eyes squinched shut, pressing my face into the security of his shoulder and neck while the tumult of the storm fell away.

Abruptly, there was nothing but silence, then the sound of a voice calling off yonder in the street, in the dark, a voice sounding sweet and silvery in the silence as though cleansed by the rain, then the silence again. I was aware, then, of the small, raw sound of Hamish Bond's breathing.

He had been leaning back against the wall while the storm subsided, propping himself that way. All at once now he straightened, thrusting forward by a heave of the shoulder against the wall. Burdened with me, he did not have his stick. With my eyes yet shut I could feel how he swung his stiff right leg forward, balancing me for the effort. It was a kind of hobbling stride, but good enough, and somewhere back in my head there was the detached thought: *He walks pretty well.* That thought was lying there in my head like something scribbled on a scrap of paper and flung down in a dark closet.

In three such contrived strides, he got me to the bed and deposited me there. Then I surmised, my eyes still shut, that he had stepped back from the bed.

For a moment there was no sound. Then some kind of a small sound, then another, a small *plop*. And I knew what that second sound was. I knew perfectly well. It was the sound of a soaked cloth being dropped to the floor.

I felt the solid sag of the bed as his good knee came down on the edge. The voice said: "Oh, Manty!" and the sound was more like a hollow groan being wrenched out of a man than like a word.

The hand was then laid to my side to grasp it, at the small part.

I remember with perfect distinctness, even now, the rasping texture of the skin of the ball of the thumb as it indented, though gently, my flesh. It was as coarse as sandpaper.

# V I

YOU LIVE THROUGH TIME, THAT LITTLE PIECE OF TIME THAT IS YOURS, but that piece of time is not only your own life, it is the summing-up of all the other lives that are simultaneous with yours. It is, in other words, History, and what you are is an expression of History, and you do not live your life, but somehow, your life lives you, and you are, therefore, only what History does to you.

That is what I have heard said, but we have to try to make sense of what we have lived, or what has lived us, and there are so many questions that cry for an answer, as children gather about your knee and cry for a sweetmeat. No, it would be better to change the comparison and say it is like children gathering about your knee to cry for a story, a bedtime story, and if you can tell the right story, then these children, then these questions, will sleep, and you can, too.

You feel that if you can answer the questions, you might be free.

What I started out to say, however, was this: how do you know how you yourself, all the confused privatenesses of you, are involved with that history you are living through?

A young girl, storm-drenched and storm-scared and lonely and confused in a foreshortening of time, is disposed on a bed by an aging man, who utters her name like a groan, and gently and bloodily does that thing to her, and she cries out. I had almost used that foul word that old Mr. Marmaduke, back in Kentucky, had used in his prediction of my fate. I would have used it in some impulse to spit upon and spurn that aging man and the young girl coupled on that bed, but something forbids. I would not spit upon them, after all, I suppose.

Well, the young girl is adjusted upon the bed, but how is what happens to her connected with some late conversation of bankers that same night in New York City, wreathed in the spicy smoke of cigars and eye-glittering with French brandy, or connected with the sweat-cold nocturnal death-fear of a politician abed in Washington, or connected with a grim-jawed old man, seated by the candle in a farmhouse in Maryland, not far from Harper's Ferry, who lifts his eyes from the Holy Writ and moves his lips stiffly in prayer, panting for the moment when the old blood-drenched fantasy will whirl again before his eyes and justify all?

Oh, who is whose victim?

And the hand of Hamish Bond laid to my side, and the spreading creep and prickle of sensation across the softness of my belly from the focus of Hamish Bond's sandpaper thumb, and the unplaiting and deliquescence of the deep muscles of thighs were as much History as any death-cry at the trench-lip or in the tangle of the abatis.

I woke not knowing, in the first flash, where I was, or what had happened, surprised by the contact of that unidentified bulk by me. Then, with the stir of memory, a flash of terror, a sense of violation, came, as though hours late I experienced, feebly but dutifully, what I should have experienced at the actual event.

By this time, in the moment of the terror, I had pulled myself free and was standing by the bed looking quickly about the room with distraction, at the broken window, the burst of early sunlight, the heap of Hamish Bond's clothing on the floor with the spreading circle of wet, the big body on the bed.

He was still asleep. He lay on one side, the face turned toward me, away from the window, the big head thrust hard against the pillow as by an effort, the bare right arm, from beneath which I had just escaped, flung heavily out. The sheet was twisted back so that, from heel to a point halfway between knee and hip, the leg was exposed. I looked at the big, hairy bare leg, with, I suppose, some remaining flicker of my terror, and I saw the scar.

There was a jagged, deep, purplish scar that ran from well up the thigh down to the knee, and across under the kneecap.

I gazed at the scar in fascination. My terror was gone. I do not know what I felt as I gazed at it. But I do know that I suddenly leaned over and kissed the scar, and as I did so, my heart was flooded with tenderness. What I mean to say is that, according to my recollection, it was not the tenderness that made me lean to kiss the old wound. The tenderness came after I had leaned. But what made me lean?

I had lain back down, on the very edge of the bed, facing away from the bulk there, making not the slightest sound, and as I lay there I tried to decide how everything in the world was different now, but in a strange way nothing was different, nothing—that is, if I did not turn over, or if I just shut my eyes, and my mind. And as I was puzzling this, I went to sleep.

When I woke up, Hamish Bond was gone.

He came back late in the morning, came up to my room, and passed me the most formal greeting. I don't know what I had expected, and I suppose I stood there, hearing the approach, balanced in a tremulous plasticity of spirit, ready to be defined by the first word spoken, the first fleeting expression on his face.

But his face expressed nothing. If anything it was stony and remote, not the face I had come to know in late months. And after that formal greeting, he said: "I have told Michele to pack your things. *The Golden Fleece* leaves at three."

While he was saying those words, I could not believe them. Certainly he had promised me freedom, but the deed done had seemed to my mind, in so far as I had thought about it at all, to revoke all. Or if I was free, it was in a different way—what way I couldn't say.

But he was continuing: "—in Cincinnati in five days or so. I have arranged all and—"

So I drew myself up, and said that I thanked him.

At the appointed hour I walked up the gangplank of *The Golden Fleece*, to the accompaniment of the festive racket. But I was not alone. Hamish Bond walked by my side. He was, he said, going up to *Pointe du Loup*.

The trip to *Pointe du Loup* was short—an hour, two, three, I do not know. We stood side by side on the boiler deck, leaning on the starboard rail, apart from the movement of people, and watched the city drift away, the roofs, the great Cotton Press structure, the spire of the Cathedral, the gold cross. Then we watched the western shore slide past, levee, open bank, levee again, forests, clearings, the rare shack on bare ground, the rare great house, in a grove, on a hillock, the sun westering beyond, all objects flat, and two-dimensional, as that light beyond defined them.

The river was at low water. On that oily and unflecked surface, from which the light reflected to our gaze, the long, ever-renewed undulation that angled back from our bows moved unweariedly forward to define, as with an index finger, the demarcation of mud and old slime exposed at the base of the levee or the margin of shore.

We did not talk during the journey. Now and then I stole a look at Hamish Bond's face. It told me nothing. I can see quite clearly that face as it was at that moment: the square jaw, the short but broad nose set between the massive cheekbones, the fixed and bulge-eyed gaze over the water to distance.

Toward dusk there was a jangle of bells. The craft lost headway, yawed in. Ahead, backed by forest visible over the low levee, I saw some sort of landing stage. At that moment the whistle let off a blast. In the stunned interlude, Hamish Bond turned to me and seemed about to speak.

In the first silence, he said: "Well, this is it."

I did not reply.

There were bell-bursts again, and a great sloshing and pother as the paddle wheel on our side reversed.

"Captain Simmons is fully instructed," Hamish Bond was saying. "He will take care of you."

A colored boy appeared behind Hamish Bond, carrying his valise, and stood waiting. The plank was rattling down.

Hamish Bond moved toward the head of the stairs to the main deck, I by his side. There he stopped, and reached into an inner pocket. He withdrew a big thick brown envelope. "Here," he said, "here is everything you'll need. The papers, and money. And Mr. Carton will attend you in Cincinnati."

He thrust the envelope at me. I took it. He stepped down one stair, as though on his way from me, then turned. Very formally, while I stood there in my numbness, he lifted my hand and kissed it. "Good-bye," he said, "good-bye, little Manty."

He dropped my hand, turned, and was down another step. People passed on the stair.

All at once, he had swung back to me. "Listen," he said, in a constricted, grinding voice, like gravel under a boot-heel. I could not be sure what was on the face that stared up at me, anguish or ferocity.

"Listen," he said, in that grinding voice, "forget everything. Everything that's ever happened. Forget me."

He went down the stairs with surprising rapidity, one hand on the rail, the other grasping the blackthorn, thumping his way down.

I stood motionless, clutching the envelope. Then I realized that he had passed beyond my range of vision, was somewhere down there, moving away.

I was not responsible for what was to happen. At least. I had made no decision for the act; it surprised me. I found myself, still clutching the envelope, dashing down the stairs. Hamish Bond was almost at the end of the gangplank before I overtook him.

He stood there at the end of the gangplank, and stared down at me. On his face was not surprise, nor incredulity, but a kind of bemusement, and a look of distance.

For a moment, I felt myself lost in that distance. Then I knew that I must have been smiling at Hamish Bond, but with some kind of shy, tremulous appeal.

He still looked down at me from his distance. Then, all at once, his face lighted in that strange way that, as I have already said, reminded me of sunlight breaking through cloud on a craggy landscape. "Well, Manty," he said, grinning, "well, I'll be darn."

He turned to the colored boy who had followed with the valise. "Boy," he commanded, "get me all that stuff from Number Seven."

The boy dropped the valise and started off.

"Hump it, boy!" Hamish Bond said.

We watched the steamboat gliding away, North, silent now in the distance, under the twin black plumes of unruffling smoke, the craft moving in shadow of the forest, for the sun was low, but the smoke steady in the high, late light.

We stood there in the wilderness, our feet on the sun-cracked mud of the old track, the incongruous luggage at our feet. Beyond the levee rose the forest, darkening now. A bird, far off there, called with a compulsive, irascible lament, musical by distance.

I stepped closer to Hamish Bond. I wanted to take his hand, I suddenly felt so lost. But I only said: "What is that bird?"

He turned to the forest, listening studiously. "I don't know," he said.

Then he looked into my face. "Pore little Manty," he said, and took my hand.

And after a moment, still looking into my face: "We're just what we are, little Manty. That's all we are."

We stood there a little while, then he said: "They'll be here soon. Times I don't get word ahead, they hear the boat blow for a landing, and know it's me."

Just then, up the levee, broke a shrill yelp. A little colored boy was up there, at the head of the track. He was dancing up there, a fantastic flickering of heels and a bird-darting and bird-swooping of hands, all against the pink sky.

We walked up the track and saw them all, coming.

Some eighty or ninety Negroes were there, various sizes, ages and conditions. When we came over the levee, they yelled and clapped hands and patted their feet, yelling, "Massa, Massa—Massa, high-juba." In the midst of them was a light wagon, two mules hitched to it, some bent poles arching over it, the bent poles festooned with flowers and bright rags, and under the bent poles, under the gaiety of flowers and rags, a split-bottom chair.

An old Negro, some sort of headman, appeared and shook hands with Hamish Bond, eying me scantwise, decorously ignoring me for all his curiosity. But meanwhile all the other eyes were full on me.

Hamish Bond looked slowly around, then back at me. "This," he said, making a gesture toward me, "is—is Miss Manty. She will be here. She will do good to you."

There was a burst of appreciative racket, clapping and stamping; "Do good—shore good—ever do good and high-juba!"

We were lifted into the wagon. Hamish Bond indicated the chair for me, under the garlands, and stood behind, holding the back. Our luggage was flung in. We started off. There was no driver. The nigh mule was led by the old boss-Negro.

We rolled and bumped over the rotting relic of a corduroy road, the blossoms and bright rags waggling over our heads. Despite the late season, some water yet stood on each side of the track, and the great roots of cypresses jagged and convoluted man-high from it, and the trunks rose high above us, draped with the old moss like a palpable darkness. The split-bottom chair jounced, and the cortege danced, clapped, and stamped about our triumphal car, chanting:

*Massa, Massa, ole Mass', he come,*
*Mass' bring good thing, gonna gimme some,*
*Massa done come, I ain't never gonna cry,*
*Gonna be hello now and never good-bye.*
*Massa—Massa—Massa, high-juba!*

Or something like that, and the old boss-Negro made up new words and called them out, to be picked up for the chant, for our adulation.

Then we were out of the darkening trees, into wide fields where sky opened enormously with the last pale light. The wheels rolled silklike now on a loamy track. On each side, the cotton plants stretched away. The bolls were opening their snatches of snowy whiteness, bright even in the failing light. Ahead of us, rising from the flatness, on a low knoll or mound, stood a massy grove. The great house, I assumed, was there among those live oaks.

But it wasn't going to be great at all, certainly nothing to brag on. Many a plain man around Danville, back in Kentucky, had a house as good. It wasn't even two-story, just a wooden house with a gallery, set high on a brick foundation. On the rear end, however, it was, as I discovered, two-story, for back there, on the lower brick level, were the winter kitchen, the dining room, and some storage. The wooden part of the house wasn't even painted.

As we drew up to the high steps of the house, all the rout of us, I saw, even in the darkness under the spreading live oaks, that the ground was grassless, as though trodden hard.

They lifted Hamish Bond down, then me, chair and all.

After supper that night—a supper of rice and soup and leathery cold venison and bowls of tepid milk—served on a great rosewood table worthy of a palace, though somewhat abused and almost a rarity among furnishings largely knocked together on the spot with hammer and nails and a predilection for the crooked line—we sat on the gallery between two smudge pots and viewed the evening. We could hear some sort of jubilation down at the quarters. There had been an issue of rum, earlier.

I said: "When you come home—come up here, I mean—"

"Yeah, home," he said. "It is more like a home, up here."

"What I mean," I continued, "is do they always do like this? Turn out and have flowers and dance and sing?"

"Listen," he said, "they always like Massa on every plantation. It's the overseer that's always a hellion, and the Massa is going to come and fix everything up nice. He does a little something in that line, if he's smart, and they think he is wonderful."

"Have you got an overseer here?"

"Not exactly," he said.

"Then they come out for you?"

"Sometimes, if I been away a long time," he said, "and it's a slack season. Like now, corn laid by, cotton-picking barely on. Anyway, they like excuse for a jubilation."

After a moment, over there in the dark, he rose from his chair, with a heavy, lumbering motion, something like a heavy animal heaving up in the brush. He took a step or two. Then he tapped the gallery floor a few times with his stick. "The mound under this house," he said, "it's Indians built it. God knows when or how, but they're lying down there in it, in the ground."

He took another step, tapping: "Yeah, and now we got nig—"

Then he stopped, and I knew he had been going to say *niggers*, and I knew why he had stopped on the word. So, quite coldly, I said it for him: "Niggers."

After a moment, then, he repeated: "Yeah, and now we got niggers on top of the Indians. And"—he hesitated—"and I'm on top of the niggers."

I heard the far-off jubilation in the quarters. And I thought of the dancing, shouting rout around the wagon, moving through forest and field, and myself sitting under the waggling garlands and bright rags.

*Pointe du Loup* was the smaller of Hamish Bond's two upriver holdings. The other, a few horseback miles to the north, called *Tarnation*, was some 2000 acres, not all under plow but with a force of 250 people. There had been a fine house there when Hamish Bond bought the place, but he had never occupied it. The house had later burned, and now there was only a cottage for the overseer.

Hamish Bond went to *Tarnation* only often enough to keep an eye on things. He referred to the place contemptuously as a "cotton camp" or a "lint station." He had, however, some deep attachment for *Pointe du Loup*, an attachment that I never fully understood, but that had some basis in the very roughness and isolation of the life there. "Home," he called the place.

Certainly, when he was there he gave special attention to every detail, riding around in a light, high-wheeled gig to investigate and supervise whatever was going on—chopping, picking, ginning, corn-pulling, farrier work, and ditching and drainage and tree-felling to win land from the swamp woods. Often I rode with him and heard his long monologues about his concerns, almost his talking to himself. Just talking to himself, he would say apologetically, and say it came from having been alone so much. "Off at sea," he would say. And once went on to say how at sea a man gets so that he has to put his words out in the air and hear them to be sure he's real, to be sure he "just hasn't melted away into things."

He would talk along, and I would listen and ask questions now and then, and feel good when he said: "Be damn, Manty, if you ain't getting to be a better farmer than me." Then he'd laugh and say he reckoned he wasn't a farmer at all, just stumbled into it, he was a sailor. And he might start talking about the China Sea, or Macao, or Zanzibar, or some other place he'd been.

We would ride along in the gig, under the beating sun, him sweating in his black coat, his game leg stuck out stiffly and a little askew, me with my patent-leather shoes set primly side by side on the curving floor boards, me wearing a dimity dress, carrying a little parasol, and I would look across the distance of white cotton and sun-dazzle to the dark forest and hear the strangeness of his voice saying the names of places away across the world.

That is one of the pictures that come back to me most vividly, summarizing that time. Another is the picture of me at evening, on the gallery, me quiet in the crook of his arm. Another is me down at the infirmary, at night, by candlelight, leaning over one of the cots where somebody lies, and Hamish Bond in the shadow, waiting, and Rau-Ru leaning and saying, "Have to cut it off—gonna have to," and the terrible wideness of the gaze up from the cot to me, and how bulging white the eye-whites were in the black face down there.

And then, after the stunning dosage of laudanum and rum, the man was strapped to the table, the tourniquet applied, and Rau-Ru cut off the mangled and gangrenous arm, knife and saw, just above the elbow, slapped on the white-hot iron to cauterize, and stepped back, looming in the candlelight, sweat glittering on the black enamel of his face, blood streaking the white blouse, the terrible, wooden-handled iron dangling from his grasp, the glow now fading from the tip. He stood there in the flickering light, staring down at the man, and he might have been the warrior with falchion in hand, pausing in the carnage, or the torturer rapt before his achievement.

He was not warrior, nor torturer, and he had done what had to be done. The gangrene wouldn't wait.

I had stood beside Hamish Bond, gripping his arm, shaking like a child, but he had patted my hand, and I had managed to stand there, sustained in some pride. After it was over, we went outside, leaving the patient unconscious, and stood a moment, while Hamish Bond lighted a cheroot.

He took a few puffs in silence, exhaling slowly. Then said: "Well, there goes a thousand dollars."

And I thought: *And the price for me was two thousand dollars.* And my hand on his arm must have started in surprise.

He swung to me, and seemed to be peering down at me in the dark, over the small glow of the cheroot. "That's just one way of looking at it," he said, glumly.


The reason I had stayed for the operation was that I had taken the infirmary as my special province and obligation—an echo, I suppose, of Hamish Bond's words when he had introduced me to the people: "She will do good to you."

The infirmary itself was a wooden building, on the knoll for coolness, a long narrow structure divided into four sections, one for men, one for children, one for women with diseases, and one for women lying in. Two handy old beldames, full of lore, sleights of the flesh, prayerfulness, and garrulity, served as nurses at need, but before my time, the head-Galen and boss-empiric had been Rau-Ru.

There is no sneer in my reference, except the sneer at my own small pretensions. As for Rau-Ru, he knew all the lore of the beldames, but had sorted out the true from the false. He knew that the emulsion of alder bark benefits a wound, that the leaf of pokeweed laid on a stone-bruise appeases pain, and that the decoction of life-everlasting brings ease to the flesh. But beyond his roots and juices he had a locked-up cabinet of medicaments from New Orleans, and a big, red-backed book, *The Planter's Guide to Medicine and Surgery.* He read that book like a breviary.

I once asked Hamish Bond how Rau-Ru had learned to read. He said he had taught him. I asked if it wasn't against the law, as I had been told at Oberlin.

"Not where I was," Hamish Bond replied. "I made what law there was."

"Where was that?" I asked.

He looked at me for a moment, a little dour, then said, shortly: "On my ship."

But Rau-Ru was more than boss-empiric. For all practical purposes he was the overseer of *Pointe du Loup*. There was a white overseer at *Tarnation*, but even in the protracted absences of Hamish Bond in New Orleans, the overseer seldom set foot on the domain of Rau-Ru. The overseer was there to be appealed to, only as a concession, I suppose, to common practice and prejudice.

"Ole Man Bond's free niggers," certainly those of *Pointe du Loup*, nearly ran their own lives. True, corn and cotton had to be raised, but under that iron necessity the rule of life was theirs—theirs and Rau-Ru's. Rau-Ru and the "old ones" were a council, but a council that would call the people together and hear them before making a decision. As for punishment, the same council served as a court, with all the people summoned for the investigation and verdict, and their moans, ejaculations, and murmurs, formed a chorus to the development of justice.

And justice was easy. The lash had hung, stiffening in its thongs, unused, on the granary door, in plain sight, for five years. The most feared punishment, past things like short pork rations or banishment from the Saturday night juba-pat, was the "finger-pointing," a kind of putting in Coventry, a system whereby no word except an order might be addressed to the culprit during the term of punishment, and at every encounter a pointed finger would accompany the wordless stare.

I have seen a strong man, famous for hunting and fishing, accustomed to loneliness in those pursuits, drop down on his knees in broad daylight, as though the pointed finger were a pistol that had delivered its slug, and cry out, "Oh, I love 'ee, I love 'ee monst'ous, oh, why doan you love me?"

Occasionally, a sufferer under "finger-pointing" would flee to the woods. But he always came back. He came back, I suppose, because in the very punishment there was a promise—the promise of the "raise-up," the moment when, surrounded by all the tribe, under the glory of pine-knot flares, the old head-man would reach down and lift the crouching culprit, and everybody would clap hands and stamp earth and chant in the common joy of restoration.

I have seen it, and the first time I saw it, I burst into tears, tears from some strange yearning despair and generous joy, tears from— shall I say?—the recognition of truth. I was standing by Hamish, and in shame at my tears I averted my face from him. But not in time. He reached his hand to my face, and drew it back to him, staring into my wet eyes.

"I reckon it's just what everybody wants," he said, "the raise-up."

Then he said: "And whatever raise-up I got, I guess it's you gave it."

I don't know how long had been required for him to develop his plantation system, nor do I know what opposition he had encountered. From him, and from Michele, came echoes of those earlier times, but the most positive one came that fall after my arrival at *Pointe du Loup,* from Mr. Jereboam Boyd, a planter down-river from us.

He rode up unheralded, got down, swapped hand clasp and shoulder slap, accepted Hamish's unfeigned pleasure in the rare exercise of hospitality, and propped back on the gallery, his feet up and the glass in his hand. I did not, of course, sit with them, but stayed where I had been, in the shady hall to catch the least drift of breeze, and went on with my sewing.

"Well, Hamish," I heard the voice say in a tone of vindication, "I got something for you."

I heard a rustle and looked up to see a hand, all I could see of the guest, reach a folded newspaper toward Hamish.

And the voice went on: "Yes, sir, Hamish, a battle going on at Harper's Ferry, and that scoundrel from Kansas—that murdering John Brown—starting an insurrection down in Virginia, and—"

Then Hamish's voice: "But the paper, it doesn't say there is an insurrection. The niggers didn't rise."

And the other voice, with its flicker of anger: "Yeah, and whose fault was that, they didn't. Not John Brown's, and—"

And Hamish, quietly: "And not mine, I reckon you mean to say."

The other: "Don't go off half-cocked and get mad. I been too easy-going, too. You ask anybody and they'll give me the name of being the easiest-going man on his force in the parish."

Hamish: "Yes, I know."

The other: "And I know this. I'm gonna quit being so damned easy-going. You and me both, we better."

Hamish: "Nobody's been whipped in five years on this place. And not in three at *Tarnation*. I haven't lost a run-off in five years. I make a bale an acre, and feed."

The other: "What the hell you aiming at, Hamish? You aiming single-handed to set every nigger in Louisiana free?"

Hamish got up and stumped a step or two. "Listen," he said, "I'm not aiming at anything. There's no telling what's coming twenty years from now. Or one year. Nobody ever knows. And me—all I'm doing is taking up a little slack. That's all a man can do. About anything. Take up a little slack."

"Slack, hell," the other voice said, "you talk about slack, and if there's any more of this John Brown stuff, there'll be war like nobody's business. There'll be killing from here to Canada. Hogs'll quit eating corn for corpses. I tell you, there'll be—"

But I heard no more. I had jabbed my needle into the cloth, and fled. I could not bear to hear more. Whatever the world was like, away off yonder—the slave under the lash, men bleeding from gunshot in Virginia—all that world was beyond *Pointe du Loup*. I could not bear to hear about it. I did not understand my own desperation.

I ran out the back door, into the dazzle, and looked around me.

I spied the infirmary. With a gasp of relief, I fled there. I sent the old nurse away. I told her to go rest. I washed the face of a cotton-hand who lay there with fever. I changed the swaddlings on a baby. I sat and fanned the flies from the listless mother.

After a while, I felt better.

When the rare visits broke our peace, visits from Mr. Boyd and one or two other neighboring planters, I always felt some deep disturbance. I heard their voices on the gallery, or from a farther room, speaking of the world, voices grim or petulant, angry or sardonic, and I fled, to some task, to a book, to the infirmary—as I had fled that first time.

When Charles de Marigny Prieur-Denis made his first visit, it was the same. The creak of saddle leather, a cheery halloo in the sunny autumn afternoon, boots quick on the gallery steps, and I looked up from my seat in the hall, and there he was, unannounced and unexpected, a graceful silhouette against the brightness.

"As quiet as the dew of dawn," he was saying. *"Mais c'est moi qui viens! Et doucement!"*

He laughed, and stepped toward me, and said, "Ah, my little

Manty," and bowed with a hint of gay parody to brush my hand with his lips. He straightened up and inspected me. "And how does the country agree with little Manty?"

I flushed and managed to murmur that I didn't know.

"But I know," he said. "It agrees very well. A little plumper—oh, so little—" and he swept his glance down my person, letting it linger for the flicker of a second on a new fullness of my bosom. Then he demanded: "But old Hamish, where is he?" And he threw his head back and filled the house with a halloo.

"He's not in," I said. "He's off in the gig."

"*Bon*," he said, "we'll wait, you and I." And he drew up a straight chair closer to me, an old hickory-bottom thing, and settled himself. "We'll talk," he announced. "You'll tell me all about life in the country."

I said there was nothing to tell.

"Oh, there must be something," he said. And toying with the edge of the cloth I was sewing, he added: "At least, there is time to think in the country. Tell me, Manty, what do you think about?"

What did I think about? That question set off, like a pulled trigger, an alarm in me.

I rose abruptly. I said I had something to do, I was sorry.

He continued to grasp, between forefinger and thumb, the edge of the cloth I had been sewing, not letting me go, looking up at me, with a kind of careless confidence.

But I was not regarding him. I was looking into myself, I suppose, into my own inward shadows, in that strange way that may come unexpectedly, even in broad daylight, from such slight provocation as his question: *What did I think about?*

Suddenly, I ceased to pull against the cloth. I let it fall into his hands, and said I had to go, I truly had to, and fled.

But bit by bit, Prieur-Denis, who came often, sometimes for protracted visits, ceased to disturb me as a voice of the world. He became part of *Pointe du Loup*, part of the whole, but a part with pleasing variety. He found that I was reading an old battered book on botany I had found in the house, and he brought me a new, fine one from New Orleans, with colored plates, and then he walked with me by the swamp-edge to gather specimens for my girlish botanizing. He brought me romances and the poems of Hugo, which he declaimed grandly, and this was a pleasant change of diet from

*Pointe du Loup's* old histories and manuals of farriery and speeches of Henry Clay and old copies of *De Bow's Review*. He told me the plots of plays he had seen in Paris or New Orleans, and asked what I thought of the characters he described.

One evening—it must have been in the early spring of 1860—Charles sat with Hamish and me. He had been riding that afternoon, putting his horse at an improvised jump on the flat below the mound, over and over, this to a gallery of little pickaninnies.

Now, in the evening, he said: "Manty, can you ride a horse?"

I hesitated on my answer, why I didn't know.

He continued: "I saw you watching this afternoon."

And with that I felt like a child detected in crime, for I had watched a long time from the grove, sure that I was unobserved.

"I could teach you," he said. "Then you could ride some with me."

With that I had a sudden flash of image from my childhood, the lawn at *Starrwood* and me on Pearlie, and I felt a yearning to be again on horseback, to feel free, to feel the surge and power, and the control of that power in the sway of the body and the light movement of fingers. I was about to come out of the recollection and say, yes, yes, I'd love to ride, when I saw Hamish's stiff leg thrust out on the floor, the leg that could never bend again to the stirrup. So I said nothing.

But in a measured voice, Hamish was saying: "Yes, let her ride. It'll be something for Manty to do. To break the dullness."

Charles left the next day, however, and I assumed that all was forgotten. Two months later he was back, back with the saddle, a fine lady's saddle, habit and boots, beautiful boots. He had stolen a slipper from me, he said, for the measure. Now he took the slipper from his pocket, with grave-faced apology for inconvenience.

And Hamish, watching, said: "Yes, let her ride. It'll break the dullness."

I began my lessons with Charles. I let him begin from the beginning, how to mount, how to finger the rein, and gravely bumbled through it all, enjoying in secret the moment when he should suddenly burst out, "But you learn so fast, Manty!"

But that slyness and vanity weren't the reason I couldn't tell him that I knew something of horsemanship. How could I tell him of *Starrwood?*

For *Starrwood* no longer existed, or existed only in a great bitterness, except for moments that trapped me, like the vision of myself on Pearlie, on the lawn. I could not bear to think of my father's voice calling out: "Oh, that's my brave little Manty!" and then think of what he had done, how he had let me be seized for the debts of his pleasure, and sold away. Oh, I hated him so, I could not bear to tell! For to tell would be to admit that he had prized me as nothing, that I was nothing.

But meanwhile I enjoyed my sly, self-flattering joke on Charles and relished his surprise and praise. We rode along the swamp-edge for my specimens. We galloped along the levee-top, for excitement. We explored the woods road, little better than a track, that led to the Boyd place. Sometimes Hamish came along in his gig, and most decorously we rode along beside him, and Charles made a great point, too condescending a point I thought, of talking to him.

And then Hamish might say, "You all get along. I've got some business."

And we would canter off.

On one such occasion, after we had ridden off, I turned to look back, and saw Hamish sitting in his gig at the edge of the wide cotton land, the westering light over him. Charles looked back, too, following my gaze.

"*Pauvre vieux,*" he said, and smiled.

I swung to him with a flash of fury. "Don't say that!" I cried.

He replied nothing. He was so beautiful and arrogant on his horse, smiling, seeming so much the confident master of all the world's delight, so far beyond the accidents of fortune and fleshly frailty. I hated him, for a moment, for that smile.


The life at *Pointe du Loup* moved on, month by month, unruffled. But it is strange how forces can gather under the surface of your own life and you do not even know they are there. But all the summer of 1860, up till the late February of 1861, when the great change came at *Pointe du Loup*, forces were gathering, too, in the far-off world. It was the summer when Mr. Lincoln made his race for the Presidency. More than once, I saw Hamish fling the paper down, and heave from his chair with his blundering force, and stump about, chewing his cheroot to a pulp.

Then, of course, Mr. Lincoln was elected, and the States began to secede from the Union. "Fools, damned fools all," Hamish said, with purpling face, and Mr. Boyd, who had just been made a delegate to the Louisiana Convention, said: "Look here, Hamish, you know I was a Whig for years. You know I was a Union man. You know I wanted to patch things up."

"The nigger thing," Hamish said with blurting ferocity, "I wish no nigger had ever been born!"

"Oh, it's not just niggers," Mr. Boyd said. "The Yankees will rule or ruin. They aim to bleed us till the light shines through like glass. And if it's war—"

"War is killing," Hamish said.

"Well, I'll do my share," Mr. Boyd said.

"I don't know what a man's share is," Hamish said.

"Well, you're not the kind to lay down and take something, Hamish Bond."

"That's not the point," Hamish said.

Whatever the point was, for himself at least, he never said, and now and then the wrangles went on, on the gallery, by the fireside. And Louisiana voted out of the Union and twenty cannon fired a salute when the State flag ran up, and the Confederacy was formed, and Jefferson Davis was President, and Adelina Patti sang in New Orleans, and the Christy Minstrel Show was there, and races at the Jockey Club at Metairie, and the Mystic Krewe of Comus paraded for Mardi Gras, and to me, who had never seen such things, it was words printed in a newspaper, words, and the flash of distress in my bosom, the fear and guilt.

I felt afraid of anything that might break the hypnotic and protective peace of *Pointe du Loup*. I felt guilty because I put my fear ahead of any prospect of freedom for all those black men in that land that stretched away in all directions beyond *Pointe du Loup,* places where this easy rule of kindness like a disease did not prevail.

But I could not admit to either the fear or the guilt. I could only suffer moments of a nameless misery, a tightening at the temples, a shadow on the soul.

Charles talked of raising a company of cavalry, and laughed, and touched his mustache and whirled an imaginary sabre, while his eyes glittered.

Then he went away, to the Carnival, with whatever picture of himself was in his head. He came back in two weeks.

It was the dead of night. I woke to the sound of dogs barking. Hamish was sitting up in bed, listening. Then I saw the topmost leaves of the live oak beyond the window picked out in a flicker of light.

"Flares," Hamish said, and got out of bed, and fumbled for his clothes. Before I could dress, he was gone.

By the time I got outdoors, the locus of excitement was down at the stables, the voices and flares. I ran down there.

There were near a score of figures there, clumped together in the uncertain light, a couple of men holding flares, a little apart, and Hamish and Charles to one side.

I stopped just outside the ring of light.

The figures in the center were Negroes, eyes bulging white and rolling in the light of the flares, big awkward fellows, half crouching, near naked, breech-clout or ragged trousers, here and there some sacking tied about shoulders, elsewhere black, slick shoulders glistening under the flares, and on the left ankle of each—I thought it was that ankle—was an iron ring, and from ring to ring ran a chain. Some of them still stupidly held a lap of chain in the hand, as they must have had to do when marching. They held it the way a lady handles her train.

Then the words of Hamish impinged upon me: "—and I don't believe your boat was leaking that bad. I think you would use me for a convenience. And I won't be made a convenience for your damned nigger-running. Do you understand?"

Charles, with the prinking gesture of a Papish priest at Mass, when he sprinkles, was smiling, saying, "Asperges me, Domine, hyssopo —oh, yes, you are sprinkled with hyssop now, but look here—" and he stopped smiling "—you don't have to be afraid now, it's all different now. There is no Yankee law now, and our law'll be changed."

"That's not the point," Hamish broke in. "Law or no law, now or later, I will not run a barracoon for your convenience."

Suddenly, Rau-Ru rose up from beyond the clump of Negroes, where he must have been crouching, and made some gesture to his master. Hamish stopped in the middle of his sentence, and went to him and looked down. Then he turned abruptly to Charles. "You damned near got a dead nigger here," he said, sourly.

Charles shrugged. "There's only one way for some to learn," he said.

Hamish said: "I tell you what I'll do. I'll buy the lot off you. Seven hundred a head, as they run."

"Seven hundred," Charles said, and smiled ironically.

"That's all they're worth," Hamish said. "Can't talk English, got home-fever, not broke yet."

"Oh, yes," Charles said, "your fancy nigger, yes, he can talk to 'em, he can break them. Yes, you'd be making a good thing."

"Good thing be damned," Hamish said. "I advise you to take my offer. And get on your way tomorrow."

He leaned down to the sick or hurt fellow, whom I couldn't see, as though the matter were concluded. Rau-Ru leaned and gabbled something. Then Hamish said: "File him out and put him in the infirmary."

I heard the click of metal on metal. Hamish looked up and beckoned one of the torches nearer. It was then he saw me.

From his face, over there in the torchlight, I thought for a moment that whatever rage had been suppressed in the dialogue with Charles would now burst out at me.

But it did not. He only said, in a grinding voice: "What are you doing here? Get to the house."

So I fled, and got to bed, trembling in something like fear, fear and lostness evoked by that unfamiliar voice.

Later, much later, I heard Charles and Hamish on the steps of the gallery. Hamish's voice rose: "Yes, I did use you. But you can't use me, not for this. Now go away tomorrow, for I don't want to see you."

When Hamish came to bed, I pretended to be asleep.

In the morning I lay abed. I did not want to see Charles.

In the middle-morning, he took his departure, on the horse that he had been leaving at *Pointe du Loup*. A little later, Hamish, very morose, came into the room. He announced that he had to go to *Tarnation*, and wouldn't be back till the following day.

He sat on the bed's edge and held my hand, wordlessly. Then he rose, leaned over and kissed me, still wordless.

I did not dress till noon. Michele came up and ate a silent meal with me. She would stay in the house with me during Hamish's absence, as usual. After our gumbo and milk, she announced that she would go to the infirmary, but she made no reference to the new arrivals at *Pointe du Loup*.

It was mid-afternoon, when, in my listlessness, I heard steps on the gallery, and looked up. It was Charles. He said he had come back to see Hamish. Was Hamish in?

No, I said, but did not elaborate.

He said that he had had a misunderstanding with Hamish and would wait.

I told him that Hamish had gone to *Tarnation,* and he said that he might ride up there later.

Meanwhile, he drew a chair up. It was the same old hickory-bottom he had sat in the afternoon of his first visit sixteen months earlier. In fact, the whole episode began to assume the quality of a recollection, a re-enactment, a muffled recollection with strange distortions, a recollection that somehow fulfilled the event recollected.

He sat there regarding me, saying nothing. Then he went to the cabinet at the end of the hall and poured himself a tumbler of brandy. He drank some, and refilled the glass. He came back to his seat, drank some more, and then asked if I would go riding with him.

I refused.

He began to toy with the edge of the cloth I was sewing, as on the afternoon so long before. He insisted that I go riding. Upon my curt refusal, he said, in French, yes, I was right, it might be better here.

When I looked at him in question, he said, again in French, that what would come would have to come, and it had been too long already. At that he seized my hand, and began to caress it. I attempted to withdraw it, but his clasp tightened like steel—he was very strong—and he twisted my wrist, just a little.

"Listen," he said, almost whispering. He whispered very slowly and distinctly, leaning at me, saying that he knew, and I knew, what would come, and the time had come.

He rose, suddenly, and leaned over me. *Maintenant!* he whispered.

I jerked my hand from him, and rose.

He again seized me, by the wrist this time, and said that Hamish Bond was nearly an old man, that I had never known what it was like, really like, and didn't I want to know?

I was struggling with him, and his whisper went on, saying I had never known, never really known. Then suddenly he said, quite coldly, in his usual voice: "Unless, of course, you have been behind the old one's back. Have you gone to that fancy nigger of his?"

At that I uttered a little gasp of rage, and jerked from him with all my might. He forestalled me, pressed me back against his chest, and put a hand over my mouth. He held me that way very firmly, then said in the same distinct near-whisper: "Now, now, in just a second, I'll take my hand off your mouth. And you won't scream. No, you won't scream at all, little Manty. Because you don't really want to scream. No, that isn't what you want."

He was still for a moment, and I could feel his heart beating against my left shoulder, and I couldn't breathe.

Then he said: "Now," in English, in quite a normal tone, and removed his hand from my mouth.

I swear, I don't know whether I screamed. It is very strange, but I simply don't know.

For the result, it did not matter. When Rau-Ru came in, summoned by my scream, or coming in by accident, I was struggling violently—or immediately began to struggle—do I know which?—and I cried out, "Rau-Ru! Rau-Ru!" most desperately.

Rau-Ru seized Charles by the shoulder and jerked him back. He jerked him so hard that he whirled sidewise, lost his footing, fell, and grazed his temple against the sharp back of the hickory-bottom chair. He lay on the floor, stunned for an instant, with a little blood on his temple.

He got to his feet, braced himself on the chair, and said: "You struck me. You struck a white man. You know the law. You know what that means."

Rau-Ru looked wildly at me.

"Don't look at her," Charles said. "She may come to you behind the barn, but she can't help you now. Not against a white man. For she"—and he looked at me and drew his lips back—"she can't testify —she's a nigger, too."

All that time Rau-Ru was looking at Charles, wide-eyed and blank. There simply wasn't a thing on his face. Then he struck him.

I suppose Charles had taken that wide-eyed blankness for terror, and perhaps it was. I suppose that any man—even Rau-Ru—has a right to terror when he feels the world fade beneath his feet. Anyway, Charles must have read it as abject terror, and therefore was unprepared for defense.

The blow was to the face. The victim didn't fall backward. He seemed to hang in the air a moment, with a sad, reproachful look at Rau-Ru, and then slumped forward and rolled over.

Rau-Ru stood there and looked down at the body on the floor. Then he looked at his hand, as at a very peculiar instrument the purpose and function of which he did not wholly comprehend.

Meanwhile, I had screamed. I know that I screamed this time. Not once, but twice, as loud as I could.

We were still standing there, Rau-Ru and I, when Michele came running in.

She did not utter a word. She looked at me, at Rau-Ru, at Rau-Ru's guilty hand, which was hanging out from his body, at the body on the floor. Then she stooped and lifted the head of the fallen man. The neck seemed limp when she lifted the head. Her gaze, and the gaze of Rau-Ru, met.

I burst out: "Hamish—he'll come—it'll be all right—"

I think that Michele was shaking her head, ever so slightly, at Rau-Ru.

"I'll send for Hamish," I babbled, "and he'll—he'll—"

But Rau-Ru had turned, had moved out of the hall, to the gallery, with his rapid, silent, purposive stride.

I ran out to the gallery. I called after him: "But it'll be all right—it'll be all right!"

He disappeared behind the oaks, toward the quarters. But I knew he would not stop there.

Charles was not dead, though he remained unconscious for a full hour after we had got him to bed and applied compresses to his head. His pulse was extraordinarily feeble, feeble enough, I suppose, to have deceived Michele at her first investigation. There was a great deal of blood, too, from his nose, which was broken.

Everything might still have been well. Hamish might have come, and browbeaten or blackmailed Charles into dropping the notion of law, and have got word to Rau-Ru. But it is strange how things develop according to an inner logic, though the details of that logic seem to depend on mere accident and coincidence.

I had sent off a rider to *Tarnation* to summon Hamish, but long before he could have arrived, while I huddled over the bed where Charles lay, I heard steps on the gallery. It was Mr. Boyd.

It was plain bad luck that Mr. Boyd should come now, but even as I recognized his figure I recognized that his coming conformed to the inner logic of the situation. He had been mysteriously summoned, as it were, by the necessity of things, by a secret voice, by a dancing wisp that led him through the bud and bird-song of the spring afternoon.

I saw him there, and even as he saw me and called out, I dashed into the room, to Michele.

"It's Mr. Boyd," I managed, in my terror.

"All right," Michele said, and hurried around the bed, toward the door.

But Charles was awake now, awake enough to grasp the situation.

I saw his face in a spasm of effort. Then he yelled: "Boyd!"

Like a fool, I had left the door open.

The yell had scarcely been uttered before Michele, outside, had shut the door.

Charles' gaze was on me with a glittering enmity.

I could hear some sort of debate outside the door, then Mr. Boyd's voice raised. Then the door flung open, and Mr. Boyd, red in the face, was inside. He leaned over the bed.

"That fancy nigger—" Charles managed to say, "he tried—tried to kill me—and they—they all—"

He must have been going to inculpate us all, in some way, and certainly Michele's attempt to block entrance to the chamber had already inculpated us. Mr. Boyd did not wait for more.

As the first words came out, I had seen the dawning intensity on his face, a sort of purity of joy. "Ah!" he said, and snapped up from his leaning position over the bed.

He strode to the door, then swung toward Michele. "I'll send the doctor. You let him die now and it'll be your neck."

Then he was charging down the hall, and was gone.

I had to go and lie down, I felt so awful.

It was late at night before Hamish arrived. Long before that we had heard a hullabaloo below the hummock, shouts and baying of dogs, and seen the distant agitation of flares.

"The Sheriff," Michele said.

The racket and torchlight disappeared toward the forest.

The doctor was there when Hamish arrived. The patient, he said, would be all right. The doctor left and Hamish dispatched some messages in writing, one to Mr. Boyd, one to the Sheriff of the parish. Then he stumped up and down the hall, for hours, sometimes muttering to himself, now and then pausing to take a drink of brandy. He was not, ordinarily, a drinking man.

Now and then I would come out into the hall and huddle on a chair, watching him. When he remembered me, he would come over and pat me on the shoulder, and once he kissed me on top of my head.

I could not stay up long at a time, I felt so bad. I knew I had fever. But I did not tell Hamish how I felt.

We got the news the next day.

They had found Rau-Ru very easily, with the dogs. He had, apparently, made no great effort to put distance between himself and *Pointe du Loup.* He might have taken a horse and gone miles. As it was, he must have waited, after all, for Hamish to arrive.

"Thought he was always so durn smart, that nigger," the deputy said, who brought the news. "But ain't none of 'em smart. Didn't even have no gun, ner knife, ner nuthin, and him just nigh kilt a white man. Caught him lak catchin a rabbit."

But that was not quite the end of the story. At the lock-up in the settlement, Rau-Ru had made trouble, so they flogged him. But he broke his bonds and killed a man. This time they did not catch him. Hamish got the news just as he was getting into the gig to go to the settlement to see Rau-Ru.

The next day Charles was up and moving about his room. We could hear him, but he did not come out.

On the morning of the next day, Hamish asked Michele how Mr. Prieur-Denis was. She said he was about all right. Then Hamish did what he must have been building up to all that day and the day before, all the times he had been stumping back and forth before that closed door, all the times he had made me tell him, over and over, exactly what had happened, word for word, leaning at me with a scary and awful avidity.

When Hamish entered the room I followed as far as the door.

Charles was propped up on the bed, dressed. Hamish said nothing at first, and Charles' eyes, over the bruised and swollen nose, followed him with a flickering wariness. Hamish stood over the foot of the bed.

"How do you feel?" he demanded.

He felt better, Charles replied, and thanked him with ironical politeness.

"Can you stand up?" Hamish asked.

"Yes," Charles said.

"Well," Hamish said, "you're going to need to."

"You needn't think I don't want to leave," Charles said. "Lend me the gig, and I'll leave right now."

"I'm going to kill you first," Hamish said and took a pistol out of his pocket.

I let out a gasp, or cry of protest, and Hamish swung toward me. "Shut up!" he commanded savagely.

Meanwhile, Charles hadn't turned a hair.

"You're a fool," he said to Hamish. "This isn't the Coast. They'll hang you here."

Hamish shook his head. "No," he said, "I got it all worked out. It'll be self-defense. Or"—he hesitated—"it'll be a duel. A sort of duel."

He propped his blackthorn against the foot of the bed, and with the newly freed left hand produced another pistol, a mate.

Charles' eyes narrowed a little, quick on the pistol, then on Hamish's face.

"You feel better, now it's a duel," Hamish said. "You've fought duels. Two. Killed one and crippled the other. You like a duel. You've practiced all your life to be perfect. Fast and sure." He paused and seemed to be brooding over something. Then: "Me, I'm not fast. But I'll be very sure."

Charles seemed about to say something.

But Hamish leaned forward a little, and said: "Yeah, you might clip me. Yeah, and that would look better when the Sheriff comes. Yes, Charles, you might hit me, but I'll be propped against the wall, and I'll take my time. Just one place you could hit me, Charles, to do you any good. Right between the eyes, Charles, but you won't risk that shot. You'll lose your nerve, the target's too little. And then you'll try to tag my heart, and you'll miss it, and I'll be standing. Long enough, anyway. You've known me a long time, Charles, and you know that when I reckon on doing a thing I do it, and you know I'll be standing there long enough. And you'll be sweating."

Suddenly, Hamish leaned forward a little more, and his voice sank. "How does it feel, Charles," he whispered solicitously, "to be sweating right now?"

Then he resumed, in his tone of patient explanation: "You see, Charles, I'm telling you all about it so careful so you'll start sweating now. So you'll start twitching now. Yes, let me tell you how it'll be after I kill you, how clean I got it all worked out. I got me a witness, even."

Charles' gaze flicked to me.

"No," Hamish said, "not little Manty. I know what you said to her about why she couldn't be legal witness. I reckon that's one of the reasons I'm killing you, Charles. For saying that. But, no, I got me another witness, white. It's my overseer's grown son. Yes, I got him downstairs in the storeroom checking my supply book, right this minute, and he's going to hear two shots, and run up here, and he'll see me against the wall, and maybe I'll be clipped a little, or the slug in the wall by me, but you—you'll be on the floor, Charles, and you'll be holding a pistol with smoke still in it, and your gut'll be shot out. For that's where I'll give it to you, Charles, a nice big target, right in the bowels. I need a fair target, for I'm not good like you."

"Give me that pistol," Charles demanded, in a hoarse voice.

Hamish shook his head, sadly. "Not yet," he said. "I got to let you get the sweats and twitches a little worse. That's why I'm explaining so careful. Besides, Charles, I've known you a long time, and a man don't kill an old friend fast. It's taken me fifteen years and I reckon I can wait a minute longer. To let the sweat and twitches build up."

"Give me that pistol," Charles said.

"I'll tell you why they're building up," Hamish said. "Because the deepest thing in you is a coward, Charles. Oh, you wouldn't be a coward in a lot of ways. Not under the Chalmette Oaks at New Orleans and the seconds watching and the referee counting and all that. Oh, that's grand, and is a picture in your head, and how grand you are. But not now, piled on the bed in a dirty bedroom and your nose is broke and a nigger broke it and that's not pretty, and the sweats are building up."

"Give me that pistol," Charles said, loud, leaned forward on the bed, and let one foot to the floor, and reached out his hand.

"Your hand," Hamish said, "look at it. It's twitching just a little bit."

Charles looked at his hand.

"Yes," Hamish said, with a detached, professional judgment, "just a little. But enough. So now I reckon we'll start."

Abruptly, he pointed the pistol in the right hand at the middle of Charles' body. "Stand up," he commanded.

Charles got off the bed.

"Listen," Hamish said, "so you won't make any mistakes. I'm going to toss the other pistol on the bed. It's not on cock. You pick it up and just take your shot any time you can. I'm going to point at your gut all the time. And now I'll just get back and prop against the wall, and count three. Then I'll toss the pistol."

He made the first count.

"Suppose I refuse to shoot?" Charles said.

Hamish studied him. "But you won't refuse," he said, finally. "You aren't that kind of a coward. You're another kind, the kind that'll be afraid not to shoot. Just like you're afraid now to yell for Tom Simpkins to come upstairs. You're afraid of the look on his face when you had to tell him why you yelled. You see, Charles, you aren't a simple coward. You got the coward all mixed up with a lot of other things. That's why being a coward hurts you so much. That's why you been sick of yourself, way down in your gut, all your life. That's why you've felt trapped, just plain trapped, all your life. And now I'm going to count, Charles."

He made the second count.

But that was all. I simply couldn't stand it. I didn't even know what I couldn't stand. I just cried out, and ran across, and grabbed both of Hamish's hands, pistols and all, and pressed them against me—the sides, not the muzzles, I mean—so he couldn't jerk them free.

I clutched them so hard I felt the cocked hammer of the weapon in his right hand pressed against the underside of my right breast, just under the nipple, and I thought: *If he should happen to pull the trigger, it would pinch me, it would pinch me horribly.*

But I kept hanging on to the pistols.

"Turn loose!" Hamish commanded.

His face was flushed dark, he was so angry, but I wouldn't turn loose.

"So you want to save that—" Hamish stopped and groped for the word of identification. "That man," he finished lamely.

I looked across at Charles, standing there by the bed, sweat on his brow, nose broken and swollen. "No," I burst out, "no—it's not for him—I hate him!"

I began to sob.

"Listen," Hamish said, "it's up to him. I'll just let him walk out the door and get in the gig and never come back. If he's coward enough not to ask for that pistol."

He looked across at Charles for a long minute.

"And I reckon he is," he said.

Then Hamish asked me to summon Tom Simpkins from downstairs, and Tom Simpkins, a big, rawboned, red-faced, and red-headed fellow of twenty-two or -three, with a shaggy cowlick, and a sly, hard, sidewise, animal glance, came in, and Hamish asked him politely if he could have the gig made ready and kindly drive Mr. Prieur-Denis over to the Boyd place. Mr. Prieur-Denis, Hamish explained, thought his health might improve faster away from *Pointe du Loup*.

Tom Simpkins looked at Charles with his sidewise look, and did not grin, and said, yes, sir, he would. Charles was still sweating.

After the departure, Hamish shut himself up in the room he used for his office. I lay down again, for a while. I still felt awful.

We managed to eat some supper, a meal scorched and ruined, but it didn't matter.

Later we sat on the gallery, silent for a long time, while a pale moonlight grew over the fields beyond the blackness of the grove. Leaning against his shoulder, I shivered a little.

"Cold?" he asked, and took my hands.

"No," I said, "I just shivered."

He was silent for a time, then said, heavily: "I reckon I did you a wrong, Manty."

I didn't say anything, but I remember that, even as I puzzled over what he meant and felt safe with my hands palm to palm inside his big hands, I knew deep inside me, maybe denied and separate from me, some hard, secret sense of advantage suddenly growing.

Ah, why do people have to be like that? Why is there that cold-eyed *not-you*—oh, you hope it isn't the true *you*—always spying from the darkest, most secret corner of your heart? But maybe it is the *you*, after all, and that thought is terrible.

Or maybe this is true only of me. Maybe nobody else is like this, nobody but me.

Would there be some way to be different before I die?

But now that I recall that moment, I see that it is like another moment, years earlier, the time in Cincinnati, when my father, after he had failed to understand my attempt to save his soul and had, to boot, embarrassed me by the quarrel with the next table, came to my room in the hotel, and sat by my bed, and apologized to me. With his sad apology, I had felt that same hard, secret sense of advantage gained.

But now I sat by Hamish on the gallery and felt it, and said nothing.

Finally, Hamish spoke again. "Yes, I reckon I did you wrong." He waited, shifted his weight. "You see," he said, "I reckon I knew all the time, way back, it would come out like it came. And I just let it come."

He fell silent, then resumed. "No, I sort of brought it on."

"Brought on what?" I asked, but I suppose I knew already, and simply wanted him to say it, and confirm my sweet advantage of having been little and precious and wronged.

With my question he heaved up from the seat, and stood there against the moonlight and stared down at me, his eyes glittering in the shadow, staring down at me with what I suddenly felt to be an accusation. And his words were like an accusation, a clairvoyant accusation. "Why do you ask me?" he said. "You know what I'm talking about. You know that I knew what he would do, sooner or later, and I let it come."

Then he said: "No, not just let it. I wanted it to come."

At that, at the thought that he had wanted the thing to happen to me, I felt some sort of excitement, a catch in the breath.

"Listen," he said, "a man young, growing up, he keeps trying his strength, trying it more and being proud of it. Then, all of a sudden—" He stopped, and I heard him take a breath.

Then he went on: "—then he's old. And he tries his weakness. He's just sort of got to test it, and see."

This time, he waited a long time, standing there against the moonlight. "I guess I just had to know what you'd do," he said.

Then: "And whatever you did, then I could kill him. No, I didn't plan it. I just sort of felt it in my bones." He waited, then added: "Because he was still young, I reckon. He was young, and I just wanted to get him dead to rights."

Then: "And I got him dead to rights." He paused grimly. "I got him," he said, "and then I didn't do anything. You asked me not to, and I didn't. But do you know why?"

I said nothing.

"Well, it wasn't because you asked me. No, it was just I could make him stand there and show you how he was empty, deep inside himself. I'd make the sweat come down his slick face, and you'd see his insides."

Then: "Do you hate me, Manty?"

I didn't know what I felt. I guess I was afraid. I had known Hamish Bond for a long time, and I guess he had been nothing but a bulk, a voice, a protecting warmth in the darkness, a pressure on my body. He had not been real, just a dream I was having, a dream I had to have and cling to.

And now, all at once, something was beginning to come real. Something had been happening in that bulk, something I had never guessed, an uncoiling of possibilities in the inside dark of that bulk, and that was frightening. Oh, it's always frightening when somebody comes real to you.

But this was frightening in a special way. If Hamish Bond had been nothing but a dream I was having, this was like finding out, of a sudden, that I myself was nothing but a dream which he had been having, and had to have for his own need. So I was nothing, and alone in the middle of nothing. It was the feeling of that old nightmare of mine, of being in the middle of a desert and the horizon fleeing away in all directions.

"Well," he said, "I'll tell you the worst. In a crazy way, I wanted you to do what you didn't do."

Then: "No, I didn't want you to do it. It's just there was something that wanted that, too. You see," he continued, more quietly, "it was like how you want to know the worst that can happen, then you feel free."

I could hear his breath.

"Oh, Manty," he burst out, his voice like a groan, like that first time he had grasped me and called my name. "Oh, Manty," he said now, crying out to me, "ain't it awful a man can be this way?"

Without warning, my heart overflowed with tenderness, and I jumped up, seized Hamish's hands, and began to kiss them.

That tenderness, that pity or whatever it was, had caught me unawares. It was like the time I had seen poor Seth Parton standing in the Turpin parlor, in Oberlin, with the snow melting on his hair.

After I had drawn Hamish to sit again beside me, he said something else.

"Free," he said, and stopped on the word, a time.

He began over again. "You know," he said, "about everything I ever set out to do, I've done. I got everything I ever set out to get. And you know, it was always just like something getting tighter and tighter around me."

And then: "I guess if a man finds his strength won't do him any good, he sort of thinks his weakness maybe will."

There is one more thing about the cowardice of Charles de Marigny Prieur-Denis.

That afternoon he had stood there and sweated and been a coward. But the war came, and, as he had said, he raised a command of cavalry, and led it into battle. He was twice wounded, the second time seriously. But he returned to his command. He was killed in 1865, on the way from Richmond.

He was killed in what I think they call a holding action. It was to help cover the retreat of General Lee's army. A wagon train had broken down and some infantry stayed to defend it till it got into motion again, some infantry and Charles' command. The Yankees came up, and began to align for the attack. Charles charged them to prevent this, and was killed. I never learned whether it did any good or not.

I do not know what this proves about Charles being a coward. Maybe Hamish Bond was right, and Charles was a coward because he couldn't be brave those times when he didn't have the right picture of himself in his head. Maybe a cavalry charge was the right kind of picture, and he could act brave then. But maybe by 1865 too much had happened for him to have any more pictures of any kind in his head, and he was just left with the things you see out there in the world separate from yourself.

Maybe that day he just looked over his shoulder, and saw the stalled wagons up the road, the skinny, hairy-faced, ragged men deploying in the old sage grass away from the road, with patches of new spring green showing between the old sage, and then he looked across the field and saw the Yankees lining up, and there was no picture at all in his head, and he just touched his left spur to the mount's flank, and did what he did.

Whatever the case, I was glad when I heard about this. Whatever Charles was, I could not bear to leave him standing in that dingy bedroom at *Pointe du Loup,* the beautiful nose broken and ruined, with the sweat coming down his face, forever.

It was the small things that began to go wrong at first. They were so small that you scarcely noticed them, like the scorched meal that night after Charles was sent away—small things like the broken dish, the tracked-in mud in the hall left on the floor, the tardiness when the horn blew for tumble-up time, the horses half-curried, the jollification fading away early on Saturday night, the sudden silence after the singing and juba.

Bigger things began to go wrong. A child was still-born out of a perfectly healthy wench and she didn't even seem to care. Hamish was sure one of his horses was being run at night, off to God knew where and for what. The new hands bought from Charles didn't seem to learn anything, despite all Hamish could do. One of them died. He just lay on his back and kept looking up at the rafters of the infirmary and died. All the days he was dying, people kept sneaking up to the infirmary to look at him. They'd just stare at him in a peculiar way by the hour, if you'd let them. Hamish forbade any to come look at him, except the nurses. But they came anyway, to stare. They'd come at night even, tired after a hard day's work, like it was something they just had to do.

Then he died. There didn't seem to be any particular reason for his dying. "Home fever," Hamish said glumly.

Then there was the awful fight in the quarters, with some bloodletting. Finger-pointing and the raise-up didn't do much good. So Hamish had a whipping. He made the whole lot come together on Saturday night and watch it, and he stood by. Lying on the bed, in the house, I could hear the yells. I counted them. There were twenty yells.

Hamish came back to the house and drank some brandy. When we went to bed I took his hand and snuggled against him, because I felt so lonesome, but he almost shoved me away. He was lying on his back, staring up at the ceiling.

In early April there was the shot from the swamp woods. Hamish was riding in the gig, and the bullet made a hole in the seat-back, right beside him. He said he didn't have any idea who it would be.

But I was sure it was Rau-Ru, come back.

"No," he said, and shook his head, "a smart one like him, he's long-gone North."

That night when I tried to go to sleep I kept seeing the picture, Rau-Ru's face surrounded by new green leaves, the face glinting like black enamel in the sun-dapple that fell through the leaves, the face peering out of the forest leaves, across the cotton fields, where a black-coated figure slowly approaches, over the bright distance, in a gig.

Just after word of Fort Sumter, we left *Pointe du Loup.* I don't know whether it was because of Sumter, or because Hamish just gave up.

He got in a regular overseer, a man very quiet in the face, with a gold toothpick always hanging out of the corner of his mouth, and a good cotton-making record.

Hamish told the overseer to go easy on the whip, the people weren't accustomed to it, and we left for New Orleans by steamboat. It was April then.

One Sunday morning, after our return to New Orleans, I was standing by the grill to the patio, Hamish beside me. Down that bright morning vacancy a young woman, accompanied by a child, was approaching, slowly, at the pace of the very little boy.

The little boy, I observed on a nearer view, was wearing a gray suit, very trimly contrived, with little gold epaulettes, and a little gray hat with a red feather jauntily on the left side, and strapped manfully at his waist was a shiny little tin sword. Soberly, he came along, and the sword banged against his uncertain little knee, much to the impairment of his martial bearing.

"Come along, darling," his mother said. "Hurry up, or we'll be late to Mass."

He hurried the best he could, with the sword.

I watched them go on down the street. Far down the street, he stumbled. His mother leaned, picked him and righted him and brushed his knees and patted his jacket into place and adjusted the sword.

"They might give him a commission," Hamish said, sourly. "He knows as much about it as some who've got 'em."

At that my heart clouded over, quite literally as though a sad cloud had drawn across the bright day.

But in those early days the city was gay. There was money to spend and people spent it. The bales of cotton were stacked up like gigantic masonry. The sugar bulged in the barrels. The long columns of profit marched with serried precision down the page of the factor's ledger. Ships cast off at the wharf, yawed to the first suck of the current, and the new flag broke from the forepeak. Wine winked in the glass. Far away, there was shouting and music, the music men march to, and in some measured lull the fife was high and shrewd, stitching and glinting like a needle busy in sunshine. Men marched along with glittering steel, and the band played "Listen to the mockingbird."

There is no way for the heart not to respond, in some way, to the joy of risk and promise.

What was promised?

I suppose that some hard-headed fellow, here and there, calculated in terms of acres and bales and niggers and gold-pieces and the Liverpool market, or even ambition, but for most the charm of the promise must have been that it was merely promise, promise redundantly promising itself, an eternity of promise, like youth, promise intransitive. And to that glittering sign of emptiness the deepest need of each heart responded for its freedom, and the most secret dream devotedly flowed into that vacuum for fulfillment.

Down the Canal Street the new regiments paraded, and passed on to their destiny, and one day it was the volunteer regiment of the *gens de couleur libres,* glittering past to the fife-sound, and from the *banquette* the eyes stared out of black faces of *gens de couleur* not *libres.* They yelled, too, and waved the old caps and the hats of campeachy.

But the spring of 1861 was the time of the fires. The fires would break out at midnight, or in broad daylight, and no one could be certain of their origin. Some, however, leaned and whispered: *the slaves.*

Perhaps it was. And in my mind I see a slave who stands on the *banquette,* with full heart, and yells, and in the dead of that night rises from his pallet and in a kind of troubled somnambulistic, marveling incredulity observes his own fingers apply the little flame to the heap of fat-pine shavings thrust against the house-timber. Later, he is the one who dashes up the blazing stairs, seizes the child from the cradle, and saves it.

I think I could understand all this. And why shouldn't that black fellow be as confused and uncertain inside his heart as we are?

Do I say *we*? I should say *you*. For I myself, I almost forgot, am one of the *gens de couleur* and was once not *libre*.

In the summer the fires stopped. Perhaps they had been caused by bad flues, after all.

I had forgotten to say that the services of the volunteer regiment of the *gens de couleur libres* were not, in the end, accepted. It remained for Yankees to use them.

Meanwhile, a little gang of outlaws and runaway slaves emerged from the swamps to harry the outskirts of the city. There had always, even in peacetime, been such little gangs, hiding in the cypress recesses, coming out at night to steal, to get supplies, to carouse at those illegal groggeries, *cabarets* as they called them, on the edge of civilization.

This gang was, however, more daring. One night at Camp Lewis they had even knifed a sentry and then poured a volley into the silent tents. Rumor had it that the leader was the fancy nigger of Old Bond.

# V I I

BY THE END OF THE SUMMER OF 1861—THE FIRST SUMMER OF THE
War—the quality of life had changed. There had been victories, the
great victories in Virginia. But the banks no longer paid in specie.
Confederate paper and shinplasters were circulated. Prices rose.
There was distress among the families of poor men off fighting.
Much money was raised for them, and I know that Hamish gave a
lot of money. More and more rarely, a ship quietly cast off and
slipped downstream to try the blockade at the Passes. The levees
were quiet now. The spars of the ships were bare like winter, like a
stripped geometrical forest. The steam towboats, snug under tar-
paulins, lay side by side under the lee of Slaughterhouse Point.

But the yards were busy. Over at Algiers, they turned a little
steamer into Admiral Semmes' first terrible command, the privateer
*Sumter.* They plated over tugs and little steamboats with railroad
rails and cotton bales to make a river flotilla to defend the city.

Meanwhile, Hamish was on some sort of committee of defense.

It was March now. Most of the troops had been called away
now, off to Tennessee, to Beauregard, and many, so many, would die
at Shiloh. Then Farragut came to the Gulf, assembling his fleet off
Ship Island, getting ready for the assault on New Orleans—Farragut,
who had once been a poor boy in New Orleans, but was now Flag

Officer Farragut coming home. At the yards on the river, the hammers went night and day, finishing the ironclads, the *Louisiana* and the *Mississippi*.

"That'll stop 'em," people said, "like a knife through butter."

But Hamish: "They'll never be ready. Farragut comes soon."

There were the forts down-river, Fort Jackson and Fort St. Philip.

"They'll never run the forts," people said. "They'll never break the boom."

But Hamish: "They'll blow the boom. What's the boom but a few lengths of chain and a few schooner hulks? And they'll run the forts. And then—" He flung out his arm in an irritable gesture of dismissal. "Then nothing but junk to stop 'em. Those made-over, floating cheese-boxes—junk."

Once Hamish took me with him to look at Fort Jackson, the big one on the right bank of the river. I sat in the barouche and saw the hulk of the old brickwork heaving, gigantic and saurian, out of the soggy savannah, a scurf of hanging grass and bushes on the rotting brick, two human forms, very small against the saffron sky of evening, on top of the parapet. The muddy river slid past. Downstream a woods grew along the bank.

It seemed a sad place for men to die.

I heard a bugle blow way off in the fort. The sound faded away, and I heard again the steady crepitation and hum of insects in all the secret marshland.

On April 18, the firing began against the forts.

I sat in the patio that morning, with Michele and Dollie, picking lint and rolling bandages. I became aware of a faint booming sound, a throbbing rather than a sound. "Thunder," I said, and lifted my head to listen.

Dollie looked at me sidewise. Then with a sly, dawning gratification, she said, "Naw, sojers. Sojers, they comen."

Michele nodded.

Dollie let the bandage fall to her lap, and suddenly sat upright on the stone bench, with her knees pressed together. "Boom," she said softly, "boom!" She began to twitch her shoulders, ever so slightly. "Boom, boom, boom," she said, and shut her eyes.

Michele regarded her. "Make your bandage," she ordered quietly.

Dollie opened her eyes, and picked up the bandage. As she

leaned over it, she said: "Ain't nobody I knows gitten shot." Then she giggled.

"It will be blood," Michele said, "anyway."

Day after day the bombardment continued. Farragut, they said, had brought up a great fleet of mortar schooners and anchored them behind the woods below Fort Jackson, and they fired day and night. Sometimes you couldn't hear at all. Then again the wind changed, and you caught the throb and mutter in the air, clearest at night.

"Listen," I said to Hamish, one night in the study, "you can hear it now."

He lifted his head to listen, then said: "It won't be long now. General Lovell's getting ready to evacuate. But folks believe in forts." Then he repeated the word *forts*, as though it were filthy and he spat it out.

He rose from his chair, and on his stick, stood in the posture of listening. Then he stared heavily down at me. "You want them to win," he said.

I was so stunned I couldn't say a word.

"Don't you?" he demanded.

I felt trapped, shamefully discovered by his question.

"Don't you?" he demanded again, and leaned at me with an avidity on his face.

When I still could not answer him, he said: "I wouldn't blame you. Not after all that's happened to you. Getting sold off. Everything." He paused and leaned lower. "Everything," he said, "including me."

He twitched his shoulders. Then he said, broodingly: "I ought to have sent you North."

At that, the power of speech returned to me with a rush, with an upsurge of anguish. "Oh, why didn't you take me North?" I cried. "Just take me away, anywhere, and be with me?"

He looked down at me, with blank astonishment.

"Why didn't you?" I cried. "If you loved me."

Never before, even in the privacy of my own mind, had I used the word *love* to describe the relation between me and Hamish Bond. He had used the word, but only occasionally, with a kind of shy obliqueness, lost and uncertain, smuggled in among the terms and gestures of endearment.

Now hearing the word on my own lips, I could not believe it. In the first flash of my surprise there was a release, a gasp of my breath as though I had risen from under water. And then, immediately, a sense of guilt.

But for what? *For what?* I almost felt like crying out defensively.

In that silence I could hear the bombardment again. I stared at the unmoving candle flames in the candelabra, and listened.

Then I realized that Hamish was listening now, too.

"You want them to win, don't you?" he demanded.

And when I didn't answer, then again, with suppressed fury: "Don't you? Don't you?"

"Oh, what are you trying to do to me?" I cried in my trouble, and tears were in my eyes.

He swung his head away from me, lifting it to attend to the distant mutter. "What am I trying to do to myself?" he said then.

That night in Hamish's bed, I lay beside his sleeping bulk and I wept. I had begun to try to think what the true answer was to the question, did I want the attackers to win? The thought of their coming was a terrible fear for me, deeper than I could define for myself.

And as I was aware of that fear, I had, at the same time, some notion, some crazy notion, images really, that my fear put a great field of crouching black people under the lash. The lash snapped in the darkening sky and the heads of all those crouching forms bowed and swayed like grain. One head lifted, and I saw that it was the anguished, accusing face of Old Shaddy. He was looking straight at me.

It was then I began to weep. I wept because I felt so alone, and trapped.

On the night of April 23, Farragut ran the forts, destroyed the made-over cheese-boxes that vaingloriously engaged him on the river, and drove on up to Quarantine, where he lay all the next day to lick his wounds and wait for troops to come upriver.

General Lovell, the commander at New Orleans, had seen with his own eyes the achievement of his enemy, and on a little steamer had barely escaped back to the city.

The news came to our house in the morning with a great clanging of the bell at the gate, then a shout from the lower hall. Hamish went down in a dressing gown, and promptly returned to begin to dress.

When he was down in the hall, I leaned over the bannisters and watched him put a pistol into his pocket, and stump out with the member of the defense committee who had called for him.

I wondered what he would do with the pistol. Would there be a last battle? Men with pistols on the levee, popping away as the big black ships bore round Slaughterhouse Point?

I could now hear the spatter of shouts far off, then a growling, grinding, throaty roar that gathered and grew toward the levee. A little later, I saw the first column of black smoke rise, and as it spread over the spring sky beyond the spire of the cathedral, that distant communal roar rose to a pitch of rage and anguish, but, also, to some tone of a deep and terrible gratification. I noticed how suddenly bright and sharp the gold cross of the spire was against the billowing, unnatural blackness of the smoke.

Then other columns of smoke rose, and more, in the aggregating pall of blackness. The lower verge of blackness, tumescent and swirling, was laced and licked with finicking flame. When I looked up, I saw the sun as a small emberlike orb in the pervasive sootiness of sky.

Dollie came up to my room, then joined me on the balcony, breathless. "Burn ever-thing," she uttered, in her breathless, bulge-eyed rapture, "dey gonna burn ever-thing—dat's de word done come—dey burn ever-thing—lak de Lawd say and de end come!"

"Are they—" and I hesitated, about to say *the enemy*. "Are they here?" I demanded.

"Sojers?" Dollie asked. Then answered her own question: "Naw, no Yankees yit, jes folks—folks and dey burnen!"

She cocked her head toward the distant roar, listening. Then she said wistfully, like a child deprived: "Shore wish me down dar."

Hamish didn't come back until late afternoon. He was disheveled and smut-streaked. The mob, he said, had begun by burning the shipping tied up along the levee, firing the vessels and cutting them loose to drift down.

The mob had gone back to work then, firing cotton. "They'll burn ten million dollars' worth of cotton by night, and figure they've done something. They figure they'll win a war burning cotton." He paused, then repeated: "Cotton."

Then: "That's what they believed in, forts and cotton."

Then: "I reckon folks have to believe in something."

But ships and cotton had only been the beginning. The sense of betrayal and the rage had passed over into a general glory of destruction. Groggeries and groceries had been broken into. Looting had started. But even the looting had been crazy, seizing for the sake of seizing. The craziness mounted. Lovell's troops, that might have kept order, were entraining for the evacuation. The Foreign Guard failed to overawe the mob, and broke before them. The frenzy mounted toward evening. As dark came on, the flames more ferociously climbed the sky. "Farragut don't come soon," Hamish said, "and there won't be anything left to come to."

After dinner one of Hamish's friends on the committee came and was shut in the study with him. I was again on the balcony, watching the flames against the darkness. Dollie again came, to steal a look from the point of vantage.

"Word come dey grabben," she said. "Folks grabben. Grab and hit's yoren. Bust de barr'l and 'lasses in de street. Lay down in 'lasses and roll fer de sweetness. Stretch de mouf and pour rum down till hit come out both years lak a bung bust. Lay down in de alley and love-up and who gonna stop 'em?"

I turned abruptly and went back into my room. I sat on a chair in the dark and tried to think of nothing.

After a little Dollie came in from the balcony. She lighted a candle, set it on the table.

She studied me. "Doan you wish," she said, "doan you wish too you down dar? And de burnen and dancen?"

So this, too, was part of what the music and cheers, a year ago, had promised. Perhaps this was the deepest and dearest promise, the most secret—the brute, communal roar, the dancing, the flames leaping in darkness. Perhaps this was the fulfillment, the freedom, that all the lifting hearts had really yearned to.

Well, they had it now. In a crazy way, I suppose, I had it, too.

Later on, Hamish came up to the room. He had a carbine, which he propped just by the balcony window. He laid a couple of pistols on the table. He said that he didn't anticipate any trouble, but just in case anybody tried to break into the courtyard, he could command the gate from here. He would sleep up here, he said.

He went back down, and I could hear him at the gate, with Jimmee, putting on additional chains. When he came back up, he carried a rifle. This, too, he propped by the window.

We made ready for bed. We did not speak during the process. Hamish Bond had not lain down with me on this bed since the night of the terrible storm, so long ago. Now, here, he would again lie down by me. The confused urgency of feeling of that night long back stirred again in me, under the present calm of.my long habituation. It was as though something had come full circle, and all that had existed between the first and the now-about-to-be last would whirl away, like a puff of smoke.

We lay on the bed, the candle out now, and watched the light flicker on our chamber ceiling.

"Go to sleep," Hamish said, almost fretfully.

"I can't," I said meekly.

"Manty," he said, "it'll be all right. Just go to sleep, Manty." He began to stroke my brow and smooth back my hair.

I shut my eyes and tried to let go, let everything go, under that lulling rhythm. But it was no use. Only by will could I keep my eyes shut and my body motionless.

Then, after a long time, he said: "Manty?"

"Yes," I said, and opened my eyes. The flicker was still on the ceiling.

"You weren't asleep, were you?"

"No," I said.

He fell silent again. I held his hand and listened to his breathing. I tried to time my breath to his. I got some pleasure, or at least some sense of safety, out of that.

Then he said: "It's like that summer."

I supposed that he, as I, in lying back down on this spot again had re-lived his own agitations of that past. So my heart, suddenly, swelled toward him, and I clasped his hand more tightly.

"I slept up here, that summer," he was saying, "to make more space for the sick ones—or to get better air—and the tar-barrels were burning down in the street and—"

"Oh, you mean *that* summer," I said, and the sweetness that had been growing in me went, all at once, dusty.

But he didn't realize the implication of my words. He simply replied: "Yes, that summer—summer of '53, it was—and at night the light from the tar-barrel burning in front of the gate showed on the ceiling here, and flickered. And the cannon fired off all the time, to clean the air, all night, too. And sometimes one of the sick ones would yell out, or something. Sometimes you didn't think morning would ever come, it looked like and when it did come, you—"

"Michele told me about it," I said, shortly.

"She did?" he asked, then fell into silence. "Michele," he said, then, in a tone of reverie, "she was wonderful. All day and all night, she'd work with 'em. All you could do, through black vomit and the dying. Jimmee, too. Work and laugh. And a lot of others, working and not caring any more, like they had come free, or something."

"Michele," I said, "she said you had kindness like a disease."

He seemed to ponder that, then echoed me: "Like a disease." He rolled heavily to his right side and peered at me under the flickering ceiling. "So Michele said that," he said.

"Yes," I said.

He dropped back and again studied the ceiling.

"Tonight," he said, at last, "it's like that night we took the village. The burning, and the yelling and—"

"What—what village?"

He didn't answer for a moment. "The name," he said meditatively, "damned if I remember the name. If I ever knew. But it was a big one. Burning, and the bodies around, and some crawling. Sometimes they'd split open a head and reach the hand in and the man still trying to crawl and—"

I sat bolt upright in bed. "What are you talking about?" I demanded.

"Lie down, little Manty," he said. "You might as well lie down."

I let myself slowly down.

"You don't even know who I am," he said.

I felt, suddenly, as if I were falling.

"Maybe I don't even know who I am," he was saying.

"Oh, but I know—I do know!" I cried, desperately, and again rose up, saying, "and you are kind!"

"Lie down, little Manty," he said.

I lay down again.

"My name," he said, "my name's not even Hamish Bond."

"It's not even Hamish Bond," he said. "Hamish—that was the name of a skipper I once did business with, and it came out a bloody business. He was a Scot with red whiskers on his face and ice water in his veins. And Bond was the name of the family of that American kin on his mother's side Prieur-Denis had. It just made it convenient to come in as a sort of cousin, a cousin from South Carolina. But who'd been off in France, and then ship-trading round the world all his life. That made it convenient in case somebody ever asked about South Carolina. You see, I never laid eyes on South Carolina."

Then: "And I never want to lay eyes on South Carolina."

Then: "I heard my bellyful about South Carolina. From the time I was big as a shucked oyster. My mother, she was from South Carolina. Or claimed so."

Then, in the flat voice: "Her."

Then: "There must have been a time it was different. But I just remember her voice going on, and my father's shoulders hunching lower."

"Your name—" I managed. "Your name—what is it?"

But he paid me no mind. He was staring up at the flicker of the ceiling.

Then: "She was a likely-looking woman. As well as I remember. Or must have been. Before her big black eyes got that crazy shine. Before one side of her mouth began to twist up all the time from the way she talked. It got so her mouth just twitched there. Even when she wasn't saying a word. It was like the words were just going on inside her anyway, and I'd look at that lip twitching and I could just hear the words, even if there wasn't a sound coming out."

Then: "I can hear 'em now."

"Your name," I said, "what's your name?"

"They called me this," he said. "Ag-lomey-klo-ha-palaver." He laughed in his throat, a sort of constricted double gasp, quickly cut off. "You know what that means?" he asked.

"No," I said.

"It's what they called me," he said. "Captain Strike-down-then-make-the-Palaver." He gave his laugh again. Then: "I reckon there was a time I was right proud of that name."

Then: "You got to be proud of something."

He went back to watching the ceiling. There was the shouting, far off.

"What's your name?" I demanded.

"It don't matter," he said, staring at the ceiling. "It was so long ago."

I jerked myself up in bed. I seized him by the shoulder and began to shake him. "I've got to know!" I cried, desperately. "Don't you see, I've got to know? I've got to know something."

He didn't seem to notice the shaking, or my desperation. But after a moment, he said: "Hinks. Alec Hinks. That was my name."

I repeated that name in my head, for its strangeness. Then I said it out loud—in a whisper, that is—for I had to know how it was on my lips.

"It's funny," he said, "hearing you say it. All these years and I haven't heard it. And now it's like it was the name of somebody else, somebody I never saw, and him dead a long time back."

He heaved up on an elbow. "No," he said, "it's not like I said." He paused, and peered at me. "I tell you what it's like. It's like there wasn't just two of us here. You and me lying here on this bed. It's like there was three. Like he was lying right here with us, and watching, and every breath I draw, he draws one, and I reach out my hand"—he reached out and laid his heavy hand on my breast—"he reaches out his hand, too."

"Stop!" I cried out, and shuddered under his hand.

"We can't help it, little Manty," he said, softly. "We can't help it if things are the way they are."

I began to weep, in desolation—desolation for what, I couldn't be sure—the tears coming silent, just running down my cheeks, the way I've seen very old people weep, easy, with no noise.

I don't think he knew I was weeping. He had lain back down now, and was looking at the ceiling. "Baltimore," he said. "I was born in Baltimore."

"Baltimore," he said, and waited. "It wasn't a bad place for a boy. Except for what happened."

"What?" I asked. "What happened?"

"Except for what happened," he said. "And if it hadn't happened —if it hadn't been like it was—then nothing else would."

Then, after his silence: "No, maybe it would; just the same. And the only difference, that I'd be lying on some other bed, in the middle of the night, and some other city, and some other fools gone crazy would be setting fires and yelling, and the light of the fool fires would be dancing on some other ceiling. But me watching them."

He stopped, then I felt his hand groping at me.

"Give me your hand," he said.

I did it.

"Oh, Manty," he said.

There was a burst of yelling, far off.

"Fools," he said. "Fools."

And: "Tomorrow. Tomorrow they'll come upriver. The fleet, black, and black spars, and the gun ports. They'll come in line."

"It wasn't a bad place for a boy," he said. "The ships, and the yards, and the going-on. The war was on and—"

"The war?" I echoed.

"That was 1812," he said, "and the British, and I was big enough boy to go down and watch the privateers fit out. Baltimore—that was the place for 'em, for the clippers. You'd see 'em laying off, low down on the water, blue or yellow or green, with black wales and trim, or all black, fair buttock line and diagonals and bowsprit like you never saw, and the masts raked and sharp-rigged, top-sail schooner or brig schooner, oversparred and so tender that if you even spit wrong even in ghost weather you'd capsize or pitch-pole. You had to know the touch. But give you a sweet one, and tender, and you could play her like a fiddle. She'd tremble under your finger. One I had once—Baltimore built, too—*The Sweet Sue*, why, she —but that was long after.

"Long after the war, I mean.

"I was a boy then, and the first year they started out just fitting the fast pilot boats, one long gun, the Long Tom, swivel or carriage, and a carronade or two, and cram a crew on till not room to stand— till after the first time you closed on a Britisher to board and after that you'd have more elbowroom.

"Then they started building the big ones. There wasn't a thing I didn't know, the name of every one, her masting and sail plan, tonnage and gun-weight and deadrise and midship section placement, and transom and tuck.

"Down to the water, it was a place to go.

"It was a place to go, and not think what it was going to be like when you went home.

"My mother would be sitting there on that chair with the brocade all nubbed down and split—the one she said came from South Carolina—and she'd set her black eyes on me and ask where I'd been. But before I could answer, she'd say: 'Oh, I know where you've been.' And she'd put the back of her hand to her forehead and lean her head back a second and shut her eyes. Then she'd say: "Yes, your mother knows. She knows you would turn your back on all she cherishes, and go consort with the vulgar.'

"And then the shine would come in her eyes, and I had the feeling I could hear a million screwed-up fiddle strings popping inside her, and she'd say: 'Go—go to your vulgar companions. Twist the knife in me. Rub salt in my wound. Torture your mother who went into the Valley of the Shadow for you. Look at her. Reduced and brought down!'

"She'd run over to that old nigger woman she had and lean her head on the old nigger's shoulder and say, 'Aunt Mattie—at least Aunt Mattie knows how I am brought down. For she was there— yes, she was there at Buckhampton Manor and loved me.'

"You see, my mother's family name was Buckhampton, and she never let you forget it. Buckhampton of Buckhampton Manor, but the Tories burnt it. Oh, yes, she had suffered for liberty, but look what liberty had done for her! Only one poor old back-broke half-wit nigger left, when once she'd had a thousand. To wipe her nose and draw breath for her.

"Anyway, she would put her head on the old half-wit's shoulder— when she wasn't cursing at her for burning the bread.

"Then she'd lift up her head and stare around that room. And God knows that room wasn't a thing to brag on. Half a cellar, with the windows high up and you could see feet passing on the street, and a carpet worn down to nothing and furniture falling apart and a mirror on the wall with the gold peeling off the frame and the glass as murky as bilge water.

"But I forgot. I forgot that that mirror was from South Carolina. Oh, yes, it had hung in the great hall of her father's house in South Carolina and a million niggers polished it every day.

"Now she'd get up and go to the mirror and look at herself and poke her face with a finger, and say, 'Look—and come to this!' And then she'd really get wound up and say how she'd given her heart to one loutish and unworthy.

"And my father would just sit and hunch his shoulders in his coat and his face would get more yellow-streaked. Which I reckon is the way you have to be if you're past fifty and a clerk in a ship-chandler's and you get poorer by the minute and you ain't genteel and your eyes are going bad so the figures blur out on the ledger and that voice is in your head even when you are asleep, and when you are dead and in your grave it'll be in your head, like a little white worm gnawing, and your son looks across the room at you and he'd like to spit on you because you are dirt.

"Your son thinks you are dirt for a different reason from the reason your wife thinks you are dirt. He thinks you are dirt because you sit there and hunch your shoulders. And don't knock her teeth down her throat.

"Yes, I'd think that, and then I'd feel so awful I'd want to cry. I'd feel like I had done the worst crime in the world.

"But nothing was ever as bad as the times at night she'd come and sit on the edge of my bed and lean over and cry. Her hair would hang down and the tears would drip down on me. She didn't want to be wicked, she said. She was just so unhappy, she said. I must love her because she was my mother, and then she would be happy.

"I loved her at those times, I reckon. Or tried to. While the tears fell on my face. But at the same time I couldn't stand it.

"Then it was over. They let me leave my schooling. I'll say this for my mother, she scraped up every penny for my schooling, and I could do Euclid and Cicero's subjunctive with any snot, and what good has it done me?

"My mother had a friend with an uncle who was rich. He got me a job in the bank and I was supposed to get rich and buy a big house and a million niggers and a gilt coach and my mother would feel at home at last and I would love her devotedly.

"The only trouble was, I looked at the faces there and they looked at me. I knew, and they knew, that in twenty years I'd be just like them, and even if I got rich I'd be gut-shot by then.

"So I just walked out and got myself a job as a shipwright helper. It wasn't easy to get a job then. The war was over, privateering was long gone, and there was a money panic. The only thing left was to build nigger-runners. Nigger-grabbing was against the law now, and the British were patroling Africa, and the only thing that could out-run the British was the Baltimore clipper.

"I could get a job just because I would work for nigh nothing, to learn.

"I went home and told 'em.

"I thought my mother was going to have a stroke. She tottered. The blood all ran out of her head so she was white-faced as whey, and then back so she was the color of a sliced beet. Then she said: 'A common laborer—my son!' She said how she was gently nurtured. She said she once had a thousand slaves and they all loved her. She said how blood would tell and I was my father's son. She cried on the old nigger's shoulder.

"What she said wasn't what did it. What did it was just getting one more look at my father.

"I cut loose. 'All right,' I said to her, 'I won't work in the yard. But I'm going away. Because I can't stand hearing you, and I don't believe a word you've ever said. And I don't believe he does either, my father, and if he was ever man enough to say so, things might be different. But he's not. And I don't believe there ever was any Buckhampton Manor, and I don't believe you ever were in South Carolina, and I believe you saved up and bought that one old nigger for only ten dollars because she is half-wit and pules in the porridge when she makes it.'

"My mother let out a yell like she had been kicked, but I went on.

"'Yes, I'm going away,' I said, 'but if you're so nigger-crazy, I'll fix you. I'll go where there's a million niggers. I'll get me a million niggers.'

"I came and leaned at her and she shrunk back, gap-mouthed and white, like she was scared I would hit her. 'Listen,' I said, 'I'll get me a million. I'll wallow in niggers. I'll be ass-deep in niggers. And then'—and I really leaned at her—'and then you'll be satisfied.'"

He stopped, and I could hear his breath. Then he said: "I'm sorry, Manty. I'm sorry for talking like that in front of you. For talking foul."

"I guess it doesn't matter," I said, staring at the ceiling where the flames flickered.

He was quiet a minute, then heaved up on his arm, as though angry, leaning at me, and I saw the gleam of his eyes. "But, by God," he said, "that was the way it was. It was that way, and that was the way it was going to be, and I can't help it, by God!"

Then he lay back down.

"Yeah, I said that to her," he said, "to my mother. Then I started for the door. I looked back just once. I saw her face, all white and her eyes staring black and her mouth making a round *O* in the middle. I saw the old half-wit nigger crouching down, and the drool. I saw my father, and he had his chin off his chest. He must have been born with a birth-cord tying his chin down on the chestbone, and they forgot to cut it. Now it was cut, you might say. Then he burst out laughing. The laugh was awful. His face wasn't laughing, but his mouth was open and that awful sound was coming out.

"When he started laughing, I made the door. I left the door open, and I heard the sound halfway down the street.

"I never knew whether I had done him any favor that day, or not. Maybe now that I got him free of the horse-apple of a lie he had lived with all that time, maybe there wasn't anything to live for now. Maybe he just dried up and blew away."

"I went down to the water. There was a new one, just finished, lying off, and I knew as well as you ever know anything that she was for me.

"She was low on the water, yellow with black wales and trim. Her bowsprit kept rising, and her masts—she was a three-master—raked back so much you just felt the wharf heave under your foot like it was a deck and she took the swell. She looked like a horse and him bunching for a jump. She looked like a hound laying out after a rabbit.

"But all the time not a breath of air on the bare poles, and not a durn ripple in the evening calm, and the yellow evening sky reflected in the water like glass, and she sat on her own upside-down reflection so clear you could see a blue-bottle fly lounging on the edge of the hawse-hole.

"There was one man on the dock. I knew he would be there.

"He was a shortish man, thick and solid. He wore a square-cut coat, long and full-skirted, dark blue, something so old-fashioned you didn't believe it, and a dove-colored waistcoat, with silver buttons, all unbuttoned except the bottom two. A big silver watch chain was hauled across his middle, big as an anchor chain. His linen wasn't anything to brag on for cleanness, but it must have cost money. He had a kind of a flattish, three-cornered hat, black, and under it, out the back side, hung a little plait of hair, red hair, tied with a black tie-ribbon at the end and chopped off. It was like you had unkinked the tail on a red hog and tied on the black tie-ribbon a third way up, and chopped off the rest, for waste.

"He was red-faced, and the face square-hacked like you had done the job out of a big chunk of red cedar with a hand-ax and hadn't been too careful about the smooth-off. His eyes were blue and squinty, under red eyebrows that would have done duty for curry-comb. He had a big silver ring on the third finger of each hand, a big ruby in each the size of a musket ball. He was taking snuff out of a silver box.

"When I spoke to him, he snapped the box shut with a sound like cocking a pistol, and looked at me out from under the red eyebrows. I can't flatter myself that he seemed to like what he looked at.

"But he gave me a good evening. He gave it like it was money and he was hard-pressed himself. It was a voice he had got up in Maine, where he came from, and hadn't improved much of the gravel out in yelling into hurricanes for forty years.

"I looked out at the beauty, which I knew was his. He had patted every plank that went in her, and rubbed a couple of fingers down it, like it was the backside of his true-love and him just back from a six-month voyage and might as well wait five minutes more just to admire the material.

"I looked out at her now, and said: 'She is sharp-rigged.'

"He grunted and never took his eyes, with their weather-squint, off me.

"So I said: 'She is nigger-rigged.'

"He put a forefinger against his right nostril, and blew snuff out the other nostril with a blast that made ripples clear out to the brig-schooner.

" 'You think you are pretty sharp-rigged yourself,' he allowed, pretty sour.

" 'I'm sharp enough to know it's niggers,' I said. 'And fool enough to want to ship out with you.'

"He looked at me in a way to make any previous look he had passed me feel tender as a maiden's dream. Then he said: 'And what do you think I'd do with a young pismire like you?' And he took a backhand swipe with his left hand at my chest. It looked like the sort of gesture you might make to brush off a fly, but I staggered three feet.

"I came out of the stagger, and did it. I lay forward, and made to knock his face in.

"I might have done it if I hit, for even if I didn't have my heft, I was coming on and wiry. But try was all, for when my fist was just six inches from his face, which hadn't budged, something clamped on my wrist, and it froze in the air. He had grabbed me out of the air, and I never felt a grip like it. Then he put his weight in the grip, and I was nigh on my knees.

" 'You *are* sharp-rigged,' he said, looking down at my face like he was studying something in the bottom of a well.

" 'Let me up and I'll kill you,' I said.

" 'Don't hurry about it,' he said. 'You will have a long opportunity. You see, you booger, it's a long way to Rio Pongo.'

"So Rio Pongo, it was. And ass-deep in niggers."

*Rio Pongo, Rio Pongo,* I said to myself, hearing Hamish Bond's voice, and tried to have a picture in my head, green coast, purple darkness descending over the gold sky.

I could hear the shouting, far off, toward the levee.

Then he said: "Rio Pongo, the first time. But I've seen 'em all. Everything between Cape Verde and Cape Saint Maria. Sierra Leone and Liberia, Monrovia and the Bight of Benin where the Benin flows in, but the niggers you get there have a liability. Eboes they call 'em. Get the sulks and sulls, or the vapors like they were ladies, and swallow the tongue, or just are melancholy. Windward Coast and Bonny River and Anamaboe, Goree, Gaboon, Gambia, Whidah, and Calabar—I've seen 'em all.

"But the first time, coming in. In the morning a squall, for that was the season, the fall not settled bright yet. Cloud lay over from northwest solid like a bridge span, gray nimbus arching over, color of a dirty sheep-belly. Then the rain came all at once, solid, like you had knocked the bottom out of a barrel, and the barrel sky-high and sky-size, and you under it. The rain tromped the ship in the sea. And the lightning, it never let up, red sheetfire and stab, all around.

"Then it was gone, like it had never happened, thin mist settling down now, like a dust-haze, brown-blue and no wind to speak of, and the sea long and greasy and dirty beer color, running out from your forefoot. Not even a cat's-paw showed. We bore in on a long tack, slow like a dream, but steady, under our kites and moon-rakers. We were under them, for there wasn't any air you could feel. But the Baltimores were light-weather flyers. They carried sail that could pick up the new breeze if a gull belched five miles to windward. They could move like a dream. A dead calm, and they'd leave a British cruiser like a cow staked out on the common.

"But coming in to Rio Pongo. Coming on evening, the sun broke astern and the light lay long out level over the water toward the east where we bore in. The light picked out the long line of the surf, white like you couldn't believe it. Then we lifted the beach, yellow, like somebody had dipped his finger in a paint pot and smeared one line, yellow and just finger-wide, across the middle of the world, north to south, and dead level. Only it broke at the river, then picked up.

"Above the beach there was the line of jungle. It was a purple-green line.

"It's always that way, up and down that coast, the surf-line, dead white on the bar, then the slack water or lagoon, the beach-line and then the jungle. Maybe a rise of ground like at Whidah. You would lay off, and the coast blacks—Kroo-men, they call 'em, fellows with red nightcaps and white drawers, and they were like a combination of a crocodile and the miracle of walking on the water—would paddle out and take you ashore. That surf was murder and you didn't draw breath for five minutes. Not in that smother. And sharks thick as herring in a brine barrel, and hungry as Hell-mouth. But those Kroo-men would take you through.

"On the beach they start howling around you—the station-niggers, I mean, not Kroo-men—young and old, flap-jawed and slack-jointed except for two or three old boogers over yonder squatting on a bone-white drift-log, black-naked and sweat-slick, with the chin nigh on the knees and the arms hanging straight down for tiredness, looking like a brace of turkey-buzzards taking siesta.

"Up yonder is the town, grass and mud and palmyra leaf or something, and the factor's house—the Mongo or whatever he called himself—and the old mud fort, if it was an old station, with half the guns spiked or rusted out long back but perhaps a couple still good for firing a salute. There's no use for 'em for anything else. Not against the niggers anyway, for if you're a slave-trader they love you. They love you the way a baby loves his mammy bringing the sugar-tit. For you are bringing that rum. That is, they love you if they are not some of the ones getting traded off.

"They are over yonder in the barracoon, back from the beach. A big palisade thing, the poles sunk six feet in the ground to prevent tunneling, and laced with iron. Some grass roofing for shade. Guard houses at the gate. Sections inside to keep the men and women apart, and nighttime the noises I've heard coming out of those places. Like dogs moon-howling and moaning. And what goes on inside, crammed in there, a thousand or nigh, locked up that way.

"Oh, they feed 'em all right. That is, they feed 'em unless rations run short. You get a British cruiser settling down offshore to a long wait to blockade the station, with your black warning flag up, and nobody will come in for a cargo. So your stock piles up, and you can't even turn 'em loose. You can't turn loose a thousand howling and gut-crazy savages on that peaceful and rum-soaked local population. It would not be, you might say, Christian.

"I have been the first ship in to a station, after a blockade broke, and I have seen the bodies floating inside the bar, in slack water. The women float face down, with the butt up and awash, for that's the fattiest part. The men float face up, just sky-staring.

"The sharks and such have long since had all they want. They just nose 'em aside.

"Well, if you've just run the surf and landed, you start up the beach. The factor or Mongo or whatever, he comes out to meet you. He is going to show you hospitality. He's got rum and brandy and claret, and if he is a real king of the Coast, that claret is going to be Margaux, nigh old as you are and laid down the right year, and the brandy is going to be older. Then he's got some cards and dice. And he's got some women. One of those real kings of the coast, like Da Souza the big Cha-Cha at Whidah, or Don Pedro, there wasn't any shape, size, complexion, nationality or condition he didn't claim to have handy.

"But they weren't much to brag on. For one thing, the climate is awful. And if it was just some fellow with a toe hold on the Coast, he wasn't accustomed to better than a half-Arab or some bush-black rinsed off a couple of times with sea water.

"But I'm talking like I had my ship already. It was six years before that. The ships I was on before that. The *Defiance*—not a clipper but an old frigate-built ship—just 280 tons burden and carried 625 slaves. Jammed on the slave decks, down in the hold, lying on the right side, one fellow's kneecaps jammed into the next fellow's hamstrings, spoon-wise. Except what women they kept on deck at night. I used to be lying on the deck with one of them. Yes, I admit doing it. And I'd look up and see the topsail drawing across the stars, steady and full with the trade, and I'd think of my mother and how I'd left her with her mouth making that paralylzed *O*, and I'd think: *well, I hope you are satisfied.*

"Then I was on a Portugee. I swore I would never be on another Portugee. And I swore that when I got my ship I'd run it clean.

"And I did. You had to lay 'em on the slave-shelves, but I gave turn-room, and all day, gang by gang, on deck for air and dancing. I hosed 'em down with sea water. Every other day I hosed down and holystoned the slave decks till they looked white as ginned cotton, and sprinkled with vinegar. I made 'em wash out their mouth with lemon and gave chew-sticks for teeth. I fed 'em like the crew, fish stew or dried shrimp with palm oil and beans with biscuits cracked up in the mess. My ship didn't smell. I never lost money by it. I landed my cargoes.

"And my crews, they stood by me. The times we had brushes, they did all right.

"It took me six years to get me a ship. How did I get it? I took it.

"It was that Scot named Hamish. He did me a wrong, tried to beat me out of my wage. I was mate then. I was sort of glad he tried to beat me. It gave me my justification. So I took his ship. Then, long later, I took his name, too.

"Ten more years and I had five ships. But them, I built 'em or bought 'em.

"I was big now. I was big enough to leave business and go to Paris when I wanted and ride round like a gentleman. I had connections there, and big ones.

"It may have been dirty but it was big now. I had skippers and factors and juniors. I had storehouses jammed with axes and kettles, knives and cutlasses, trade-guns and cloth, chintz and calawapores and braul—that's a blue-stripe the nigger top-men and cabosheers favor for head-turbans—and spearheads and fishhooks, powder in half-barrels, and iron bars. Geneva gin and Yankee rum in puncheons and ankers. Great God, the rum.

"Forty bars—iron bars—a head, that's what we paid for a good one, young, joints clean, no teeth missing. Or what calculated at forty bars, say five ankers of brandy. And the rum.

"They'd come marching 'em in, out of the jungle, a coffle a half-mile long, thongs neck to neck, but the child-size and women not tied. Each one carried something on his head, ivory if it was a rich trade-chief coming in, or yams and hides and such. Guards with

guns alongside the coffle. The trader—a head-man or chief or ca-
bosheer, nigger or half-Arab or what—he'd lie in his litter and fan.
There would be singing and dancing out front, when they broke
from the brush.

"Then the trading would start. That is, after we'd given 'em *dash*
—presents, that goes to say—and soaked 'em in rum. They'd trade
anything. They'd trade mother or father. Son or daughter. The poor
ones, that is. The rich ones, the kings and such, they had the war-
raids and the criminals. It was a crime to move a fetish-feather off
a path. Even if you didn't know what it was.

"Well, I didn't make the world that way. That's what I said to myself. It was that way a million years. They raided and warred back
and forth, and cut throats and drank blood like buttermilk, and
chopped off heads for some mud-post of a Bo-god, who is nothing
but a human man-part, and heel-hung 'em like a slaughter pen to
honor a granddaddy's grave, and if a British cruiser set free a cargo
and landed 'em they'd be sold again in a week, and be sold for Liverpool trade-guns and Lancashire cotton, and if they put 'em in Liberia, where there was a free and civilized nigger country we fixed
all up just like the Land of Liberty, those black Sons of Liberty
passed their black brothers on to traders waiting on the border. It
was all like that, and nobody cared, and don't let anybody tell you
different, and if you took one of 'em off to pick cotton five thousand
miles away, you did him a favor. If saving a man's life is ever doing
him a favor.

"You'd do God a favor if you sunk that country under the sea. He
may have made it, but it's got out of hand. That's what I used to say
to myself.

"And I said, I didn't make this world and make 'em drink blood. I
didn't make myself and I can't help what I am doing. They drove me
to it. And I'd see in my head again how it all happened. I would
wake up in the night.

"Well, you can always go back to sleep."

There was the shouting at the levee and in the streets. It was
nearer. I hung on to Hamish's hand, tighter, and tried not to think
what he was saying. If I thought too much about that, I didn't know
whose hand it was, and I felt that if I let that hand go, I would slip
off the edge of something and go falling.

"Listen at 'em," he said.

Then: "Maybe it would be a favor to God to sink this country in the sea, too. Maine to Texas."

"If I hadn't gone inside," he said, "maybe I'd be there yet. If the fever didn't get me. Or the British hang me. But I went inside.

"Three ships I had, empty, and couldn't get a cargo. I raked the Coast. Even at Whidah. Except for the mackrons, the beat-up and sick just good for shark-bait. 'You'll have to wait till the wars start,' they said at Whidah. 'It's not the season for the wars.'

" 'Going to war is not planting potatoes,' I said to that yellow-face Portugee, with the gold rings in his ears and the lace shirt.

" 'The king will go at the season,' he said.

" 'I reckon I will go see the king,' I said. 'He may be a king, but he is a nigger-dealing king, and he would sell his mother, and I have three empty bottoms laying in the Bight with sails clewed up and crews lazy.'

"The Portugee shrugged. He had lived there a long time. Maybe he was born there. Maybe he was half-bush. Anyway, he took that king pretty seriously.

"The king lived at Agbome, a long march in.

"I took three men off *The Sweet Sue*, volunteers for prize-pay, armed 'em so heavy a man could scarce stagger, packaged up some *dash* for that king, brandy and beads and a rocking chair and a lady's feather fan, the ballroom kind, pink, and some striped silk shirts, got together a file of bearers, hammock-men and stool-toters, and I was ready to start.

"The night before I started, two men came to me. They looked in the face like a cross between starvation and malaria, and their bones were done up in black coats. They were Wesleyites, missionaries. They wanted me to take 'em to the king.

" 'What do you want there?' I asked.

"They said they would expound him the gospel and persuade him from selling slaves and making blood sacrifice.

" 'I am not personally in the blood-sacrifice business,' I said, 'but I am in the nigger business. I am in it in a large way, if I may say so without indecorous boasting. Do you still want to go with me, and be defiled?'

"They looked at each other. Then one of them rummaged in his head and found the right text for the occasion.

" 'All right,' I said.

"They asked what the charge would be.

" 'Listen,' I said, 'I'll deliver you to that king without mark, weal, wen, cat-scratch or bullet-hole on your body. All you have to do is pray for my soul.'

"Then you know what one of those boogers did? He looked at me, and he said: 'Brother, morning and evening I shall name you in prayer and beseech that your eyes be given vision and your soul find peace in the infinite mercy of God.'

" 'Cheap at the price,' I said. 'But you better pray short tonight. We leave at dawn.'

"At dawn we were in the hammocks. Hammock pole nine feet long, running from one nigger-head to the other, and you swing under the pole, with a red-and-blue awning with fringe rigged over and tilted against the sun. It is like being trussed in a poke and bounced off the ground every three paces and the sun bears down through that awning all the time and what the hammock-men are saying about you and your relatives you are happier not to understand the lingo of.

"Seventy-odd miles of that, past bombax trees 100 feet across and palms standing separate and fine, the soil red with dry grass neck-high on the dry ground, and here and there a *marigot* to ford, stinking like a horse-pond in August, and a swamp like old coffee grounds bordered with fern-forest the color of arsenic.

"In the open you hit the maize fields, then some town. Bo-posts and fetishes, grass huts and a swish house—mud, that is—for the caboosheer or muck-a-muck, with a rooster crucified head down on a cross over the door, and the feathers falling off and his bouquet no help to your appetite. The caboosheer comes out and snaps fingers at you for politeness. They set up his stool and red umbrella, and your boys do the same for you, and you all swap rum and compliments. They fire off a few guns and do the beheading dance in your honor. When time comes to butcher a goat for supper, the buzzards who have been sitting along the swish wall where the skulls are stuck on the wall as regular as brass tacks in a chair back—well, the buzzards come down most obliging and help pull the guts out.

"But all that is nothing to Agbome, the capital. Agbome is in a plain, where there is drinking water from mud-holes, but way off, you can see the blue where the Kong mountains begin. They say it is cool there, with water, and the wind blows fresh.

"It is not cool and fresh here. The sun bears down on a mud wall miles around, buzzards sitting on it, and a dry moat below, and mud palaces inside, sixty feet high, with skulls, a million of 'em, set in the wall, and jawbones, and skulls to make pavement for the king to walk on. There are 20,000 live people.

"You ought to see that king. That is, the one they had then. His name was Gezo. He had been king for fifteen years about, and he had beat all the tribes around and broken their towns. Of course, he had half depopulated his own country and shrunk the maize fields, so he was a king sitting in the middle of a desert, or nigh, and proud of it. But he was a king, and as a matter of fact, he wasn't a bad looking sort of a king, rather firm-faced and with strong-made joints but with a skull sloping back a little too much for beauty. He was middle-aged. I figured he would be worth about thirty bars on a good market.

"I saw the booger sitting in front of his mud palace, with the million skulls, sitting in a pavilion thing, with a score of umbrellas around, propped on a couch covered with clothes of all kinds and colors, smoking a silver pipe like a steam engine. He wore a violet-colored skullcap, a green silk handkerchief round his waist, and shirt made out of a red-flowered damask that had been a table-cover in Liverpool before it got promoted to Africa, and a jewel-hilted rapier hung round his neck on a blue sash.

"In front of him, on a table, were four skulls mounted in gold—or brass—to look like things, one like a ship, another like a flower, and so on. These were the skulls of special enemies the king was doing special honor to by drinking out of. There were a dozen more brass pans—neptunes you call 'em—of skulls stacked up, enemies not special enough to drink out of. Then, of course, the trees and posts had skulls hung up, with flags and banners or just plain colored rags.

"Beside the king was a big brass spittoon. You won't see a finer in the Saint Charles Hotel.

"His women were behind him, all ages and shapes and hair-rigs, some cropped short and stained blue or red, some short-plaited to make melon-stripes down the skull, showing the hide between rows, some in twisted spirals like cloves stuck in ham, and some built up solid like a block of wood hung with leopard-ears and bird-feathers.

"A lot of his ministers and cabosheers were around, wearing their gewgaws and carrying Bo-sticks and trade-guns and butcher knives, and there were gangs of hunchbacks and jesters and about ten

thousand of those Amazons. You see, this king had women-troops—
as I had heard tell down on the Coast. Amy-johns they called 'em.

"They were divided up in companies and regiments, the razor-
women, who make a nice specialty of carving off heads, then the
gun-women, who would make a specialty of shooting, if those trade-
guns and blunderbusses were any good in the first place and they
had ever learned to aim in the second, then the skull-breaking
women, who had iron-nubbed clubs and the biceps of blacksmiths,
and the bow-and-arrow women. They were all supposed, in a manner of speaking, to be wives of the king, and if one of them ever got
caught irregular, there was hell to pay for all concerned.

"But the king never touched them himself. The notion was, you
might say, that you didn't want to get the minds of those ladies off
the business of bloodletting. But it looked like those ladies had got
the bloodletting and the other thing all mixed up, when they started
firing off guns and dancing and squatting and waving their hips and
beating gongs to honor His Highness.

"You see, it was the time of the big celebration, what they call the
Year-Customs. It goes on for days, and I had to sit through it.

"It was bigger than an election barbecue.

"The Amy-johns were dancing by squad, gang and regiment, slung
all over with bullet-bags, powder-calabashes, water-gourds, fetish-
sacks, pipe-cases, and human jawbones, to bounce and bang, and
waving razors and firearms. All the ministers danced. The cabosheers
danced. The hunchbacks danced. There was a steady firing-off of
trade-guns, and now and then somebody overcharged one, and it
blew his hand off. This was regarded as very funny. Some old ship-
guns, carronades, had been hauled up from the Coast, seventy-five
miles, and stuck in the ground, and they fired them off. The big men
and the head Amy-johns stood up and made their brags. Everybody
drank rum, and yelled.

"The king drank his rum out of the gold-or-brass-mounted skulls.
Then he danced, and ministers and cabosheers lay on the ground
in front of him and put dust on their heads.

"Some days they showed off the king's treasure, marching it round
and round to make the populace bug-eyed.

"It was a walking pawnshop. Copper pots, a big mirror with a
crack across and gold peeling off the frame—just like my mother's
mirror from South Carolina—a couple of iron horns five feet long,
colored apothecary jars, a lot of dry goods strung out to be admired,

a Paris barouche pulled by a sweating team of citizens, for there's not but one horse in the country and he's too weak to pull anything, a green chariot of some kind, with lions painted on it, an Ohio trotting wagon with the leather hood rotting off, a sedan-chair with the gilt gone, a ship figurehead, a full-busted lady with a trumpet, carved and painted, mounted on a platform supported on the heads of bearers, a child's hobbyhorse, a violin with the strings snapped long back, a few pieces of silver plate, a silk hammock. Then, behind everything, was my rocking chair. On a fellow's head.

"The rocking chair was a great success. The next day the king sat in it and rocked. That gave me hope we could do our private business. But there was still a lot more public business.

"The big part of that public business was killing off the sacrifices. There was a whole pen full of those fellows, dressed in white cotton Mother Hubbards and white caps on their heads, eyes bugged out, whites rolling, admired by the populace and well fed, waiting to be bastinadoed or throat-cut, and sent on to report to the king's father. Every night or so—Evil Night—they finished off a few. The king set the example with some expert butchery, and then the right officials took over. The blood collected in ditches dug for the purpose. I had heard tell that they collected enough blood this way to float a canoe, and did. With the king in it. But that is a cruel libel. There was no canoe in it with any king. But one or two old boogers drank blood out of a calabash. They politely offered me a swig, but I politely declined.

"In fact, some of the sacrifices weren't bled at all. They simply got hung up by their heels on racks and beat to death. But blooded or not blooded, all the fellows got left on display. The buzzards, who sat around all the trees and the palace wall, like senators waiting to vote, would flop down for tiffin. The dancing and gun-firing didn't faze 'em. The naked children paddled in the special mud over by the palace gate, and made little mud Bo-gods, or mud-pies. The Wesleyites didn't like it. They prayed quite a lot.

"The women sacrifices were killed private in the palace to maintain decency, so I didn't see any of that.

"But my business, I worked it. The last day, I was invited to dance before the king. I did it. I stripped me down to the waist, and I danced for two hours. I did hornpipes and reels. I walked on my hands and waved my legs in the air. I did back somersaults. I waltzed slow and sang to myself, with my eyes closed and my arms like I held a lady and I was in Paris. I jumped in the air and clicked my heels three times before hitting ground. The tricks I did those poor untutored savages had never thought of. They broke bones trying.

"I lost twenty pounds in two hours, but that Gezo took a shine to me. He made me sit on a stool to one side of his rocking chair, under the big red umbrella with the silver fringe. I knew I had him then.

"Meanwhile, the king wanted the Wesleyites to dance. They shook their heads and looked sick. They had been looking sicker every day, and I must admit I hadn't been too sympathetic. When some booger would get hung up and beat to death, I'd say: 'Now, brother, do you think I ought to leave him here, or maybe buy him to pick cotton?'

"But I did them a favor now. I told them if they wanted to get on the good side of Gezo they had better dance.

"They said dancing was against their religion.

"I pointed out that Gezo was getting cross.

"They said they feared no wrath of the heathen.

"I said, that might be true, but they had come here to soften up the heathen, and it looked like dancing was the only way. I pointed out that there was good precedent in King David.

"They said they would dance.

"They got up to dance, the brace of 'em, and that made me even higher in favor with Gezo. He was fanning himself now with the pink ballroom plume fan I had brought.

"They started dancing, if you call it that, two coast-fever skeletons sweating in black coats, doing a kind of slow shuffle in the tramped dust, with a lot of naked, hung-up black bodies and turkey-buzzards for a background, and naked pickaninnies paddling in the special mud, and the Wesleyites sweating and singing.

*"Oh, let us be joyful, joyful, joyful,*
*When we meet to part no more.*

"That was the last I ever saw of them.

"Next day I was off on my business, a special-early war-raid that I had talked the king into. We headed inland, the army and I. That is, the part of the army old Gezo had assigned me, a gang of blunderbuss Amy-johns and razor-women and a sprinkling of the other kind, and some men fighters and a lot of men bearers. We straggled across the open country to the jungle, me and the three men off *The Sweet*

*Sue* banging in our hammocks, the army yawking and whooping like kids out of school. Then we came to the jungle.

"The jungle on the way to Agbome was an old maid's verbena garden compared to this. Trees a hundred and fifty feet high, and vine hanging down big as your body. You never saw such rigging. Ants on the ground the size of a fice dog, with mudhouses six feet high and a smell like a backhouse. Daylight never comes in there. Bats hang on those high sycamores, way up, so thick you can't see the white wood. Butterflies the size of soup plates drift out of the shadow. They are red and black and gold. They move so slow you think they are asleep in the air, just lying on shadow. When they do move, they are so big you hear the wings creak like tackle.

"Meanwhile, the army is yawking and yammering. Their big idea of strategy is to yawk and yammer as much as possible, and go right by the town you aim to break, and then squat down a few hours in the bush and come back at night. It is a surprise attack, which depends for its success, you might say, on the fellow who is to be surprised being deaf, dumb, paralyzed and stupid.

"He must have been. The surprise worked.

"We hit just after midnight. We burst through the thorn wall around the town like it wasn't there, and went to work.

"I stood in the middle and watched it. They threw burning billets on the thatch of the houses and waited for people to run out. They shot 'em and clubbed 'em and razored 'em, this in the middle of the gigantic bonfire which that town had by now got to be, and with yelling to split the eardrums. Enthusiasm was at such a pitch that a lot of valuable two-legged property was being destroyed. There might not be enough of a cargo to be worth marching back to Whidah.

"But by now they were working on the wounded. Those Amy-johns ran from pile to pile, and they didn't kill 'em quick. They killed 'em slow. They carved 'em with razor-work of the greatest tact and delicacy and left the deprived objects still crawling. This was extremely funny. They cracked open heads and dipped their ribbons and rigs and furbelows in blood and plastered more blood on the gun-stocks to stick cowrie shells in to keep tally on your killing.

"I stood in the middle, and saw it, and heard the yells and watched the flame leaping to light up the jungle-top, with a million disturbed bats wheeling and weaving in the upper light, and it was all like a dream. I could not believe it was true, and yet when I looked round and saw those three men I had brought off *The Sweet Sue,* I knew it was true. They were not lily-fingered and they were not lily-livered, I knew for a fact, but they certainly had a lily-complexion now. They looked sicker than Wesleyites.

"I said I couldn't believe it was true. It was like a dream. It was like a dream you had had long back, but didn't know you had had until, suddenly, now you remember it, and the dream is coming true. It is coming true, just like, deep inside you, you had known it would. Known without exactly knowing, that is.

"I said: *This is not me.*

"I said: *They drove me to it.*

"I saw the picture of my mother's face in my head, that last day, and I said: *I reckon you are satisfied now.*

"They were howling and working on the wounded.

"Then it happened.

"I was looking right at a pile being sorted out by a couple of Amy-johns with a man helping. They razor-worked a few of them that were about gone anyway. Then they uncovered a woman sort of propped up on somebody under her, with her eyes wide open. She was alive, all right, and on the ground, right in front of her, was a baby. It was a baby just born. I stood and stared.

"They dragged the mother a couple of feet and carved her. It looked like I couldn't move.

"But I moved. I moved when that fellow who was helping the Amy-johns lifted up his spear to take a poke at the baby.

"I moved in on him, and grabbed the spear-haft with my left hand, and hit him in the face with my right. Meanwhile, one of the Amy-johns made a pass for the baby. I just shoved her a little.

"It was very peculiar, the way you have a habit. I shoved her gentle because she was, in a way of speaking, a lady, and I had learned manners back in Baltimore. Here she was, a crocodile-hided, blood-drinking old frow, who had been in her line of business for twenty years, and I caught myself making allowances for a lady.

"She disabused me. She took a swipe at me with her razor-knife and got me in the right leg, a long, jagged swipe. I didn't feel much, but I let her have it. I gave her the butt of the spear in her leathery old bread-basket, and I did not spare honest effort.

"I reckon I was a little crazy by then. I reckon that in my way I wanted some blood, too, by now. I reckon I stood there a few seconds, whirling that spear-haft around and holding off a couple of other razor-women. Then the chaps from *The Sweet Sue* were by me, and fired off a couple of rounds into the ground just underfoot of the pair coming on.

"It wouldn't have done any good against the mob, whatever hot lead we had to offer, but it gave pause. Then one of the head Amy-johns came up. She took my side, to my great surprise, assuming, I reckon, that that rocking chair had put me in special status with Gezo.

"She waved back the pair that had been given pause, took a couple of clouts with a gun-stock at the head of the lady on the ground, the one I had broke-winded with the spear-haft. She clouted so hard that she bounced off a couple of those trophy cowries plastered on the stock with dry blood.

"Then she picked up that black infant, and thrust it at me. I was so surprised I dropped the spear and took it. I just stood there, bleeding down the right leg, with the flames still leaping up from the burning town, but not so high now, and the bats whistling and chirruping in the quiet that had come on just for a second as everybody watched me, and I was damned if I knew what it was all about. Maybe the head Amy-john thought I wanted to eat the brat.

"Well, the bloom was off the party now. The revelry died down. One of the chaps off *The Sweet Sue* bandaged up my leg. It was all right for a few days, moderately sore, but by Agbome, it was swelling bad. By Whidah I was off my head. But they were putting some kind of brew on it and plastering it with farina and a leaf for a plaster, and I pulled through.

"Meanwhile, we had taken on cargo. Not a full one, though, even after all that time and energy. But I ordered the two other brigs to work the Coast south, and I laid course for Cuba. As I say, I didn't have a proper cargo, but I wanted to get into open water."

"My leg never did get good. It makes some difference in a man to have an infirmity come that way, right when you are stoutest and don't give a damn. It's not just that it slows you down.

"The big difference after the trip in was that I felt I had come to the end of nigger-trading. I don't mean that the praying of those Wesleyites did me any good on High. And I knew that nothing I did would change things on that Coast. It was just that I had finished a thing I had had to do, and now I had to do something else.

"It was during that time I got acquainted with Prieur-Denis. A cousin of his in Paris was a great gentleman—oh, yes—but he made secret investments with me. Well, he wrote me a letter saying he had a young cousin who had come to France from New Orleans, who was in debt, was not straight with cards, and was in a business swindle. He was, in general, a personality that would do better on the Gold Coast than in Paris. If fever got him, so much the better.

"So Charles de Marigny Prieur-Denis came to me. And when I left the business I sold him one of my brigs, part on credit, but then he came into his inheritance in Louisiana, and went back.

"I had left the business. I kept just *The Sweet Sue*, and knocked out the slave decks. I tried trading two years in the East. But I came back to the Coast. I simply got drawn back. But now I had a legitimate station and plantation, pineapples, malagetta pepper, yams, pineapples, and such, and traded for palm oil, hides and gold. But nothing felt right, not now.

"Then I got the idea. Or rather, it seemed like one more thing, maybe the last, I had to do. So I wrote Prieur-Denis in New Orleans. I told him I had a most important document to send him. The document was, I said, from his grand kinsman in Paris. And he understood.

"So I came to New Orleans as Hamish Bond, the dear cousin of Charles de Marigny Prieur-Denis. He didn't have much choice. He knew, and knows, that the scandalous document from Paris and the stuff about the Coast are in the hands of a lawyer in New Orleans, to be opened if my death should occur under peculiar circumstances. He doesn't want to be known as a sharper, a swindler, or even a slave-trader. Slave-trading is not respectable. It is just respectable to own them. The more you own the more respectable.

"Yeah, my mother always wanted me to be respectable."

Hamish Bond's voice stopped. For a couple of minutes he said nothing, looking at the ceiling. Then he said: "I've been respectable a long time. I've owned a lot of niggers." He stopped again. Then: "I've always tried to treat them fair."

Then: "None of 'em ever hated me."

But he suddenly raised on an elbow. "Except," he said, "for Rau-Ru." And repeated: "Rau-Ru. You're right, he was the one shot at me. And he had least reason. He was that one that lay there when the town was burning, that new-born baby. He was the one they cut my leg for saving. And I raised him the best I could. Like a son. I swear it."

"What's a *k'la*?" I said.

"A *k'la*," Hamish Bond echoed. "That's a kind of special slave. It's almost like a brother or son or something. It's the one you tell your secrets to. It's the one when you die that dies with you. Maybe they kill him. Maybe he just sits down and dies."

Then, after a little: "A *k'la*, he's sort of like a part of you. He's sort of like another self."

And paused, then said: "Yeah, I reckon that's why he hated me."

I thought of Rau-Ru, and the shot from the green woods. Well, now Hamish Bond could admit it was Rau-Ru.

His voice was saying: "I always reckoned Rau-Ru was a Koromantine. That's the best kind off the Coast. He wasn't the right tribe, but he must have been part. There's a lot of slave-stealing back and forth, in those tribes, and maybe his mother was a Koromantine. I always reckoned so.

"Koromantines, yeah, they're fine-looking, brave, you never saw the like. When there was to be branding, they'd drive their chest on the hot brand-iron, and laugh. Not that I ever branded. You be fair to a Koromantine, and he'll die for you."

I wasn't really listening now. I was thinking, all at once, of something else.

"Michele," I said, "was Michele a slave?"

He did not answer for a minute. Then he said: "I know why you asked that."

I didn't answer. I felt ashamed of myself, somehow.

"If you just had to know," he said, "why didn't you ask long back?"

When, again, I didn't answer, he said: "Well, you're right. It was Michele for a long time. And would have been longer, but I got the notion of marrying. Oh, my fiancée was respectable. But she was poor. And Hamish Bond was rich. But Michele, when I wanted to free her, to sort of make something up to her, she wouldn't do it. She said she would lie down at the door. So she married Jimmee, and stayed. And me—" He paused.

Then continued: "And me, I didn't get married."

"Why?" I asked.

I was surprised at the sound of authority in my voice. I had a feeling that everything was shifting and changing, dancing like the flickering on the ceiling above us, but even in that disorientation, some excitement of power had suddenly grown in me.

"Why?" I demanded.

He waited a long time. "I just don't know," he said, then.

"But I'll tell you this," he added after a little. "I did that girl a wrong. I did her what they say is the worst wrong you can do a nice, young, respectable, Catholic, priest-loving, beautiful, aristocratic Creole girl, and I did it to her the first chance. She was cold as ice, and suffering like a martyr.

"But me, I was cold, too. I did it in cold blood. I was cold as arithmetic, and I did it like I was doing sums. It was something it looked like I had to do, to wind up some business. It was like a revenge. But I don't know for what. She had never done anything to me.

"Then I told her I wasn't going to marry her. She went to a convent. She was that kind."

I waited a while, listening to his breathing, which was heavy and slow, while he stared at the ceiling. It had begun to rain now, just a drizzle at first, but building up steadily. The flickering was fading on the ceiling, as the fires, way off yonder in the city, were wetted out.

"What made you buy me?" I asked, very deliberately.

I had let loose his hand a while back. I was lying apart from him now. I felt cold and detached from everything. I didn't feel like myself. I didn't feel like anybody.

"What made me?" he said.

I thought he would never go on.

But he did: "I just happened to be in there, in the Saint Louis Hotel. I just happened to see you standing up there. You looked so little standing up there. You had your feet set close together, side by side, I noticed. And your arms just hung down straight at your sides."

"What made you buy me?" I demanded again.

"You were standing up there, and I saw that fellow. That fellow who started up to look at you and paw you. Hair greased down and diamond rings on his fingers and turning his toes out. It looked like I couldn't stand it. I just did it."

"Kindness," I said, I don't know with what degree of edge or irony, if any. "Michele said you had it like a disease. That's what she said."

"I used to think it might be kindness," he said. "About you that day, I mean. I wanted to think so. But it wasn't. No, I just saw that fellow going up there, going up there to put his hands on you. Yeah, he was young. And I suddenly felt I couldn't stand it. I wanted to make him draw a knife on me. So I could knock him down."

He paused a minute, then said: "Like it was about Prieur-Denis. I wanted him to do what he did. To you. So I could test something. It was like I had to test it."

He waited. "Yes," he said, "I tried to think it was kindness, or something like that. That day at the Saint Louis."

"Yes, kindness," I said, "and you brought me here. To torture me —yes, to torture me—"

"I tortured myself," he said. "That's what happened. You were here, in the house, and you were so little, and young. All my life just seemed like nothing. I felt old. My leg got to hurting. It hurt at night. I didn't know what to do."

"Oh, you knew how to torture me," I said. "You knew to make me wonder, every day—I didn't know, could I escape, could I be free— and I didn't know what would happen—and every day I felt more caught and desperate—oh, yes, your kindness."

I suddenly sat bolt upright in the bed. Vindictively, I said: "I wish you had beat me. Till the blood came. Then I would have known what to feel."

I could hear his heavy, painful breathing, but I didn't look at him. The breathing stopped an instant. He seemed to be collecting himself. He said: "As soon as I knew how you felt I was ready to send you North. I guess I had always meant to do that. As soon as I could get up my nerve to be by myself, in this house, again. You have to grant me, that, I was going to set you free."

"Free!" I cried out, and some unknown, deeper anguish burst out. "Yes, free. When it was too late—too late."

But I didn't know what had been too late. I just knew the upsurge of the anguish.

"Yes," Hamish Bond said, soberly, "a lot of things come too late."

He reached over and took my hand. I let it lie passive in his grasp.

"Even too late," he said, "maybe it's better than nothing. Maybe nothing is ever too late. If it really comes. Oh, Manty, we're just what we are. Listen, Manty—that day upriver at the landing, at *Pointe du Loup*. That day I was leaving you forever and you ran down the gangplank after me. It looked like to me my life might just begin there. Begin over. Like nothing that had ever happened, had happened. Like it was all a bad dream, when I was a boy and ran away, and all that came after. Oh, Manty, do you know what I mean?"

He pressed my hand, but I said nothing.

"Manty," he murmured. He rolled on his side and reached over to lay his other hand on me.

I jerked my hand free, and pulled back from him.

I guess it was my jerking back that caused it. He seized me. He was kissing me, but it was like he hated me. I struggled against him. But then I stopped struggling, even though I knew I ought to keep struggling against what was so awful, all of a sudden, and degrading. He was rough with me, not like he had ever been before. I was extremely frightened. It was as though there was a confusion of the terrible things he had told me, burning and screams at night, but somehow I was wickedly involved in it, making it come true. But I was extremely frightened.

I cried out, I was so frightened.

# VIII

I SUPPOSE THAT I OWED IT ALL TO GENERAL BUTLER—BEAST BUTLER, as they used to call him in New Orleans, and as far away as London, after his notorious General Order Number 28, that any woman showing contempt for any officer or man of the Federal forces should be treated like a woman of the town plying her vocation. Or to go back a step before, I may have owed it to the New Orleans lady, whoever she was, who got on the horse car—they were really mule cars—one fine spring morning with her little girl. Or back another step, I may have owed it to Flag-Officer Farragut's fine gold braid, which was an invitation to the little girl's fingers, when he sat down beside her. She stroked the braid, and said to her mother, "Look, pretty." At which, the conqueror patted her on the head and called her a dear little child. So the patriot mother spat in his face, and Butler issued the order.

And then one day I came down the street.

It was early autumn, almost six months after the fall of the city, the kind of day in Louisiana when summer lingers and the blossoms of rose montana and bougainvillaea yet loop in tropic brilliance, but the air freshens off the sea and tingles deliciously in the throat like the exacerbation of wine. I was walking down the street, in a kind of dreamlike detachment which, even in those days of the furious excitement around me, made me regard the events of the world almost as something seen through glass. I knew that I did not belong in that world.

I was carrying a parcel in my hand. The parcel contained some fine linen undergarments, two corset-covers, to be exact, which I was to embroider. For now, in my decent little room on a back street, I earned my living after that way. The corset-covers, needless to say, were not the property of Confederate ladies. Not that I would not have accepted a commission from a Confederate lady. The Confederate lady, simply, had no money, and besides, her mind was not likely to be on new vanity, but on the son off in Virginia, or the husband dead at Shiloh—who would never again admire embroidery and toy with corset-laces. No, the corset-covers I carried were to conceal the rigor of whalebone that held in place the loyal Unionist bosoms of ladies of Federal officers.

For more and more, the tone of life set by those as yet unblooded heroes who had come with Butler a week after Farragut's assault was a tone of complacent ease. Let the tide of war roll far away. Upriver, to Baton Rouge, to Port Hudson, to Vicksburg. God had given them victory. As for Butler, he was too busy overawing civilians to commit troops to Farragut's projects.

So I got a chance to embroider new French corset-covers.

When, with my parcel, I turned the corner I found myself face to face, quite unexpectedly, with three Federal soldiers, two tousled red-faced farmer boys, with tunics askew and yellow ringlets shyly showing under manly campaign caps, the third rather the counter-jumping type, a corporal with sharp nose, tight-lipped, pale face, and the cap set mathematically on his head, as on a fence-picket. I almost charged into them, uttered a gasp, and for an instant was frozen to the spot.

The farmer boys were frozen, too. Or, as is more likely, their naturally ruminant responses were a little more deliberate than usual by reason of a morning dose of rum. Anyway, they stood there, flat-footed, unbuttoned, and askew, and stared at me from great round blue eyes, slightly bloodshot. I uttered my gasp, came unfrozen, and jumped off the *banquette*, pulling my hoops aside to let them pass.

The farmer boys mumbled something by way of manners, and one of them gave me a slack, engaging grin, full of gums and teeth. I smiled back, and the encounter was over.

Only, it wasn't.

The pale face of the counter-jumper type was there before me, and a pale finger, quivering in schoolmasterish rage, was pointed into my face, like a pistol.

The pale lips, slightly quivering, too, were saying: "I am a soldier of the United States of America, and you have insulted me!"

My jaw must have dropped wide open. I couldn't say a word.

My accuser swung his face toward his companions. "Look," he exclaimed, "she insulted you!"

The farmer boys looked at him, they looked at me, they looked at each other.

"Stupid!" the pale corporal exclaimed vindictively to them. "Don't you see she insulted you?"

The farmer boys simply grinned, weakly, under that lash of a voice.

"I didn't see nuthin," one of them then said, and shuffled his feet.

The accuser gulped, and made the appeal to reason. "She got off the pavement," he demanded, "didn't she?"

The farmer boys nodded.

"Well," the accuser said, setting the nail-head deep in the wood of argument.

But one of the farmer boys had had time to think it over. "Maybe she jist aimed to git by," he said.

That was too much for the pale corporal. I thought he was going to faint. But he mastered himself and went back to first principles. "Listen," he asked, "this is New Orleans, isn't it?"

They nodded.

"If this—if she—" and he looked at me with a shudder of loathing, "if she lives here, she is Secesh, isn't she? She is a rebel, and if she is a rebel, she owns niggers and thinks she is a lady, and if she thinks she is a lady, she thinks you are scum, Yankee scum, and a lady don't get off the sidewalk, oh, no, not for anybody, don't you know that—or don't you know that?"

But he couldn't wait for it to sink in.

"And if she got off for you, she means you are scum and she wouldn't touch you. And she wouldn't touch me—"

He had forgotten all about the farmer boys. He was sticking the finger in my face again, shaking it, saying, "Yes, you—you think I'm scum—scum!"

I was trying to say something. In fact, there was too much to say. The craziness of the comedy was mounting in me. If the idiot only knew me. Me, a slave, an ex-slave with precious manumission papers, me, a nigger, a nigger gal Old Bond had cut down, me, a child of bondage this man had come to set free. I must have been about to burst out laughing at the craziness.

"So, you'll laugh at me!" he screamed. "Well, I'll teach you, you—you whore!"

And he seized my left arm.

So I slapped him. It was a good round, ringing smack, solid on his cheek, and I gave a grunt when I hit him, I hit him so hard, and when I took my hand away, there was a rosy glow on the pale cheek. I felt suddenly gay, like giggling. It was a strange, funny sense of tightness, then release; as though I had, after minutes, hours, years —how long?—broken out of a stupor, a spell.

As I said I felt gay, but I knew it was very serious.

It began to be awful. He grabbed me by the other arm, too. He said I was arrested. He said I was an insulting rebel whore. He was shaking me, hard. Then I heard the voice.

Then the voice said: "Corporal! Attention!"

But the corporal did not let go.

Then that wonderful, clear, ringing, bugle-loud, beautiful, strong voice: "Corporal, release that woman. Release her, or I'll see you under court-martial!"

The voice broke through the corporal's rage. The hands came off me. The corporal stood at attention. His face was whiter than before, the nostrils were twitching, the lips were twitching. Then the lips managed to say, "I was acting under General Order 28, sir."

"General Order 28 does not authorize you to commit mayhem upon ladies," the voice said, and I turned my head a little, and there he was, at least all I caught of him in that moment, a tallish figure, blue-clad, slender, erect, broad-shouldered, young, a captain, with flashing eyes.

"I was arresting her," the corporal said. And his hysteria began to return, he leaned forward, he pointed at me. "She insulted me!" he almost screamed.

"At attention!" the captain ordered.

The poor corporal pulled himself up, shaking.

The captain was addressing the farmer boys. "Did this lady insult you?" he asked.

The farmer boys thought it over. "No, sir," one of them finally said. "She was jist aimin to git by, best I figger."

Back to the corporal, the captain turned, asked for name and command, wrote down the information.

I watched the corporal's white, twitching face, and all at once I thought that whatever long rancor and outrage in him had made him burst out at me, was now confirmed forever by that pure, bugle-toned voice, the voice of easy command and clear certainty of the handsome captain, the voice so unlike the corporal's nasal and rage-ragged own.

But the handsome captain was turning to me. "Madam," he said, "you may be called upon to make a statement."

I was suddenly weak in the knees, disarrayed. "Oh, sir," I said, "just let him go—I just want to go home—you see, I was going home—"

I was aware of another figure that had suddenly stepped up beside the captain, from behind me, and was peering earnestly at my face, under my bonnet brim. I was so upset that I just saw the blur of a face, no more. Then the voice cried out: "Oh, Manty!—Miss Starr!"

The voice, and the face, were Seth Parton. It was the first time he had ever called me Manty.


They saw me home, Tobias Sears, of Litchfield, Massachusetts, graduate of Harvard College, a captain, aide to General Benjamin Butler, and Seth Parton, of New Hope Corners, Ohio.

Seth no longer had his old piece of Oberlin drugget about his shoulders, no longer had snow melting down on his bare head, no longer wore poor, old, heartbreaking boots to offend a tidy parlor carpet or crunch the snow. He was a lieutenant now, his long neck now military out of the trim collar, not gawky now, his high, bony face with the air of command now as well as spiritual aloofness.

But it was, I suppose, the ghost of the other Seth, the Seth with the drugget and the snow-damp hair, that made me feel safe again as we walked down the street, that made my heart stir with a nameless hope.

It was different as soon as they had left me at my door, or rather, as soon as I had entered and closed the door behind me. I heard their boot heels on the paving of the patio. I heard the last scrap of their voices. Then I faced the dingy room, the couch in the corner with its tawdry chintz, the creaky chair, the carpet, the little safe where

I kept my eatables, the brazier where I cooked, the oil lamp by which I leaned in the evenings to do embroidery for ladies.

I had lived here in this room, lived some kind of life, and had never noticed it. But now every object rose up in miserable mockery. Oh, why had my eyes been opened? Opened to an unhappiness that I could not name.

I wished they had never interfered with me and the pale, rage-bit corporal. A cell would be better than this, and all contempt. They had saved me, only to walk away, happy and discoursing together, dear friends together, leaving me.

Then I thought of the corporal again, and my distress, and sense of bitter comedy, returned. I remembered how when old John Brown of Kansas had raided Harper's Ferry the first man he killed was a free Negro. Oh, the Southern papers had made much of that! Suddenly, everything that had ever happened in the world, all history, seemed nothing but a savage comedy.

I went to rummage in a valise and take out the papers, the manumission papers, that Hamish Bond had made out so long ago, before we went to *Pointe du Loup*. They had been in the brown envelope which he thrust into my hand as he took leave of me on the *Pride of Cincinnati*, as she swung in toward the landing for *Pointe du Loup*. But that first night at *Pointe du Loup*, I had laid the envelope on the table in the hall. That was the last I ever saw of it until the morning in May, a week or so after the fall of New Orleans, when I took my leave of Hamish Bond. He gave me the envelope then.

Now I looked at the papers. They specified my name, condition, and provenance, and declared me now, after all, free.

Free—from what? For what?

I lay down on the faded chintz of the couch, and could have wept. I had the wild impulse to get up and run out and seek Hamish Bond. He might take me in the crook of his arm and be gentle with me.

The night of April 23, 1862, was the night when Farragut ran the forts, and the next night was the night of the riot and fires, and the night when Hamish Bond lay by my side, under the flame-flickered ceiling, and dreamed back to the old fury, and then seized me with that violence that had made my heart stop.

Afterward, he had plunged into sleep, as one might plunge over a precipice, or plunge into a black water. The breath drew in and out of his bulk with a grinding, irregular râle.

Still shaking—shaking with what, with cold, with fear?—I rose and flung on a wrapper and went out of the room. I wandered about the house, numbly, touching an object here, an object there, as though to assure myself of what familiarity there was in life, stopping dead still now and then in the middle of a room. But there was no sound except, faint and far off, the last twitching disorder of the vanquished under the dawn rain.

That wet, gray light grew in the house. I found myself huddling, at last, in the darkest room, the study, where the jalousies were closed tight, huddling in a big chair, huddling in the last dark, while the brass of the great ship-compass strove to draw to focus the dull light, and the crooked wickedness of those blades that bedecked the walls began, soberly, to glint. The rain was steady beyond the jalousies.

In many houses in the city, behind the closed jalousies, people must have huddled that morning, sleepless, dry-eyed with grief, sick with some deep, ineffable wound to the spirit, and to vanity, waiting for light to grow and the black hulls to move upriver. The ships would come, and they, the people who had been free, would be free no longer. But at that moment I was not thinking of their suffering. I was thinking of my own suffering, my disarray of spirit, my disorientation and fear, even as the forces of my liberation were moving upriver under the rain-gray dawn.

It was mid-morning when I woke. I was still in the chair.

There was Michele. I noticed that a light shawl had been laid across me. I thanked her.

She shrugged. "Don't thank me," she said. "I did not even see you here."

As I fingered the shawl, she went out, closing the door behind her. I did not know what to feel about the fact that Hamish Bond had come in—had, no doubt, hunted me in the house—and had covered me. I shut my eyes and thought of Hamish Bond standing there, looking down at me asleep.

But it wasn't Hamish Bond. It was Alec Hinks. Alec Hinks was his name.

Then I realized what had just now waked me. It was cannonade, nearer. "Michele! Michele!" I cried, and ran to the door.

She came down the hall, toward me. "Don't be afraid," she said, and took my hands.

"What is it?" I demanded.

"Chalmette," she said. "They have come, and they are firing cannon at the little fort at Chalmette."

It was not long before the firing stopped.

Michele was right, it developed. The earthworks at Chalmette, disposed so as to impede an overland advance between the river and swamp toward the city, where Pakenham's redcoats had once been slaughtered in another old war, were of little use against the water-borne batteries of Farragut. When the fleet made the bend and came within the half-mile range, the little 32-pounders of Chalmette, supported by the neatly arrayed infantry, had opened. The fleet drew on, slowly, then gave the first broadside. So it continued, until the last of the ammunition at Chalmette was burned. The supporting Confederate troops there disappeared toward Lafourche, and the long line of ships, whose pace had scarcely slackened, moved on.

This much from Hamish Bond, when he got home late in the afternoon. Later I heard that only one man of the fleet had been hurt, for all that expense of Confederate gunpowder. He had been whiffed overboard by the breath of a passing shell. They fished him out.

As soon as the fleet passed Chalmette, the Mayor ran up the flag of Louisiana on the City Hall, the red-white-and-blue stripes and the big, pale yellow star in a red field.

"There was that durn mob on the levee," Hamish said, "and all the burned-out hulks—those that hadn't floated down, and the busted molasses barrels, and the busted rum barrels, and the last, black, half-burned cotton bales that the rain hadn't quite put out, and the rain was getting set to begin again. That durn mob just stood there, jam-packed, and not a sound. It was so quiet you could have heard a corset stave creak if a lady drew breath. It was like that, waiting.

"Then they came, coming in line, and not a sound off those ships, the crews lined up like inspection, and the guns laid level out, and the gunners holding the lanyards. The river was just sliding by greasy like brown beef gravy, high water near levee-top, and the ships, all thirteen of 'em, sliding up past the levee, steady as a funeral. It began to rain again, hard. Thunder, a-sudden, like cannon, and lightning right on your head.

"Then from upriver she came. It was the *Mississippi*. Oh, yeah, we were going to build a ram that nothing could sink, the biggest ram in the world, covered with iron, and it would sweep the river. Nothing could withstand her. And here she came. Adrift, and afire, flame standing up forty feet in the rain and the lightning, the durn thing blazing like a grate full of coal.

"The crowd sort of bunched together. And then, the howl. It was like one single howl out of all those throats. You know when a hound sits back on his tail and gives a moon-howl, and all hope gone. Well, this was it, you multiply by a million, and it didn't look like it would ever stop. That was their God-durned last crazy hope floating by."

And Hamish Bond took another drink of the glass of brandy, and looked over beyond me, as though I weren't there at all, and beyond the wall of the study.

Then: "They had figured on cotton. They had figured on forts. They had figured on the river-boom. They had figured on the *Mississippi,* and nothing could sink her."

He stopped, then said: "They just never figured on something inside themselves."

He stopped again, looking beyond me.

Then: "That howl didn't stop till she was round Slaughterhouse Point. She yawed round the Point, broadside and blunderbuss to the current, still blazing.

"But there wasn't a sound, not a sound, off Farragut.

"He anchored off, thirteen ships, two hundred and fifty guns, or nigh, not more'n half-pistol-shot and a spit offshore, guns looking straight in the first-story windows of every house back of the levee, the ships laying in bow-and-quarter line, broadside available.

"It must have been one o'clock, by then."

Hamish sank back into himself, set down his brandy glass, and took a bite of his sandwich of cold meat and bread. He had had no food all day. With a couple of others of the defense committee, he had gone to the Mayor's office when Farragut sent ashore his demand for surrender.

A Captain Bailey and some lieutenant, I didn't catch his name, even if Hamish mentioned it, came ashore to the levee. The mob yelled and hooted and shook their fists, Hamish said, and the little boat came on, and the two officers got out. They stood there on the levee in the rain, in the middle of the hoots and the fist-shaking and the shotgun-waving and pistol-waving. The mob shouted, "Hang 'em!" and shouted, "Kill 'em!" The mob followed on down the street after the two officers, hurrahing for Jefferson Davis and General Beauregard.

They just followed in the rain, on behind the fat captain and the young lieutenant, who didn't know their way in the strange town, yelling to hang them.

"Heroes," Hamish said. "Yeah, saving the country and yelling. And then we got to the office, there was old Monroe"—Monroe was the Mayor then, and again after the war—"and Captain Bailey asked for surrender of the city, and old Monroe, he started hemming and hawing like a lawyer, saying he was just a mayor and the city was under martial law, they'd have to ask General Lovell, and so they sent for General Lovell, and meanwhile Pierre Soulé made everybody a lecture on international law, and the mob was beating on the doors and yelling to hang 'em.

"Lovell finally got there, riding down the street the way he always does, with so much stirrup leather he can stand straight up and show off—that little banty rooster of a general. He said he never would surrender. Oh, no! But he said he would get out of town, and Mayor Monroe could do what he liked.

"What he liked," Hamish repeated. "What do you like when two hundred guns are looking down your throat? One broadside from Farragut, and this town would be like the nub of a dandelion after you blow the fuzz off.

"I just left. It got so I couldn't stand all that talking."

Hamish never went back, but they kept on talking for nearly a week. They talked in the Mayor's office and they talked on the deck of Farragut's ship. Monroe wouldn't lower the flag, and Farragut said he would bombard the city, for Monroe to evacuate women and children, and Monroe said that was impossible, you couldn't get them out, and for Farragut to go ahead and be a butcher if he wanted. Meanwhile, in spite of the fact that negotiations were in progress, a Federal detachment came ashore and, unopposed, ran down the Louisiana flag on the Mint Building, the red-white-and-blue flag with the one big yellow star, and put up their own, and a crowd gathered. As soon as the detachment had left, a man named Mumford climbed up and took it down. The crowd tore up the new flag for souvenirs. It was for this that later on Mumford got hanged.

In the end, of course, Farragut had his way.

But that was all to come later. Meanwhile, the talk went on, talk about the surrender.

"Surrender," Hamish said, "what in damnation's name are they talking about? Like a bankrupt man borrowing money to hire a lawyer to make his will."

He stood in the middle of the floor of the study, bulky and dour, his secret anger coiling deep within him—anger, but anger at what? —anger and the dour satisfaction that something was proved now— something, something he had always wanted proved. "Fools!" he said, and struck the floor with his blackthorn.

But I scarcely heard his words.

It was the afternoon of the last day of that week of talk and bicker about the surrender. All that week I had scarcely seen Hamish Bond. Every day, he had gone out into the town, leaving before I came out of my room. For I had come again to my room the night after the riot and fires, and had shut the door and bolted it—bolted it as for the first time, ever—but there had been no step and tap in the hall, all night.

It was now a strange parody of the early times in this house, the time of my languors and fears, of hope for escape and fears that were like hopes, the time when all my plans and efforts had been, deep inside me, like the jerks and spin of a June bug on a thread to amuse a child, and I had known, most deeply, that the days, and nights, glided like doom.

The days and nights were gliding by now, too. During the day I might see Hamish Bond, but I would scarcely hear what he said, because of a deep, distracting process going on in me, and at night I would lie in the dark, by myself, my door locked, afraid but not specifying what I was afraid of, afraid simply, in a way, of endings and beginnings, but afraid of something else, too, and I would hear the voice of Hamish Bond again, as I had heard it on this bed a few nights before, telling what had happened to Alec Hinks, and I would see the flicker of flame on the ceiling again, flame of the ships and cotton burning, far off, and the cries of the mob, or flame of the nameless village in the jungle, and the screams. I would remember what had happened on this bed, remember that heavy-bulked, raw-handed, stertorous, brutal stranger—the raw hand seizing my hair, compelling me, that compulsion outside me evoking some new compulsion inside, like a terror. And, remembering now, I would be filled with my shivering shame and defilement, even in broad daylight as I stood before him, before Alec Hinks, scarcely hearing his voice.

"Surrender," he said, again, "lawyer's talk, and two hundred guns charged and shotted and looking at you—and did you ever see what a broadside can do?—and they talk, and talk, and try to save something, some fool notion in their heads." And again he struck the floor.

I could hear his breathing.

"Why can't a man—" he demanded, but stopped in the middle of the question. Then resumed: "Why can't a man just see a fact? Just the fact he's ruined, say, the fact something's over, the fact all he ever did is nothing, nothing—why can't he just see the fact, and him just say, well, that's that? Say that, and maybe feel free."

He was looking down at me, and his eyes began to shine a little in the shadowy room.

"Stop talking and forget it," he said.

Then he took a step toward me. I knew what he was going to do.

"Just plain forget," he was saying, and took another step.

I knew how it would be. So I said, "Don't," but he had his hand on me. He dropped the stick on the floor. I heard the thump. Then he was on the couch with me.

I said, don't, and I told him not to, please not, but it didn't do any good. I was, quite literally, terrified of what he was doing, all that dishevelment and tearing of cloth and wrenching of me.

Then I cried out, "Oh, I know—I know—it's just you want to make a nigger of me—that's what you want—a nigger—a nigger—like those niggers you had, off yonder in Africa—oh, you want to make me filthy like them!"

For a moment, even after my words had stopped, I kept on struggling. I guess his hands were still on me, still gripping, perhaps, but they were no longer forcing me. He was looking at me, in a peculiar way, as though I had struck him and he was defenseless.

Then I realized that his force had just drained away. All at once, I saw that his face looked like an old man. It was funny, how it was still his face, full-fleshed and heavy-jawed and ruddy, in the last flush of strong life, but you saw how it would be when very old. It was as though twenty more years happened, were happening, in a flash, under your gaze.

His hands had dropped away from me.

He was looking at me as though he had never seen me before. Then he lifted his left hand, not saying anything, and made a gesture of repudiation, a slight backhand wave as though to say, begone, but he too weak, somehow, for the words.

Then, in a hoarse, throaty voice, not much more than a whisper, he said: "Go away."

I went out of the room quietly, almost on tiptoe.

Upstairs, on my balcony, I looked out over the city. It was about sunset. I felt very calm now, drained and tired. I looked down at my torn and disordered clothing. I made some perfunctory efforts to straighten myself.

I stood there quite a while, looking out over the city, as light failed. I saw the flag off yonder on the City Hall, the one the victors had run up after Mumford's vainglorious exploit. It hung torpid in that late light.

It was Dollie who came to fetch me, quite a while later. "Say fer 'ee to come down," she said.

"Thank you," I said. Yes, there was nothing to be afraid of now. Nothing except my own blankness.

"Ain't long now," she said, " 'fore nobody gonna say come, and nobody gonna say go. Naw, Lawd, gonna be parlor-time, gonna be rockin-cheer time, set in de parlor, rock and fan. Fedder-fan. Dis Lawd's chile."

I didn't say anything.

"And you," she said, "ain't long 'fore you won't have to lay on de bed fer ole him."

She kept on looking at me, as though to read something. "But sojers," she said. "Dey done come. Come totin freedom. Come drippin freedom, lak sweat and a hot day." She stopped, cocked her head on one side, peered into my face. "Sojers," she said, "ain't you seen them pretty sojers marchin?"

"Shut up!" I burst out at her, and ran from the room.

When I entered the study, Hamish was standing in the middle of the floor. He motioned me to a chair. Then, with the tone of dry impersonal announcement, he said, "Manty, it's time for you to go."

I made some motion in my chair, and he lifted his hand as though to stop any remark. But I had not been about to say anything. I suppose that my movement was simply a way of my body's saying, *Ah, here it is.* I had not said it to myself. I had simply known it.

He stumped over to the big Empire desk, garlanded and scrolled with the rich bronze, and fumbled in a pocket for a key, and opened a drawer. From the drawer he took a metal box, unlocked it, and took out a brown envelope. He came and placed it in my hands.

"The papers," he said. Then added, drily: "I don't reckon you'll need 'em forever."

I held the envelope in my hand.

He said, "Oh, I forgot," and went back to the desk. From the metal box he laid papers out on the desk, then picked up a little bag, a chamois bag. He came, and stood before me.

He opened the bag, and took out a coin. He held it up between thumb and forefinger.

"Look," he commanded, "that's gold." Then said: "Look good, for it's the one thing no matter who wins a war or who loses a war, it don't change. It's the one God-blessed, God-durned thing nothing ever happens to in this world."

He dropped the coin back into the bag. There was the minute, solid chink of the metal finding contact with metal. He drew the strings of the bag. "Take it," he said, and thrust the bag at me.

"It's not any fortune," he said, glumly, "but it'll help you start." He looked down at the bag in my hand. "No," he said, musing, "not much. That's why I don't really figure why I held it out. You see," he said, "I put what I had in Confederate. Yeah, I did that. Win or lose, I did it. Something in me just made it that way. I put it all, except this." He paused, still studying the bag in my hands. "It don't make sense," he said, shaking his head. "Just to hold out that much. Why don't I hold out a lot, to do me some good? Or nothing? But, no—just this piddling much."

He brooded a moment, on the bag. "Funny," he said, "I always reckoned I was a fellow when he did something, did it all out. I led a rough life, and one sure way to be laying face down in the bush, or floating face up in the Bight, was to do something halfway. Yeah, from the time I saw my mother's face freeze up white with the yell still hanging in her round mouth, and I went out the door and never came back, I never aimed to do anything halfway. But this"—he pointed at the bag—"just halfway."

Then: "It looks like a man is just going to hold a little something back. Just to be holding."

Then: "Even a fellow marches right into the cannon. He can be holding something back, too. Even when he takes the grape in the belly."

Then: "Yeah, even him."

Then: "That stuff—that gold—get it out of the house. I reckon I'm glad you're getting it out."

He lifted his head, suddenly. "Listen," he said, with an abrupt change to the tone of business, "this is what you do. Pack one valise. Jimmee will carry it for you. You go to the Saint Charles, or the Saint Louis, and get a room. Say you are from up in Tennessee, or somewhere, and your brother was at Shiloh, and you heard he was wounded and sent down here. Then tomorrow you go out and get yourself a room somewhere. You got to wait till things quiet down before you head North. A young girl hasn't got much business trying to get through picket lines, no matter whose picket lines, and if you stay at a hotel, that gold will be gone like a snowball in August. Do you understand?"

I nodded.

"I'll send Jimmee to the hotel tomorrow with your other valise and stuff."

I nodded again.

"Now, go."

I got up, and stood there, holding the little bag in my hand. I didn't feel anything. I knew there was something I ought to feel. But I didn't know what. I stood there, and I saw a part of my life whirl away, like a leaf blowing in the wind, and I didn't feel anything.

"Go," he said. "Go on!"

I went to the door, slowly.

Just as I laid hand on the doorknob, he spoke. "Listen," he said, now in that grinding, gravelly, constricted voice, "wherever you go, whatever you do, I don't want to know. Do you understand? I don't want to know where you are."

I was in the hall, before the feeling came. Was that all, was that all to take away now? Was there nothing of any tenderness in the dark, any protective peace? In my despair, I suddenly felt that this was like dying with nothing, oh nothing, to take away.

Then I became aware of the little chamois bag in my hand. Well, I could take that, I thought bitterly.

A little later, in the upper hall, I encountered Dollie. I was about to step past her, when she reached out to touch my sleeve, saying, "Yeah, Jimmee—he done tole me."

"Told you what?" I demanded.

" 'Bout Old Bond," she said, " 'bout him sendin you off."

"Yes," I said, irritably, anxious to get her hand off my sleeve.

"Gonna be free?" she demanded.

"I guess so," I said.

She looked intently at me, peering in the shadowy hall. Then she demanded: "Me—you reckin I'm gonna be free?"

"I don't know," I said, and pulled away, and turned down the hall.

But she ran after me, seizing my arm, saying, "Free—you git free —but doan fergit ole Dollie. Fer I ne'er meant nuthin. Nuthin agin you ner nobody. I jes wants you to love me."

And with that, she burst into tears, staring up at me beseechingly, her eyes wide and the tears running down the cheeks.

Something seemed to break in my bosom, quite literally. And I heard my voice say: "I love—I do love you!"

And then my own tears came, and I turned and ran from her.

So I left the house of Hamish Bond and found my dingy room, in the dingy patio, and waited. I did not know what I was waiting for. For things to quiet down, Hamish Bond had said, so I could go away. But where? Where would I go? Where would I belong?

I stood in the street, and saw the raw jostle of life. I saw the victors move bright and clattering, hoof and steel. I saw those who had once been masters now move with the sullen down-glance of the enslaved. I saw those who had been enslaved standing on the street corner, just standing all afternoon in that delicious emptiness of sunshine. On May 1, when the transports of troops came up the river, and General Butler disembarked, there was the great crowd of Negroes on the levee. There was the laughter, the high giggle, the shove and scuffle, the cry, "Amen! Lawd God, amen!"

Ah, Jubilo.

I saw men, or women, under the guard of troops, marched down the street to the Custom House and the trial—if you could call it that—before Butler's military commission.

I saw them hang Mumford.

He was the man who had, before the settled surrender and occupation, pulled down the United States flag from the Mint Building. Butler had sworn to hang him. "You better catch him first," Farragut had said, thinking it all a joke.

But it was no joke.

In June Butler hanged him. He offered so many justifications, did

Butler. Mumford was really a gambler, and you had to put down vice. If he didn't hang Mumford, the mob would think he was unable to govern. He had been threatened with assassination if he hanged Mumford, and he had to prove his contempt of such a threat. He had to hang Mumford to defend the honor of the flag.

But later, when I met General Butler, it crossed my mind that none of the justifications made sense, or enough sense. I saw him, a shapeless man of indeterminate middle age, and stooped middle height, the dress uniform sacklike on him, the gold braid too important, the last thin gray hair brushed back over his somewhat flattened, shiny skull, the thin compressed lips slightly twitching at the corners of the mouth, the face white and almost hairless, the hazel eyes cockeyed and disturbing, never still, the hands restless and plucking. Yes, he had to hang Mumford. He would, no doubt, have hanged the entire world if there had been neck and rope for the job.

So Butler hanged him. The scaffold was in front of the Mint, where Mumford had exhibited his bravado, and the mob had cheered. Now the mob was silent, facing the hollow square of fixed bayonets, and the muzzle of cannon. Mumford, handcuffed, wearing a white suit, carrying his head high, marched up the steps of the scaffold. He conferred briefly with a clergyman. The officer in charge read the sentence. Mumford addressed the people. The drop fell, a communal groan was uttered. The white-clad body swayed, then was still. The drums were beating.

At first, it all seemed like a show to me, on a stage. I was far back, on the very fringe of the crowd, and I was not tall enough to see very well. I saw the figures up there, black for the clergyman, blue for captain, white for Mumford. I could barely catch a word now and then of the reading of the sentence, or what Mumford said, which was, as people later declared, very dignified and brave, and up there the figures were little, like dolls. When the white-clad body fell and jerked, I was sure that it wouldn't hurt, a little old wooden doll, way off yonder, jerking.

Then I knew that it did hurt. All the waiting for it, and then the moment. Oh, what did it all mean? Had Mumford felt that it meant something? Or had his words been empty even to himself, standing up there, talking, sweating, desperately wondering if it was he, really he, who had climbed the flagstaff, really not believing that it was he who had taken down that rag of color? Oh, what were those colored rags men put on sticks and made music under, and died following, in the smoke?

I was full of a sadness, because it all seemed so far away, so little.

Then my sadness was, all at once, a grinding misery, deep in me. I was miserable not because there was no meaning to put against the sweating and the pain, but because there was, perhaps, a meaning. But a meaning that somehow I could not understand.

Oh, that was my misery! I was outside some meaning that other people had, even if only for a moment—Mumford at the moment of his fine words, the crowd at the moment of the communal groan, all the nameless ones plunging through the smoke-swirl, the nameless ones lying on last sickbed, watching the dawn-window grow gray, with a calmly growing, incredulous joy for the first, peevish bird, the last they would ever hear.

I had a strange dream that night. I saw Mumford. He came to me wearing his white suit, somewhat stained and disheveled. Around his neck was the great noose, still tight, but with a frayed end hanging loose down his left shoulder. The noose was set deep in the flesh of his neck, and the flesh was raw and bruised, but his face was calm. He had something to tell me, he said, and laid his hands on me. He began to make love to me, and I felt the expectation of joy, but, suddenly, somehow, he was like Charles, Charles Prieur-Denis when he had seized me that last day in the hall of the house at *Pointe du Loup,* and I woke ready to cry out.

But next day the figure of Mumford was only the memory of that little white-clad puppet, way off yonder, jerking on the end of a string, and I was living my life as best I could, and watching the life around me.

People hummed "The Bonnie Blue Flag," and went to jail, or wore the Confederate colors, red and white, and went to jail, or whispered Confederate victories, and went to jail, and the blue troops swung past in formation, sun on bayonets, or lounged in front of groggeries, full of strychnine-whisky—"damnation," people called it—or simple rum.

Runaway Negroes—*contraband,* Butler had named them, back in Virginia—crowded into the lines, into the city, groping toward what, toward freedom. But were they free? Nobody had said they were. And Butler ordered that no more be admitted through the lines, had even sent some back in chains, from Lake Pontchartrain, to Confederate masters. But they kept on coming, like a tide. They starved in the back streets, squatting in mud or dust, according to season, stretching out the hand, waiting.

Butler—and his brother who came down to help in a business way, so people said—got rich, licensing gambling, licensing groggeries, buying confiscated cotton cheap from the government agent under his command and shipping it North at war prices, taking share-money of debts collected for Northern creditors, smuggling supplies to the enemy.

People whispered that Confederate pickets—lanky, gray ghosts squatting at the swamp-edge or sitting gaunt hammer-heads in the dappled shadow of live oak—were only ten miles out of town.

There was much destitution in the city. In a miserable room opening on the patio where I lived, was a woman with three small children. Her husband had been killed near Corinth. I gave her one of the gold pieces. Later, when I had the embroidery, I set a little money aside each time, a few pennies, for the children. I felt I was buying something, something almost illicit, for myself.

So the summer passed.

Then all was different. But it is strange how a new quality of feeling, of your life, may be defined, unawares, by its very opposite. So it was when Seth Parton and his friend left me alone in my room. My sudden despair, the sense of absolute isolation from life—all this was, I suppose, a perfectly logical thing to happen.

After all, Seth had been the object of my first, and only, girlish passion and dream, and his reappearance, and turning away, simply re-enacted my old story. But he not only re-enacted, and took away, the meaning of my past. He took with him, their heads bowed together in an intense colloquy, the hope of my future—or rather, the image of what must have been a secret, unacknowledged hope, the fine shoulders, the flashing glance, the bugle voice, the air of command of the liberator. Captain Tobias Sears had descended from the glittering cloud to save me, had saved me, but then had faded with a smile of Godlike casualness, worse than contempt.

But that despair on the faded chintz of the couch was the birth of hope. I discovered in it that I could live no longer without hope. I suppose that I had snuggled into my isolation, and even as I suffered from it had felt it also as a protection from the raw risks of the unhinged world I saw around me. Now I lay on that couch while the day wore out, and light faded, the baby next door wailed in its unassuageable, feeble grief, two soldiers, drunk, wandered into the courtyard, laughing, and one pressed his face against the bars of my window, and stared at me lying there, and I saw it was a Negro face, and did not even feel alarm or anger, and then the face was withdrawn, and at last I fell asleep. I slept till morning.

I was very calm when I woke up. I felt weak, but weak and pure, as you feel after an illness, and ready for life.

Tobias Sears called on me that afternoon.

He came, he said, to get me to sign a statement about the episode of the corporal. I said that I didn't want any trouble for the fellow. He said there wouldn't be much trouble, that the corporal had a splendid record in battle and would have had a commission long ago if he had been able to control his nerves and his temper. "It's a peculiar type," he said, "so nervous and angry, he's made for war and war's made for him, the kind that's a hero in battle. But when the war is over he'll go back to Illinois, or whatever place he came from, and whatever small occupation, and he will die young of dyspepsia."

In the end, I signed the paper.

He lingered a while, I continued to work at my embroidery, telling him frankly that it was a commission promised for tomorrow, and would he forgive me? He sat on his rickety chair and looked out of place in the dingy room. I made no apologies. Not even when, after he had lingered a long time, I offered him what purported to be tea, but wasn't, and was offered in a cracked cup.

He talked about Emerson. He asked me if I had read the essay on Transcendentalism, and when I confessed ignorance, he said that I must, that he would bring it to me.

Two days later he brought it, and again sat on the rickety chair and drank the vile infusion which was not tea. When he rose to go, he asked when he might come for his book. He should like also, he said, to know my views.

As I hesitated, his face suddenly broke into a warm, boyish smile. "Miss Starr," he said, "you see through my poor pretenses. I do not want the book back. I want you to have it. What I really want is to see you again."

I hesitated a moment. I wanted to see him again, I wanted that very much, but out of that new calmness of spirit I had to assess, even though fleetingly, the context of my own desire.

As I hesitated, he said, "Please," and again flashed that boyish smile at me.

I did not return the smile. "Captain Sears," I said, "you have already done something very important for me. No," I said, as he seemed about to interrupt in deprecation, "I don't mean the matter of the corporal. What you have really done for me is greater, and is my secret. And I shan't deny that I should like to see you again. But if I properly read your character, it is possible that you might enter upon a"—here I imagine I hesitated, in my own mind at least, on the word—"upon a friendship with me, with a false assumption. Therefore—"

"Miss Starr—Miss Starr," he broke in, "I assure you—you do me a wrong—I assure you—" His face was scarlet. He was leaning at me a little, his military bearing gone, and I thought that I detected a sudden perspiration on his brow.

He was a tallish man, broad-shouldered for all his litheness, and I am not even average in height, but suddenly I felt that I had touched some secret spring that gave me power over him. My heart leaped.

I stopped him with my lifted hand. "No," I said, "it is now you who do me a wrong. For I impute no baseness to your motive, if that is what you imply. Captain Sears, there are some persons who perform an act from simple decency, and then because of that act feel committed to the person who has received their kindness. I would not have you feel so about me. For I think that now I can live without help. Somehow—I don't really know how, Captain Sears—you did that for me, you made me realize that I could live. So you see, Captain Sears, you need do no more for me. But for what you have done"—and I put out my hand to him—"in all gratitude I thank you."

My speech, I would swear it, was without calculation. But I am sure that the shrewdest calculation of event, and of the soul of Tobias Sears, could not have been better designed to bring on what I most deeply desired. I wonder if it is paradoxical to say that my releasing Tobias Sears from the bondage of his own magnanimity worked in him such a secret relief, and gush of gratitude, that he had to prove his magnanimity all over again, had to prove it to himself, to be himself, the self that stood forever beautiful, naked, and pure, like a white marble statue, in his innermost eye? For if Hamish Bond, as Michele had said, had kindness like a disease, then Tobias

Sears, I might hazard, had nobility like a disease. And if once you know what secret disease of virtue a person has in him, then you have more power over him than if you had spied his most concealed and disgraceful vice.

Anyway the effect of my speech on the captain was extraordinary. When I offered him my hand, he seized it and leaned—no, *leaned* isn't the word, his knees seemed to bend and give too, and the fine shoulders hunched a little. He kissed my hand several times, with extreme fervor, no, not with fervor—with a cold wildness, but a wildness on leash.

Then he straightened up and was, all at once, himself. "Miss Starr," he said, "when I come again, you can be sure on what terms I come. And when I come"—here he gave me that high smile that had such sweetness and wisdom in it—"I should like to hear your views of the book. I really should, you know."

With that, he saluted, with a faint touch of self-conscious comedy in the act, of gaiety, and was gone.

When, after his first visit, he had left, the articles of my room had risen before me in an anguish of ugliness. Now, as I stood there in the first moment of being alone, each object, the chair, the couch, the table, the empty cup, seemed to glow, with a subdued, inward incandescence. It was as though a secret light were being shed from everything, on me.

I went to the chair he had sat in, laid my fingers on the back, gingerly, as though afraid of some start of sensation. Then I sat down in the chair. The teacup was on the little table beside me. I picked it up, turned it slowly in my hand to look at it, then I placed my lips to it, where his had been.

I set the cup down, and looked at my hand, the right hand, the one he had kissed. All the while I supported in it my left hand as though it were precious, or injured. The preciousness, the sweet injury, seemed to flow out from it over my entire body. In a funny way, my entire body felt bruised. I looked at my hand, and saw him leaning over it, and thought: *oh, he is beautiful.* And that beauty seemed to flow into, and involve, me.

For four days I was alone. But all that while my mood did not change. I walked through my days, and slept through my nights, in perfect certainty of joy. On the fourth day Seth Parton came.

If the old Seth Parton, rag of drugget on shoulders, broken boots, on feet, snow melting on his head, had appeared miraculously before me, I don't know what I would have felt. My new joy might have seemed like a betrayal of that old moment in the Turpin parlor when pity had flowed over him.

But as it was now, there was only the new Seth Parton, rigid in the blue cloth and gold insignia of the conqueror, with no snow on his hair.

Seth was very formal with me. He sat bolt upright in the chair, his hat on the table beside him, and inquired of my health. I asked about his war experience. He had not been at Oberlin when the Oberlin command was formed, and just as well that was, too, for they had all been killed or captured in Virginia at their first brush with the Rebels. No, he had been in Massachusetts, sent there on business for the Church, when the war came. After prayer and fasting he had divested himself of his cloth, and volunteered for combat. "I was not so sure of the purity of my heart," he said, "that I might shield my poor flesh behind the flesh of Christ which had bled for me."

Yes, he had seen combat. He had seen much blood. "It is hard to learn how to pray in the midst of blood," he said. "It is hard to find your purity of heart."

He was silent a long time. Then staring directly at the blank wall across the room, he said, "Miss Starr—" and stopped.

"Miss Starr," he began again.

"Yes?" I said.

"Miss Starr," he said, "it behooves me to inform you that I am married."

*It behooves—it behooves me to inform,* he said, and at that preposterousness I almost broke into a gale of laughter.

Did he warn me, warn me that he was not for me? Or did he release me, absolve me? From what?

But I didn't laugh. I was so far away in the presentness of my own life now. So I said, quite evenly: "I wish you all happiness."

He looked at me in a peculiar, uncomprehending way. I even thought that he hadn't heard me. Then, irrelevant and abstract, he said: "We have two children."

"That is wonderful," I said. "What are their names?"

"Seth," he said, "and Hannah." Then added: "Hannah is the name of my wife. In the godly language the name means grace. She is a godly woman."

"It is a pretty name," I said.

"Pretty," he said soberly. Then leaned to me, and said with ferocity: "It is a godly name!"

"Excuse me," I blurted out, absurdly.

Then he retreated into his own thoughts.

After a moment I offered him some tea, but he didn't even answer me. Instead, coming suddenly aware of my presence again, he said: "I am a friend of Captain Sears."

"So I assumed," I said.

"He is my firm friend," he repeated, "and I have found much in him to the comfort of my heart. He is learned and—" He interrupted himself: "Listen, you remember how I once believed that man, even in this world, may put on perfection and perfect joy? Do you remember?"

I nodded.

"I still believe," he said earnestly, and stared at me.

He stared at me, then burst out: "But, oh, how hard it is! How long the path, and rocky, to joy!" Then: "But Tobias—Tobias thinks that that perfection, that joy, may come easy in this life. But he reads too much philosophy, not enough the Scriptures. He thinks that joy quivers behind the veil of things. But, oh, his hope is too easy! I would tell you how in the night I have sweated and prayed, and—" He stopped. "Listen," he said, "Tobias speaks of you."

"Yes?" I said, and my heart lifted like a fee-lark.

"He speaks well of you."

He rose from the chair, and picked up his hat. He turned it in his hands once or twice, then looked probingly at me. "I have not told him," he said.

"Told him what?" I demanded.

"Have you told him?" he demanded.

"Told him what?"

He looked at me. "About you," he said then.

*About me:* what he said restated itself in my mind—no, in my body, in the sudden bruised constriction of my heart, in the cold clutch of my vitals.

"I feel it my duty to tell him," Seth was saying.

I heard the words far off, and I felt the solid earth about to slip from under my feet. I saw, suddenly, the craziness of my joy. I saw myself, the stain of the black blood swelling through my veins—yes, I actually saw some such picture in my head, a flood darkening through all the arteries and veins of my body—no, a stain spreading in a glass of clear water.

I saw myself for what I was, the half-caste, the child of the nameless woman, the slave child, the nigger gal Old Bond had cut down, ignorant, rejected, stuck in this dingy room. And I saw the face of Tobias Sears smiling in pity, but withdrawing, withdrawing into distance. Oh, lost!

But my voice said: "Tell him!"

"I would not tell him without your knowledge," he said. "That is why I am here."

"Oh, I know why you are here," I burst out. "You are here to destroy happiness. Couldn't you be satisfied with what you did to me long ago? Oh, you could have given me happiness—but, no—no— and when I was in trouble—when you told me my father had died— then you turned from me—"

"But you said—you said you never wanted to see me again," he essayed.

"Yes," I said, "but you—you should have understood—in simple humanity—"

"I prayed," he said, "I prayed for guidance."

"Did the Lord tell you not to come after me?"

"I didn't know where—where you were."

"Well, I'm glad you didn't," I flung at him, "and now go tell your friend what you want to tell him. Then you will be sure that he knows."

I stepped closer to him. "And tell him this for me," I said. "That if that knowledge has any meaning for him, tell him never to come here again. I should spit upon him for the vilest of hypocrites. And as for you—"

At that I may even have lifted a hand as though to strike him. For he stepped back, his eyes fixing deep on mine as though fascinated by my fury and accusation.

"As for you," I repeated, "as for you and your fine virtue! Well, you may find that you have done Captain Sears a wrong, you may find that he is not swayed by blood, as you are—"

"But there is—there is defilement of blood," he managed, staring at me as though rapt.

"Go away!" I cried.

He kept staring at me. Then, not really to me, more to himself, he said: "I'll go pray."

"Go pray not to be a fool," I slashed at him.

He really fumbled his way out, reaching out a hand behind him as he took backward steps, his gaze still on me.

As he reached back to fumble for the latch, I said: "And one more thing. Tell your precious friend that if he does call here again, I want no mention, then or ever, of this topic. Tell him that!"

He backed out the door, drew it to, and in the last crack before the door engaged the jamb, I saw his eyes still staring into mine.

The next afternoon, there was a knock on my door. I opened it. There was Captain Sears. He came in without a word. I looked into his face, the high, beautiful face, pale in the shadowy room. I could find no word, in that frozen moment before I should know my fate. I am sure that my heart did not beat.

I retreated from him, toward the center of the room.

He reached out a hand toward me. He stepped toward me, and touched me on the shoulder.

The sob of joy had burst from the deeps of my being even before his arm was around me, drawing me toward him.

A little later, that afternoon, after he had asked me to marry him, he said: "I revert to a subject that you have forbidden. No, I don't revert directly to it. I refer to Seth Parton."

"Yes," I said, bitterly.

"Forgive him," he said. "What foolish pain he caused you—and me —springs from the intensity with which he strains for virtue, with which he wants all things to be laid open in truth. Will you forgive him?"

He took my hands, and laid one against his cheek. "For my sake," he said.

"Yes, yes," I cried, in the fullness of my joy.

And I had, indeed, good reason to forgive Seth Parton. For I am sure that it was Seth Parton's word of revelation that had sent Tobias to me and made him take me in his arms. Seth had touched the trigger of Tobias Sears' deepest secret.

There was one more interview to be remembered from the time before I left forever that room where dinginess had come to glow for me with the promise of all happiness.

It was the middle of the afternoon, the afternoon of the first autumn rain. A knock came at the door. I opened the door, and there stood Hamish Bond.

But for a moment, I did not recognize him. Even had he been unmarked by the months since our parting, even if his face had not gone slack and gray, I suppose I should not have recognized him. For how could any part of the past intrude into my dream of the future?

I looked directly at the bulky, black-clad figure at my door, at the man holding patiently a black hat in his hand while the rain fell on his thick, iron-gray hair and ran down to gather on the jowls. But then the stranger said, "Manty," and I knew him—knew him in a benumbed, incredulous way as though time itself had slipped askew and suddenly what had been past was about to become future, to be re-enacted, but re-enacted without feeling, mechanically, emptily, fate drained of meaning.

"Manty," he said again, with some echo—or was the echo only in my head?—of the wrenched, groanlike utterance of the name he had made when, that night of the old storm, the thrust of his knee had made the bed sag and his hand had first been laid to my side.

I made a gesture for him to enter the room. He did so, then peered searchingly into my face. "I had a hard time to find you, Manty," he said.

At that, in a flash of anger, or bitterness, I almost retorted that it was his own fault, he had driven me off, he had said he didn't want me, didn't want even to know where I was, I might have died for all of him.

But as though humbly answering my thought, he was saying: "I have thought of you, Manty. I have been wondering how you were."

He peered more searchingly into my face, saying: "How have you been, Manty? Have you been well?"

"Yes, thank you," I said, and knew that some trace of ironic bitterness was in my voice.

But he ignored it.

"Last spring," he said, hesitated, then went on, "I just don't know—" Then he stopped.

"Don't know what?" I asked.

"Don't know what was wrong with me," he said in a tone of calm detachment. Then with a flash of intensity: "You know, when Farragut lay down in the Gulf, waiting, sometimes it looked to me I'd just go crazy I got so mad at the Confederate damned foolishness.

Getting ready to throw it away—the fools. Getting ready to give it away to him—all of 'em from Jeff Davis down, like a passel of fools. But when he came—Farragut came—it looked like in a way I wanted him to blow the damned place off the earth. Broadside at fifty yards, two hundred guns, and keep on till the guns were hot and nothing stood, blast it down, then cut the levee and me in the middle for all I cared, for why I ever came to this hell I don't know."

He stopped, leaned heavily on the blackthorn, and seemed to brood over what he had said. "Yeah," he said then, "and you know what I ought to done?"

I didn't answer.

"I'll tell you," he said. "At the very start, way back when the killing started, I ought to fought. I could handle a regiment. I can make men do what I say. At least, one time I could. When the killing starts you might as well go and kill and get killed, and be done with it. But no—" He leaned and slapped his right thigh. "But, oh, no! I had this thing. But you know something?"

He leaned at me: "I'll tell you. This leg—it was just an excuse. Oh, no—not the way you think. Nothing I planned. And not because I was scared of getting killed. No, not that either, for I'm not, and by God, I've proved that much in life if nothing ever else. But deep down in me just some kind of excuse. But for what? For what?"

His attention seemed to wander from me. Then he lifted his head sharply, and stared at me. "But I'm glad of one thing," he said.

"What?" I asked.

"I'm glad I told you," he said. "About myself, I mean. About being Alec Hinks. Yeah, Manty—I'm glad you know who I am, even the worst. Not that I planned to tell you, I don't claim that. It just came busting out, me laying up there and the durn fools off yonder yelling and burning ships and cotton, and the fires a hundred feet high. But I'm glad you know now. But, Manty—Manty—"

He took a step toward me, leaning at me. "Oh, Manty," he said, "I'm sorry for what it brought on. I didn't want to make you feel filthy, I didn't want to make you a nigger, like you said. You see, it just came on me and—"

"Hush! Oh, hush!" I cried out. I couldn't bear what I felt, but I didn't know what it was, all the confusion of all the past time, and his face looking very sorrowfully at me.

"I only want you to be my little Manty," he said.

"Don't call me that!" I cried out, I couldn't bear it.

He straightened up, and stared soberly at me. When he spoke, his voice was again the voice of calm detachment, strong and regular. "I came here for a purpose," he said. "That is why I have told you all this. And I must tell you something else. In all likelihood, when the fool killing is over, I am going to be a poor man. But for my purpose in coming here—" He hesitated, then collected himself. "I am here, Manty," he said, in his strong voice, "to ask you to come back. We will live the best we can. I want you to come back. And marry me."

I heard the words as though from a considerable distance. That was the effect of my incredulity. Or rather, of the fact that the words seemed to be spoken to a person who was not the person that I now was. But the next instant came a sweetness, a tenderness, a yearning, I might say, toward identity with that self I no longer was. All mixed with a lostness because I knew that that identity was impossible, that the sweetness came too late to salve old wounds and repair old rejections.

Then I thought, quite clearly: *But what has all this to do with me? I have my life.*

So I said: "Next Tuesday I am being married."

I was aware of the calmness of my words, and was a little proud of it. And I suppose some vindictiveness was in the pride, too, a way of saying: *See, my time has come, I can spurn all you have to give.*

He was looking soberly at me, but his face betrayed nothing.

So I said: "I am marrying a captain in the Federal army."

But that invidiousness, addressed to him, to one of the vanquished, an aging man, hat in hand, drops from his rain-matted gray hair working unnoticed down his face—that invidiousness, too, did not alter his gaze. But then, after a moment, soberly nodding, he said: "Yes, Yes. That's the way it was bound to be."

"His name is Tobias Sears," I said, as though that information, somehow, would confirm something, would strike him.

Ignoring my words, again nodding, he said as to himself: "Yeah. I ought to known."

Then, coming aware of my presence, he said: "I ought to known. But I had to come, anyway."

Then he leaned at me, over the blackthorn. "Do you know why?" he demanded.

"No," I said.

"It was just something it looked like I owed myself," he said.

I said nothing.

"Yeah," he said, "just like I owed it to myself to set you free so I—"

"Free!" I cut in, bitterly, not knowing why.

He lifted a hand to command me, then said: "Yeah, I know. I was a long time getting to it. After that first time, I mean. And even then, way down inside I didn't reckon you'd go. I was just testing something. Just like picking a scab. And later, I just locked those papers away in a box. I never even looked at those papers again. I knew they were there, and that was something to my conscience, I reckon. But they might as well been torn up. You see, I reckon I was just afraid to free you, to lose you. And when I did free you, it was a mean way."

"Oh, yes, you freed me," I said.

"Mean or not," he said, "I owed it to myself. So I could come here, in the end now, and ask you. Because, like I said—"

He looked down at me for a moment, but not as though expecting an answer. Then he said: "I never figured on anything. It was just to clear up something in me, I reckon."

Then he leaned, took my hand, kissed it quite formally, straightened up and said: "I want you to be happy with your captain, Manty. Promise me to be happy."

With that, he turned away, with the tap of the stick.

With his hand on the door, the door already opened, he turned. "Manty," he said.

"Yes," I said.

"Remember the old boy," he said. "The best you can."

Then he went out.

After the sound of his passing had ceased on the stone of the patio, I stood in the room and remembered that long ago, on the steamboat bound North, when he had turned away, thinking to leave me forever, his last words, in a grinding, strangulated voice, had been: "Forget me—forget everything."

But now, leaving me, really forever, he had asked me to remember him. What was the difference? Because now, at last, he had really set me free?

*Free:* I thought, and joy swelled. Free, and what had I to do with any confusions and brutalities and anguishes of old Hamish Bond.

For I was not now the lost, lonely child flung into the world, dependent on his appetite or kindness. No, I was, at last, Amantha Starr.

But it was not old Hamish Bond who had set me free.

No, it was Tobias Sears who had done that. His own clarity and freedom had made me free. Free from everything in the world, all the past, all my old self, free to create my new self.

I saw him before my eyes, smiling, filling the dingy room with light.

Ah, he was so beautiful!

What had the past to do with me? Nothing, I told myself, and believed it.

But for a moment, on my wedding day, my belief wavered. For there before me, seemingly untouched by time, the stem of the waist as willowy as ever and the movement of shoulder as fluid, the chin lifted to exhibit the white, unmarked throat, the eyes as blue and innocent as ever, was Miss Idell. Only she was not Miss Idell, not Mrs. Herman Muller, any more.

No, for when I looked up to meet that smiling stranger, and felt the stab of recognition, the name pronounced in introduction was Mrs. Morton. Colonel Morgan Morton was the handsome, mustachioed leader of men, who had, the moment before, kissed the bride.

For this was in one of the parlors of the Saint Charles Hotel, at the little reception after the ceremony, with cake, and flowers, and champagne in the lifted glitter of glasses, and gold braid and sword tassels and the swish of silk, and I felt the blood in my cheeks, and everything swayed and flickered in the gleaming, tear-bright mist of my joy.

Then there was that face before me. All the bright objects that, the moment before, had been swaying and dancing suddenly froze into immobility, and I was sure that every eye was fixed on me, and every ear inclined for the first words to be uttered by the woman who confronted me.

"Ah, Manty, little Manty!" that woman exclaimed, and leaned to kiss my now icy cheek. Then she was looking at Tobias—Tobias by my side—saying, "Oh, Captain, isn't she beautiful? You know, Captain, I knew her as a child, and I said she would be beautiful. Look at those eyes, I said long ago, those beautiful brown eyes—" And she gave Tobias the full benefit of her own most blue-eyed gaze. "That's what I said to her father, and—"

"So you knew her in Kentucky," Tobias, very much the embarrassed groom, managed to say.

"Oh, no, in Ohio," Miss Idell said.

"In Cincinnati?" a voice suddenly demanded, and I turned to see the face of Seth Parton—he was groomsman to Tobias, and yet stood by his side. The face leaned down toward Miss Idell, staring avidly, inquisitorially, at her.

"Oh, I beg your pardon!" Tobias broke in. "May I present Lieutenant Parton, my dear friend."

Miss Idell murmured acknowledgment, but Seth, ignoring that, leaning at her, only repeated, more peremptorily: "In Cincinnati— did you say Cincinnati?"

"Why, no," Miss Idell replied, as bland as cream, "I didn't say Cincinnati. But it was Cincinnati, in fact, and how clever of you to guess it! Yes, that's where I knew dear little Manty—just a child then—" She reached out to touch my cheek, as you touch the cheek of a child, caressing me with the slick, white kid of her glove, continuing: "But of course, Manty doesn't remember me—not really, do you Manty?—but I am so much older that I remember everything, literally everything about you." She was looking straight into my eyes now. She said again, more slowly, more directly: "Literally everything, Manty."

The words coldly echoed in my head: *Literally everything.* And the floor seemed to slide beneath my footing.

But in that moment of terror, Miss Idell smiled most sweetly at me, and leaned to kiss me again, and murmured at my cheek, as though confiding a secret: "And I do so want you to be happy, Manty. Do you understand that, little Manty?"

Oh, yes, I understood everything.

Then somebody tapped on a glass, and announced that General Butler would say a few words for the happy occasion, and the man with the shapeless body in victorious blue and gold, with sharp nose and askew glance, and never resting hands, spoke, and spoke well, saying that he wished happiness and saw in this union the symbol of the reuniting of our nation, of the North with what was beautiful and loyal and true in the South, and on and on, and all the while my terror would not die.

Oh, yes, I had understood Miss Idell, her threat and her bargain.

Then, while the General's remarks continued, some voice of reason in me asked what I feared. What was the dark shadow of "literally everything"? And the voice replied that I had nothing to fear. Tobias knew me, what I was, what my fate had presumably been. Seth had seen to that. And my heart surged with gratitude to Seth, crazy, cranky old Seth. Suppose, suppose somehow, I had stood here and the threat had come and I had not felt confidence in Tobias and his knowledge!

And besides, the most secret voice inside me said: *If Miss Idell knows your secret, you know hers, what she was.* And I found my glance, in confirmation, seeking her out in the room.

She stood over yonder beside her handsome colonel. She had her head lifted to catch General Butler's remarks, the face at a slight angle, serenely and beautifully exhibited to the world. Then I observed that to one side and slightly behind her was Seth Parton. His head, too, was in the posture of listening, but he was not listening to the speaker. He was staring covertly, but most fixedly and avidly, at Miss Idell. His gaze would be steady on her face, then slip down over the high offering of bosom, down the stem of the waist, over the swell of hip, down the flow of blue cloth to the floor. Then his gaze, with its secret rigor, would return again to her face.

Suddenly, with perfect clairvoyance, I was sure I knew what was happening inside Seth Parton. He had decided that this was the woman in whose bed, in whose very arms perhaps, my father had died. And there he stood, probing and rancorous, in the mysterious entrapment of that moment. He was stripping himself, laying himself down naked, living and dying that moment, over and over again, the soft bed, the shaded lamp, the white bosom, the terror and blackness.

I shuddered with a chill, and shut my eyes, and saw Seth dying on that white bosom—no, it was my father dying there, and Miss Idell's face was smiling in triumph, and a gust of hatred shook me like a leaf.

I opened my eyes and fixed my gaze firmly on the high, clear-cut, beautiful face of Tobias. It was as though if I kept my gaze there, all would be well. And I was right, for as I watched him, whatever dark disturbances had been in me passed into a pulsing, inward expectation of joy. I felt the blood beat in my wrists. I felt like offering the very blood in my body.

*This is love,* I thought.

*This is love,* I thought, standing in the middle of the floor of the room in the Saint Charles Hotel, where Tobias had conducted me after the reception.

I stood in the middle of the floor still holding my flowers. They were pink roses. Tobias kissed me on the brow, and I thought: *this is love.*

He turned away, casually, and went and pulled the curtains together against the afternoon sunlight. It was, then, dusky in the room, with just one bar of sunlight falling in where the curtains did not quite meet, and the gold motes danced in that shaft of light.

He walked past me, not noticing me, and went and stood by a chair.

Methodically, as he did everything, he unbuttoned all the bright brass buttons down his blue tunic. Then he hung it on the chair back. He adjusted one of the gold epaulettes. Then, methodically, he undressed. He put all the clothes neatly in place. He set his shiny boots side by side in front of the chair.

I held my breath and I could hear his breathing. He turned toward me then and started to move toward me. He had no clothes on, and he looked like a fine statue. He looked like the statue of a Greek athlete, and every muscle swelling strong and true in the white marble. For he was white and slick-looking, like marble, except for the crisp and precisely arranged black hairs of his body. He looked like a beautiful, strong, narrow-hipped statue walking toward me in the dusk of the room, setting his white feet down on the red carpet, coming toward me, smiling.

Each morning I woke with the expectation of happiness. Whatever shadow lay over my heart seemed only the shadow of the war, the possibility that tomorrow Tobias would be called away, to Texas, to Virginia, up the river. But the weeks passed, and he was not called. When, in December, a month or so after my marriage, General Butler was removed, the whisper was that Washington had acted because of Admiral Farragut's complaint of the General's administrative corruption and military lassitude, and that now there would be action, that we would now drive upriver, to Port Hudson, Vicksburg—and victory. But I was selfish enough, and faint-hearted enough, to feel no joy in that promise.

"Will there be fighting now," I asked Tobias, "with General Butler gone?"

He said he didn't know.

"Maybe there won't be," I said, "maybe it wasn't because he wouldn't fight that they removed him, maybe it was just the way he ran things, and the cotton-jobbing and trading with the enemy and those things."

Then I saw the look on Tobias' face, a sudden hardening, the look he always got when somebody mentioned the Butler gossip. "We don't know the truth," Tobias now said, and shifted his gaze from me.

"But there's so much talk," I said.

"I don't want to hear the talk," he said.

"You are on his staff," I said, "you feel you have to be loyal. Even if you see something."

"I don't see anything," he burst out, in the nearest thing to anger I had found in him. "And if there is something, if something is true —just if, mind you—you have to remember that he has done much for the cause and—"

"You mean freedom."

"Yes, that's what I mean, and back in Virginia General Butler took slaves into his lines when other commanders sent them back to the slave-masters and—"

"But," I said, "right here in Louisiana General Butler put chains on escaped slaves and sent them back."

"He's just a general. He can't control Mr. Lincoln, and if Mr. Lincoln does not see that the only way to justify things is by freedom, then all we have is just a lot of burning and butchering and men screaming when they get hit and—"

"Stop!" I cried out. "Stop, I can't bear it."

"I'm sorry," he said, and groped for my hand. Then he went on: "But it's so hard right in the middle of things to remember that the power of soul must work through matter, that even the filthiness of things is part of what Mr. Emerson calls the perennial miracle the soul worketh, that matter often retains something of its original tarnishment, that history is a movement of matter, and that even if history is the working out of the design of the Great Soul, the redemption of matter is not always complete, that imperfect men must fulfill the perfection of idea, that—"

"You mean you think General Butler has done those things he is accused of?" I said.

While speaking, his gaze had wandered from me, though he still held my hand. Now, at my interruption, he swung sharply at me, and stared. Suddenly his body stiffened. He rose abruptly, turned his high, white, carven face from me, and left the room.

Something still nagged inside me, and when, after an hour, Tobias, very silent and calm now, the dampness of mist from the winter river on his tunic, came in, and wordlessly kissed me, I felt awful. But I said to myself that I had just been nervous because he might get sent away to the real war, and I began to run my fingers through his damp, crisp hair and feel the precious narrowness of the back of his neck just before it swelled out into the curve of the skull.

General Butler left. He made his speech about how merciful he had been in not having fired any live rebels out of cannon, as his critics, the British, had lately done to Sepoys; took his fortune, however he had made it; and sailed away. Sailed away to get bottled up on a Carolina peninsula by an enemy force half his size, to go to Congress as a hero and lead in the impeachment attempt on President Johnson, and to spend the rest of his life trying to be Governor of Massachusetts.

General Butler asked Tobias to come with him on his staff, but Tobias declined. I suppose that Tobias' refusal of the flattering invitation may have been, in some way, the result of that mysterious near-quarrel that he and I had had about General Butler. I suppose that he understood it no more than I, and wanted, simply, to make some gesture to say that he loved me. And he did love me, I am sure, in the way that it was his fate to love.

So we stayed in New Orleans, to our fates, and General Banks came. Swapped the Beast for the Dancing Master, people said, for Banks was charming, Banks gave balls for the local gentry, Banks released Butler's prisoners, Banks would mollify all, and two high officers resigned their commissions to marry local heiresses, for if you married a few thousand bales of cotton and you were a Union man it wouldn't get confiscated.

But there was to be gunpowder, after all, and Tobias was to get more than a whiff of it. He was to get it in late May—May of '63, that was—clambering over the cunningly felled trees of the long

approach, while grape ripped the air, running across the murderous
openness of space then, plunging through thickets of blackberry,
plunging toward the batteries of Port Hudson, the black muzzles
visible over yonder, across the greenness of grass, wreathed in
smoke, outstabbing with flame. Oh, I could see it all, and my heart
just stopped.

They tried it six times, Tobias said. They would get almost there
to the guns, then break, and go back. But they would re-form, try
again, and as they plunged forward, try not to notice the dead ones
from before.

"It's just the first time that's so hard," Tobias said to me. "After
that it's like a dream. You are afraid, but it's like being afraid in a
dream."

They tried six times. And it was Negro troops that Tobias was
leading—that is, Louisiana *gens de couleur libres*.

"That proves it," Tobias said. "It proves a colored man can fight."

For nobody had believed that they could.

And nobody had wanted a black command. Worse, if you took
one, you'd be half-ostracized.

"Yes," Tobias had said, the night he came home and announced his
decision, "it's going to be ostracism, or something near— Oh, the
swine, the filthy swine!"

"Don't worry about me," I said.

"Darling," he said, and put his arm around my shoulder. But after
another moment, he said: "Today, when I met Major Smythe—he's
just back from upriver, from Baton Rouge—he very pointedly pretended not to see my hand when I offered it to him. Oh, he's from
West Point! And Colonel Morgan Morton, he professed a fatherly
interest in my career. Said I could resign the black commission, it
hadn't been forced on me. Said I was a gentleman, and Banks would
understand. Morton, they say he's rich, a speculator in New York, or
something. I've never liked him. Anyway, I don't think they'll ask us
to dinner again, even if she is your old friend. I was short with him,
today. I told him I wasn't interested in my career, and that I hoped
I was more interested in being a man than in being a gentleman.
Thank God, I had one fact to give him anyway. I could tell him that
I had refused a majority just so nobody could say I had gone nigger
—yes, that's what they call it—to get a promotion."

Tobias seemed to be brooding over what he had just said. All at once he jerked free, and stood up.

"It's awful," he said. "You try to believe there's something—try to live for something and—" He stopped, then almost savagely continued: "Why don't I say it out straight right now? Why am I ashamed to say it?" Then as though squaring himself, continued: "You try to believe in some idea—that's what I mean. In truth—yes, and you might as well say the word. You want to see truth work out in the world, but every day it's something like this, and you feel yourself getting lost in the confusion of things, and then to keep from getting lost you try to do something and then you have to explain yourself. That's what's so awful, you feel like a Pharisee."

"Sit down, darling," I whispered.

But he was saying: "No, the awful thing isn't you have to explain yourself to other people—it's awful you find yourself explaining to yourself."

Then under my drawing hand, he sank down beside me.

"No," he said, "that's not it either. The awful thing is that you feel, somehow, cut off from the world."

"Darling, darling," I was whispering. I was whispering into the distance where he was, wanting to comfort him, but jealous too, jealous of what could draw him into the distance—yes, jealous of truth, his truth.

I began to move my hands over his face, then round his shoulders, and moved myself against him, pressing myself against him. I shut my eyes, and got his image into my head, and held it there, all the while caressing him, the actuality, but in the darkness behind my tight-shut eyes, yearning toward an image, the brilliant whiteness, the beautiful whiteness, of that image that overhung my mind like a bright cloud.

It was, I must confess, what amounted to a seduction. But, in a funny way, it was not only Tobias Sears whom I had to seduce and draw out of his darkness. It was also myself. There was the need to overcome, by the bright image, some coldness and desperation in myself.

Yes, the act we performed in that unaccustomed spot was, in some aspect, cold and desperate, and veined through with a kind of angriness. I clutched him hard, and one of the buttons of the tunic got turned sidewise and cut into me like a knife, toward the inside of the right breast. I had to insist on that pain. I had to thrust myself at that pain. It became more important than any pleasure, for only by that pain could I justify, as it were, my pleasure.

Afterward, while we rearranged our dishevelment, he was avoiding looking at me. And I was careful to keep my eyes from him. Then I pretended to be arranging some books on the table, but Tobias remained as he was, sitting on the couch, elbows on knees, wrists hanging.

Then, suddenly, he got up.

"Those damned niggers better fight," he said.

That was what he said: *niggers.*

That night, late, after we had eaten a meal and talked in idle decorousness of nothing, after we had gone to bed and after I was sure Tobias was asleep, I heard his voice, all at once, in the dark.

He said: "You know, I've never been in a battle. Not a real one, just a skirmish in Virginia. And that—it was like an accident, it was over so quick."

He was quiet a time. Then: "I guess you never know what you'll be like."

I seized his hand in the dark. "I know," I said. "You are the bravest thing in the world."

I kept on holding his hand. His breath fell into the regularity of sleep. But I couldn't sleep. Lying in the dark, I was wild with fear. If he were dead, oh, what would become of me!

Tobias need not have worried about being brave. Or about his men being brave. And Colonel Morton asked us to dinner again. And, still holding his wineglass, after the first appraising sip, the Colonel said, "Well, Captain, it seems your niggers did all right."

"They died under the very muzzles of the battery," Tobias said, coldly. "If you call that doing all right."

"That's doing all right," the Colonel said, nodding his head sagely, and took another appraising sip. Then: "So now would be a good time to get out."

"Out of what?" Tobias demanded.

"Out of the nigger business," the Colonel said.

I saw Tobias stiffen, and the white, sharp lines appear at the corners of his mouth. Colonel Morton smiled—he did have a fine, engaging smile until you noticed that his eyes were watching you respond to that fine smile—and lifted his hand, saying: "Now, don't fly off the handle. It's just I take an interest. I've got a majority for you, all arranged with the General. A white majority, Captain." Then before Tobias could reply, he turned to me: "Yes, Mrs. Sears, that's what we are here for—to celebrate the promotion. The promotion of a hero."

He lifted his glass. "I give you Major Sears," he said.

Miss Idell, smiling, her white fingers delicate on the delicate stem of the glass, lifted it, murmuring, "Yes—to the hero."

And I, too, had my glass half up, infected somehow with the smiles, with pride, with the air of gaiety. Then I saw Tobias' eyes fixed on my lifting hand.

"I don't want the white majority," Tobias said then, his eyes still on my hand.

I let my hand sink down, the wine untasted. I was flooded with shame. I had almost betrayed Tobias. That was what his look had said: *You are betraying me.*

"Listen, Captain," Colonel Morton was saying. "You think Port Hudson proves niggers can fight. But look here, Captain, those weren't niggers. They are Louisiana *gens de couleur libres*. They've been free God knows how long. They are people. Take an average and every man in the outfit would be worth $25,000, cash and property."

"Money in the bank never stopped a bullet," Tobias said.

"What I mean is," the Colonel said, "it's blood that counts, and damn it, a lot of that gang hasn't got a spoonful of nigger. Why"— and he looked round the table, from face to face—"a lot look as white as anybody at this table."

I was sure that his eyes had come to rest on me. I was sure that Miss Idell was staring at me. That Tobias was looking at me. I was sure, but as a matter of fact I didn't see those eyes directed at me, for my own eyes were lowered. I had lowered them the instant that Colonel Morton's gaze had reached me.

Then the talk went on, the Colonel saying just wait till somebody tried to take those real gumbo blue-gums into battle, and Miss Idell cut in with laughter, and I still could not lift my eyes.

That night, walking home, past the clinking patrols and civil police that kept the streets clear of toughs and aimless blacks, Tobias said he wondered why he accepted Morton's hospitality, when he didn't like him. I said I wondered why the Colonel put himself out so much for Tobias' promotion.

"Oh, he has his reasons," Tobias said. "And no doubt his reasons have something to do with the fact that my father is rich."

He walked on another block in silence. Then he said: "You know what I want."

"No," I said.

"I want to get a blue-gum command. I want a real gumbo, blue-gum commission."

He pronounced each word with a peculiar, lingering relish, but a self-torturing relish, as though each syllable were foul on his tongue but he would suffer it as long as need be before the ejection, as long as needed for some nameless expiation.

He got the blue-gum commission.

He went up into Mississippi, to Vicksburg, where Grant was now closing in for the last grim days, to join a regiment assembled from the runaways and contraband that had been sucked into the wake of the Federal passing. He had a majority now. But a black one.

And I became a schoolmarm.

If the lingering, self-torturing relish with which Tobias named the kind of command he wanted was an expiation, I suppose that my becoming a schoolmarm had in it something of the same need, expiation for the moment when, at the table of Colonel Morton, my hand had lifted the wineglass to toast the majority of Tobias, the white majority. But it was days later before that need came on me, one afternoon as I stood beside Tobias, in the middle of a camp of Negro refugees, a contraband camp at Kenner, where he had had to go on business, or for his own mysterious need. And where that need had made him take me.

So we stood in the middle of the camp, under the blazing sun. There were the crazy shacks—rotten board, palmetto leaf, sacking— the discarded army tents, tattered, rotting away. There were the faces. The old faces, the scrofulous, grizzled polls, the yellow-veined eyes, the claw-hands, gray flesh dry in the palms, reaching out to us. The sick faces, staring at us or beyond us, at nothing. The baby faces with skin too tight on skulls like big gourds, the necks not strong enough to hold up the heads, the bellies distended.

"There they are," Tobias said.

I looked around me.

"They don't even know if they're free or not," he said.

"There's the Proclamation," I said.

"Oh, that," Tobias said. "It just applies inside Confederate lines. It doesn't apply here." Then: "And it won't ever if Banks has what looks like his way."

For Banks was getting able-bodied contraband back on plantations, by steamboat load, by gang down the big road with fixed bayonets behind them, putting them to work, for pay, sure, but what pay, and to loyalists, sure, but back on plantations.

A woman, a white woman, middle-aged, nondescript, gray hair drawn back tight, came across the dust carrying a kettle, behind her a colored woman with a basket of hardtack. They passed by us, steady in the dust, not noticing us.

"Who's that?" I asked.

"One of the Missionary Aid women," Tobias said. "Down here trying to do something. Work with the sick. Teach school." He pointed far off, over the hot dust.

"The school's over there," he said.

I felt the land just stretching away from me in all directions, just stretching away forever, like a bad dream.

"It's a picnic now," Tobias said, "compared to the winter. The rain coming down, and no fire. Huddling together, coughing their lungs out. But more kept on coming. God, you couldn't stop them from coming. Sometimes the road just black with them coming. And at night, walking crazy at you out of the dark. Listen—I never told you, something I never—" He stopped.

"What?"

"When I was at Carrollton, and the general order was to receive none in the lines. I was on routine inspection, to report back to Butler on contraband control. It was night and I was making a round of sentry posts, just myself and a sergeant. Just as we came up to one post, there was a shot.

"A shot, and the scream. We came up, on the double, me getting my sidearm free. The sentry was leaning forward, staring out beyond a clump of scrub.

"It was moonlight, and I came rushing around the clump, my sidearm ready.

"There it was. There was the body on the ground, face down, right under my nose, not more than ten feet. The sentry had fired point-blank. Later, he said he had warned three times. Anyway, there was the body. And around it, in the moonlight, crouching down, squatting on their hams, staring down at it, staring up slow at us then, there they were, six or seven Negroes, contraband, runaways—men and women, squatting there in the moonlight, not making a sound, staring.

"Now a lieutenant and a squad was up, the lieutenant demanding what had happened, the sentry rattled and not very coherent, a green boy from up in Illinois—it was an Illinois regiment—saying over and over how the last time he was on duty they just came walking right over him.

"But now the thing began to happen. Over yonder was some woods, woods fringed by undergrowth, and out of that absolute blackness, into the faint moonlight, they came walking. One first, then another, and another, a woman carrying a child, more men, men and women. They kept coming, slow, out of that black woods over there, not making a sound, and they moved as slow as sleep-walkers. It looked like it would take forever for them to cross that moonlight.

"There must have been about twenty-five or thirty of them. They had simply up and walked away from some plantation. Or maybe the planter had sent them, driven them off. Oh, yes, that happens sometimes when we get close, the slaves won't work, just slow down —shiftless, as they say—and the slave master simply drives them off so he won't have to feed them. Sure, he expects to recover them, after the war. One even sent in a letter by an old man, addressed simply "Yankee Commander," describing his lot, asking for a receipt, and saying he hoped the Yankee Commander would be able to get more out of them than he had lately, but not to beat Old Billy.

"God," Tobias said, standing there in the heat-shimmer, "and don't beat Old Billy, and it's all crazy.

"But that night," he resumed, "they came out of the woods and the dark, this other gang. About twenty-five, but you felt that the dark woods over there was full. That they would keep on coming out, forever, walking at you slow and steady in the moonlight. You couldn't take your eyes off them.

"But I did manage to look at that lieutenant." Tobias paused. "Well," he said then, "I imagine my face might have looked something like that, at Port Hudson, just before we started across, the first time, for the battery. But now this lieutenant, he was staring at those fellows coming across the moonlight, and not a sound. 'Ready,' the lieutenant ordered his squad, and I heard the rustle and rub as the rifles came up, the soft slap of the hand on stock, that sound you get to know, but I didn't look. I was watching the lieutenant's face.

"The lieutenant called out: 'Halt!' It was a very military voice, but they kept coming, slow as ever, not a sound. Except suddenly I could hear feet swishing in the tall grass in the heavy dew. You know that sound, a silky sound, walking in dew, in grass, at night in summer?

"The lieutenant called out again. It didn't do any good. They were almost up to the place where the body lay. 'Halt!' he called again, still military. But they didn't stop for another six or eight feet, not till they got where the body lay, with the others crouching there. It was as though that defined a mystic line. They came up to that line and stared at us. In the moonlight you could now see how white the eyes were in the black faces.

"Then they started moving forward again, a slow step.

"'Stop! I tell you, stop!' the lieutenant called at them, but the voice was not very military now.

"They hesitated, then another step. It was then the lieutenant fired. He fired his pistol over their heads.

"That stopped them. It brought them up short. Then they seemed to bunch together. I heard the lieutenant give a gasp, as though he hadn't been properly able to get a good breath before. It was the sound a man makes for the first good breath, coming up from a deep dive. I suppose that I, too, sucked in a good breath. I suppose we thought, he and I, that it was settled.

"But one of the ones crouching by the body, an old man, rose up. He put out his hands. It wasn't a gesture of supplication. It was more like a disinterested, a scientific act, to show the hands as empty. He took a step forward, and then the others rose from beside the body and moved, then all, all together somehow, not as individuals, but like some inorganic mass, moving. Yes, it was like that—like some great mass of matter, like earth, like rock, something like that moving slow, so slow you couldn't believe, in a kind of black, deep, inorganic sleep. You know what I mean? That's what it was like.

"'Aim!' I heard the lieutenant's voice calling.

"It was a matter of feet now, and I waited. I was perfectly cold. I was thinking—no, not thinking—something in my very body, in its coldness in that sweat-sweltering night, a real Louisiana night, was saying: *Well, you've come all this way, you have lived all your life, for this.*

"It was an agony to wait. They swayed toward us another step. I couldn't wait for the next step. For then it would happen.

"But it didn't. No, the lieutenant cracked. He cracked in a most frightful, and frightening, kind of way. He swung toward the squad, waving his arms, but not managing a word, his face working. The squad stood gap-mouthed and stared at him, and the Negroes simply came on, and went past them, past us, through us, you might say, as though we were diaphanous, or they were, and moved on into the camp, way yonder, in that same motion, in what there was of moonlight. The lieutenant, as in a catatonic stupor, just stared after them.

"Then, all at once, he was out of it. He went over to the corpse, looked down at it, and began, quite systematically, to kick it. I got to him, got my hand on his arm, and that was what did it. Suddenly, it was a frenzy, the kicking, and he was screaming, 'Oh, the bastards, the bastards!' He struggled against me, yelling, 'Oh the bastards, the dirty black bastards!' "

Tobias stopped, looked away from me, from the moonlight scene in his head, to the camp around us. "The sergeant," he said, "he and one of the men took him off my hands."

He seemed about to say more, then didn't. Instead, he gave enormous attention to an old woman squatting directly before us, an old woman scratching her belly, under her rags.

"Free," he said. Then: "That's one thing a thousand proclamations can't do."

He took his eyes off the woman, and looked far away, over the flat land toward the river, beyond the river, the land shimmering into distance. "You've just got one life," he said. "You'd like to make it mean something."

And so, one day after Tobias had gone to his blue-gum majority, I climbed into a rejected commissary wagon that was still good enough for the Aid Society, and so left New Orleans, staring up the dusty road over the bony and lash-bit rumps of a team of rejected army commissary mules—staring up that dusty road, past the great oaks and sad, mauve-gray festoons of moss, past the fields green as arsenic, staring toward a life I could not in my wildest imagination have previsioned.

"Crazy to larn, crazy to larn," they said, the young ones, the hand not really big enough to hold the pencil while you guided it, the old ones, grizzled, claw-handed, clutching the book till the knuckles cracked, staring at the page, moving the pendulous gray lip in silence.

"Done set up all night," the old woman said, "set up a-studyin. Press the larn-book on my haid—I press hit lak this, Missie—press on my forehead, and pray Lawd-Jesus, all night, Missie, pray Him to make hit soak inside, let the larn-rain soak in this old dry haid, and the drout break."

"Too old, Missie," the oldest one said. "Too old to try, but gonna set in the door, jist set on the floor, Missie, and ne'er no 'sturbance, jist set and watch 'em nibble the larn-cake. Uncle be happy, watching they mouf move."

Crazy to larn, they said, "larn so won't sign nuthin' fer Massa come slave me." Crazy to larn, they said, "to read the Good Book and the Promise." Crazy to larn, they said, "how folks come here, over the water, us black folks, and the land they come from." Crazy to larn, they said, "be lak white folks." There were the thousand reasons and always behind other reasons the reason that to learn had been forbidden. But perhaps not behind the reason the young boy gave. "Gotta larn," he said, "gotta larn and know how come dew on the grass at night at fust frog-peep."

When things happened, I tried to remember what he said. I tried to remember when they moved across the country, the blacks, singing and jubilating, never gonna work no more, stealing, begging, waiting for rations, not crazy to larn. When Federal troops—Connecticut—stripped black men of the uniform on the streets of New Orleans. When at Ship Island the Federal gunboat *Jackson* fired directly into the black troops it was sent to support. When the Negroes aimed to take over the country, it was theirs. When Federal troops scoured the country—black troops, sometimes—to seize Negroes for conscription, and the Negroes ran for the woods and swamps, and they shot them like beasts for running. When they broke contracts and the crops rotted in the field. When the lessees of confiscated land—men come down to make fortunes—drove off the old, the children, the sick, not to feed them. When the scum and adventurers came, when they sold them the red-white-and-blue sticks to set in the ground and claim land. When, in the end, riders raked the country at night, under the white hoods. What the boy had said, it was something beyond the day's disgrace, or effort. It was like a promise of happiness.

It was the promise I returned to that terrible day when the little girl seized my hand and I did what I did.

It was morning, and as every morning they were holding out their hands to me to show they had washed them, and I would go from one to another murmuring my approbation. I had just come to the little girl, and she was grinning at me, saying, "Look'ee, hands clean and wash, Missie."

Then she said: "Look'ee, my haid comb out, Missie—look'ee, no nits, not no more!" And she seized my hand and pressed it on her head.

Suddenly, I thought I was going to faint. A nausea assailed me, a frightful sense of defilement, not just defilement of the hand seized and pressed on that coarseness of hair, but a total defilement, a crawling foulness on my scalp, a pricking of skin down my spine, a twitching revulsion to my last nerve-end. And I heard my voice crying out, "Don't—don't touch me!"

And I had jerked my hand away, and was standing there with it held in the air before my gaze. I was staring at its whiteness. Yes, it was white.

It was the sob that broke the spell. I heard it, and looked down into the child's face. She was staring at me, directly up at me, and sobbing now. And I was aware of all the eyes—wide and bulging, the whites of the eyes so bulging white in the black faces—the eyes fixed on me.

I dropped to my knees by the child and embraced her desperately, saying, "Darling, darling," over and over again, while I kissed her, over and over, pressing my desperate kisses against the skin of her face and against the coarse hair.

That evening as I walked home through the mud, under the cold sunset—home to the shed-room, the wind-creaking slab wall—I found myself saying it out loud, over and over, clinging to the promise: *know how come dew on the grass at night at fust frog-peep.*

I found myself saying it, and tears came into my eyes.

But sometimes when I was most aware of the promise of happiness, something would stir darkly in the very depth of my being. It was like something at night, in the dark, stirring in the next room. It got so I was afraid to name my happiness to myself.

So I learned the trick of sinking into the day's occupation, into the human commitment, into the night's dream, the dream of Tobias' return. He would come again, step down from the golden mist, high-faced and smiling from his victorious cloud, and save me.

But save me from what? Not save me from the happiness I had learned now, and his own pride in me: *Dearest Manty, how can I say how happy I am in knowing that everything you do there in our poor human effort for Truth is, across distance, a kiss of the spirit.*

But, oh, it was so long till he came!

That autumn Seth paid me a visit, down from Vicksburg, a captain now, silent about the war he had seen, silent, in fact, for most of his mysterious visit. But when we were sitting by the fire in the miserable house of the family where I boarded, while the mother worked in the lean-to kitchen, Seth, after a long silence, with the tone of a man coming last to difficult business, said: "There is something I would show you."

He handed over an envelope. First there was the picture of a woman, a daguerreotype, a woman with a round face sagging in the cheeks, a low forehead with hair drawn back, a wide-eyed stare out of the picture at you, as though you weren't there, as though nothing in the world were there. "That's my wife," Seth said.

"Oh, I know her," I exclaimed, for I had seen before that same world-canceling stare. "Why, she was at Oberlin—Hannah, why, of course, she was Hannah Schmidt."

Yes, I remember her, the formless girl, sagging flesh, bulging flesh, flesh straining fabric and button with its melancholy mass, flesh not happy in its bulging, not pink-and-cream, but a cheesy white, faintly splotched, smelling faintly, you know, of cheese, smelling like clabber-pans before washing, the buttocks moving in massive fatalistic retarded rhythm as the feet were lifted and set sadly down, on snow, on grass, on board, the breath coming slow and sad with an adenoidal murmur. Hannah Schmidt—of famous piety and famous stupidity.

*Oh, poor Seth,* I thought, with a burst of painful pity, *oh, why did it have to be her!*

And my eyes must have betrayed something, for with a sudden vehemence, he said: "She is a godly woman."

"Yes, yes," I said, and made the quick pretense of again studying the picture, and murmured as best I could, "and she's very handsome."

"Handsome," he echoed, in a grating voice. "She is not handsome." Suddenly, he stood up. "Why would man bend to the corruption and the snare?" He paused, then added more quietly: "It is the end of man to seek perfection and the perfect joy."

He leaned over and snatched the pictures from me, as though to get them from contamination.

"Oh, the children," I cried, in some sort of desperation, "I haven't seen the children!"

"Yes, the children," he said absently, and returned the pictures to me.

I looked at the children. They were the children of Hannah Schmidt. I could not find anything to say, so silently I passed them back to Seth.

He sat down, sank into his own silence.

When the time came to go, he said: "Have you a message for Mrs. Morton?"

For a moment, I could not grasp the notion—Mrs. Morton. Then the name came clear and in my surprise I burst out, "Miss Idell— oh, you mean Miss Idell—why ever are you seeing her?"

"I had to find out how to reach you," he said. "I addressed myself to her for information. She is interested, she says, in your welfare, and wishes me to report to her. I can do no less, in courtesy." He paused. "I know she is a worldly woman," he said. "But it is courtesy."

"Yes," I said, "but why couldn't you have asked the Aid Society about me?"

He stared at me narrowly, then said: "I didn't think of that."

I walked out with him to the road, to show him a short cut to the house of a neighbor where he would stay the night before leaving for New Orleans.

We said good-bye.

He took a couple of steps away from me, then turned and came back. "Do you know why I came here?" he demanded.

"Yes," I said, bumblingly, for I suddenly felt as mysterious what I had taken for granted, "—yes—because we are friends—old friends, Seth."

"I wanted to see you in your godly occupation," he said.

With that he swung away again, and again hesitated, turning to me. "I have prayed for you," he said, "I have prayed in the night." And with that was really gone.

My life flowed on, day after day, and the echoes of the world came to me, muffled by distance, victories and defeats, Chickamauga, Missionary Ridge, the Wilderness, Spottsylvania, Nashville, the flash of cannon beyond horizons I could not see, and each name, at some moment, was a constriction of my heart.

Meanwhile I went back and forth to my shack of a schoolhouse while men killed each other and then tried to put back together the world they had knocked apart. Mr. Lincoln wanted the states back in the government, any state where one tenth of the voters were loyal, and General Banks set up an election, and politicians sprang up like jimson weed, and a man named Hahn became Governor, and a man named Wells his Lieutenant-Governor, and there was a gala inauguration, with banners naming General Banks a hero, and within a little while he marched off, with music, to conquer the rest of Louisiana. The Confederates hit him at Mansfield and Pleasant Hill. They hit him so hard he came back to New Orleans and stuck to politics and let the war alone.

But back in New Orleans he had enough politics to keep him occupied, for he had set up a convention of loyal Union men to draw a new constitution for Louisiana. The Convention sat almost three months, abolished slavery, debated whether or not all Negroes should be pushed off the soil of America, established free schools, guaranteed the vote to all white men, tried to decide exactly how much black blood made a man a Negro but gave this up as a too ticklish job, and presented the state with a bill for $5000 for carriages they had ridden in, $8000 for paper they had written on, and $10,000 for whiskey they had drunk.

I read about the Convention, idly, now and then, in the newspapers that strayed in, days late, to the quiet corner where I lived. How could I know that the goings-on in Liberty Hall, the free whiskey and cigars and oratory and schemes and ambitions and— even—dreams for justice, more than the battles and marches far away, were shaping my fate? And anyway, what could I think about but Tobias?

# I X

THEN TOBIAS CAME BACK.

He had done his share, Chickamauga, Nashville, Franklin, the nameless skirmishes, the dreary convoy duty, the night surprise when Forrest's cavalry rode right over the pickets, and the men nearly panicked.

But all that was over now. And my schoolteaching was over. We were together, to start life over, to make our own world of love and loving-kindness.

But the world outside, that world was coming to us. Miss Idell came, once alone and once with her Colonel, bringing fruit and wine, laughing, laughing when she talked about Seth, but calling him charming. (Charming, I thought, what a word to apply to Seth!) And officers came, full of war and politics, one of them planning to settle in Louisiana and full of his scheme. "Yes," he said, "it's a sure thing. Why, I know a man came down two years ago and leased 2000 acres of confiscated land from the government, and by George, you know he's rich now. Gets niggers from the government, just what he needs—yes, that's the beauty of free labor, just what you need—"

"Eight dollars a month," Tobias said sardonically.

And another officer: "Yes, but anything's too high if they won't work. But now the niggers know they start malingering the Provost Marshal's men will snatch 'em off to public works with not a dime of pay."

"We can't keep an army down here forever," Tobias said dryly.

So the world came into the shadowy recess of my happiness, Miss Idell's smile borne like an offering more precious than fruit or wine, the schemes and arguments and gold braid of the officers, and I hated them all.

Even when Seth came—that was just after Appomattox and the murder of Mr. Lincoln—I felt, as soon as the excitement of his arrival had worn off, the same resentment, and felt guilty for feeling it. After all, he was my husband's best friend, a strange friend but the right friend, for Seth's cranky, cold, self-anguishing intensities seemed the right contrast to the beautiful, calmly spreading light of Tobias' spirit, and each seemed to fulfill the other in the passion for the good. So they sat there and talked, and I moved my needle with care and tried to conquer the wickedness of my nature, and didn't succeed too well, for when Tobias asked Seth what he would do now, would he get out of the army, I found that wicked inner voice saying that I didn't care what he did just so he did it far away, and left me to be happy.

But Seth was saying that he didn't know exactly what he would do. He did not know that he could return to the ministry. Did not know but that in the violence, even in the combating of evil one did not assume contamination, and he might have to wait long to purge his own soul before he could speak again of that peace which passeth understanding. His large, bony hands worked slow and plucked at his blue-clad knees, torturing the question. "Meanwhile," he said, "I shall keep my commission, and do the duty of the day, and think on those who have died."

"Oh, but your poor family," I exclaimed, aware of my glint of malice, "your poor wife!"

He turned a sober, painful stare upon me.

But Tobias said: "You can bring your family down here."

Seth turned to him. "Yes," he said, "yes."

At that Seth sank again into silence. Then, abruptly, he stood up. "I must go," he announced over our heads.

"Nothing of the sort," Tobias said. "You will send for your kit, and you will stay right here."

"I must go," Seth reiterated.

"Look here," Tobias ordered, "look right down here at me."

Slowly, Seth obeyed. Tobias was looking up at him smiling. "Look," Tobias said, "I'm your dear old friend, Tobias Sears, and you will sit right down."

"Yes, yes," I urged, on my feet now, "of course, you'll stay, please stay!"

Seth looked right at me. "I regret it isn't possible," he said. "You see," he said, "I have accepted an invitation to stay with Colonel and Mrs. Morton. They had written me ahead."

I suppose I gasped.

In the moment of ensuing silence Seth stood there, stiff as a ramrod. Then announced: "I must go."

He shook hands with Tobias, then moved toward me. I conducted him into the hall, toward the outer door. Just at the door he paused, looking severely down at me.

"Tobias Sears," he said, "is a man of deep spirit. He has a great work to do. We must do all to make that work possible, under God's hand—"

I felt resentment blaze up in me, but I spoke evenly. "I do not need to be instructed in the worth of my husband," I said.

He did not flinch from my anger. He kept looking down at me, intently and curiously. Then he said: "Nor do I need to be instructed in your worth."

I was so taken aback that I gaped at him. I was still gaping, when, in his most rancorous, inquisitorial manner, he demanded: "Are you happy?"

I was trying to say, yes, yes, I was happy, but more severely than ever he said: "I want Tobias and you to be happy. It is important for you to be happy, and happy in moving toward that perfection of joy, that perfection of which I spoke once to you, and—"

"Oh, I just want to be happy," I cried, "just like people—like everybody—oh, you know what I mean—like people you see in the street—like—"

"People—" he echoed, and paused. The word seemed to bemuse him, and he repeated it.

Then, all at once, he said good-bye, and was gone.

For a moment, I leaned with my head on the jamb, letting the nameless agitation of my being subside. Then I went on toward the back sitting room, where Tobias was. "Gosh," he said, "what did you all find to talk about all that time?"

"You," I said, and laughed, "just you, darling. Poor old Seth, he wants to be very sure that you are happy. Oh, are you happy, darling?" And I did a litle improvised dance toward him, swinging my skirt in two demure hands, singing, "Are you happy, darling, happy, are you happy now, my dear?" watching his face break into its beautiful smile, and his hands reach upward to me, feeling some leap of my own heart, a true leap.

Oh, why did the world intrude?

But the world was there, creeping in like cold air under a door, collecting like lint in the corner, crowding in on us like the camel in the tent, the people, the words, the papers, the letters, letters from the friends in Cambridge, arguing, giving advice, the letters from Tobias' father, in Litchfield, the old friend of Emerson, the mill-master, the man who had sent money and rifles to Bleeding Kansas, the holder of investments, the reader of Greek, the reformer of factories, the believer in Christ as the Perfect Man, the daring yachtsman, the handsome old face in the picture, scholar's brow, eyes deep but corner-crinkled with weather, nose bold as a pirate's cutlass, straight mouth, jaw-jut softened by chop-whiskers, the face of the son without the gleam of beauty, but the rock from which that beauty had been hewn, the picture the son held out to me, saying, "Look, it's Father," adding, "You ought to know him, he's something for a fellow to try to live up to."

Every week the letter from the father came, thick letters, written with black ink in a strong hand, defining the world: "—and as I see it, there is one argument against your notion of a limited and progressive suffrage for the black freedman. True, your notion that the Republic must depend upon the instruction of the electorate is sound. All men are capable of the Light, else why had God set a model of human perfection on earth for us to strive toward? *Nulla gens tam fera. . . . eius mentem non imbruerit deorum opinio.* The suffrage itself will school the black hand holding the ballot, and we shall stand by with primer and musket to preside over him and protect him in his right. But we shall not want to keep troops forever in the land of sedition and darkness to protect the freedman, for it were a great expense and aggravation. The ballot, once established, will be its own protection. And further the black ballot will be a ballot for the Republican Party, and will prevent any conspiracy between the conquered South and the raw and impulsive West to repudiate the National Debt and upset the fabric of our economy and liberties. I would not seem to speak for the cash-box and not justice, but you, my Son, know where my heart lies, in the last hope of human Brotherhood. But God hath so wrought the world to harmony that, though Virtue comes into the world seemingly a ragged beggar, she always in the end is the good citizen paying an honest way."

Tobias read it to me, as he read most of the father's letters, and at that point paused, and I noticed, or thought I noticed, the little V-shaped wrinkles come between his eyebrows, decisive in that clear forehead, the way it happened when something disturbed him. Anyway, he laid the letter aside, unfinished.

But he was to pick up the same letter, go to his desk and get it, one evening when Colonel Morton and Miss Idell were there, and others, and the argument ran high.

Colonel Morton had been arguing for the limited suffrage—"More won't stick," he kept saying, "not when half the states up North don't give 'em the vote at all."

"Yes," Seth said, "but in the North there is enough virtue to permit self-reformation, but here"—he spread his hands out, palms down—"we must enforce virtue."

"Oh, some of these rebels," the Colonel said, "they're not such bad fellows. I've been talking a little business with some of them."

At that Tobias rose to get the letter. "Business," he said, "I'll give you an argument for black suffrage based on business. My father, he's a businessman, too."

He read the letter, folded it with an air of fastidious finality, and said: "What do you make of that, Colonel?"

The Colonel gave it thought. "Coming from a man like your father," he said, "yes, that's important. But now it's my humble opinion—as of the moment, mind you—we have to sort of let things work themselves out."

"Work themselves back into slavery!" Seth said.

"Oh, no," the Colonel said, in his good humor, "once things stabilize down here—the people, the better sort, I mean—they won't be wanting to repudiate the National Debt. No, they'll have a stake in things."

"Virtue through self-interest," Seth said in massive contempt.

But the Colonel benignly ignored that, continuing: "It's a patriotic duty to help develop this section. I'm thinking of settling down in Louisiana, myself." He turned to me: "Mrs. Sears, I've made Tobias a little proposition. To come into business with me. Now you're a Southern flower, you don't want to go to cold Yankee-land, do you?"

Tobias stood up. "I'm not going there," he said.

"Ah," the Colonel said, and took a fine military step toward Tobias, putting out his hand, smiling, saying, "ah, so you've decided to come with me!"

"No," Tobias said, still smiling, but I caught a hint of the jaw-jut of the old man in the picture.

"No, Colonel," Tobias was saying, "I've decided to join the Freedman's Bureau."

I saw the Colonel's smile go empty, the hand still out-thrust. But no surprise was, I suppose, as profound as my own. For in so far as we had plans—plans beyond the dream of being together, my dream of the silken-haired heads at my knee, the smile over the white linen of the tablecloth, the sweet hand on the counterpane, in the dark—those plans were to go to Massachusetts, back to his country, back there and study and teach at some college, and in my mind's eye I had seen myself walking down a street shaded by elms, nodding to the faces that passed, kind faces, strange blue-eyed faces, feeling safe, safe by the very strangeness of those faces, safe by the distance from all I was and had been, safe with Tobias walking by my side, under the elms.

Now, in my surprise, there was some sense of entrapment, a sense of the walls of the candle-lit room closing in on me, of the warm, perfumed darkness of the summer night intruding through the jalousies, stifling me. I had the crazy impulse to jump up, then and there, to run out from them all, to be free.

Then my eyes settled again on Tobias, so straight, so high-headed, and my feeling went into anger: *Why hadn't he even told me?*

He seemed to be lifting, withdrawing, into distance, still smiling beautifully.

But it was the Colonel at whom he was smiling, saying: "But let's shake hands, Colonel. If you'll shake hands with a nigger-lover."

Then I heard his voice saying: "And Colonel, I might as well confess, total suffrage is my line."

And the Colonel said something—oh, he was himself again, they had shaken hands—but I didn't attend to that, for I suddenly remembered that Tobias had been for the limited suffrage, progressive suffrage, he called it, under education and supervision, and that that view was what had called forth the letter from his father. Then I remembered how when he had started to read the letter aloud to me, he had laid it aside, with the little V of wrinkles sharp between the eyebrows, just after his father's argument about the National Debt and the remark how virtue, in the end, always paid her way. Well, had his father convinced him now?

But now Seth was saying: "I am for total suffrage because I believe it to be totally right. There is no other argument."

No, his father had not convinced Tobias, I guessed. Nor had Seth convinced him. Colonel Morton had convinced him. Convinced him to flee the serving of the interest of Colonel Morton. But that meant he had to flee the serving of another interest, that of his father. And so he had burst out with the decision to go with the Bureau—had seized on that idea, that very instant, as the escape, the escape from both, from the Colonel, from father. And I suddenly had some vision of Tobias straining to break out of something, straining to rise from something, a clinging mass, undefined, gray, viscous.

And Tobias was saying: "Yes, Colonel, I'm back in the nigger-business. And you know who was the bravest man I ever saw? He was the blackest. His name was Oliver Cromwell Jones, and he made the rally that night Forrest surprised our convoy. Yes, the Rebs surprised us, whoever's fault it was, and my men nearly panicked. Sure, they were black, but you've seen white men panic, too, and who wouldn't feel panicky that night, with those hairy-faced crazy devils plunging out of the dark and riding right over you, with that crazy falsetto halloo—come clean, Colonel, don't you hear it in your sleep sometimes? I confess, I do. And suppose you were just waked up and no gun in your hand yet, and you a black man, with all your memory of being black, and those devils are riding you down, hallooing, and yelling, 'Bedford, Ole Bedford!' and you know who Bedford is, right out of the Pit, and they are yelling, 'Death to the niggers.' You are a nigger, and those devils lean from the saddle and the shotguns blazing right in your face and no quarter, the torches swinging into the rope-cut tents with men struggling under the canvas, and the wagons afire.

"Well, Oliver Cromwell Jones stood up in the middle of it, clubbing a musket—clubbed two of those devils out of the saddle, by George—and rallied our boys. I got him a commission. Though I had difficulty, even in a black command.

"Well, Lieutenant Jones will be in town this week. Come to dinner with him. You've shaken hands with a professional nigger-lover, now will you shake hands with a nigger?"

The Colonel slapped Tobias on the shoulder. "Old Tobey," he exclaimed in his heartiest voice, "when you go in for a thing, you sure do it up brown. No, black!" he amended, and gave a fine laugh at his own wit.

Miss Idell was looking at me. "Are you really having him to dinner?" she asked.

"Of course," I said. "Why not?"

She looked sweetly at me. "Yes, why not?" she said.

Lieutenant Jones was a little late. When he did arrive, I was across the drawing room with other guests and did not see him until the voice of Tobias broke in, saying: "Darling, here is Lieutenant Jones."

I caught the impression of blue uniform and gold braid, the height of form, the blackness of face, in that instant a kind of anonymous blackness. All this, in the flicker of an instant, as I put out my hand —with perhaps a slight excess of cordiality—and framed the words to greet the stranger.

But the words simply froze on my lips. For the black face looming there above me, somehow looming with all the blackness of the blackness beyond the room, beyond the suddenly frail walls, beyond the house, looming with the blackness of faces, of deep earth, of thicket, of fear, of night, was, all at once, not anonymous. Lieutenant Oliver Cromwell Jones was Rau-Ru.

My hand was in the air before me. The black hand took it. I felt the dry creases of the palm firmly against mine. Rau-Ru was looking straight into my face.

Then, with great gravity and detachment, he said: "I am very glad to know you, Mrs. Sears."

In the deepest sense, it had not been surprise that froze my greeting on my lips. In that moment, the surprise was the superficial thing, the veil, quickly penetrated and rent, over the recognition.

I do not mean my recognition of Rau-Ru, the man, standing there. I mean the recognition of the *fact* that he was there, the recognition that somehow I had been waiting for that fact to emerge from the realm of undifferentiated possibility into which, as into woods and darkness, Rau-Ru had walked that afternoon at *Pointe du Loup,* so long ago—leaving the form of Prieur-Denis on the floor, leaving my voice calling after him. Yes, he had walked away to be fixed in the uniqueness of the past event, to be left fixed in the darkness of the past, as I have read of the bodies at Pompeii caught in the descending darkness of the volcanic ash.

But no, that darkness of the past into which Rau-Ru had walked was not, I suddenly knew, the darkness of the thing fulfilled. No, it was, rather, a teeming darkness, straining soundlessly with forms struggling for recognition, for release from that dark realm of undifferentiated possibility.

At that moment of recognition, with Rau-Ru there before me, I would have been surprised at nothing, at no involution of Time, not even had Old Shaddy appeared there in a puff of magician's smoke offering me poor unbeautiful Bu-Bula, had I felt my father's hand plucking me from night and storm, had I seen my never-seen mother come walking toward me across the polite room, in her stained grave dress—ah, what would that dress have been, some poor simple thing, white no doubt, dimity, to wear when she sat with my father, a ribbon in her hair?

But what necessity would summon them? Standing there before Rau-Ru in that frozen instant of recognition, I did not propose that question to myself, but the answer was there in the frozen moment: *You summoned them yourself.*

But I was saying: "And I am very glad to meet you, Lieutenant." I denied the past.

Tobias' work with the Bureau took him often from New Orleans, for he was an inspector, and even when he was back in New Orleans, there were the endless letters and reports, long past the hours of the office, late at night, under the lamp in our sitting room, the endless interviews with all sorts of people, General Fullerton, who was the new agent for the Bureau, and accused of being pro-Southern, local businessmen and planters, politicians like Hahn, the Bavarian who had once been a Confederate and then became Governor under Banks, Dr. Dostie, the dentist from up North who had become an organizer of blacks, violent and opinionated—a Robespierre, Tobias called him—*gens de couleur,* and Stewart Pinchbeck, son of a white man who had sent him to Cincinnati for education, now a gambler with gambler's manners, eloquent and ambitious, bound for greatness, black freedmen with the mark of lash or chain still on them,

Lieutenant Jones, now an employee at the Custom House and already a voice, a force, in that strange swirl of rancor, opinion, aspiration, fear, calculation, generosity, and ambition that was the life of that time.

I bore the pressure of the world with as good spirit as I might. I knew it was a bad time, all the ruin of the war and now the fading of all the old, grand hopes in the grind of the day, and especially a bad time for the Bureau itself, the one thing, as Tobias felt, and I suppose rightly, that stood to redeem the war and might make some of the hopes come true. But meanwhile there was the bad management and corruption, the Provost Marshal's office short-handed or political, or levees down, jungle creeping over the rich land, crops rotting in the field, new men come in to take land—and always, behind all, the Rebel planter, unreconciled in his heart, oath or no, hungry and hard, waiting his time, waiting with vagrancy law, legislative enactment, lash, estopment of wage, terror, but strongest of all, merely his presence, his hovering hand, his arrogance, his humor, his strange violence and stranger forbearances, his flash of understanding, his stroke of justice, all in all, the sign of some cranky order and accommodation in the world.

"Massa monst'ous mean, but me and him, we git'long"—so Tobias quoted one of his wards to me.

And burst out: "What can you do? What can you do to make them feel that freedom is responsibility, when that old master is there calling them back into the world of nonresponsibility? Even if there's the lash with it and ten hours a day under Louisiana sun. But why shouldn't they feel that temptation? I admit I felt it, even in the worst of the war, just being part of a process, a machine, part of the falling motion of the world, just the pebble in the avalanche, just grinding in darkness—just not to think!"

I suddenly was aware of the vehemence of his pronouncement. I saw the rigidity of his neck, as he turned in his chair to me, the tension in the tendons above the collar, the blue wideness of his gaze on me—if it was on me, and not through me. And then the thought: *How lonely he must be, must have always been, to long for that dark and suffocating and grinding, overwhelmed depth of the landslip to make him feel part of something! Oh, what is his loneliness?*

The sense of that loneliness swept over me, and in that instant I loved him in a new way. I cried out, "Oh, darling, don't be lonesome! Oh, darling, I'm with you!"

And I rushed to him and, as he sat in his chair, cradled his head in my arms.

If that moment could only have lasted! But Tobias lifted his head.

I was almost ready to blame something on the fact that Tobias lifted his head. But that isn't fair. Everybody, even the most confused of us, must have such moments of vision, glimpses of a beautiful possibility of life. But the truth must be that you can't live by the moment of vision. You have to be the vision, not see it.

But anyway, Tobas raised his head, and in that instant I felt that somehow I was being repudiated, denigrated.

"But you have to think, if you are to make all that butchery mean anything," Tobias said, with the same vehemence, as though the moment when he had sunk into my arms had been, somehow, a concession to weakness.

I jerked my arms from his head. He didn't even notice.

"I'm writing Senator Sumner right now"—he was saying—"to say how the black question and the white question here aren't separable. I don't mean to say that now you can withdraw troops. But you can make the occupation a process of educating the Negro and white to live together in justice, not a process that assumes that one must dominate the other. We must give up vengeance. Oh, I know, it's difficult, but it can be done, let the states back in the Union but enforce justice while justice is being learned. Oh, that will be hard, but—"

His voice trailed off, and he fingered the pen.

"Yes, darling, I'm listening," I said.

But Senator Sumner wasn't listening. Nor President Johnson. Nor Congressman Thaddeus Stevens. Nor Tobias' father. Nor the planters of Terrebone and Feliciana. Nor Dr. Dostie. Nor all the millions of others.

I had said I was listening. But I wasn't.

We were all just ourselves.

So the autumn after the war, and the winter passed, Tobias deeper and deeper into his work, and his hope, clinging to it despite moments of despair about the Bureau, despite the mounting rancors and hints of violence as the idea of the hard peace of Congress gained ground over that of the soft peace of Mr. Lincoln. I saw the faces of those men who came to the house and heard their words, but it was a muffled world I was living in and the voices came from a distance, and I strained to catch their meaning. And sometimes, even when Tobias laid his hands upon me in love, and drew me to him, I had that feeling of all the world being muffled.

But it was a time of great tenderness between us. I clung to him, and he to me, but in a strange fashion each acted toward the other with some air of secret consideration, as though kindness were necessary as a concession to weakness in the other, as though that other were barely coming out of a deep grief, or a sickness.

I said that it was a muffled world, a world of waiting. Once or twice when Seth and Miss Idell and Lieutenant Jones were present, I would look from face to face, and have some sense of almost unbearable suspense. Each face would have, in that moment, its characteristic quality, a quality seemingly then refined to an almost allegorical simplicity, as though a painter had caught that central, secret moment and fixed it forever: Seth's cold intensity, head high and eyes looking through you, with some impression always of a snowy woods, a snowy sky, behind that head; Miss Idell's smile and the lift of the chin to show the white, unmarked throat, and the lifted white hand with its promise of a soft compelling grasp, such softness and yet, you knew, with the knife-sharp, needle-sharp provocative nails in the midst of that softness; Lieutenant Jones's head with the hair crisping to the rounded skull like a cap or casque, the whole head and face rounded into a strange economy, the head large but nothing wasted, the features strong but somehow reserved and drawn into the basic shape, the ears close to the skull, the nose strong but less protrusive than need be, the eyes, with their positive whites, always watchful, as though watching from a thicket, from a door ajar, from the inwardness of that reserved, fulfilled sculpture of head, from the smooth, enamel-slick blackness.

I would look at them, not thinking, really, of the time in my past when each had come into my life, and say—no, feel: *they are here.*

And I would be breathless with my waiting.

Waiting to know what? To know my life, myself. It was as though your life had a shape, already totally designed, standing not in Time but in Space, already fulfilled, and you were waiting for it, in all its necessity, to be revealed to you, and all your living was merely the process whereby this already existing, fulfilled shape in Space would become an event in Time.

You wait breathlessly, because you cannot see that shape standing in its coiling shadows, just an outline here, a bulge there, quickly blotted out.

You will make it out only at some very last—but something in you is certain that that shape exists there out of Time and will be transposed into Time, and this something in you, the thing that makes you sit breathless in a chair, in the noise and brightness of company, and stare at a face, straining for its meaning—well, this something in you is longing for the kiss of Fate.

So I might sit, bemused and waiting, and look at the face. Or I might make an occasion to speak to the face, seeking the word that might provoke it to divulge its meaning, its role, for me. But that is not an act you plan. It is as instinctive as breathing.

As when I said to Seth: "When is your wife coming, Seth, with your children?" And watched him narrowly, not knowing what I watched for, but somehow relishing the instant of painful hesitation, before he said: "She cannot come soon. She is with her mother on the farm. Her mother is a widow and is not well."

Or as when I said to him, watching: "Seth, Miss Idell—Mrs. Morton—she says you are charming."

He turned upon me a face of such pain that I recoiled from him. It was like catching an inward glimpse through a chink in a shutter. It was as though that pain I glimpsed through the chink had some separate, identifiable being, had its own body and that body were stuck on a spit to writhe and revolve slowly, not over flame, but slow and glimmering white in the cold darkness of Seth's mind.

Then I caught myself peering at his face, waiting, you might say, for another glimpse inward, straining to see that body of pain in the darkness. I had the need to give it a name. Hannah—was it Hannah?—that heavy, bulging splotchy-whiteness turning and turning in infinite sadness on that spit in the cold darkness. No, not Hannah, not splotchy-whiteness, but sweet whiteness, pierced, transfixed. It was Miss Idell, twitching with anguish, and suddenly I felt a thrill of elation, the thrill of justice.

But Seth was saying: "Why do you hate her so?"

"What?" I burst out, coming out of my instant of vision terrified by his own clairvoyance. And at the same time the thrill of elation that I had experienced became the spit in my vitals, myself the victim turning forever there in that cold darkness. But no, no, it couldn't be I.

"What makes you think I hate her?" I said.

"You hate her," he said, staring down into my face. "You hate her because she killed your father," Seth said.

"What do you know about anything?" I demanded, not sure what that *anything* was.

"I know that she was Mrs. Muller. In Cincinnati. I remember the paper. Your father, and her husband the convict. I guessed who she was, from the first."

"All right, all right," I said.

"You don't have to hate her," Seth said. "You see, she is sorry. She is not the woman you think. Or I thought. A worldling. No, I have prayed with her. I have seen tears of contrition."

"Oh, you have been talking together, you two," I interrupted, and had the vision of their heads leaning together, and felt disarmed, conspired against.

I looked across at Miss Idell, across the room, laughing over there like a flash of music, scattering brightness.

"Don't be a fool," I said. "That woman, when she found out you knew something, she had to quiet you. She'd make you pray."

"If you hate her so," he said, "why do you see her all the time?" With that he turned away.

She had my secret, that was it, and I feared that if I turned my back it would not, somehow, be safe.

And knowing this, I hated myself in an arid, dusty way.

Yes, in that time of waiting, I might fumble into the coiling shadow to touch the shape of my life that stood out of Time, or might seek the word to provoke a face to divulge its meaning. As when, on an unpremeditated impulse, I spoke to Lieutenant Jones.

It was late afternoon, toward dusk, the spring dusk of Louisiana—spring of '66 now—and the group in the garden had begun to drift toward the house again, taking their talk with them, the talk of the forthcoming election of city officials. "Certain to be Confederate now," Judge Durrell—he had been chairman of the constitutional convention of two years before—was saying, and Tobias said: "You feel history being wiped out."

The only hope, Judge Durrell was saying, was in loyal men staying away from the polls to prejudice the election.

"Not if we could vote," Lieutenant Jones said quietly, and the eyes all turned to him. He stood there in his quietness, his shadowy, shuttered watchfulness.

For an instant nobody said a thing.

"Not if we could vote," Lieutenant Jones said again, and suddenly turned away from the group, stepping back soundlessly, leaving the eyes, seeming to fade toward the shadowy margin of planting beyond the area of white crushed shell—fading into the japonicas, tree-size, black now with evening, heavy with perfume, mimosa, myrtle.

Somebody spoke, and all the eyes had left Lieutenant Jones standing over there.

No, all eyes hadn't left him. I was watching him, and it was that act of withdrawal, neither insolent nor humble, an act of withdrawing into some secret fullness of self, that drew me a couple of steps across the shell. The group over there was drifting toward the house.

Lieutenant Jones looked at me, but said nothing.

Then, on the startling impulse, I said what I said. I said: "Why, when you first came to this house, did you deny knowing me?"

As he stood there, in his dark, ordinary civilian coat, with the darkening mass of foliage and paling of blossom above him, and looked down at me, scanning my face, I thought that he had not heard me, and the face seemed, on the instant, absolutely strange to me, even inimical, as though the past we shared, and the debt I owed him out of that past, were something I had merely dreamed.

Then he said: "The world has changed."

"What do you mean?"

"You are Mrs. Sears," he said, and moved his shoulders with the faint, muscle-rippling hint of a shrug under the cheap cloth of the coat.

"Well, if you mean to imply—" I began, not quite knowing how I meant to go on. But there was a crunching of shell underfoot, behind me, and I swung round, and Tobias was stepping toward me, smiling, with a hand already reached out to touch me.

"Darling," I said, "darling—" I felt the rush of relief.

Tobias' hand was on my shoulder, the fingers moving ever so lightly to caress secretly the flesh under the thin fabric, and he was saying for me to hurry, to come in, the guests were waiting.

So I hurried.

In the course of the evening I sought to avoid the eyes of Lieutenant Jones, who had been Rau-Ru.

But the eyes were there, that night and for the two weeks before he came again, to talk some Bureau business. We had, however, scarcely been served our coffee when a man came and wanted to talk to Tobias. It was urgent, he had ridden half a day to come. So Tobias took him into his study, and Lieutenant Jones and I sat silent, sipping our coffee, aware of the weight of the spring night outside, the unremitting vibrance of the insects needling the darkness of the garden, the heavy, flesh-sweet odor of blossom out of the dark penetrating through jalousies into the candlelit room.

"Do you remember our last conversation?" I said, finally. I had to brace myself to say it.

He turned toward me, and I noticed again how the hair was like a casque on the reserved modeling of the skull, how close and economical the ears lay to the skull.

"It was not only our last conversation," he said, with detachment. "It was our only one."

"What do you mean?"

"I mean we had never had a conversation before," he said, indifferently.

"But I had known you so long, and—" I began. But that was getting off what I had meant to say. So I said with great factuality: "Be that as it may. I meant to go back to what we were saying when we were interrupted."

"Yes," he said, "when Major Sears interrupted you."

"Yes," I said, and remembered him coming toward me, smiling, his hand out.

But Tobias didn't come in, and so I said to Lieutenant Jones: "I was not sure of your meaning in that conversation, but I want to say that if you meant to imply that there is something withheld—some—some—"

"Some secret," he said.

"I meant to say that if you implied such, you were wrong," I said firmly.

He set his coffee cup down in the saucer, with a precise, definitive click. "Well," he said, "you had denied having known me." He waited a second. Then said: "So you told him afterward?"

"As a matter of fact—" I began. "As a matter of fact, I did not. But not for anything of importance—you know what I mean. What I mean to say is, my husband knows who I am. Certain things— certain details—we have not discussed. It is just because—certain painful memories—you know, associations—"

I was looking down at my cup, which I held in the air before me as I tried to say what I meant.

"You mean," he said, in his low, husky voice, "you mean you can't stand being a nigger?"

I felt the blood come into my cheeks, and saw the cup there before me quiver in the air, ever so little.

"Oh, it's not that," I managed.

"You mean that Major Sears can't stand having a nigger for a wife?"

I set the cup down on the table.

"Listen," I said, leaning at him, knowing that if I had a weapon I should strike him, "listen, that is unjust. You know my husband. You know his character, his being, his idealism, how little he cares for opinion of the world. You know how—"

He shrugged in his slow, rippling way, and I hated him. "I suppose he does the best he can," he said.

"You talk that way about your friend, your admirer," I said hotly.

"Nobody can do better than the Lord lets him," he said.

"Well, leave him out. And as for me—"

"Well," he said, "I don't blame anybody for not wanting to be a nigger. Do you think I liked it that time they caught me and took me to the jail and laid on the rawhide? Well, I'll tell you—" He rose suddenly from the chair.

"Oh, that's why you hate me!" I cried out.

"Hate you?" he said, and looked soberly down at me as though to find the answer to the question in his voice.

"Yes," I said, "hate me. Oh, it was because of me—of trying to help me—that you had to leave, that they whipped you."

"I don't hate you for that," he said. "I owe you thanks."

"Owe me?"

"It wasn't Mr. Lincoln who set me free," he said. "It was you."

"Me?"

"Yes, you," he said, "you and that Charles. And then that man with the rawhide. Oh, yes, if it had not been for you, I might have been there yet. Ass-kissing Old Bond. Oh, yes, I was the k'la—I was the k'la!" And he swung his right hand out in a sweeping gesture of revulsion.

"But he *was* good," I found myself crying out.

"Yes, good," he said, "and that was the worst. Worse than the rawhide. Old Bond being good—yes, that makes me hate him most."

He leaned at me, staring at me. "Listen," he said, his voice low and husky now, "tell me the truth. Don't you hate him most for being good to you?"

"No," I said, "no," with some flash of desperation in me, some feeling that if Hamish Bond were here, Hamish were here, I might be safe, might be protected from something.

But it wasn't Hamish Bond who came in.

It was Tobias at last, his face strained and preoccupied, some papers in his hand. "It's worse than I thought—" he began.

But I had cut in: "Oh, you ought to have heard Lieutenant Jones, what he was telling me!"

"What's that?" Tobias asked politely.

"It's terrible," I said, "how he was a slave. He was flogged. They tied him to a post and used a rawhide. On his bare back." I turned to Lieutenant Jones. "That's right, isn't it?" I asked. "On your bare back?"

"Yes," he said, and I thought a kind of grim smile was on his lips.

"They struck him again and again," I said. "It laid the flesh open, till his back was bathed in blood."

Tobias laid his hand on my shoulder. "Yes, darling," he said quietly, "yes, it is terrible, but I am sure that Lieutenant Jones doesn't wish to dwell on it now."

"The scars," I said, "it left most frightful scars."

And I saw it in my mind, the healed-up scars, great corded scars, rough as hemp rope, rough as oak bark, black with gray scaling, humping out, interlacing mathematically on the bare, black flesh. I could just feel how rough that surface would be if you ran a finger down it.

"Rough as oak bark—oh, it was terrible what they did."

Tobias' fingers had gripped my shoulder, quite hard. "Darling," he was saying, "I am quite positive that Lieutenant Jones does not wish to dwell on it. We all have new problems now. Just tonight, now this man—" He stopped, patted my shoulder now. "Besides," he said, and smiled down at me, "what we all need is some more coffee. Some good, wonderful, poisonous Louisiana coffee."

So I went to get some more coffee—Mathilda would have been off duty by this hour—and made it, quite calmly, brought it back, *café brûlot* now, and they drank it, and I tried to but couldn't.

It was quite late when Tobias came to bed. I had been sound asleep, an exhausted sleep, and didn't wake until he lifted the *moustiquaire* and got in with me. When I stirred, he drew me to him a little, with my back toward him, my head on his right arm, my body arranged as though I were sitting in his lap. It was a way we often slept, his right arm under my head, the left arm laid over me, and I was so much smaller than he that his long body bent around me. I felt safe.

Outside, there was moonlight. Some filtered in through the jalousies. A mockingbird was singing in the garden. I knew he would be singing for hours, with that moonlight. I wished he would stop.

"Tobias," I said.

"Yes, darling."

"I love you, darling," I said.

"I love you, too, darling."

"Let's go away," I said. "As soon as we can. Go to Massachusetts. Go somewhere." I had a glimmering vision of a street of bare trees, night, but the night was bright with snow, and myself walking down the street, Tobias by my side.

"My work is here," Tobias was saying.

"Oh, it's so mixed up," I said.

"I have to do it," he said.

"Oh, but it's so hopeless," I said.

"I have hope," he said.

"That Lieutenant Jones, even," I said, "I don't think even he has gratitude."

"Why should he? His back scarred, why shouldn't he be bitter?"

I thought of the back with the horrible scars.

"As for gratitude," Tobias was saying, "one does not work for gratitude. One works in order to be able to live with oneself."

*To live with oneself:* The words seemed, in a strange, bright way, to be healing a wound, a wound in me. Then I saw them like a bright miraculous unguent laid over the weals and humped, corded scars of the black back. As soon as it was laid on, the scars were gone, simply gone. The back was there with its unmarked sheen and molded musculature.

I felt purified somehow, forgiven.

I grasped the hand of Tobias that lay folded over my breast. "Oh, darling," I whispered, "darling, you are so good."

That was the way it was, he was so good, and the night passed, and after a while the moon was down and the mockingbird didn't sing any more, but I was asleep well before that, and the season passed, the last japonicas were gone, the last azaleas, but the myrtle was on, the bougainvillaea coming, summer came, the gray clouds, the color of unwashed wool, came in from the gulf in the afternoon, and the rain fell in a black torrent across the brilliance of sky, then the sun struck stunningly again, it was three o'clock, and the roof-tiles steamed, and all the world, day by day, night by night, seemed waiting for the force of summer to collect itself, to fulfill itself, there was talk of fever, and Mr. Monroe, the old Confederate Mayor, was Mayor again, for President Johnson had given him a special pardon.

President Johnson, he and all those other men off in Washington —Sumner, Stevens, all the rest—were preparing the fate of Louisiana, and preparing, too, my fate.

As for Louisiana:

The President wanted to accept the state as it was organized under the Constitution of 1864, and admit its men to the Congress, but Sumner and those people they called the Radicals wanted to reduce the state to a territory until it should give all Negroes the vote.

Concerning motives there was all kind of talk. Johnson, they said, was a Southerner after all, and had stood by the Union only because as a poor, unlettered mountain boy he had hated the low-country aristocrats. But now, they said, those aristocrats, blood still on their hands, came to the White House, and flattered him, and in his old hate and deprivation there was so much sad, secret longing that now he was ready to betray the Union. But the countervoices said that the Radicals wanted only power, only the tariff, only hard money, only the Republican Party, only the National Debt.

"But I cannot be responsible for their souls," Tobias said. "I can only be responsible for my own, and be a Radical for my own reasons."

"As for me," Lieutenant Jones said, and fixed his gaze steady on

Tobias, "I'm a Radical for only one reason, and that reason is that I can't be anything else. Not with this face." And stabbed a forefinger brutally into the flesh of his own cheek.

Whatever the motives, the Fourteenth Amendment to the Constitution was passed by Congress in June, making the Negro a citizen.

"A citizen who can't vote," Lieutenant Jones said.

"Yes," Tobias said, bitterly, "and you know why the franchise isn't in the amendment? Because if it were written in, not half the Northern states would ratify."

The amendment didn't give the Negro the vote, but it was understood that it would get him the vote in the Rebel states. Failure to ratify, failure to give the vote, would mean the refusal of Congress to admit representatives. The happy fate of Tennessee made that clear. Tennessee ratified immediately, and immediately, in July, her representatives were seated in Washington.

But in Louisiana it was different. The legislature wasn't in session. No special session was called. The Democrats didn't want a special session because they still hoped, perhaps, that President Johnson would win, that the West would help him, that the Fourteenth Amendment would fail of general ratification. As for the Radicals, at least most of them, they didn't want a special session either, for ratification would, presumably, leave the present incumbents in office in the state.

No, they had a bolder plan. They would cut the present government off, root and branch, and cast it into the fire.

They would create a new state constitution, total black suffrage with assurance doubly sure by barring ex-Confederates, or barring at least certain large categories. But how get a convention to do this when the state, under the present suffrage law of the Constitution of 1864, would certainly send up a Democratic majority?

There was a simple and brilliant way—oh, so simple: call back to life the old Unionist Convention of 1864, to write a new constitution. They would take the state, and do—for all their various reasons, good and bad, noble and ignoble—with ballot and convention what, apparently, bullet and bayonet had failed to do.

There was, of course, the question of legality.

But even the president of the old convention, Judge Durrell, did not believe the reconvening would be legal.

"You aren't afraid, are you, Judge?" Dr. Dostie demanded softly and leaned his mad eyes into the circle of light from the lamp. The lamp was on the center table in my drawing room. It had a white porcelain base, wreathed in painted roses.

"Not for myself," Judge Durrell said, "but for what may happen."

"Ah," Dr. Dostie said, and leaned into the light.

Yes, Judge Durrell had done what he could. He had telegraphed the Radicals in Congress—Thaddeus Stevens himself—and now, days later it must have been, there was only silence. He had been to see General Sheridan, the commander of the district, and Sheridan had refused protection for such a convention.

But Dr. Dostie said, "Ah," and rose up. "The war's not over," he said. "But we don't need you, Judge. Nor you and the Bureau, Sears. Nor General Sheridan. We are ourselves!"

"Yes," Lieutenant Jones said, "ourselves," staring into the light, not looking at anybody.

"Let it come!" Dr. Dostie said, and flung out his arm.

Let it come, he said, and did he feel already the quick, slick—oh, so easy—slip of the sword-blade into the viscera, the numbing chunk of the pistol ball to the spine? Did he see, not us now under that lifted arm, but others, the thousands of faces he was to see one night soon, black faces sweating under the flares, staring up at him, while his veins tingled like wine, and he cried again, to those faces, let it come if it must, let blood come?

Or was there nothing tonight across the room, beyond the lamplight, but the severe face of Justice?

It was tonight that Lieutenant Jones stopped me in the hall, just outside the drawing-room door. "For curiosity, Mrs. Sears," he said, "I should like to know if you are for or against the convention."

"I agree with my husband," I said.

"You mean you are against the convention?"

"I mean," I said firmly, "that I agree with Tobias—I mean that there must be Negro suffrage, but—"

"But what?" he cut in.

"But there must be no *coup d'état*. We must have justice in law, we must have—"

My words withered away under his heavy, sardonic gaze. "You talk funny," he said, "for the little nigger Old Man Bond flattened out."

As I stood in my stunned silence, he leaned again at me.

"Was that how you learned about white folks' justice that you like it so well?" he whispered.

"Oh, you are vile!" I said.

"Yassum," he said, in broad obsequious parody of the field hand, "I'se vile."

"I will tell my husband to forbid you the house," I said.

Lieutenant Jones bowed ceremoniously. "It is the privilege of Madame," he said.

That night, I lay in the hot dark, unable to sleep, with Tobias asleep beside me, and I asked myself if there was no justice, only the white man's justice?

I rolled my head from side to side against the stickiness of the pillow. *Oh, whose side am I on?* I demanded, and stared up through the shadowy white of the mosquito net into the darkness.

And all at once my head was full of the old image, the flames leaping up, the carnage, the jungle bats circling and whistling in the high periphery of light.

I called out Tobias' name. I rolled over and seized his shoulder, and shook him awake.

He asked me what was the matter, and I told him it was nothing, just a frightful dream.

The summer was on us, the talk of fever, the black burst of rain off the sea, the heat. Somehow, this year, I couldn't stand the heat. Tobias had even suggested that I go to Massachusetts, to his father's summer house. There would be cool sea, sailing, friends who would like me, his father would love me, and the thought of that powerful, not beautiful old face in the picture, with the weather-crinkles at eyes, cutlass nose, jut-jaw, filled me with a cold flash of terror, or something like terror. And in that instant I had looked at Tobias and wondered—in the sudden clairvoyant sympathy of my own feeling—if something like that lurked deep in Tobias, too.

No, I couldn't think of going away, alone. Being without him here for a few days at a time when he took his inspection trips, that was bad enough. And sometimes when he did come back I would feel that he was not really with me, his face strained, his mind on the report he would have to write that very night—perjury in some Bureau court, irregularity in an account, a freedman's body rotting in a bayou, bullet in head.

In June Tobias went away for a long inspection. The heat was worse now.

But Miss Idell, when she came to call, seemed untouched by it. She sat there with her expensive blue dress unwrinkled, the lace at her bosom white as foam and crisp as frost, her gaze blue and cool like distance, the ice in the frosty glass of lemonade in her hand making the faintest tinkle, sitting there superior to time, weather, fate, and human considerations.

Seth was not very well, she said, and I realized that I hadn't seen him for weeks. He was working too hard, she said. "Now, Morgan," she said, "he works, too, but he knows how to relax."

Yes, Morgan Morton—Mr. now, not Colonel, for he was out of the army and was in business—knew how to relax. I had seen him stand in my little drawing room with glass in hand. I had seen him drive past behind his pair of matched bays, the smart rhythm of the pacers unspooling down the avenue, the red spokes of wheels flashing, reins and silver-mounted whip in hand begloved in yellow dogskin, rosebud in lapel of discreetly checked coat, mustaches glinting black, hard black hat on head.

Yes, Seth was working too hard, she was saying, he was too stirred up about that Constitutional Convention business. Now Morgan—Morgan certainly was pleased to see that Tobias was taking a more moderate view. It wouldn't do anybody any good to stir things up. Morgan was glad Tobias shared his view.

I thought of Tobias flinching from that approbation, Tobias struggling in the gray, viscous matter that threatened to suck him down, all the world that might suck him down.

And I thought of the stiff black finger of Lieutenant Jones stabbing brutally into the black flesh of his own cheek, him saying:—*for only one reason—this face.*

Suddenly she began to put on her gloves. She had to go, she said. She invited me to dinner the next night. Do come, she said, for they wanted to cheer up the little widow. "Poor little Manty," she said, and kissed me fleetingly on the brow, touching me as you touch a child. "Poor little Manty," she said, "to have to sleep all by yourself two more horrid nights, and no man."

I looked up into her smiling face, then flinched from her, aware of my shortness of stature, angry at that, and at the tone of condescension, but flinching away for more than that. It wasn't some hint of impropriety, either, in her remark, though I am sure there must have been some surprise at it, surprise because there had always been in Miss Idell's conversation a most sedulous avoidance of anything not perfectly, even priggishly correct—as though that sweep of thigh, that lissomeness of waist, that high offering of bosom might otherwise be guiltily misconstrued by the world.

No, I flinched from what I saw, or thought I saw, on her face now, a glutted drowsiness, as though the cheeks had gone fuller, swollen—but oh, so little—with their blood, the lower lip lax and fuller, the eyelids drooping to show the faintest azure in the depth of their modeling, to give the impression that something of the color of the eyes thus veiled yet shone through the purity of the eyelid's flesh.

That look on her face was quickly gone, like the shadow of a bird's wing sweeping over, but it struck me as the shadow of her night, the night she was moving toward, the night from whose depth of dark, lax satiety, previsioned in that instant, she might cruelly taunt my loneliness, and I suddenly saw in that same instant, her head on an arm, the yellow hair loose over the man's arm, over Morgan Morton's arm, over Herman Muller's arm tangled with his yellow beard, over Seth's arm—no, that couldn't be—over my father's arm. I saw her head move in the shadow of my mind, shift itself luxuriously, and it was my father's arm.

I was absolutely quivering with that entrapped hatred, which I could not express.

Tobias came home, and all was as I had imagined, he was sweet to me, and for a little everything was different. But the world was there, in the threats and boasts of men standing at bars, it was there, in the tobacco smoke and brandy reek of hot rooms at night where men leaned together in their conjurative sibilance and burgeoning dreams, there in the laughter of Negroes at night, walking down the middle of the street, there in the marble corridors far off in Washington, there in the wolfish glance of the ex-soldier standing on the corner of the street, motionless in the glare of midday, with nothing to do.

Meanwhile the Convention had met, at the Mechanics Institute. But there was only half a quorum. The others, out of fear, conviction, or cunning, had stayed away. But the half quorum elected a man named Howells as president, a clever man—clever enough, they said, to devise the brilliant stroke in his formal proclamation reassembling the Constitutional Convention: the Convention was to rewrite the constitution, yes, but also—and here was the brilliance—to consider the Fourteenth Amendment. The date set was July 30.

Then Judge Howell went off to Washington, off to get the blessing of Thaddeus Stevens and the rest, and to confirm what was the general gossip in New Orleans, that the original idea itself for the Convention had come from Washington. So we waited, all the city waited, for Judge Howell's return.

Tobias went away on another trip, and I was alone.

The next day Miss Idell and Seth called on me. Seth was very quiet, and yellowish in the face. He had a touch of fever, he said. He was thinking of asking for leave, of going home. "Poor Seth," I said, "poor old Seth, you must."

He stared at me with a numb distress, and I saw his tongue come out to wet his dry lips. The lips looked, quite literally, gray.

Tobias came back. There was still no word from Washington, only the wild rumors. More troops would be moved in. The present government would be arrested. No, not the Governor, for Wells was too sly—against black suffrage only a year ago, but now gone over to the Convention. But Judge Abell of the District Court, once a member of the Convention of 1864, had switched his allegiance and had charged the Grand Jury that the new Convention was dangerous to public peace. They said he would be arrested for treason.

Tobias received a letter saying, "Be silent or flee." The picture of a dagger, crudely drawn, with gouts of blood dripping from it, was the only signature.

"Why you?" I asked, "oh, what do they bother you for, you're against the Convention."

"I am a Yankee and a Bureau man," Tobias said.

Judge Abell was arrested for treason.

"Fools," Tobias said, "fools!"

Judge Howell returned from Washington. "He will dine with us tomorrow," Tobias announced to me. Then added: "I have one last idea."

So Judge Howell came, and the others, two men I had never seen before, Seth, Dr. Dostie, Dr. Horton, Lieutenant Jones. Before dinner, Lieutenant Jones, standing at my side, a little apart from the others, leaned and said: "Have you told him yet?"

For a second I didn't know what he meant.

Then he said: "Have you told him to forbid me the house?"

"Why do you come here to insult me?" I demanded, whispering. "I come only on business," he said, and turned away.

Tobias explained to them his new idea, his last hope. The idea was simple. At behest of the Convention, Governor Wells had just issued a proclamation for an election in the fall to fill vacant seats. Therefore it was logical to postpone assembly, till a full Convention had been gathered.

There was not a word, only the cold look of Judge Howell, of Dostie, on Tobias, the other looks.

But Tobias only lifted his head a fraction higher, let his clear gaze touch fleetingly each face, then said: "What would be lost, gentlemen? And much gained. First, the charge that the Convention is a rump will be obviated by the election. Second, the passage of time will mollify the tempers now exacerbated, the danger of—"

"Mr. Sears," one of the strange men said, "Mayor Monroe is issuing writs of arrest for every member of the Convention. He is swearing in a thousand grog-soaked Irish bullies and demobilized Rebels as special police. If we knuckle under now—"

"General Baird," another said, "what are his troops for if not to protect us?"

"You know General Baird's position," Tobias said. "I went to see General Baird and—"

"So *you* went to see him?" Judge Howell said, with irony.

"Yes," replied Tobias evenly, "and for your information, I tried to see Governor Wells, but he is not to be located."

And another: "Oh, he'll hide out to see who wins!"

"But I did see Lieutenant-Governor Voorhies," Tobias said, "and he has telegraphed the President for information on the role of the military in relation to writs against the Convention. And Baird, he has telegraphed Secretary Stanton, but there is, as yet, no reply and—"

And another: "What's the Secretary of War for, if he won't show authority?"

"And as for Baird himself," Tobias said, "with his superior away, with Sheridan off in Texas—"

And another: "What's he commander for? What's he doing away in Texas?"

"With his **superior** away," Tobias repeated calmly, "Baird feels that he can go no further than to release any members arrested by Monroe."

"Mr. Sears," Judge Howell said, "it seems that you have busied yourself unnecessarily."

Suddenly Tobias' head—how fine it was in that instant—lifted a little more, the nostrils flickering ever so slightly with the stir of spirit, and he said: "Judge, what I have done I have done in my poor best of conscience."

"Was it your conscience made you write to Washington to try to block our efforts?"

"Ah," somebody said.

Then Tobias: "I take it as my duty to inform my Bureau of anything bearing on the fortunes of the freedmen."

"I saw a copy on the desk of Thaddeus Stevens."

"I did not suggest that it go there," Tobias said, "but I hope you read it."

"I did," Judge Howell said.

"I hope that you noted that I expressed my concern for full suffrage, that I—" Tobias suddenly stopped, then flung his gaze over the group. "Gentlemen," he said then, "we are together on our best hopes. And believe me, all I have wished is to see peace in justice—"

"With Monroe's Rebels?" Dr. Dostie demanded.

Tobias stepped in front of Lieutenant Jones. "Word comes to me," he said, "that you have gathered members of your old—your old group."

"My outlaws," Lieutenant Jones said, sourly. "When we were runaways in the swamp."

"I beseech you," Tobias said, "to let no armed man go near that Mechanics Institute. I have confidence that General Baird will be instructed. But I beg you to use all influence to let no freedman, no black man, go near. That will be our strength."

"Our strength," Dr. Dostie said, "it will be ten thousand in the street!"

Tobias paid no attention. "You know me," he said to Lieutenant Jones. "We fought a long war together. I know you are brave enough for peace."

He held his hand out to Lieutenant Jones. For a moment Lieutenant Jones looked down at the hand. Everybody was watching.

Lieutenant Jones took the hand.

"Fool," Dr. Dostie whispered. Everybody heard the whisper.

They had shaken hands all around. Even Dr. Dostie in the end. Judge Howell said that he would make representations to General Baird for protection. He would assure, on the part of the Convention, peaceful assembly. Then they were gone.

All, that is, except Seth. At the last moment, Tobias had quietly motioned him to stay.

Now Tobias said he wanted him to do a favor. Tobias himself had to go to Carrollton for a Bureau matter, and wouldn't be back until Sunday afternoon. But would Seth try to see General Baird, and undertake to do what could be done for military protection?

Seth hesitated.

"Oh, Seth," Tobias said, "I know you don't agree about the Convention. But I want you to know that I've tried to see the right thing. You see, Seth, you are my dearest friend." And he put out his hand.

Seth was about to take the hand, his own hand was out-thrust. But all at once a shudder took him, his face went streaked and white under that new sallowness of ill health, and he sank down into a chair. Tobias had seized him by the arm to support him. I rushed to bring a glass of cordial.

By the time I got to the chair, he had recovered a little, though his breathing was heavy and his color ghastly. I offered the cordial, but he waved it away.

He even tried to rise, but Tobias gently restrained him. "You must stay here tonight," Tobias said.

Seth shook his head. Suddenly, despite Tobias's restraint, he was on his feet.

"I must go," he said.

The next day was Saturday, and on that day I made it a practice, unless some special occasion precluded, of giving the servants freedom from noon until the next morning, except for one to prepare the dinner and, if I was alone, sleep in the house. So when the bell rang about three that afternoon, I myself went to the door.

"Why, Seth!" I cried. "How do you feel now?"

He said he was much better. And indeed his face was different. Despite the sallowness, it was calm and pure, like the face of one who has been ill but now mends past the crisis.

All at once, he stepped across the threshold, ignoring me as though I were a flunky, and was two full paces beyond me into the hall.

"Wait," I called after him. "Tobias isn't here—if you have seen General Baird—"

"Tobias is in Carrollton," he replied, flatly, not to me, to the air, the shadows of the hall.

"Yes, of course—" I began, but he had turned from me, and was walking down the hall, toward the drawing room.

I stepped quickly to catch up, but he was there before me, and had entered. He was standing in the middle of the floor.

"Did you see General Baird?" I asked.

"No," he said, "no," and twitched his head, in annoyance.

Then he said: "My furlough is arranged."

"Oh, Seth, that's wonderful, oh, you'll be well now," I said.

"I leave tomorrow."

"Tomorrow!" I exclaimed. "Why—why, Tobias won't see you."

"I don't want to see him," he announced.

Then, in my silence, he walked back to the door, and closed it. He returned and stood before me.

"Last night," he said, "did you see?"

"See what?" I asked, bewildered.

"I could not take his hand," he said.

"Poor old Seth," I said, and reached out to touch his sleeve. "You were ill."

"He called me his dearest friend," he said, staring at me.

"Well, you are," I said.

"Listen," he said, and leaned rancorously at me. "It was when he said that."

"What are you talking about?"

"When I found that I could not take his hand," he said. "Then I knew that the deed was already done."

"What?" I was demanding, caught by the glitter of his eyes.

"For what is done in the heart is done already," he was saying, with the air of careful instruction, "and if the deed is done in the heart it should as well be done in the flesh that the vileness of the heart may be confirmed. For only in vileness is the beginning, and therefore—"

But he stopped. All at once, like a man shot, he dropped to his knees.

He seized a fold of my skirt, and stared up at me. "Oh, spit upon me," he cried out, and shut his eyes, waiting.

He was waiting, his eyes squinched shut, but then, all at once, they were open again and he was speaking in a low rapid voice, as though against time, saying: "I will explain to you. Once I sought immortal perfection in mortal life, for the Book says it is possible, and I told you that we two should seek it together for our final joy, but I did not know what I know now, that only in vileness may man begin to seek, and now to seek we must confirm what vileness has been enacted in my heart."

He was now tugging at my skirt, as to draw me down, saying: "Now—now." Then: "Now—on this spot—on this floor," whispering, still tugging, harder and harder, with one hand while with the other he patted the floor, and the motion of that hand had something of cajolery, as when you try to wheedle a child to sit beside you, and you pat the spot.

It was that absurd motion of cajolery that broke my spell. "You are ill, Seth," I said quite calmly. "You have a fever. Now stop tugging at me, do you understand, and go right to a doctor."

He rose from the floor, crankily like an old man, but still clutching the wad of my skirt, drawing it a little high for decency, had it not been for my petticoats.

"Drop that skirt," I commanded him.

"It would have been just once—just one time," he said, sadly, not releasing the skirt. "That I might be free. Free to begin to seek."

Then more sadly than before, distantly, as to himself: "I did not want to have to force you."

So I jerked back. The skirt drew taut.

He shook his head. "No," he said, "not that kind of force. For I have knowledge that will compel you. You see, I could tell Tobias."

"Tell Tobias what, tell him what?"

He looked most piercingly at me from under his inclined brows. "What you have not told him. What you are."

For an instant I simply didn't know what he was talking about. Then I burst out laughing.

"You are laughing," he said, stupidly.

"Oh, Seth," I said, "I don't want to laugh, not when you are so ill, but Seth, it's so crazy—you told him yourself."

"Told what?" he demanded.

"Poor Seth," I said, "your fever, it's made you mix things all up, now and the other time when you came, and you asked if I had told Tobias, and I got angry and told you to tell him yourself, and you did, and he came to me. He came and took me in his arms. You see, he didn't care, even if you are such a fool, even if you told him, even if—"

"Even if what?"

Thinking back on that instant, I now know that I must have hesitated, trying to find the words that would somehow put it so that I could say it. Then I said: "Even if my mother was—was a slave."

"I did not tell Tobias that," he said.

"Then what in God's name was there to tell him—what?" And that question sprang with a surge of nameless apprehension, but apprehension for what, I didn't know, for with what other secret did I live?

"I told him about your father," Seth was saying. And then while I groped at the meaning of that, he explained: "That he was of libidinous nature, that there was a taint of immoral blood, that he—"

"Get out!" I commanded.

"—it was that which I told him—I did not know this other until later, but now I know it, for Mrs. Morton—"

"She!" I exclaimed. "Oh, I might have known! Now get out, get out and go to your precious Idell—yes, go and pray with her some more, and maybe she will lie on the floor with you, but I won't."

He was looking at me quite numbly, standing there with the little wad of skirt still in his hand.

"One thing more," I said, "for your information. The instant Tobias enters this house I shall tell him. About you. About myself. About my mother—yes, I'll be proud to tell him. For you know what?" And I looked up at him, thrusting my face upward toward him to my full height, triumphantly. Then I answered myself: "He will take me in his arms."

At that I reached out and released the skirt from his fingers, as though I had been passing down a country lane and it had merely caught on a briar.

He looked down at his hand, studying the empty fingers.

Then he turned his face to me, with such a sad and suffering intensity that, even in that moment, my heart was touched. He said, his voice not much more than a whisper: "Why didn't you spit upon me?"

After he had gone I stood there in the drawing room, and felt grow in me a slow, sweet joy.

I clasped my hands before me and thought how I would say to Tobias what I had to say, and how he would put his arms around me.

The rest of the day passed in some sort of dream, a sense of lightness, of release, like a dream of flying. I busied myself around the house in the most casual and unnecessary little tasks, sorting linen, mending a shirt of Tobias, but all the while I saw my hands as though through the wrong end of a telescope, far away and small about whatever silly little task.

I had not finished my coffee after my lonely dinner, when the bell rang. My servant returned to say that a lady was waiting in the back sitting room. It was, I should have surmised, Miss Idell.

"Well," she said briskly, "you did have an afternoon!" And she leaned to pat my cheek, saying, "Poor little Manty."

"Don't touch me," I said.

"Well, I had some trouble, too," she said, ignoring my remark.

"Did you two pray together?"

"Don't be acid," she said, still smiling, and quite calmly, she seated herself. I remained standing.

"Oh, sit down, dear," she said, and before I could reply, continued: "As for the praying, since you are interested, you know I just did it to humor him—you know, he's so compelling—he's so—"

"You prayed with him," I said, "to shut his mouth about your past."

"My poor past," she echoed pityingly, drawing off a glove and inspecting the white hand. Then she looked brightly up at me: "But I'd better tell you why I came."

"I can't imagine why," I said.

"About Seth," she said. "He's really ill. He's at my house, and in a distressing condition. Now when you tell Tobias—that is, if you—"

"Tell him!" I cried. "I can't wait to tell him. You see, I thought he knew, I thought—"

"Yes, yes, of course, my dear Manty," she interrupted. "But when you do, why not just fail to mention Seth's—Seth's unfortunate proposal. It will just disturb Tobias, and in Seth's condition and—"

"Why should I do anything for you?" I demanded.

"Now, Manty," she said, reprovingly, "I know you are a little outdone with me. You think I talked behind your back. But you know, it was just a misunderstanding and in a very funny way, too. Several times Seth got me alone, and he kept making dark hints about something. I didn't quite know what. A lot about the blood and about your father and how your father had done a wrong. So I just jumped at the wrong conclusion. I said, yes, it was pitiful, to be arrested right at your father's grave, I had seen it, and—"

"Yes," I said, "you saw it. And didn't do a thing."

"Now, Manty," she said, "we'll come to that. But right now, it's how I made that slip with Seth that's made you so furious with me. Well, as soon as I said that, Seth said, what, what, but I didn't catch on fast enough, and the first thing I knew the cat was out of the bag. But what Seth had in mind, it wasn't you—I mean, you know what—it was about me and your poor father. It seems that was preying on his mind, how he died, and—"

"I hate you," I said, and felt a flash of delight in having said it.

"Why, darling," she said, "I know you do. For a long time, darling, and I can't say I blame you. You thought I let you get sold off, but you know, I didn't have a penny. After they arrested poor Herman, I had even pawned my rings. I would have done it and tried to get you off, but I was living on credit, and you know I never would take anything from your father, and—"

"I hate you," I said.

"Yes, darling, you hate me because of him, too, and that's only natural. But, darling, if you cared for him, you ought not to hate me, for I was nice to him. I was as nice as ever I could be. And you know, he was the only poor man I ever really felt that way—"

"Poor?" I echoed, in some kind of question and bewilderment and, actually, deprivation.

"Oh, he wasn't rich, darling, whatever you may have thought. He may have looked rich down there in the country, but you know, it is different up where there's more opportunity. And your father was lot poorer after Herman got him mixed up in things. But your father—he was sort of sweet and old-fashioned. He wanted to marry me, you know, but I couldn't go down and get stuck in some mudhole in the country and a drafty old house. But he'd do anything to please me, even wearing those funny new clothes, and the rest of the men, they just want to please themselves, but your father—sure, he was getting a little old, but—"

"I hate you," I said, standing there calmly on the floor.

"Now, Manty," she said, sweet and reproving, not looking at me, taking off her other glove, inspecting the hand, "I was just saying how I was nice to him, even if he was poor. Now, I don't mean to say that because a man is rich, he is anything to me necessarily, but

If there's a lot of money it's funny how it just makes things nicer, even in bed, you just feel softer, somehow. Sort of more comfy. It just improves the way you feel, sort of slow and easy, you know—oh, Manty, you look so shocked!"

I don't know whether I looked shocked or not. All I felt was a kind of disorientation, as though the objects around me had begun to shift of their own volition.

Miss Idell suddenly rose from her chair and stepped to me. She patted me on the shoulder. "Darling," she said, "you needn't look so shocked, I'm just talking natural, and I always say what is natural oughtn't to be shocking, and now it is just a kind of vacation, you might say, for me to be talking natural—outside of bed, I mean—for you know how I got started?"

I was staring at her in discomfited incredulity.

"Well," she said, straightening herself to her height, touching the lace at her breast, lifting her chin in that characteristic pose of proud exhibition, "I was fifteen years old and well developed and I had already been flattened out on a pile of grain sacks in a room off the tavern stable and it happened as quick as a wink and twice as easy and just one little scared squeak out of me before I saw the advantage of it. But I didn't want to be laid out on grain sacks the rest of my life. I was a barmaid, but I caught on quick. I got the right kind of a dress. I'd go stand in a lobby at the big hotel and watch how ladies did, and I'd practice it, and shucks, darling, there's nothing to it, anybody can do a lady's tricks, and it is sort of more fun if you have been a lady all day, and then when you kick your shoes off, you can just let go and take a vacation for fun. And sweetheart, I've had my fun and I'm going to have plenty more of the best kind and when my legs get so much rheumatism I can't spread 'em, I'm going to start eating all I want and who cares, and just think of all that peach cobbler and whipped cream waiting, and I'll love myself all fat and white, getting fatter, and you never guessed I wasn't a lady, did you, darling?"

I just stared at her, at that triumphant slim coolness, the filmy black bodice, the white froth of lace, the blue-eyed distance.

"And do you know why I'm telling you now?" she was saying. "So if you are mad at me and want to tell people about me, you can tell it all. For I'm leaving this place, I'm leaving that Morgan Morton, for he's just a tin-horn feeling big down here where they're beat up and don't know business, and thank God, I never married him. Yes, tell 'em that, too. And tell 'em they can just kiss the you-know-what!"

And she was, all at once, no longer in that cool, blue-eyed distance, she was right before me, slouched over, arms akimbo, head cocked a little to one side, lace at bosom askew, one buttock up a little, a blowsy jollity on the face that looked rounder and pinker, eyes dancing as she tapped herself gaily on that perfect rondure of the you-know-what.

"You are going away with him—with Seth," I said, almost whispering, bemused, somehow, by the emergence of that fact from the shadows of my imagination.

"Oh, you hate me for that, too," she said, and was herself again, the cool lady, and the gay, blowsy barmaid was gone. "But you needn't," she said. "You see, you had your chance. But you didn't want your chance this time any more than the first time, when you two went out in the brush."

"Did he tell you—tell you about that?" I asked, and felt almost sick.

"Oh, yes, the poor boy had to talk to somebody. How he was going to be pure as Jesus and all. But look here"—and the blowsy jollity flickered before me for an instant—"there's a lot more to that boy. All he needed was just somebody to start him right." She hesitated.

"Well, you had your chance today," she said. "But I guess I knew you'd do like you did. What I meant to say, I guess I let him come on to you because I knew he'd be easier to thaw once he got the nonsense about you out of his head. Well, he's thawing. He held my hand to tell me—it was sort of pitiful. But when that boy thaws! Well"—and the jollity was really back now, the akimbo arms, the dancing eyes—"when it happens, that boy will really be a bed-breaker. Once he gets the notion folks are built for fun. And money—well, once he realizes it is not just something to put in the collection plate—with that head of steam, he'll take it all. There won't be any left."

"Please go away," I said. I didn't feel anything now.

She looked at me. "Just tell me one thing," she said. "Honest Injun, didn't you get just a little bit tempted today, seeing him get so worked up?"

"Go away," I said.

She seemed about to go, then turned back. "Darling," she said, "don't forget not to tell on poor old Seth. Just tell about yourself, if that will make you feel good, about you having a little dash of the dark brown. And don't you worry, darling, about Tobias. You know, deep down he'll probably like the idea. A lot of men like it, you'd be surprised. Anyway—" She leaned at me a little. "When you do tell him, why don't you get him to bed first, just sort of start getting reacquainted, then tell him."

"Go away," I said.

She got as far as the door, moving across the carpet with her fine carriage, the head high, the shoulders straight and just wide enough to define the wineglass stem of waist, each step defining the sweep of thigh under the rustling cloth. At the door, she looked back. "Your father loved you," she said.

"I hate you," I said, mechanically.

"I could tell you why he didn't set you free," she said.

"I want to die," I said.

"Poor little Manty," she said, with pity, and was gone.

It was the middle of the next afternoon when Tobias got home. I did not wait. I led him to the sofa in the back drawing room, and sat beside him, and held his hand to my bosom, and told him. I told him first that long back I had thought he knew all from Seth, and he remembered perfectly well how Seth had come to him. Then I explained to him how I had thought all the time it was something else that Seth had told, the fact of my blood. So now I told him quite simply, about myself, who I was, how I had been seized and sold. All this time I did not look into his face. I simply sat in the crook of his right arm, holding his left hand against me, looking off across the room at the sharp definition of a Sèvres vase against dark rosewood, somehow clinging to that factuality.

I stared at the vase, and said: "I was bought by a man who was not a bad man. In one way he did treat me like his slave, but he was kind to me. His kindness, and the hopelessness of my position, are the only extenuation I have for not making more desperate effort to escape or for not doing away with myself. In the end, he set me free."

I waited, and tried to understand something from his breathing. I could hear nothing. He did not seem to be breathing at all.

Then I said: "I would not have deceived you. Not even to have my heart's desire."

A weakness had come over me, a languor like sleep. It was as though some terrible grip that had been holding me all my life, like a closed hand, was, all at once, released. I felt my head fall back on his arm, my body slip a little. My strengthless hands had released his hand and had dropped to my sides. His hand lay, motionless, of its own weight on my bosom, as though I had abandoned there some inanimate object. Then I brought myself to look up into his face.

The face seemed very far away. It was very calm, very carven and beautiful, but for an instant I had the apprehension that he had heard nothing, that he had been thinking of something else, not me, not my poor story, or he had been thinking of nothing, that fine head merely the head like a statue.

But in that very instant, I was saying: "That is what I am. Whatever it is, it is totally yours. You may do as you will."

It was dawning on his face, a clear luminosity, a light from within, as though blood began to pulse in and mollify the beauty of marble. The smile that grew in that light was of some wonderful innocence and benignity. I felt the same smile growing on my face, as though the smile, and the luminosity, were reflected on me, in me.

He said: "You are what my deepest heart desires. More now than ever. More now than ever."

At that he kissed me, but once lifted his head to say: "You are given to me for a sign."

At about seven-thirty, after a quick supper, Tobias left the house. He had to go to a meeting, he said, a meeting of great importance for the Convention the next day.

"Hurry, darling, hurry," I said, and scanned his face, wondering if there I detected some alienating cloud of preoccupation. I did not see how I could wait for him.

But such is the paradox of the soul, that as soon as he was out of the house I was, in a way, glad. Suddenly I needed solitude to try to come to terms with what had happened to me, the sense that a wall that had stood between me and the fullness of my life had been thrown down. I needed time, as it were, to look out over that rich landscape. Or to put it otherwise, it was almost a need to get acquainted with my own body, a body that this afternoon had found at last the full blaze of its exaltation, and now in contemplation of that fact had slipped into a new sleepy, delicious, shadowy flow of being, spangled somehow, as by light. I felt like touching myself—my face before the mirror, my bosom as I walked about the room—to verify something.

Wandering the house, where evening now encroached, I suddenly wondered why, if I had thought all the time that Tobias knew me, the telling now should make such a difference. There was some vague discomfort in that question, something unreconciled. I suppose that I had never faced the simple question, whether or not I had truly believed that Tobias knew my origin. Had there always been some cheating, niggling comfort in the hope that he didn't know, some comfort in an ambiguity of believing and not believing at the same time?

Be that as it may, that night as I wandered the house, it suddenly came to me that his knowing would never, in itself, have been enough. I had had to tell him myself. *Ah, truth,* I thought, *it isn't enough just to be true, we have to say the truth to make it living truth.* And I suddenly had the grave thought that the shadow of truth unspoken, though known, is darker than the shadow of a lie.

With that thought came a great elation. Why did anyone ever suffer, when joy was so easy, when this was the deep secret, the healing of all self-division, of all self-wound?

*Oh, Tobias, Tobias,* I was saying to myself, wandering now in the dark, begging him to hurry and come to me, come to me, seeing him before me, bright in the dark, leaning at me, smiling with that benignity, his body white and glimmering in the dark.

I found I was clenching my hands so hard the nails were driven into my palms.

In the silence of the house, I heard the latchkey. As I sat in the hot summer dark of the drawing room, waiting, that little click plucked the central nerve of my being. I did not move, but sat hearing his tread down the hall—I had left a lamp in the hall—hearing it approach the door, approaching me. When he entered the room, I called his name, very softly.

"Oh," he said, "what are you sitting in the dark for?"

"Waiting for you," I said. But as I heard him fumbling at the little table by the door, I felt some tiny little spot in me go numb. Then his match flared.

He brought the lamp to the center table and came to kiss me. "Darling," I whispered, "darling."

He straightened up.

"It is terrible," he said.

"What?" I demanded, thinking: *what? what?*, in a nameless apprehension.

"What may happen," he said, and looked down at me. "That Dostie—he's crazy. And Hahn. Tonight they got nigh ten thousand of them to the meeting, and then—"

"Who?" I demanded. "Ten thousand who?"

"The freedmen—who else?" he said savagely. "They get them there—Dostie, Hahn—and say it will be blood. The Convention is ours, they say. We are 400,000, they say. Let blood come if it must, they say. Come in the streets. And there they are, thousands of them, ignorant and blind, listening, under the flares there and the night hot as an oven and their faces shining, yelling to hear that."

I saw the crowd, the black faces sweating, and somehow, in the silence, heard the throaty roar.

Then, quietly, Tobias said: "Don't they see it would be easy. To have victory without blood. Let Monroe arrest the Convention, peaceably. Blair has promised to release the members and arrest the Sheriff. Then Blair would be committed to protecting the Convention, because violence had been practiced upon it. Then all could be achieved in peace. But no—Dostie—does he want blood?" He paused.

Then: "My God, do they all want blood? Does Congress want blood, and President Johnson want blood, and Secretary Stanton—why in God's name doesn't he telegraph Baird?—and my father want blood, and the fine gentlemen here—oh, they won't be in the street tomorrow, they won't have to be, but they want blood, and there will be blood, for this is a city of blood, a city of mob worse than Paris ever was, and the mob will do the gentleman's work, and Dostie's work, and Congress's work, for they all want blood—and every cullion and footpad and Irish bully and *âme-de-boue* and slungshot boy and demobilized Rebel who didn't get killed at Shiloh and nothing left but to hate niggers—oh, they'll be there."

He stopped, looked down at me, and said, calmly: "You know, Manty, it will be the freedman's blood again. Yes we freed them. Then we flung them into pits to dig, we kidnapped them for bounty men so some coward in Ohio would not have to run from Rebels, we seized them when they came in the lines and sold them to state's agents to fill quotas, we wouldn't lead them in battle, for they weren't men, our gunboats shelled them in the back in battle, our soldiers stripped them naked of uniform in the street, men in blue uniform sold them out of Texas to Brazil after the war was won, we stole their rations, rascals sold them red-white-and-blue sticks to mark the land they had been told the lie they'd have, politicians use them for vanity. And now—"

He paused again: "You know, Manty, you remember that book of Emerson I gave you?"

I nodded.

"In that book," he said, "he speaks of a spirit above our heads that contradicts all we say. Now Emerson meant a spirit better than we. But I tell you he had things reversed. I would tell you that we said fine things—oh, yes, we promised ourselves all virtue—and a spirit sat over our heads and contradicted all. We went out to do fine things but there was that spirit of darkness above us. Oh, Manty, we undertook to do good in the world, but we had not purged our own soul."

I got up, and went to take his hand. "You are tired, darling," I said.

"Manty," he said, "my friend Shaw from Harvard, he took the first black command. Fifty-fourth Massachusetts. He was no longer respectable. He was killed at Fort Wagner. Flung in a ditch with his niggers, off in Carolina. I almost wish I were Shaw. No—" he hesitated. "No, I'd rather have been a slave-master and blind to all but the enemy, and ridden at him, to kill, or be killed. Then if I didn't get killed and came back, I'd at least have something. I'd at least have my defeat. I wouldn't have to endure victory."

I was holding his hand. "Come to bed, darling," I said.

He made no reply, so I leaned and blew out the lamp. We went into the hall, and up the stairs toward the spot of light that the night lamp made in our doorway. We stopped on the landing, and I put my arms around his body. I wanted to comfort him. He leaned over, in a second, and began to kiss my hair.

In the room we did not light a proper light. In that dimness of the night lamp we began to make ready for bed. I already had on my nightdress and was brushing my hair, when he spoke.

I suppose it was the tone that gave the first little tremor of warning, a tone that evoked in me a faint stir of the disappointment I had felt upon his return tonight.

I looked around at him. He was sitting on the edge of the bed, facing me, clad now only in his drawers.

"One thing," he said, "one last thing I might do."

"What's that?" I asked, and laid down the brush.

"I might go to Monroe. With the justification of the meeting tonight—he might regard it as justification anyway, Rebel justification—he might be persuaded to serve peace warrants beforehand on the officers of the convention and the ringleaders. Hold them to prevent trouble." He paused. "I might go now," he said.

"Oh, not now!" I cried.

"I should go now," he said. "Monroe would need time. To arrest them by dawn. To notify Baird and explain why."

I had risen and gone to stand over him, waiting. "Darling," I said.

"Oh, it may be no use," Tobias said, not looking up at me. "There's no reason to think Monroe would do it. No doubt he wants blood, too."

I laid my hand on his shoulder.

Still not looking up, he said: "And I would feel like a traitor, going to Monroe for this." Suddenly he looked up into my face. "Oh, Manty," he said, beseechingly, "would I be a traitor?"

"If you went, yes," I said, feeling the elation of victory. But with that sense of victory, I could give comfort. I sat down beside him on the edge of the bed, and said, "Oh, darling," and took his hand. I looked at the hand.

Tobias had wonderful hands, sinewy from his life of action, but smooth-skinned, the smoothness sprigged with the crisp brown masculine hair, the fingers steel-hard but tapering long to the deep-set square-cut nails. I loved to see that hand. I loved to feel the delicate, powerful articulation.

But now, for an instant, I scarcely recognized it. What I saw was nails bitten into the bloody quick, the flesh by the nails drawn bloodily back, the blood fresh, and the fingers, as though they had a life of their own, trying to bend themselves over, to withdraw themselves, to hide their secret distress, their guiltiness, from my gaze.

That sight did a peculiar thing to me. I felt a fear, a sense of betrayal, a sense that all my new joy of that afternoon had been a fraud, all his words a lie, all the release and surrender of my body a deception before an iron grip settled on me. Those bloody tortured fingers were the mark of the betrayal, the lie.

Oh, I could not bear it.

So I was clutching his hand, covering its shame, saying, "Oh, let's forget everything—everything—let's just be ourselves, only ourselves!" And I saw his face with its startled, white-streaked question, as I fell back on the bed, curling my body over, clutching his hand, drawing him.

He was not resisting me, but in that very lack of resistance, in some dead weight, there was something worse than resistance. Then, when he began to respond, even the response marked a more terrifying alienation.

Had what I had just that day discovered been lost so soon?

And in the desperation of that question, even as we clung and strove, my mind was filled with a crazy vision of flame and shadow leaping on the ceiling, as on the night when the bales were burning, and the ships—no, it wasn't that, it was the village in the jungle aflame, flames fifty feet high in the night, higher, the great bats swinging among the white, gigantic uppermost treetops in that savage illumination.

For a moment it was as though Tobias himself were caught in that crazy vision of flame and carnage and screams and the bat-crying. There was his guttural breath, his hand wrenching my hair back. But, all at once, he pushed me aside. He was crouched on the edge of the bed, one foot on the floor. "I can't," he said, "not now, not now!"

I was clutching at him, but he was standing now, beyond my reach.

"Oh, don't you see," he cried, "I've got to go!"

"Wait," I said, "wait," but he was fumbling for his garments.

I was sitting up in bed by then. I was sitting there in a kind of nightmare of blankness. Suddenly across that blankness, there was, almost literally, a flash, and I was saying: "Oh, I know you! Oh, yes, you'd be a traitor—oh, it's white folks' justice you want."

He was standing there on the floor, holding a shirt now, or something. He was saying he loved me.

"Love," I said, "love," leaning toward him from the middle of the bed, him over yonder beyond the night-lamp, white in the face.

"Yes, you say love," I cried, "but I know you. This afternoon—oh, as soon as I really loved you, loved you for the first time—as soon as there was nothing but you to me—you thought that was nigger—the nigger in me—and it scared you—and you went away and you bit your fingers till they bled—and now—and now—"

He was coming toward me, his hand out to touch me, saying darling, saying he loved me.

So I said, all at once, quite calmly: "I hate you."

He stopped where he was.

I had read somewhere that the mouth of a head just struck off by ax or guillotine may move to speak, or to try to speak, to utter some last thought or cry. Now his head was there suspended against shadow in the rays of the night-lamp, and the eyes were staring. The lips were moving, but I didn't hear a sound.

Perhaps there was a sound, and I simply didn't hear it. Perhaps he was saying that I was his darling, that he loved me, that I was the sign given him, that he had to go to prevent blood, that he would come back soon. But it didn't matter what he said.

"Go away!" I commanded.

At that I flung myself face down on the bed, to cut off the world.

I don't know how long he had been gone, when I got up and dressed myself. I went downstairs and out into the street. It was all done with perfect calm, without thought, with a strange precision in every detail of action. There was nobody on the streets. It was a long distance, for Tobias and I lived in the new American part of the city.

I came to the patio, entered, climbed the short stair. I did not even knock on the door. I simply went in.

He was sitting at a table, wearing a dark coat, facing the door. An oil lamp, with a tin base and tin reflector, was on the table. He was eating something from a plate. A glass of beer, or some other brown liquid, stood beside the plate.

He stared very steadily at me, and did not say a word.

Then I reached behind me, not turning, and fumbled to shut the door.

At that he took out a handkerchief and wiped his mouth. Then I could see him move his tongue over his teeth, inside the closed lips.

"It took you a long time to come," he said.

That was what he said. I studied him across the distance to the table.

"I want to see the scars," I said.

"The scars," he repeated, thoughtfully.

"Yes," I said, "where they beat you."

He rose from the table, very deliberately, his face showing nothing, and walked toward me. He stopped in front of me. Then, with a slashing motion he flicked the back of his hand across my mouth. The blow was not really hard, just the weight of his finger-knuckles striking, but I tasted the tinny taste of blood, just a little oozing through the teeth back to my tongue. I wondered if my lip would swell.

"Do you still want to see the scars?" he asked.

I said, yes, and so he did it again.

# X

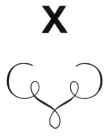

UPON THAT SECOND BLOW TO THE MOUTH—SCARCELY A BLOW, MERELY a flick, even if the black man's finger-knuckles were heavy—I stood there quietly as before, and ran my tongue along the inside of my teeth, tasting the ooze of blood.

Then Lieutenant Jones—who was Rau-Ru—leaned slightly toward me, and demanded, most solicitously, almost in a whisper: "Does it hurt?"

When I made no answer, merely staring up into that strange face, his right hand came out very slowly, fastidiously, and touched me on the shoulder. I flinched, ever so little, and his hand, with the delicacy of response of an insect's antenna, almost in the same instant, had lifted from the contact, hovering in the air.

"Remember," he said in that husky whisper, "remember, you made me carry that valise? You stood on the *banquette* and looked down at me. You passed the valise to me and walked away and I followed you down the street, carrying it."

The hand had descended again to my shoulder.

"Wait," I said, jerking back.

He made a slight noise in his throat, the slightest exhalation.

"Wait," I was saying, very hurriedly, "you know what—he has gone—he has gone to Mayor Monroe and—"

"Who?" he demanded. The hand was not touching me now.

"Tobias—Major Sears—he's gone to Mayor Monroe, he wants to stop everything, he wants Mayor Monroe to arrest all the officers, the chief men, tonight, now, yes, he got right out of bed and went —yes—"

"The betraying white son-of-a-bitch," Rau-Ru said, very slowly.

"No," I said, "no!" the protest bursting suddenly out to surprise me.

"If that's what you think," he demanded, "then what the hell are you here for?"

At that question my heart absolutely stopped. Then it gave a funny jump inside my hollowness.

"Look," he was saying again, "he does know you're a nigger, doesn't he? You didn't lie to me about that?"

I kept staring at him.

"Answer me!" he said.

I nodded.

"Well," he said, "whose side are you on?"

I kept staring at him.

"Well," he said, "if you can't say it, I'll say it for you. You are on the nigger side."

I felt something closing in on me, to suffocation.

"And," he said, "I'll tell you why."

He leaned at me, grinning suddenly with an implacable, glistening, glittering malevolence. "It's because you haven't got any other side to go to."

The leaning face jerked back from me. The grin was gone. He swung from me, toward a chest of drawers. He opened the top drawer and took out a revolver. He inspected the cylinder to see if it was loaded. He turned to me, thumbing the cylinder. "The son-of-a-bitch shook my hand," he said. "Oh, yes, and I was going to keep my word. I was trying to stop 'em. I swear to God, I was. But now" —he said—"now, we'll be right there."

He dropped the weapon into his pocket, took a folding knife from the drawer, and dropped that into the other pocket. On top of the bureau was a white hat. He put it on his head, took it off, searched around in the drawer, and found a black cap.

"I've got to go," he said. "I've got to let Howells and Dostie and the others know."

He was meditative for a moment.

"You know," he said, then, "I don't believe that's what Monroe wants. I think Monroe wants it in the street."

He jammed the cap on his head. "All right," he said, "it will be in the street."

He came and stood in front of me, very matter-of-fact. "I can't come back here tonight," he said. "For if Monroe does act, he'll want me, too. And you—it wouldn't be pleasant for you, if you were here when they came."

He moved toward the door. "Come on," he said, over his shoulder, indifferently. Adding before I could move: "If you want to."

I followed him down the dark stair, across the patio, into the street. He did not look back or abate his long, gliding pace. I had to run a step now and then to keep up with him.

He went down an alley, stepped into a kind of alcove, fumbled in his pocket, produced a key. He opened a door, motioned me in, followed, shut the door, struck a match, found a candle.

"It's a place I had," he said, "just in case."

I looked around. It was a medium-size, bare room, plaster walls, high windows in back, sparsely furnished.

"There's a big bolt on the front door," he said. "And don't open unless you hear my voice or somebody says my name." He pointed toward a corner of the back wall, a sort of recess." There's another door back there. It goes to a passage to another street. That is the beauty of this room. Two ways out. Keep that door bolted, too. Somebody will come to that door in the morning. It will be an old woman. She will knock and say her name. It is Jubbie. Let her in. She will bring you some grub. She will want to tell your fortune or make *gri-gri* or cook you up a medicine to catch hot love. She thinks she is voodoo, but she is not. She is just a pore old black bitch with nothing in her head for importance, but she will do what I tell her. Just send her away."

He cast a glance about. Nothing else seemed to demand comment. He set the candle down, and turned back to me.

"I will be mighty busy," he said. "I won't be back till it's over."

I didn't answer.

"If you ever want to," he said, "you can walk right out the door."

I looked over at the door.

He was, all at once, studying me. "You know," he said, "back at

*Pointe du Loup*—" and stopped. "You remember that thicket down beyond the stables," he said, "where the mimosa was?"

I nodded.

"At night," he said, "I have squatted down there, and wondered what you were like. I squatted in the bushes down there and heard the owls hoot and I wondered what you were like. Up there in the bed, with Old Bond."

"That Dollie," I said, "that Dollie—was that baby yours?"

He was still studying me. Then he shrugged his shoulders with the indolent, rippling motion. "What's that to you?" he demanded, and went toward the door.

Not looking back, he went out the door.

I ran to the door, and leaned against it. I had the impulse to run out.

But I continued to lean against the door. Then my hand found the old iron of the bolt. Under my fingers I could feel the caked rust. It made a grating sound as I thrust it home.

The rest of that night and the next day, the period of my stay in that room, was like nothing so much as the period immediately after I had been seized at my father's grave. There was the same blankness, or if not blankness in the period itself, a blankness in my recollection of it. I remember blowing out the candle and lying down on the cot and falling into a confused sleep. I woke once, feeling sick, got a match lighted for the candle, found a slop jar and suffered some minutes of dry retching. Then I was suddenly tired, peacefully tired, and went off to sleep again. But again the sleep was confused and fitful, dreams merging into images recollected in the dark, then images fading into the deeper perspective of dream.

In the morning the old woman with nothing in her head for importance, came, with the food and drink, offered me her quavering services, and went away. I ate something, lay back down, and the day passed as the night, shadowy, intense with the question: *what?*

For how was I to know what was happening in the world outside that bolted door?

It was years later before, in any detail, I would know, years later before I should happen to pick up the book from the desk in my husband's study, where I had gone to fill the inkwell, and feel my heart stop as I read the title on it, *Report Of The Select Committee On The New Orleans Riots in 1866.*

For there had been, of course, a Congressional investigation.

There was that Select Committee, and they summoned hundreds of people to testify, all kinds of people, and they told the truth, or lies, or lies that told deeper truth, or truth that was lies, each by his nature and convenience, and then it was all printed up in a big book, every word, and the books were laid aside, scattered here and there over the continent, in dark cupboards and attics, to rot with damp, to go yellow, page by page, the yellow creeping inward from the margin year by year, and what had happened had happened a long time ago, and was something people had forgotten, and painfully wanted to forget, in the long rush of history, of brute happening, of old blindness and new betrayal, of perennial hope and devotion.

I, too, most painfully wanted to forget, but how could I forget when, suddenly, there it was, myself and what I could not bear to remember, bound between faded purplish-brown buckram, with scaled gold stamping, and I opened at random. The name leaped off the page:

*General ABSALOM BAIRD sworn and examined.*

There was the question, Number 6497: *State your position in the army.*

And the answer: *I am assistant inspector general, with the brevet rank of major general.*

And question Number 6498: *State what was your position in July last and where you were.*

I laid the book down, filled the inkwell and fled. I fled out into the yard, in the dusk, and stood there, waiting for my husband to go into his study and pick up the book, waiting for my daughter to go into the living room, waiting for myself to go back into the house, for there was no place else for me to go.

So, after a while, I went back in, and sat down by the lamp and picked up my sewing, a dress for my daughter, the first grown-up sort of dress she had ever had, a pretty dress, deep rose color for her paleness and darkness. I did so want it to be a pretty dress.

She came into the room, very soft-footed, and sat down. I stole a glance at her. She was sitting almost back of me, far away. "Darling," I said, "come closer, you'll ruin your eyes in that light."

"I'm not reading," she said quietly.

"But, darling, your book—"

"I'm just holding it," she said. "It's just something to hold."

And with a stab of fright, a bruised sensation at the heart, I realized that it was true.

So I said, "Come here, come here and look at your dress!" I held up the dress.

She looked up, but did not rise. She did, however, smile, and say: "It's going to be awful pretty."

I jumped up and ran to her, somehow touched by her smile, and knelt beside her, and cried out, "Oh, darling, I do so want you to be happy!"

She was looking at me, and I was suddenly aware of pity in her look. "Dear mother," she then said, "I know you want me to be happy."

I went back to the sewing. I could not look at her again. I was afraid of the spinning out of the sandy distance, the dimness of distance, between us.

After a while I went to bed. I lay there in the dark, and thought of my husband downstairs, bending over the book, and in my mind I saw the page turn, and I stiffened, waiting, waiting to see what was there on that next page, under the light:

AMANTHA STARR *sworn and examined.*

Then the question: *Are you Amantha Starr?*

But the answer, the answer, I could not see the answer, and I lay there sweating in the summer night.

Later, long after my husband had come to bed, I slipped down to the study. I lighted the lamp, closed the door, and began to read the book.

But, of course, my name was not there.

The Convention was to meet at noon, Monday, July 30, 1866. That morning, Mayor Monroe issued a proclamation beseeching order. Early, about ten o'clock, Lieutenant-Governor Voorhies, according to his own testimony, took to General Baird the answer President Johnson had given his own telegram, to the effect that the military were expected to sustain the local courts. But Secretary of War Stanton had not replied to Baird's telegram, therefore Baird would not allow writs of arrest. The General did agree, however, to provide troops to keep order. According to Baird's testimony, however, Voorhies' first request for troops came at 12:30, not some two hours earlier.

While the Lieutenant-Governor was thus employed, Governor Wells, who had returned from his cautious absence, went to his office, stayed a few minutes, listened to the rumors of impending trouble, called at General Sheridan's office, to discover what everyone else knew, that the commander was in Texas, and then retired to his own house. He had a telegram in his pocket from President Johnson, demanding on what authority he had assembled the Convention. But no, he hadn't assembled it, he was merely a servant of the Convention, for the Convention of 1864 had drawn the Constitution under which he was Governor, and Judge Howell had merely reassembled that Convention. No, Governor Wells was not responsible.

His son, of course, was at the Convention. The father may have assumed that there would be no danger for white men inside. The military would take charge. Later there was testimony that members of the Convention had appealed to Baird for protection by troops. Baird testified that no appeal had ever been made.

But at noon, the advertised hour for the formal assembling, when the Convention gathered at the Mechanics Institute, there was no quorum, not even the quorum of the original hardy ones who had constituted the rump. The twenty-odd members waited. Dr. Horton offered a prayer. Still no one came. The meeting adjourned until one o'clock. The sergeant-at-arms was sent out to locate the timid and the wavering. Most members waited in the hall, but Judge Howell went down to the Governor's room, a floor below. Governor Wells, of course, was long since snug at home.

Thomas E. Adams, Chief of Police, had assembled his force, including the specials, at headquarters.

General Baird's troops were at Jackson Barracks, three miles from the Mechanics Institute.

All was ready.

The procession moved toward Canal Street, a flag and a drum at the head. It was a procession of Negroes. The procession began to cross Canal Street.

At the corner of Canal, a white man bumped against one of the Negroes. The Negro struck him. The white man produced a revolver; fired almost point-blank; and missed. The procession moved on. It was noon now.

The procession reached the Institute. Along the walls of the buildings opposite, in the shade, white men lounged. There were police, not many. There was at least one news boy, for according to some testimony, it was this boy—the nameless street brat—who began all.

He baited the procession. A policeman arrested him. In the crazy irrationality of all, in that moment under the blazing noon of Louisiana summer, it was a Negro who fired at the policeman for arresting the white boy and thereby protecting him. It is crazy enough to be true. Or almost.

There was, then, silence. The Negro, too, had missed.

Across the head of Dryades Street, toward the Institute, on the double, they came, the police, the specials. Their clubs were waving. They were met by brickbats, still no gunpowder. The procession broke, ran into the convention hall.

Three times the police charged the doors of the hall, and were beaten back, upended chairs against clubs. Then the serious work began, the pistol work. There was return fire from within. Dr. Horton was waving a white handkerchief, crying, "Arrest us, arrest us! We do not defend ourselves!"

"We don't want any prisoners!" yelled somebody.

A bullet found Dr. Horton.

The police charged again, the last time, firing.

Negroes began to jump from the windows of the hall. Some were shot as they jumped, some as they tried to climb a fence at the back, some in the streets.

The wild firing abated. The swirl sank down, sullenly. Chief of Police Adams was to testify that with his own hand he had knocked down five of his men to restrain brutality. Arrests had now been made. The ex-Governor Hahn, who had spoken at the mass meeting the night before, was arrested, already beaten and wounded. The mob—for by this time the mob was there—howled for his blood, but the police got him safely through, him and the other conventionists. Only one delegate was dead, a Mr. Henderson, a man of no great consequence. The dead and wounded of that faction, black and white, were piled on drays and hauled off.

All in all, some forty persons were killed, some hundred and fifty wounded, including seven police suffering from pistol wounds.

Dr. Dostie had said, let what may come, come. He lay now with a sword cut through his stomach, a pistol slug in his spine. He died slowly.

At last, at two-thirty, more than two hours late, the troops which General Baird had promised to hold in readiness for any disturbance, arrived, the General himself in command.

The hour of the meeting of the Convention had been announced, over and over again in the public press: *noon, Monday, July 30*. It had been on every tongue, at every bar, in every lobby, on every street corner: *twelve o'clock, noon*. General Baird was to testify that he thought the meeting scheduled for six o'clock. He was, apparently, the only person in the city to labor under that delusion. He was not the only person to suffer for it.

The procession that marched toward the Mechanics Institute, with flag and drum, they had been on time.

The high officers of General Baird's command rallied around him handsomely. They signed a joint statement that obfuscated everything in a golden haze. It almost obfuscated the fact that, even after the orders had been received at the barracks to send troops, there was a strange delay, a delay that no one even tried to explain.

When under martial law, troops were, however, put out to patrol the streets, General Baird used a black regiment. This seemed to extenuate something, justify something, prove something. At least, it provided the last irony for the summer day.

Two days after the event, General Sheridan arrived from Texas. Immediately, he pronounced the event a massacre. But, impartially, he pronounced Hahn and his friends agitators and bad men. Governor Wells, he said, had shown none of the man at all. Of General Baird, he said nothing.

Meanwhile, he allowed the writs of arrests against the conventionists to be served. They were indicted for creating a riot.

It was all crazy.

Toward dawn, when the robins had begun to stir, as I sat there in my husband's study, I came to the findings of the congressional committee. There was, naturally, disagreement among the members. The majority report found that all was the result of a fiendish conspiracy among Mayor Monroe, Chief of Police Adams, and Lieutenant-Governor Voorhies. The minority report found that the Convention was illegal, that there was a conspiracy among Hahn, Howell, Dostie and their friends, abetted by members of Congress,

to seize the state government, and that the intention existed to provoke an attack on the carefully inspired Negro demonstration in the
street to serve as an excuse for congressional action against the state
government. The attack, was, of course, to be suppressed by the
military before lives of the white conventionists themselves were
endangered.

Sitting there, in that dawn, I suddenly thought that maybe both
reports, with their lies, omissions, and distortions, majority and
minority, were right. The conventionists had not taken the way of
peace, the way that poor Tobias had besought. Monroe had not
taken any course for peace, nor the last risk for peace that Tobias
had risen from my embrace to go urge upon him. Yes, it was strange,
two counter-conspiracies, each devoted to the same end, and to fulfill that end the procession follows flag and drum down the street
toward that moment in front of the Mechanics Institute.

Then the thought grew in me that around those conspiracies
charged by the reports, there was so much else looming, darker,
deeper, taller than shadow, all the other questions, why was Sheridan in Texas just then, why had Sheridan not given explicit instruction to Baird, why had Stanton never answered Baird's telegram, why
had not President Johnson wired directly to Baird and not merely
to Voorhies, why was Baird the only man alive not to know noon the
fatal hour, why, in the end, were the troops delayed at the barracks?

No, not just those two little conspiracies, two little conspiracies
conspiring together to the same end in blood. No, all things conspiring together, the most distant things, the most trivial things,
leaning together, vibrating in a communal gust, from the most remote periphery or personal irrelevance—Tobias snatched from my
arms—all sucked toward some center, caught in the great, whistling
up-draft of history, like a chimney.

No, it was different from that, from the image of the chimney,
and all at once, more sinister. It was as though everything were a
great blossom, an enormous thing, white, blossoming in perfect silence, in darkness.

It was foolish therefore to ask a question such as why were the
troops delayed, at last, at the barracks. No, that event was not an
event independent and discussible, it was part of the great slow,
white process, swelling in darkness, and when the order came it was
as though, under some entrancing spell of fate, human muscle, hu-

man members, human will, might move only in a dreamlike, submarine retardation till all had been fulfilled.

Things merely happened, that was all there was to it.

You must have seen pictures of those tropic plants—great, fat-petaled, luxurious blossoms in jungle darkness—that entrap and devour insects and small animals? Well, in that instant, with the vision of the great blossom, I knew myself the victim, the insect, the animal, struggling among down-spiked hirsuteness, against the sweet fetidness of dark secretions, against the constriction of the great gullet of time, caught in that corolla of history. I was being digested, being dissolved from my own bones, the marrow from the bones and the gray matter from my skull being deliciously extracted.

It is awful to know that everything in the world is just something that happens, and it is all happening to you.

But what was happening to me now, as I lay all day in the shadowy room where Rau-Ru had left me, out of time and out of life, was that I did not know what was happening, and did not know what had ever happened, involved in a flow of images, a dream of the past, one image evoking another by some portentous logic that always seemed about to declare itself in a burst of light, but never did.

The old woman came again about dusk. Again she wanted to tell my fortune, and I declined. Would I like *gri-gri?*

I said no.

"Doan want no *gri-gri?*" she said.

I shook my head.

"Doan you hate nobody?" she demanded, scanning me with her weak eyes.

"No," I said.

Would I like one of the potions? "Put heem in cup-café," she said. "Put heem in rum. Make man come crawl lak dawg. Crawl on belly and moan to git you."

I shook my head.

"Doan you love nobody?" she demanded, sad and peering.

I shook my head.

"Den I make sumpum you drink yoreself," she said, whispering, insinuating. "Six bits," she said, "six bits," and leaning at me she began to make a little whining, anxious, breathy, whimpering noise.

"You drink hit," she said, "and you love somebody, you crawl lak dawg."

"Get out!" I cried, "Oh, get out!"

She got out, I slammed the bolt shut, I scraped the food, untouched, into the slop jar, as though it were one of her crazy brews, bat-droppings and rat-gizzard and what, and I lay down on the cot, wanting to be nothing, and I was next to nothing, the slow unspooling of all the images of my life, with no feeling, no reason.

Then the knock came.

As I leaned at the door, I heard the name: *Lieutenant Jones.* It was a voice somehow familiar, but not his.

I slipped the bolt, opened the door a crack, the figure there suddenly slipped in, like a shadow through that crack, actually pushing the space wider, closing it behind him, but all with spectral deftness, in an eye-blink.

With the door shut, the candle unlit, only the trace of light from the high windows at the back, I could make out nothing of the visitor. I moved toward the table, fumbling for the matches and candle, hearing the breathing in the room behind me. I lighted the candle, and turned.

In that instant it was as though, out of the hours of that blank reliving of all my life, a figure had suddenly stepped, not a dream, not an image from my wide-eyed staring at the darkness of ceiling, a figure rather slight, narrow-shouldered, a little stooped, the face dark and seamed, the head preternaturally big with swathing of white cloth, like a turban, all familiar, terribly familiar.

Then I knew. Shaddy, it must be Old Shaddy, Shadrach, with his broken head bandaged like a turban, who had been whirled away in the flesh-merchant's gig, oh, long ago, because I had told my father, because I had told on him—but told what? told what?—and they had broken his head, and now he had come back to me, he would show me the head. This, all in a flash, as I stood there, not yet out of the entrancement of that solitude of self.

"Stop lookin' me lak I was a spook," the voice said.

I couldn't speak.

"Ain't yit," the voice said.

I couldn't move or speak.

"But tain't no fault of them bastards," the voice said, and a hand went up to touch, gingerly, the turban.

"Oh," I breathed.

It was Jimmee.

"Come on," he said, "we got to git."

"Where is he? Where's Rau-Ru?" I demanded.

"Lieutenant Oliver Cromwell Jones," Jimmee corrected.

"Where is he?"

"Layin' out," he said, "and we got to git."

I was about to ask again, but he seized me by the arm, saying, "Come on, gotta high-tail, maybe they wuk on him some, but he ain't daid yit, and he ain't daid you still better do what he say, and he say come," all the while drawing me toward the door, out the door, with his free hand closing the door behind us, leaving the candle to gutter down in that room.

Still gripping my arm, he proceeded down the alley, toward the corner, stopped at the corner, peered round it, drew me around the corner into the street proper, and said, "Git in."

There was a rickety surrey, two horses to it, a man on the front seat with the reins. I started to climb to the back seat, but Jimmee said, "Up front. I gwina drive, and you up front."

I obeyed him, the other man climbed down and got behind, Jimmee took the reins, we moved off.

"Where are we going?" I asked.

"Whar he lay," Jimmee said.

"Is he hurt?" I asked.

"Take a lot to daid-hurt him," he said.

"How bad?"

"You see," he said.

He seemed disinclined to speak further. He sat up straight on the seat, holding the reins smartly, the whip erect, as long back, in the summer evening, out the shell road, past the flickering hut-fires and smudges, the wheels rustling deftly on the shell, he had done it, conducting the barouche of Hamish Bond.

The street was empty till we encountered the first patrol. They came marching toward us, four men and an officer, way off, behind them the light of a distant street lamp. Jimmee slowed the pace, the detail swung past us, the faces black, a little light on the bayonets, eyes straight, except for the sergeant, black too, who surveyed us.

Jimmee saluted him, with elaborate expertness. "Forty-second Tennessee," he sang out, "sah!"

And I almost said: *that—why that's Tobias' old command!*

The officer had returned the salute, we were drawing away, that measured, authoritative tread diminishing behind us. Jimmee, not turning, jerked his head to indicate the patrol. "Our'n," he said. "Our'n," he repeated bitterly, "yeah, and we could shore used them gizzard-stickers this afternoon. Yeah—but them white bastards, they wouldn't let 'em come."

"Is that the Forty-second Tennessee?" I asked.

"Naw," he said, "but I waz."

And I almost said: *why you knew my husband—Major Sears—you must have known him.*

"I wuz," he was saying, "atter we left the swumps. Rau-Ru, he taken us in."

"You were with Rau-Ru?"

"Lieutenant Oliver Cromwell Jones," he corrected. He paused, clucked at the horses, continued: "Yeah, I run off to him, to the swumps, taken a hoss and lit out, when she done hit. Yeah," he said, flicked the whip-spat, "yeah, all that-air time, sweet to me, and all 'twunce she crawl out my baid. Yeah, him come back to the country, upriver, ole lak a ole man, ole and sick to lay down, and she crawl out my baid, just up and go to him, she lay in his baid and—"

"Who?" I demanded. "Who?"

"Ole son-a-bitch Bond," he said, and spat.

He plunged into his silence, staring up the long street.

Far up the street was a human figure, moving up the *banquette,* a man. Slowly we overtook it. It was, apparently, a man of middle age, the stride not elastic. He was not well dressed, he carried a little pail, probably a mechanic of some kind going home, late. We drew even with him, pulling over close to the *banquette.*

"Mister," Jimmee said, "good ev'nin', mister."

The man looked up. Jimmee bobbed his turbaned head, bowing and grinning in imbecile servility. "Mister," he repeated, and asked for the time.

The man fumbled for a watch, and found it. The light was bad, and he leaned over to peer at it, his head, with a little cloth cap on it, bowed directly under Jimmee.

It was simple. All in one motion, Jimmee had up-ended the whip, seized it some two feet above the butt, and slashed the butt—the butt must have been heavily loaded from the sound it made on contact—down on the man's bowed head. The man dropped without a sound.

It was all so fast I did not have time to cry out. Even as I gasped, Jimmee had dropped the whip across our feet, and had seized my wrist with a startling grip, twisting it a little. "Shut up," he said.

Another patrol, eight men and an officer, had swung in from a side street, some thirty yards up. We drew toward them, Jimmee still gripping my wrist, still twisting it. Then we were upon them, and they were black, too, the officer, too. Jimmee let go my wrist, gave his salute, grinning, saying, "Good even, Gin'l, good even," leaning confidentially, saying, "Done left you a package back yonder, Gin'l."

The officer peered up the street.

"Jist a feller insult this-heah lady," he said, and the officer looked at me, and Jimmee was going on, "—yeah, and she a colored lady— yeah, she doan look hit in a pore light, Gin'l, but she long-heel, Gin'l." And he swung to me and laid his hand on my knee, squeezing it, saying, "You, ain't you long-heel, Honey?"

"Move on," the officer said.

"Forty-second Tennessee," Jimmee sang out, "sah!" and we drew away.

The tread was fading behind us. Jimmee whistled softly through his teeth, the teeth showing.

"Oh, why did you do it!" I cried out.

He stopped whistling and looked at me. "Ain't no why," he said, "ain't never no why, just done hit, Lawd's sake and no why."

"He never did anything to you," I said.

"Ain't never gonna, neither," he said, "not him ner his brother." And he looked away from me, clucked to the horses, and again began whistling through his teeth.

"He was just going home," I said, "home from work, and—"

He swung ferociously at me. "Look!" he commanded, "look here!" And touched his hand to his head. "Look here, and they bust me. Not doin nuthin and they bust my haid. Shoot ole Jelly and him yellin surrender, shoot him in the gut and they stomp him. Stick a swored in Patty-Jack, and him yellin surrender. But Rau-Ru, he never yelled no surrender, fit 'em, bullet all gone and bare-hand, and they shot him in the shoulder and club him and break his arm and him still fightin, but we save him, git up the alley and git 'em down what chase us, and save him, and who you think care? Ain't nobody care, and them black sojers—oh, no, them gin'ls, they wouldn't let 'em come—oh, we fit that freedom war, but them white gin'ls, oh, no they wouldn't let 'em come."

I felt cold, sweaty cold. I was seeing the face of Tobias, twisted white, in the air, the mouth moving. Oh, nothing, nothing, nothing, had done any good.

"White gin'ls," Jimmee said, and spat.

We had probably gone near a half mile—out in the country now— when he stopped that awful whistling.

"You know who Oliver Crom'ell was?" he demanded.

I didn't answer, I felt so bad.

"He was a gin'l," he said, "back yonder, crost the water, and he fit and killed the white folks."

I heard my own voice saying far off, mechanically, that Oliver Cromwell was white.

"Huh," Jimmee said, "huh," and spat. Then: "Him white, then what Rau-Ru got that name fer?"

So we went on, toward whatever spot Rau-Ru lay, Lieutenant Oliver Cromwell Jones lay, slug in shoulder, arm broken, what else cut or broken. We were out in the country, beyond the shacks, the road a dusty track now, beside a bayou of absolute blackness in cypress shade, moss from the cypresses, behind us dust rising pale, spectrally climbing the motionless, hot, rot-sweet, swamp-sweet air of the night. I looked back once, and saw the paleness of that dust against the blackness of the cypresses.

A man rose from the darkness ahead of us, and moved to stand in the paleness of the road.

Jimmee drew up even with the man, and the man took the bit of the near horse. "Git down," Jimmee commanded me and I obeyed. He himself got down. The man in the back seat of the surrey, who had made no sound all those hours, got down and went to replace the other at the head of the horse. That other climbed to the driver's seat, took the reins, and the horse-holder stepped back.

The surrey turned scrapingly, turning too short in the narrow track, getting over into weeds and ditch, then pulled off, back the way we had come. An owl was whooping back in the swamp.

"Come on," Jimmee commanded, and moved off into the darkness of cypress by the bayou.

I followed, the other man behind me.

"You step on sumpin," Jimmee said, "and hit heave, hit's a cotton-mouf." And he sniggered.

There was a movement ahead, a flicker of light, then a beam of light touched us, flickered away from us and indicated two pirogues, drawn up at the bayou-edge.

"Git in," Jimmee commanded, "git in dat nigh p'rogue."

I obeyed this by the light of the dark-lantern directed by an unseen hand on the bank. Jimmee ordered me forward, got in himself, and shoved off. We sat in darkness, rocking a little on the blackness of water. The lantern was cut off now. The owl was whooping again. I could hear the men get into the other pirogue and shove off.

"Me follow you, Blue-Tobe," Jimmee said.

The beam of light broke out again, probed down the bayou, showed for an instant the heaving, anguish-contorted, Gothic-groined, antediluvian roots of the cypresses, three times man-high above the black water, pale against the caverned darkness beyond. The light found the break where the bayou disappeared into the swamp, and the other pirogue, paddles plashing softly, moved ahead of us. I could hear the silky slither of water at its bow, as it drew past.

They had fixed the lantern toward the bow of the other pirogue. As they swung into the track under the cypresses, I could see that the beam struck out through a whirling, glittering mist of insects. Then we fell into line behind, and I could see the light only far ahead seeking the channel that was only black water spreading and threading insidiously into the blackness that vibrated, whirred unrelentingly, with a horrid unseen life of air, like a nerve being tortured inside the enormous blackness of night. The owls were calling, far off.

When the owls weren't calling, I could hear the water whispering against the wood of the pirogue.

Once a great owl swept downward out of darkness, eyes glaring, into the beam of light ahead, flattened its flight over the heads of the first pirogue, and swept over us, right down at us, just a whoosh of appalling air, darker than the darkness. This all in one instant.

It was then that Jimmee ordered me to cover my head against the gallinippers. "Git yore dress up," he said, "up over yore haid, jist so you kin breave."

I bowed forward and drew the skirt up over my head, holding it close to create my own airless, inner darkness, and be safe in it.

The sounds from outside came more dimly now. I could feel, however, the untiring rhythm of the paddle, the gliding lunge of the
pirogue on the stroke, the silky glide from that impetus failing toward the instant when the paddle should again enter the water.

It was all happening in the darkness of my head.

That was all there was, and it was a long time, until the halloo
from ahead, and I dropped the dress and looked up.

Over yonder some forty yards, there was a hump of darkness with
some light on it, fires glowing a slow red, an island or something,
and the halloo came again.

"Ole forty-two," a voice called from the pirogue ahead.

Jimmee gave several prodigious strokes, drew up even with the
other pirogue. "Dar 'tis," he said to me.

"What?" I asked.

He gestured with the paddle. "Whar we laid out," he said, "long
back."

He made a couple of strokes. "All dat time," he said, "and hit's
been waitin. Lak hit knowed."

I could see two or three figures on the bank beyond the glow of
the fires. The fires were reflected in the glossy blackness of the water.

"Waitin," Jimmee said, "lak hit knowed we'd come back.'

We were gliding in close, now. The front of the pirogue nosed
into the mud, a squishy-soft sound. A man stepped from shadow, a
man with a rifle in one hand, and leaned and with his free hand
seized the rope of the craft and drew it higher. "Git out," he said.

I got out and looked at him. He was a colored man, a mulatto,
sick-looking, wearing a campeachy hat, a red shirt, a vest, pants
stuck in what seemed to be old cavalry boots.

Jimmee was getting out. "How long you been?" he asked.

"'Bout an hour," the mulatto said.

"How he do?" Jimmee asked, and nodded vaguely off toward the
black hulks that I now saw were huts beyond the fires.

"He do," the mulatto said. Then he turned to me. "He say you git
on in thar," he said.

I hesitated, and perhaps threw Jimmee a glance of question.

"Git on," he said. "He say git, you better git."

"Hit's the nigh one," the sick mulatto said.

I moved toward the nearest hut, skirting the smudge fires on the side away from the three other men. They stared at me, over the red coals, through the upward unravelment of the smoke.

The rear hut was a small thing, round, nine or ten feet in diameter, sloping inward, rounded toward the top, something like the shape of the Eskimo's igloo, but not of ice in that airless, breathless night heat, covered with moss and palmetto leaves, many rotten and scaling off, as I could see even in the bad light, no door, just a low opening, with some sacking hung across it, the sacking new, brought out tonight no doubt in this flight back to the old time, after the day's disaster.

I was hesitating before bending to that sack-covered opening. Then I was aware of a movement behind me. It was Jimmee. He thrust something at me. "Take hit," he said. It was the dark lantern, the blind drawn over the light.

I took it.

"Open hit," he said, and I did.

"Git on in," he said, and so I bowed low, thrust the sacking aside, and had entered.

The beam of the lantern, on the first instant, found nothing but the trodden earth, the sloping wall, boards, tin, palmetto. Then I swung the light left, and there he was. He was propped on a sway-backed military cot, wearing a white shirt split open to allow for bandages on right arm and shoulder, sweat standing on his face, blinking slow as he stared at me, or rather, at that focus of light which would have obscured me behind it. Not thinking, I kept the light on him, my gaze fixed on him.

Then he said: "So you waited."

"Yes," I said.

"Get that light out of my eyes," he said.

I obeyed, swinging it to one side. An up-ended cartridge box served as a table, I saw. A tin cup was on it.

"They near ruined us," he said.

"How do you feel?" I asked.

"They gave it to us," he said.

"How bad are you hurt?" I asked.

"The troops didn't come," he said.

"How bad are you hurt?"

"It's always the ones on your own side," he said, "the sweet talk and the lie."

"Are you hurt bad?"

"It is always the sweet-talking ones that promise you, then fix it so you get ruint," he said.

"Won't you tell me how bad you are hurt?"

"What do you want to know for?"

"I've got to know!" I cried out.

"So you got to know," he said.

I found I was passing my tongue over my dry lips.

"Come a little closer," he commanded.

I moved slowly toward him, a step or two.

"Stop there," he said.

I stopped.

"Turn that light on your face," he said.

I did it.

"Hold it out farther."

I did it.

"Look right into it," he said.

"What do you want?" I said. I was, I suppose, afraid, suddenly.

"Nothing," he said. "Except just to look at you."

The beam was on my face, but after a moment, I let the light waver.

"I said hold it," he said, sharply.

I held the light and stared into the beam. I could hear the rustle of his breath over in the dark beyond.

"How does it feel?" he demanded, almost whispering. "How does it feel with the light on your face, and not seeing anything but the light and the dark around the light, and knowing I'm over here, in the dark, and you can't see me, but I'm looking at you, I am looking at you all the time?"

"Oh, I can't stand it!" I cried out, and jerked the light from my face, flinging the beam wildly about.

"You couldn't stand it?" he questioned, softly.

"No," I said, "no!"

"Put the lantern on the box," he said.

I set it down.

"What are you going to do?" I asked.

He looked meditatively at me. "Something," he said, "something that just came over me I got to do. I got to do it now."

"What?"

"It came over me, me over here in the dark, looking at you."

"But you're sick," I said, my words pouring desperately out, "yes, you're sick, you've got fever, you ought to be quiet."

"I'll be quiet later," he said.

"But you're sick, you—"

He had drawn a cord from inside his shirt, on the cord a whistle, and the blast cut across my words.

I stood there in absolute silence, looking at him, he not seeming to notice me any more, till the sack-curtain was lifted.

"What you want?" Jimmee demanded.

"Pack up," Rau-Ru commanded.

"But we just come, we—" Jimmee began, but Rau-Ru cut him short, with a quick, violent gesture.

"Pack up!" he said.

"But what—"

And very quietly, leaning forward on the cot, Rau-Ru asked, "Do I have to start getting your permission for what I'm going to do?"


By day the swamp was a twilight. The moss hung down like twilight from the high cypresses. We moved, as before, by some secret channel among the cypress stools, Rau-Ru and two men in the pirogue ahead, then Jimmee and another man and I, then two more pirogues behind. The cottonmouth, not bothering to array its cumbrousness, would drop fatly off the cypress root, an overripe plop into the water. Once, on a hummock, a white heron leaned forward on the improbable ricketiness of its legs, thrust the neck jabbingly forward with the wing-beat, and rose. It moved ahead of us, white over the black water, under the gloom of moss, far off.

We stopped twice to eat. We ate in the pirogues, munching the cold corn pones, the cold side meat, washing it down with water from the canteens that were passed around. During this process the pirogues were drawn up together. There was no conversation. Rau-Ru was propped in the middle of his pirogue, sweat beading his face, and sweat coming through the white shirt to make it stick to his skin. Once I asked him how he felt. He looked at me from some meditative distance, then shrugged his good shoulder. "I'll make it," he said.

Then he turned from me, ignoring me.

I slept most of the afternoon, on the bottom of the pirogue, my face down, hidden in my bent arms.

Just at dusk, we stopped again, ate, drank some of the tepid water. The paddlers lay back and rested for a half-hour or so. Then Rau-Ru looked at his watch. Without a word spoken, the paddles began their motion.

The swamp was thinning here, the trees smaller, less moss, more land visible, and some underbrush, sycamores and other trees now, the sycamores very white in the dusk.

It was not really swamp now, rather a marshy forest threaded here and there by bayous. Looking up I could see the sky now. Stars were coming out.

Very late, they made a camp, with smudge fires. When broad day came, we went on.

In the middle of the afternoon we stopped again. Long since, the bayou had given place to swamp, then swamp again to forest. We were in forest now. They drew up the pirogues, and tied them to trees. Then, with Jimmee leading, Rau-Ru next, me next, we took a faint trail into the trees. After a while we heard dogs barking. We had entered a sort of clearing now on high ground. Jimmee stopped, turned his head over his shoulder. "Here 'tis," he said.

Rau-Ru nodded. He walked away from the trail, across the little clearing, some twenty feet, and sat down, propping himself against a tree. The group edged over toward him. They disposed themselves, some simply dropping down, head on arms, asleep by the time they hit ground. I propped against a tree. Rau-Ru's eyes were closed, but I did not think he was sleeping.

There was not a word spoken until near dusk, when we ate again. It was the last of the food. There was no talk now, now and then the shifting of a body, the slapping of a hand against bare flesh where an insect had struck. At length one of the men got up, and began to gather bits of stick and wood for a smudge fire. He arranged the material, and struck a match.

"You light that fire," Rau-Ru's voice said from his shadow, "and I'll shoot you between the eyes."

Not looking up, very carefully, the man blew the match out and dropped the stub. Night had come on very dark now, and cloudy.

I went over and away from the others, and covered my face with my skirt again.

It must have been an hour later when Rau-Ru rose, and wordlessly moved down the trail. We followed him. A half mile or so on, he stopped. We were, I suddenly realized, on the edge of the open, just a fringe of brush screening us. But it was very dark. I could make out nothing.

Rau-Ru turned. "Blue-Tobe," he said, "you stay here. You stay here and keep her." He nodded toward me, paying me no other heed.

He moved out into the open beyond the brush, the other men following. "I'll send back when I'm done," he said, over his shoulder, not even to me I felt, to Blue-Tobe.

The men had moved off into the darkness of the field. "What's he going to do?" I asked Blue-Tobe.

"Ain't said," Blue-Tobe said.

"Do you know where we are?" I asked him.

"Ain't knowin," he said.

So I stood there, for a little. Then I crouched down and covered my face again. I could hear the man moving about, now over here, now there. I could hear the owls, then the wail of some other night-crier. I crouched there and didn't know where I was.

Not for some forty minutes, I suppose, when I stood up. A little after I had stood up, the moon broke through the clouds. It was just a rift, rather a kind of sluggish dividing of that low-hanging swollenness of dark, then the mass drew together, coalesced oilily again, and the light was cut off. It had, however, been long enough. I knew now.

But I had not made a sound. I stood there, hearing my heart beat, and said very casually: "I'm just going to step over here a minute."

"Ev'ybody do," the voice in the dark said, and sniggered.

I moved into the brush, made some deliberate noise shuffling it, then moved as silently as possible into the open. I moved up the edge of the field, crouching, each step a calculation. I proceeded this way for some fifty yards, still at the margin of the woods, for shadow in case the moon broke. But it did not break.

I looked back once, saw nothing in the dark, then plunged away from the woods. It was a cotton field. I was running between the rows, stumbling on the clods, hearing my skirts swish against the dew-heavy leaves. I heard Blue-Tobe calling in the dark, far back. I fell two or three times. Several times I had to stop for breath, my chest hurt so. When you run that way, your chest can hurt you till you want to die. But it's funny, it is like it is hurting somebody else.

As I approached the hummock, that darker mass in the dark beyond the field, I kept thinking maybe just the oaks cut off any light there might be in the house. Then I had managed up the incline, using my last breath, it seemed, and there was the house, not a light showing.

The house was shadowed by the absoluteness of the oak-darkness. I stood there at the foot of the steps to the gallery, clinging to the rail, staring up at the house.

For a moment, clinging there, I had the thought that maybe he was lying inside there, asleep in the dark, not knowing I had risen and run out into the dark fields, and run and run, falling in the dirt, all breathless and sick, and had now come back, now here I was, and I would go in now, and lie down, and he wouldn't wake up, but he would shift a little and take my hand. It was just a flash of that kind of craziness.

Then I heard a sound, what I didn't know, distant beyond the house. I had some breath back now. I ran around the house, under the darkness of the live oaks, around the kitchen porch, and there I saw down the hill.

I saw light flickering on the high boughs of pine trees beyond the barn and granary, above the bulk of the buildings, toward the quarters. I ran down the slope. A dog was barking off down there.

I ran around the corner of the granary, and stopped stock-still.

Two men held fat-pine torches. The other men stood around, with rifles. Beyond, ringing round, were forms, shadowy forms, people from the quarters no doubt, eyes staring. There in the space was Rau-Ru. I could see his white shirt. He was near the old pine tree. He was looking up at something. I saw something, then knew it was a wagon, something big on it. A man stood at the head of one of the mules to the wagon.

I came closer, not running now, stepping up slow and quiet. The dog was barking near the wagon, barking at something up there. Now I could see it was a cotton bale on the wagon. But I knew the dog was not barking at a cotton bale. I felt I couldn't bear to go closer. I just couldn't bear.

But I went closer. And there it was, but it hadn't happened.

I cried out, and I ran toward Rau-Ru, and I grabbed him, crying out, no, no. I shook him, and I beat at his chest with my fists. I called his name, and said, no, no. But he didn't even look down at me. He just grabbed me by the arm with his good hand, and held me in that grip, and kept on looking up, with some sort of intent, rapt look on his sweat-beaded black face, as though my hitting him on the chest were nothing.

So I quit hitting him, and quit calling out, no, no. It was as though his fixed look up there, which seemed to draw him out of himself and just leave his body standing there like a post or the trunk of a dead tree, fire-black out in an empty field, and my hitting his chest did as much good as hitting on that dead tree trunk. It was as though that look involved me, somehow, too, and drew me out of myself. As I said, I stopped striking his chest. I just stared up there, too.

Hamish Bond was standing there on top of the cotton bale. He did not have his blackthorn stick, balancing up there without it. He wore a nightshirt stuck into trousers. His hands were tied behind his back. A rope was around his neck, disappearing up into the shadow of the pine boughs, which wavered with the flickering of the torch flames. It was Hamish Bond, but if I hadn't known it was Hamish Bond, I might not have guessed, he had changed so much. He looked so old.

Hamish Bond did not seem to notice that his hands were tied, or that there was a rope around his neck. He was peering down directly at me, a slow, studious, sadly inquiring look.

"You," he said then, looking right at me, across the distance.

"Oh, Hamish, " I cried, "it's me!"

"Yes—you," he said, from that sad, speculative distance.

"Oh, Hamish," I cried, "I'll save you!"

And I swung toward Rau-Ru, clutching his shirt, jerking at it, calling his name, pleading.

It was the crazy laughing up there that broke across my pleading, that jerked my gaze back up there to the top of the cotton bale, and the shadow-swaying pine boughs.

Hamish Bond, his head thrown back, uttered that laughter up there that seemed to blow the whole world away in a gay, demoniac gust.

Then, all at once, the laughter stopped, and he looked square down at me, square at me, as though discovering me for the first time.

"All niggers," he said then, and his lip curled.

"You, too," he said, and laughed.

"Ass-deep in niggers," he said.
And jumped.

It was strange, the way he had jumped, not like a crippled man, but with a force and lightness, as in the old days when he would put the foot of his good leg on the step of the barouche, and swing up, laughing, swinging up above me with the lightness of youth, crying gaily, "And did I skeer you, Manty? Did I skeer you, little Manty?"

It was that light motion now, like a young man leaping, but the leap was an old man's leap, out from the old angers, the old self-torturing kindness, the contempt and self-contempt, into the stunning blaze of release, into the apocalyptic pain, into quietness.

The dog, down below the bale, began barking again.

After the event, several things happened. Rau-Ru's hand had released my arm, and in the silence he had moved away to go and sit on the chopping block by the woodpile. For a time he kept staring up there, but then he began looking down at the ground, between his feet. He simply seemed outside of what was going on now.

Some of the men had gone to the smokehouse and broken open the door. Then they broke open the granary. Then they went into the stables. After a time, Jimmee led out a horse harnessed to the old high-wheeled gig I had used to know. Jimmee hitched the horse to a tree and came over to stand in front of Rau-Ru, very quiet, as though waiting for further instructions. By this time, some of the men had worked the bale off the wagon, and were leading the wagon toward the meat-house.

Meanwhile, the people from the quarters—whoever they were now, new ones, some of the old ones from slave-time who had stayed on—stood very quiet, in the background, in the shadows, watching.

I was standing there in the middle of the space. I simply hadn't moved. It was as though all my life were over, as though I were dead and the only thing alive in the whole world were the suffocating pain in my chest.

Jimmee touched Rau-Ru on the shoulder. Rau-Ru looked up at him with a slow, dazed look, then rose. He went to the gig. Jimmee started to help him up, but it wasn't necessary. It wasn't as though

Rau-Ru were weak. It was, rather, as though he moved in some heaviness of sleep.

Jimmee came over to me. "Come on," he said.

I followed to the gig. I felt that I, too, was moving in that same, dazed heaviness of sleep. I simply didn't feel a thing now, just a sad heaviness, beyond everything.

Jimmee helped me up, then motioned to another man, the sick-looking mulatto. "You get 'em loaded up," Jimmee ordered, "and come on down thar." Then Jimmee climbed up, shoved me over, and took the reins. Jimmee was a skinny man, so he didn't crowd too much.

After we had moved beyond the hummock where the house was and had gained the track between the west fields and the woods, I cast a sidewise glance into the darkness. I really can't be sure that, in my numbness, I had the notion of trying to leap from the gig and run off in the dark. Perhaps I did have the notion, or the possibility was there in me without being even a notion. Anyway, at that moment, I felt the sudden grip of Rau-Ru's hand on my arm. In alarm, as though he had read that notion, or possibility, I looked at him. He was paying me no attention. His face was fixed up the track, into the darkness. But his grip on my arm did not relax.

We had reached the spot where the track branched off through the woods to the Boyd place, the spot where Hamish Bond, accompanying Charles Prieur-Denis and me, would always turn back with the gig and let us ride on. I recognized the spot, even in the dark, the heavier, higher massing of the darkness of the forest. We entered it, the road felt more even, Jimmee touched up the horse, we bowled along in the dark.

After a time the moon broke again. By now we had turned off, again between fields. But I could see that they were uncultivated, water standing here and there. "Levee," Jimmee said. "Levee done cut long back, and nobody keer."

We moved on, and Jimmee spoke again: "Ole Boyd, he doan keer. He done daid."

Then: "Git on his hoss and ride off to kill Yankees."

Then: "Done daid."

There was the darkness of a grove ahead. We entered it; the moonlight showed what had been lawn, or garden, part under water. Over yonder was a broken statue, white and headless in the moonlight. There was the mass of the house. Half had fallen in, just the chimney of that wing standing.

Jimmee nodded toward the ruin. "Yankees," he said.

We drew up the drive, stopped in front of the undamaged section of the house, and got down. Jimmee lighted the lantern and led us in. The rays of the lantern showed that some of the furniture was yet about, much abused and broken. The windows were broken out. Part of the hall showed the marks of fire. I wondered, numbly, how the fire had been put out. Had it broken out while the Yankees themselves were here and they had put it out? Had the Negroes put it out, stirred by some old fidelity? Had it merely rained opportunely, a Louisiana torrent?

Jimmee led us into a room off the hall, what must have been a back sitting room. There was a kind of couch there, Empire, the scrolling off, the upholstery much faded and ripped. Rau-Ru stood in the middle of the floor. Jimmee went up to him, and pointed at the couch. "Lay down," he said. And Rau-Ru propped himself there.

Jimmee provided a candle, lighted it, and set it in its own grease on the marble of a tabletop. "Dey's a crick back de house," he said to Rau-Ru. "Done tole 'um to bring the p'rogues up de crick, we load 'em here. Doan have to tote so far."

Rau-Ru wasn't paying attention, not really.

"Done sent two of 'um, and dey's Blue-Tobe down thar."

Rau-Ru looked at him. "Get out," he said.

Jimmee went out into the hall.

Rau-Ru motioned me to sit down. I sat down on the floor, and leaned against a carved and scrolled leg of the table. I stared across the room at a big pier glass. There were holes plugged in the glass, as though by pistol slugs. The flame of the candle was reflected murkily in the glass. The glass was dirty and much cracked, and it was as though I looked through that webby impediment to vision into a farther room. In that room yonder beyond the glass there was a candle, and two human forms. It was as though this room here did not exist, just the room yonder, and I was one of those motionless, shadowy forms beyond the webbed and dusty glass.

"You killed him," I said.

His face turned soberly at me, but he said nothing.

"You killed him," I said.

For a long time he looked at me, over the distance.

"You were the *k'la*," I said, and waited.

"Yeah," he said, and stirred heavily on the couch. "Yeah, I was the *k'la*."

Then: "I reckon it was because I was the *k'la*."

He kept on looking at me from that sober distance. There was no air moving, and the candle-flame was steady.

"No," he said, then, "no," and sort of shook his head.

"You were the *k'la*," I said.

"It wasn't just because I was the *k'la*," he said. "It was because of what happened."

He waited, collected himself. "Because of what happened day before yesterday," he said. "Yeah, it's always the same, " he said, "those on your side, they give the sweet talk and the promise, and we got shot in the street. Yeah," he said, "and the soldiers never came."

He sank into his meditation. Looking into that farther room of the mirror, where the candle and the two shadowy forms were, I saw his head sink a little on his breast. Then he lifted his head.

"No," he said.

I looked at him.

"No," he said, "not just because of that, either."

"What?" I demanded.

He stared heavily at me. "You," he said.

He heaved himself up a little. "Yeah, because of you," he said. "If you hadn't come and stood there in front of me, I never would have remembered how at night I used to squat in the brush down by the barn, near those God-damned mimosas, and wonder about you up there with Old Bond. If you hadn't come and stood, I never would have done it."

He sank back. "But you came," he said.

"I didn't make you do it!" I cried out.

He seemed to think about that, then pushed up, and said: "You didn't make that Charles do what he did, either."

Then said: "Or did you?"

Then said: "Or make me do what I did to Charles then, and they ran me in the woods and they whipped me?"

He stared slowly at me. "You're just the way you are," he said, and sank back.

*The way you are, the way you are;* the words were in my head, and I wanted to scramble up and cry out that I wasn't that way, no,

I wasn't. But what way was it? But you are the way you are, that is only logical and can't be otherwise, whatever way that is and you don't know what it is, oh, you never know what it is.

I felt as though the walls were coming closer and closer.

But I sat very quiet on the floor, leaning against the leg of the table. The carving and the scrolls cut my back. I was there when Jimmee came in.

Behind him was the sick mulatto.

"Tell him," Jimmee ordered the mulatto, and Jimmee was leaning over the couch, watching Rau-Ru's face, avid, waiting for vindication in the words coming out of the mulatto's mouth. That Michele woman, he was saying, she had got away. She had got away long back, nobody knew how long back, she had got a horse, for there had been a horse down in the little side lot.

"I told you to lock her up," Rau-Ru said to Jimmee, tiredly, "or tie her up, so she couldn't get out."

"You ought to let me cut her thote," Jimmee said, "her layin up there and nary a stitch. You ought to let, and now you see what's done come. You ought to let me drug her out and hung her up in the pine tree and nary a stitch, and her light-skinned and kickin. Her and Ole Bond, that the way she wanted hit. Yeah, and now what's come, you listen to 'um!"

He turned to the mulatto. "Tell 'um!" he commanded.

The mulatto told him. Some white men—bushwhackers he called them—had broken up a Negro rally the day before, a rally got up way out in the country to celebrate the Convention. They beat up and shot up some people, but nobody killed. Now some of the bushwhackers were camped over toward *Tarnation*, not far. Now they figured that Michele had gone to the bushwhackers. They figured Michele would guess about the Boyd place. So the mulatto had sent the provision wagon to the woods, instead. They'd tote what they could to the pirogues, and come up the creek here and get Rau-Ru and the rest. But they better leave fast. No telling how long Michele had been gone.·

"You gotta leave fast," Jimmee was saying, leaning over the couch, "you gotta leave fast."

But Rau-Ru wasn't listening to him.

Jimmee insisted: leave fast. Rau-Ru shook his head irritably, saying he would leave in a minute.

Now, Jimmee was saying, now.

Rau-Ru ordered him to get out, to wait in the hall. So he went out.

Rau-Ru sank back on the couch, staring over at the wall. I had stayed on the floor. I heard voices out in the hall, Jimmee and the mulatto. Then somebody went off down the hall.

Rau-Ru shifted his weight on the couch. "I might never have done it," he said.

"But you did," I said.

"No," he said, "no. I had him up there and the rope on him. I had to get him up there and look at him, like I could do it. I had to feel I could do it if I wanted. But I might never have done it."

"But you did," I said.

He was propped up now, looking slow at me. "No," he said, "no. I didn't do it. You did."

I couldn't find breath for a word.

"Yes," he was saying, "you coming out there. He never would have jumped if he hadn't seen you."

Jimmee came back in. "Come on," he said, "come on." He came over and plucked at Rau-Ru's sleeve, wheedling. It was as though Jimmee might cry.

Rau-Ru said he would come in a minute.

Jimmee said he himself was going to go now. He was not going to wait and be chewed up by no bushwhackers. He was not going to wait.

But he did wait.

He waited out in the hall again, and that was where they shot him.

# X I

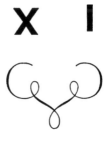

HE WAS NOT MUCH OLDER THAN I, JUST A BOY REALLY, TALL AND bony, with a hard, hungry-looking face and a wispy mustache. Even if there was a moon, I couldn't now see what his eyes were like, for his hat had a broad brim. But back in the house, in the instant when he had grabbed my arm and said for me to come on, I had caught a glimpse of them, the slit eyes, eyes used to peering close, to squinting into distance.

Now I looked down and saw that his right hand, the hand that held the rifle, was small, too small for his frame, and finely formed, and this surprised me, for when he had first laid hand on me his grip had been hard as steel. But now, standing in the moonlight, his left hand light on my arm, we might have been sweethearts wandering to this spot for the romantic shiver of the ruined house, or for the privacy of our embraces.

You could see into the hall of the house, and way down there a little light showed from that back sitting room. We were both watching that light now. We had come down the hall, his grip tight on my arm, past the humped-up form of Jimmee on the floor, and out the front door. As we now watched the light, we heard the yell.

At the yell, I felt the grip on my arm tighten spasmodically. Then he was looking at me, with what in his eyes I couldn't know for the hat brim, but I saw his tongue wet his lips. "Lady," he said, "five years now, Lady, and I have been all over Hell and found it handsome. I have seen it all, but you get tired, Lady."

I heard the horses stir, then an owl again.

Then he said: "Lady, perhaps some of my friends found Hell even · handsomer than I did, so I am making a suggestion. I don't care if you are black or white, but I just suggest you jerk loose from me and shove me down, for I shove mighty easy some times, and you grab one of those horses and tear out. Some of my friends are rough."

I felt his touch on my arm go light as a feather.

"They won't like it," he said, "but I can handle 'em."

I did it.

I looked back just once, just for an instant, far down the drive. It was when I had heard the burst of firing, and the shouts, then more firing. It must have been the men from the pirogues arriving. I wondered if they got there in time to do any good. Any good, that is, for Lieutenant Oliver Cromwell Jones, who was Rau-Ru.

My mount was going at a dead run, not back up the road to *Pointe du Loup*, but south, a strange road where I had never been before, running blind under the shadow of forest.

I was riding with my last picture of Rau-Ru in my head.

The shot in the hall had been our warning, the shot that got Jimmee. There had not been, of course, much time between the shot and their appearance at the door of the back parlor, but whatever that time was, I am of the impression that Rau-Ru made no attempt to move. There was a rifle propped against the table, and I suppose he might have fired it with his good hand, or tried. And he did have a pistol. But he simply waited, whatever time there was to wait, and there they were.

"That's him," one of the men said, a black-bearded man, but even before the words, the rifles were already on him.

Rau-Ru had lifted his head a little, looking at the rifle muzzles, then slowly, studiously, up at the men.

Then one of the men spied me, sitting on the floor, propped against the table leg, in shadow.

"What the hell?" he demanded, his rifle on me.

I came unfrozen.

I know that scientists have put a galvanic current through the leg of a dead frog and that the galvanic current will make the leg move as in life. It was something like that with me. It was as though a strong galvanic current had been passed through my being to jerk me out of my torpor, to jerk me scrambling up, not in fear, in some deeper necessity, uttering the unplanned words, the words that burst out of me.

The words were: "I'm not nigger, I'm not nigger—I'm white, and he made me come—oh, he made me!"

I was shuddering now, as with that galvanic current, and pointing at Rau-Ru.

At my cry, the eyes of all had turned on me, but now, with my pointing finger, they were fixed again on Rau-Ru.

Rau-Ru shifted a little on the couch, looking at me. The big mirror was beyond him, cracked and pistol-plugged and gray-webbed. Rau-Ru was staring at me, the candlelight showing the sweat-beads on his face, staring at me from some sad, dark, pitying depth.

"Yes," he said, in his husky, whispery voice, tired-sounding now, "she's not nigger. And sure, I made her come."

The black-bearded man turned to the tall boy. "Git her out," he commanded, and the boy had laid that small hand with the steely grip on my arm and said for me to come on.

That was the way it had been, and that was the picture that I had in my head as I rode away. I don't suppose anything different I might have said would have changed things, anyway. Those men knew what they were there for.

But the funny thing was, I hadn't said it because I was afraid. It had just burst out of me.

Before dawn I got so tired I couldn't stay in the saddle. The forest was over now, a country of woodlots and corn patches, and I huddled in the protection of an old corn-crib at the edge of a field, and listened to the night, then saw the dawn coming up the color of blue-watery buttermilk, and the stars paling out, and some pine trees off yonder eastward lifting their crests against the buttermilk blue looked incredibly black, as though sketched in India ink on that color of dawn, and I felt nothing, absolutely nothing, for there is no blankness like the blankness of the dawn hour. Then, I slept.

It was broad day when I awoke. The stamping of the horse woke me. I ate some half-green corn and drank water from a creek, and it is a wonder I did not die of it. Toward evening, I took shelter in the shack of some piney-woods people, telling them I had come down from Tennessee to trace a brother who had been wounded at Shiloh and had, word now informed me, been sent off to Louisiana. Telling that tale of the brother wounded years back, whom I must now find, or whose grave I must dew with my tears, I began, almost, to believe the tale myself, feeling emotion about it, some sweetness at my own fidelity, an escape into another dimension of being, and then, in the very moment of that feeling, I realized that it was the tale Hamish Bond had told me to tell at the hotel in New Orleans to explain my presence, after he had sent me from his house.

So rapt had I been in the telling of the sweet lie which made me not me, that I did not notice the faces of my auditors, the people of the shack, the man, the woman, the old woman—the tightening around the mouth, the narrowing of the eyes. Then the old woman said: "We wuz Union." And she folded her arms across her breast, like closing a door.

"Yeah," the man said, "two year in the army, fightin Rebels." He spat on the ground, and turned his thin, fever-sallow face away, looking off across the starvation corn-patch to the pines. Then he looked back at me, saying: "Them as is dead is dead. You kin come in."

Next day I rode again. I passed through the dust and dazzle of August, saw the blackness of bayous, caught the nose-tingling disinfectant smell of pine woods broiled of resin in that savage heat, heard the metallic whirr of insects in the fields and brush, whirring forever. I had some feeling that this flight had happened before; everything, the bend of the road, the fall of a leaf, the cant of a face, seemed to have happened long back.

Then staring ahead through the dazzle, I knew. I knew that this was the flight I had not made, a heroic flight from the house of Hamish Bond, long back before anything had happened, and in my mind, suddenly, there was an image of snow, of coldness, of icy woods, nights bright with ice-glitter and joy, as though, untouched and triumphant, I were fleeing toward that. It was, in a way, as though the thing not done—the flight not made—is always done, too, and never releases you from the grip of the old possibility, and you can only escape from the done, never from the not-done, which in its not-doneness is always there being enacted forever.

But I knew I was not riding toward the image of ice, of joy. I was riding south, back toward New Orleans.

I sold the good horse, and the McClellan saddle, at a settlement outside the city, getting cheated and knowing it, for a young woman in the wreck of expensive clothes, clothes designed for a city street, who comes riding up, astride, on a McClellan saddle, on a travel-broke good horse, with no baggage to her name, and who doesn't even bother to lie about herself, is in no position to bargain. Anyway, I couldn't tell my lie again: the sweetness I had felt in the first telling was now nauseous to me.

I took what few dollars I could get from the transaction, not knowing whether or not I would need the money. My plans were of the most shadowy. I would go to the house—the house where Tobias Sears and I had lived—and I would get some decent clothes and what money there was in the house, not much but enough, I imagined, to set me on my way. If I encountered Tobias, well, I should simply brave it out. Actually, the thought of that encounter stirred an excitement, the image of the encounter—his walking in on me in the hall or bedroom—yes the bedroom was better—and asking what had happened, saying he had been desperate, asking where I had been.

And I should say: *You left me because I am a nigger, and I left you because I am one.*

I should say: *You left me for your niggers, and I left you for mine.*

Yes, I could see his face again before me, stricken and white, the lips moving but the words not audible, the face hung there in the air, and a joy suffused me.

Oh, I should say: *Yes, you left me for them, and what good did you do?*

But with that the words returned to me, addressed to me, like an echo from a dark cavern: *—and what good did you do?*

None, oh, none, for what I had sought, whatever that was, I had not found, and that was why I had fled, and was fleeing. It was why I would take what money there was in the house where I had been happy—or had I been happy?—and I would go away. I would flee into the commonness of life, the life of people one saw on the street, into the common meaninglessness, or meaningfulness, it did not matter which so long as it was different from whatever had been. I would escape into the averageness, the dullness, I would hide in the daylight, I would hide in the commonness of daylight, which is a darkness deeper than the darkness of sleep and of nightmare, for that darkness is a blaze that lights up everything.

I would go to a strange place and I would walk down the street and be like everyone else, I would live in a cocoon of quietness, I would move in the sweetness of wanting nothing but the quietness, and nothing would ever have happened.

From the settlement outside the city I got a ride, on a wagon. I paid the man two dollars to take me in. I made him let me down a block from the house, on that street of fine white houses set back in gardens of magnolia and crepe myrtle, the myrtle now blooming, and the man looked at me with the blunt wonder in his eyes as to what I, torn and filthy and disordered, would be doing here.

I found the front door unlocked. I went up to the bedroom, laid out clothing for myself, bathed, and dressed. I was going down the stairs, to Tobias' study, where the little safe was, when I saw the cook in the dim hall, standing there staring up at me, her eyes wide with surprise in her black face.

I had come down another step or two before she could speak. Then she managed: "You—you—Miz Sears—"

"Of course," I rejoined tartly, "why not?" As though defending my right to be here at all.

At the foot of the stairs she rushed toward me, reaching out her hands to me, putting an arm about my shoulder in comfort, saying, "Chile—chile—been huntin you everwhar—chile, you pore chile, and him nigh dead."

"What are you talking about?" I demanded.

"Him," she said, "dey nigh killed him, him layin dere all dis time, not knowing nuthin—not nuthin—and caint find you—you pore chile."

"Who?" I demanded, but knowing the answer, thinking as echo: *lying there not knowing.*

"Mister 'Bias," she said, "him tryin to save de pore colored, but de white folks, dey nigh kill him."

*Lying there not knowing:* and I said: "Where is he?"

"De 'firmary," she said, "whar de sick sojers."

I was almost to the front door, then turned back. I hurried upstairs, and made a package of my ruined clothes. This I took out with me. I would get rid of it somehow. Yes, on my way there I would do it, somehow.

I had assessed, in a flash, at the moment of the echo in my head —*lying there not knowing*—the probability that Tobias Sears had not come home after leaving me the night before the riot, that he did not know, and did not ever have to know, that I, too, had left the house. I assessed that probability, and acted upon it, but I did not assess the need that led to the action. But *need* in the singular is not accurate. Oh, if needs ever came simple and single, how easy happiness might be, even in defeat, for even defeat would be definition!

No, there was more than one need. To do myself justice, there was the welling up of pity, of the desire to reach out to that beautiful, strong, white face that lay like marble, with the eyes closed, to touch it and heal. But even that desire was, I now surmise, not only the desire to heal, but to be healed: to be made free.

But what had become of my resolve to flee into the commonness of life, to hide in the light of common day, to find freedom in that anonymity?

Nothing had become of it, for this was it, too. Tobias sick, Tobias wounded, Tobias maimed, and me leaning over him, day by day, night by night, bringing him life, or death, in my devotion—yes, that would not be nightmare but escape from nightmare. That would be to create the deep hermitage to which I would flee, the grot to which I would carry his white, unconscious form to restore him, and in restoring him bind him forever with the invisible chains of love. In that devoted story I would find power and freedom. And vengeance on him, I suppose, and on fate, for his having failed, somehow, to free me.

And that was the story.


Tobias was sick a long time. He had been severely beaten, and twice stabbed. He did not regain consciousness for two days after my arrival at his bedside, not until a week, that is, after the injury. When he did come to, even though I sat by the bed holding his hand, he did not at first recognize me. As a matter of fact, I thought he was blind—one of the blows had been to the head—and with the awfulness of that thought I had some fleeting, submerged sense, like the white flash of a fish-belly in deep water, of fulfillment, of vindication: I should lead him, always, by the hand.

But a moment later I saw the recognition come into his eyes, saw the faintest smile touch his face, and leaning above him, saw his lips, soundlessly, trying to form my name: *Manty.* And watching that soundless effort, which nevertheless was my name, was me, **was** all the best of me, I burst into tears of joy.

It was another month, early September, before Tobias could be moved. The weather was still brutally hot, and on that excuse I had him taken upriver, toward Baton Rouge, to a plantation which a Northern man had bought, a man whose admiration for Tobias' courage now prompted an invitation. I had, of course, long since closed our house, surrendered the lease, and gone to live at a hotel. I had given the servants handsome sums by way of parting, and they, carrying whatever knowledge they had of me, had sunk without trace into the dark, teeming tide of their lives. As for the physicians at the hospital, I had told an adequate story, adequate because of its very sinuousness and shadowy complication.

We were at the Hartwell plantation until late fall. Tobias' health improved, but despite his efforts at concealment, it was clear that he suffered periods of depression, even sitting there on the deep veranda, looking out over the level lawn, down the avenue of live oaks dripping the gray elegance of moss to shade the marble forms of gods and goddesses, unquenchable images of power, fertility, and love—Tobias sitting there and staring out into the clear, wine-bright, sunlit season that would never, it seemed, change, looking out on a world that seemed to have escaped all time and the jostle of history.

On Saturday nights the darkies sang down at the quarters, the tidy brick cottages painted white like the big house. One Saturday night after Tobias had gone early to bed, I sat by him, reading aloud, but his mind was clearly not on my words. Far off, there was the singing.

"Damn it," Tobias broke across my rotelike words, "do they have to sing?"

"Does it bother the reading?" I asked.

"No," he said, and I resumed.

But after a little he broke in again. "Well," he said, "at least he pays them wages."

"Mr. Hartwell, you mean?"

"Who else would I mean?" he demanded, testily. Then: "Hartwell—and five years from now he'll be voting the straight Democratic ticket."

The singing died away. I went back to the reading. Then I heard the first rustle of rain. The cloud had come over the moon, in my mind I saw the clouds drifting over, the moon had been obscured, the first tentative drops had fallen, the singers had ceased, and withdrawn. The rain became steady.

Suddenly, Tobias said: "We've got to leave. I've got to leave this place!"

"Yes, darling," I said.

I had waited for this moment.

I had waited with only one apprehension, that Tobias might want to go back to Massachusetts. My earlier dream of our going to New England, of living in a clean, crisp college town, of escaping into a vision of starlit, snow-bright night, of walking on Tobias' arm under the tracery of bare elms, past the lights of houses—I had given up that notion. I had given it up because now I not only would flee from the place where I had been what I had been, but from old Leonidas Sears as well, from that face of jut-nosed force, for now I felt, instinctively, that within that orbit Tobias, sick or well, would never be mine, and therefore I could never be myself, be free.

The old man had written Tobias suggesting that he come back, come back and "accept your responsibility, for here at the center of power and with that small instrument of power which I, under God's will, have created, you will be able to serve best our mission of Virtue. For here you will not be subject to the vicissitudes of the perimeter, but will, by your slightest motion, sway events in those far-off parts with influence multiplied through distance in a Divine leverage."

Several days before, Tobias had read me that letter. He had said nothing, and I had said nothing. The letter had lain on the table, emanating silence.

"I've got to leave this place!" he cried out now, and asked for pen and paper. Propped up in bed he wrote a letter, then without a word, sealed it and laid it on the table by the bed. He slipped down, suddenly pale and exhausted, making some feeble motion with his hand, saying, "Darling, I'm so tired."

Naturally, under such circumstances, I could ask him nothing. I dimmed the lamp, made ready for bed, and lay down on the couch in his room, where I might hear him if he stirred.

The next morning he announced that we would not return to New England. "Yes, darling," I said, and nothing more.

The rains lasted two more weeks. By the time they broke, the reply from Tobias' father was at hand: "—and though disappointed in your decision, I would not press you. I reflect that in that western part to which you go, men of our section and sort may do much to inseminate responsibility and to mollify that rawness of pride and rash selfishness of gain which, if unbridled, may in the end do as much to unsettle the social fabric which we, in God's name, have created, as ever did the Slavocrat in his crime."

St. Louis was that western part to which we planned to go.

Neither Tobias nor I had the slightest knowledge of St. Louis. That was, I suppose, the reason we were going, and why the going was a restoration, a joy, a birth. We would go to that strange place, and nothing, nothing that had ever happened, would have happened. My heart, and mind, closed on the past, like a valve.

The fair weather had returned. Sun gilded the lifting water that we breasted so powerfully. The first night aboard we stood on the deck and saw the sparks from our twin stacks spiral back like flaming nebulae in the dark shadow of the bluffs of the Mississippi shore. Then, unhurriedly, the moon rose in imperial gold above the bluffs. Tobias' hand tightened upon my own.

He drew me to him and a little later, his arm about my waist, led me to our cabin. There, on a little table, was a silver bucket of ice, in it a bottle of wine. Wordlessly, a boyish smile on his face, a smile almost of waggery, he left my side, opened the bottle, and filled the glasses with the frothy, vital liquid. He handed me my glass, and as I looked at him over that gleam, he lifted his own glass, his face went serious and high, and he said: "To you, dear Manty—for you are all to me."

"You are all to me," I said, and we tasted the wine.

We had both spoken truth, no doubt, and that was the terrible thing.

We spoke truth, he tossed off his glass, and drew me to him, and then with a free hand fumbled to pour himself another glass and lifted it as he held me close, and drank it, holding me tight the while, drawing me out of all the past into our mutual necessity and doom, and that seemed joy. It did not seem—it *was* joy. For when is the reality of a moment to be defined? In act or consequence? And in what consequence?

But even in that joy, in the very act of love, in some brief valley of awareness between the crests, there was the flicker of thought: *Had he brought the wine to ritualize our joy? Or to make joy possible at all?*

The next night I took two glasses before we disposed ourselves, side by side.

A little time after our arrival in St. Louis, I knew that we were to have a child.

As for St. Louis, in its raw, ragged bustle there was life for us. The bustle made it possible for Tobias to practice his law with enough success to have leisure for his more congenial and bookish pursuits, and the very rawness of that bustle made our withdrawal into our own little circle more snug and complete. At the very center there was our son, named Leonidas for the grandfather but looking like Tobias, and then, one on each side like a photograph, were Tobias and I, holding hands across the cradle and staring down in perfect bliss, untouched by fate and history. I suppose I actually saw it that way, like a picture—life frozen in quietness, in eternal stasis, out of time, no past, no future, no beat of the heart.

But even in its quietness and decorum our life was not quite like that. We had friends who made a small circle around us, delightful friends, some learned, some witty, young men all, some just out of Harvard College or Amherst, some out of the war, boyish colonels and majors wearing wound or reputation with gay disdain, all with the air of men touched by the finger of destiny, all what old Sears had called men of "our section and sort," all spilled like bright buttons out of a button-box in the westward heave of the continent.

We lived in a nice, small house in a good section of town, and I poured tea for friends out of a beautiful silver service which had belonged to Tobias' mother's mother, and the talk flowed on around me, and now and then I caught an echo of poor Herman Muller pulling the golden ringlets of his Bavarian cheese-farm beard and leaning at my father to say, "Aaron, there's money in it, much money," but no, these young men did not talk like that. They said, "an interesting possibility," "a potentiality of development," "the duty of expansion," "the logic of the situation." No, they were not like poor Mr. Muller: none of them would ever go to prison.

Even so, when they talked, I now and then would see the hardening of Tobias' face, a withdrawing, and the old image would come to me that had come the night of Tobias' declaration of his intention to join the Freedman's Bureau, the image of him struggling in some gray, viscous matter that would draw him down. But when Tobias spoke, even in criticism of the way the world wagged, these young men listened most respectfully. He was, of course, the son of old Sears, as I once or twice reminded myself, then accused myself of disloyalty and remembered that Tobias could command anyone's respect, he was the most learned of them all, the one clearly marked for fame beyond the presidencies of banks and the building of railroads, and remembered that these cultivated young men respected the talents that would lead to such higher fame. They heard him read his poems, over the tea cup or port glass, before they saw them in the newspapers or even, now and then, the *Atlantic* magazine.

Yes, the poems impressed these young men, for the poems were of the War, and these young men themselves had plunged across the blood-soaked barnyards and disordered corn fields which, now, were history, and the poems lifted such old moments of fear and rage, quieted them in the glory of an ideal fulfilled, in the pathos of death. Yes, the hero of those poems, whatever his various names and avatars, spoke always from the grave beside many a sad pine grove, by many a moonlit water, spoke in accents of sober dedication veined by melancholy sweetness. The young men who had emerged from the old smoke-wreathed and blood-splashed dream into the coziness of our little drawing room were always quiet after the reading, flatteringly quiet, then they spoke their praises and happy predictions, and Tobias thanked them, and sometimes, as they turned back to the vigorous concerns of the present, I might see him sitting there, more withdrawn than before, the sheet of paper in his hand.

I was, of course, proud of the poems, and of the praise. The most famous piece, one of those printed in the *Atlantic* and quoted everywhere, "The Dead Vidette," I cut out of the magazine and framed and hung on the wall, and that pleased Tobias, even though he was embarrassed by the moral weakness of his own pleasure and, when I called attention of guests to it, pretended to scoff a little at my fondness.

But the time was to come when at the brink of such a moment, he would turn his head away from the guests as he waited for me to say, "Yes, that's a poem Tobias wrote long ago—when he wrote poetry"—waiting for me to say that in a cruel echo, which I recognized and hated myself for, of the old tone of wifely pride.

Then one morning I noticed that the frame was gone from the wall. It had been there the night before when I had shown it to

Judge Talley, so Tobias must have risen from my side during the night, and gone to remove it and, no doubt, destroy it. Now in contrast with the pale rectangle where the framed poem had been, I saw how discolored and old the wall paper in general was. We really ought to repaper, I thought. But I knew we couldn't afford it. But this was later on, after we had moved to Sill's Crossing, Kansas.

Meanwhile, the life in St. Louis was lived in itself, and in its own satisfactions. Little Leonidas throve, a strong, fine child, and we had a daughter now, Martha, with big brown eyes and curly hair, and people said she looked like me, but truly, I could not believe it, she was so beautiful. I loved my children, I enjoyed serving tea from the noble silver tea things that had come from the time of George II, I admired Tobias' face across the drawing room and at night I was not lonely, lying in the crook of his arm. We were, in short, a charming young couple, very devoted—oh, yes, I saw us as a charming young couple, posed eternally, as I have said, for a photograph. And myself was the photographer eternally taking the photograph, I suppose, for the photograph is what we need to prove the reality.

Then came the moment of Tobias' fame. It wasn't the poems. It was the book that, unknown even to me, he must have been working toward for ten years, and suffering toward, in the privacy of his study, into which I never intruded, and the wakeful hours on his pillow, into which, too, I rarely intruded, all the years while the world was besmirching his youthful dream of the Idea that was to redeem all evil and butchery. His book was called *The Great Betrayal.*

Now in 1877 he said the Idea of Freedom had been betrayed. Big Business had betrayed it, first by putting corporation lawyers on the Supreme Court to protect the National Debt and then placate the South by reinterpreting the Fourteenth Amendment, and second by making a deal with Southern Democrats to let Rutherford Hayes go in as President in return for the withdrawal of troops and the handing over of the Negro to the planter's mercy.

But that, Tobias said, was only a symptom, however heinous, of the Evil. There had been a time in New England—Tobias said he would speak specially of his own section—when men had aspired to live for an Idea, of God, of Good, of Truth beyond the Veil of Appearances, of Human Brotherhood, of Progress, of Freedom, of values beyond the Worship of Things. Men, he said, had fought a bloody war for the value of Ideas, but in victory they had betrayed all to the Moloch of Thingism, and now in a land that had once produced statesmen, prophets, explorers, scientists, poets and seers, we found politicians who were gate-keepers for pelf, judges who were janizaries for the National Debt, courts that were a Swiss Guard for credit, prophets who were prophets for six per cent, scientists who were subsidized tinkers, teachers who were cataloguers of libraries and philosophers who would justify all.

"We fought to save the Union," he cried out, "and we saved it, and it is a league with dollars and a covenant with death. We have saved the Union, but have we lost our own soul?"

Whether or not we had lost our souls, we came near to losing our friends. Those young men—not so young any more, and some already entering upon their destiny of Success—came less often to our cozy drawing room, and came at all, I sensed, because Tobias Sears was, even in his craziness, the son of old Sears. If they could have smelt out the rancorous correspondence then accumulating between father and son, they probably would not have come at all.

And six months later they did not come. We were not there for them to come to. We had fled, and those young men had been proved right in their deepest instincts.

There was in St. Louis, during those years, a rising young man of business named Bryce Caxton, an imperious, driving sort of man, not of the best blood but of the brightest prospects. His wife, a lovely, pale creature, was, I was informed, of the very best blood, having been a Miss Colfell of Cambridge, but her only prospects, as I could well determine without any informant, were to be overawed and sneered at, not always subtly, by Bryce Caxton, and he particularly chose to sneer at what was her greatest solace, what he termed her "lovely Love of the Beautiful." Bryce Caxton made it all seem very silly, her albums and engravings and oils and bronzes and plasters commemorating the years she had spent growing up in Rome with an old aunt, in a *palazzo* stuffed with antique treasures, local aristocrats, and traveling savants. But it was not silly. She was learned and devoted, and if, to her, art was too much, it was so, you felt, only because life was too little, and that through no fault of her own.

The time came when life was not only too little for Irene Colfell, but was less than little. So at ten o'clock one morning, having seen her husband off to his appointed triumphs and dismissed the servants for some hours, she dressed herself carefully, disposed herself on a couch in her dressing room and turned on the gas.

Somebody found her in time. But they found, too, a note. She had been having a love affair with a gentleman, one possessing the delicacy of soul to appreciate all she appreciated and whose personal beauty touched her being as wind touches the harp, but who, she had found to her disaster, lacked firmness of purpose. He had planned to flee with her, to flee to Italy where she had been happy, but at the last minute he had cruelly canceled their plans, and their love. Perhaps all was for the best, she added, perhaps they might not have had happiness on terms meaning sorrow for others. So she was content to die. She did not give the gentleman's name.

She did not have to. Bryce Caxton got it out of her in no time at all, by methods I can abhorrently imagine. The name was, of course, Tobias Sears.

Bryce Caxton blazed the thing, letter and all, far and wide. He had clearly wanted to get rid of his old bargain, and here was the way, heaven-sent, and within a matter of months there was a new Mrs. Caxton. But there was, no doubt, another motive for fanning the scandal, in seeing that it was in every paper and on every tongue, the motive of Bryce Caxton's dearest vanity, for he was the chief local apostle of Thingism, and if the author of *The Great Betrayal*, that savage attack on Thingism, was nothing but a cheap adulterer, a lily-livered aesthete not having even the courage of his manly appetite, and a cruel cheat to boot, then what became of his fine ideals, his fine Worship of the Idea? Thingism was, somehow, justified after all. That was the implied conclusion in every reference in the press, from Boston to New Orleans. Yes, Bryce Caxton was right, you needn't worry about Tobias Sears any more. The sky was the limit. Or would be, as soon as the little money depression was over.

They didn't have to worry about Tobias Sears.

But I did.

I had to lie awake in the night and realize that for ten happy years the forgetfulness of the past had not been a forgetfulness at all, but a thin shell, like a glaze of ice, over the darkest and deepest remembering. I had to realize that the happiness itself was but the gilt of the scab over the old sore. I had to remember that Tobias Sears had once before fled from me, and why, oh, why? In revulsion from a taint in my blood, in fear of the dark passion of my blood which honesty to him had unbound, in answer to a noble obligation, in desire for some truth which was not in me to give or understand? Had the old reason, or reasons, for his flight now been lived over again?

And then came the chillingest thought of all. Not his reason for flight from me had been relived, but his reason for coming to me in the first place. Only now it had not been to me but to Irene Colfell that he came, seeing her lost, seeing her unhappy, seeing her rejected, and in his white high magnanimity he had leaned toward her. That thought was so chilling that, literally, I lay in the bed and shook. I had been nothing to Tobias Sears, nothing at all, nothing but the excuse for his magnanimity. Oh, my life was nothing.

I rose and walked the dark house. It was familiar even in darkness, but even in the dark I knew that it was whirling away from me, for we could not stay in St. Louis. I went into the room where my baby slept and leaned over her shadow-shrouded perfections as for the last time. I went to the room of my son as for a last farewell. I longed for some farewell, no matter how tragic, if it could be total. Why did I not die? Why did I not kill myself? Did I have to live on and on, and see everything repeated over and over again? Was life only that, a perpetual re-enactment of what you thought you could not bear, but which was, somehow, the very essence of what your self was?

Caught up in those thoughts—or rather, feelings—I wandered the house. Dawn was coming up. I saw the glimmer of light on the glass over Tobias' framed poem, "The Dead Vidette." I mournfully ran my finger over the glass, taking leave of that, too, or rather, of my old pride in it, my old sense of having some share in his achievement.

My eyes, in the dimness, happened to pick out the first line: "I who, alone, through night and cedarn glade."

*I who, alone:* and all at once I knew that I had never had a share in Tobias' poems. No, for their hero of the hundred names, or namelessnesses, who had died into the hundred graves, by sad pine grove or moonlit water, had been Tobias dying from me, dying in perpetual, self-perpetuating flight from me, dying in a constantly re-enacted suicide and infidelity, fulfilling in imagination what blade and blow of the New Orleans *âme-de-boue* and plug-ugly had failed to fulfill in the old first flight from me, dying always into the beauty of Idea, into the nobility of Truth, dying into the undefiled whiteness of some self-image.

And crazily, there in the dawn grayness, it was as though I saw Tobias again moving toward me as he had in that room in the Saint Charles Hotel, that day of our marriage, moving at me white, naked, glimmering, setting his white foot down, smiling.

It was too awful. I did not know what I felt. I did not know what would happen.

Except that I knew that Tobias and I would be to each other as we were, for we were already reconciled. He had come to me as soon as word of the attempted suicide was out, before there had been any indication of his culpability, and telling me the facts, had said: "It seems that I have lost the capacity to do good to anyone. But at least I have come back to you, if you will have me. For you, dear little Manty, are all to me."

And he was all to me, and the reconciliation, which might have been joyful and renewing, was not. Despite the lies I told myself, I knew, deep in the unlit center of my heart, that it was not, that our tears were like tears spilled on desert sands, as quickly soaked up by circumstance and as irrelevant, that our caresses were a charade. I knew this because I knew that our reconciliation had been inevitable.

It was inevitable because, unless I could say to him, "Look, I fled from you once," I should always have to accept, in the blind logic of things, his own flights from me.

But I could not say it to him, or to myself.

So we fled, to Sill's Crossing, Kansas. The tight times after the money panic were better now, and Tobias got some law practice. He had a little money, anyway, money inherited from his mother, and so we were comfortable. And for a time he was so affectionate to me, so careful of my every whim and sentiment, that I could not but be happy—happy, except for those rare moments of blackness when I had the impulse, never acted upon, to outrage him in some way so awful that he would tear aside his mask of affection and consideration and show me the truth of disprizement, which I was so sure, at those moments at least, was there.

And at those moments I would think that he should have fled with Irene Colfell, would wish that he had, and would take some kind of sad solace, like the recognition of justice, in a vision I conjured up of Tobias and Irene Colfell, hand in hand, sailing through the highest light, totally fulfilled, bathed in glory, moving high over blue waters toward that land of joy and beauty, leaving me to die.

But he had not left me to die. He was with me, and was kind to me, and worked hard at the law, and worked hard, night after night, in his study, on a book that was to affirm the Idea in our History, so he said.

Then old Leonidas Sears died. He died, and his will cut Tobias, the only child, off without a penny. The reason was clearly stated: "—not for reason of libertinage or lack of filial duty, but because unaware of the obligation which wealth entails."

"Yes," Tobias said, "he means *The Great Betrayal*," and he folded the letter from Boston, from his father's lawyer. "Well," he said, and laughed shortly, "he ought to have waited to read my new book."

So Tobias went back to his law, and his work on the book, and was kind to me and sweet to the children, and all was as it had been before, for he had never been much concerned with money, and in a strange way I was happier because the old man had repudiated the son, for it seemed to make the son more completely mine, confirmed me in my possession.

But how blind I was! For subtly, how subtly by that repudiation, had old Sears drawn Tobias from me and delivered him into the hands of that exigent goddess: Success. Or was it into the hands of that other goddess, the twin goddess Failure, whose rites are even more exigent and mysterious? And so Tobias, even as he sat behind the closed door of his study anatomizing the evils of our time, became himself the child of the time. For one evening, not going into his study, he said: "I've recently become acquainted with a Mr. Lawson, a very well-informed person, not one with whom you might find too much in common but well informed about—about local developments. Now it seems that there will be a branch line of the railroad built down to Morden. There is a chance to get in, as Mr. Lawson puts it"—and Tobias' lip curled slightly in an irony not wholly at Mr. Lawson's expense—"to get in on the ground floor. This is, as Mr. Lawson puts it, inside stuff, and if—"

And if it had been true, we might have been rich. But it was not true, and we were poor, or at least, not as well off as we had been.

Then Tobias got the idea for a better kind of mechanism for tying sheaves of grain on a binder, and set up a little shop to work at night and on Sundays. He did not perfect the invention in time, though it once seemed that a big company might buy it. But he began to study mechanics seriously, now and then saying, with something of the same ironical twist to his mouth that I had discovered when he quoted Mr. Lawson about the ground floor, that all you had to do was settle on some simple thing the world needed and then go and invent it. By this time I knew that there was a bottle of whiskey in the top drawer of the desk in Tobias' office downtown.

That bottle, however, remained untouched for a time in Blair City after our son died. The death almost killed Tobias, and almost killed me, too. For weeks my body just hurt all over, and I couldn't help but remember that, long back on the steamboat coming up to St. Louis, Tobias and I had taken wine to lie down together, and so now I felt that somehow, somehow, a falsity and death had been in the very conception of our son. And perhaps Tobias felt the same thing, for I am sure that he didn't touch a drop for some months, those months in which he and I moved in a muffled, fog-bound world, glimpsing each other now and then as the fog parted, reaching out to each other in those brief intervals of visibility, then lost again in the muffledness. But when the bank closed—we had come to Blair City to establish a little bank—Tobias began again with the whiskey.

The next year we left Blair City. There was no reason to stay there, where all that remained of our boy was the hump of raw earth on the edge of the prairie, where the building Tobias had put up for his bank was having new letters in gold on the window to say it was a bank again, but not Tobias', and where the house we had bought was now occupied by a most poisonous woman who was effusively nice to me whenever we met, and with whom I suspected Tobias of having an affair.

So we moved to Kiowa City, and Tobias dabbled in wheat farming, some good years and some bad, and practiced his law, and at night shut himself up in his study to work at what I didn't know, if it was work at all. For a while I still used to go into the study after dinner and lay out the pens and see that the inkstand was full, but when I gave up the habit Tobias didn't seem to notice. He was never unkind to me, was even sometimes gay with me, for strange as it may seem, in those later years, a sort of humor emerged in his make-up, sometimes sardonic and sadly self-satiric, but sometimes gay. And he remained a handsome man, the ungrayed lock still falling over his fine brow in a rather poetic fashion, his skin still firm though gone a little sallow, his face composed, but with a little tic on the left cheek. He was courteous to everyone, was generally admired as a gentleman, and was much in demand as a speaker for high-school commencements, Fourth of July barbecues, and G.A.R. rallies. He even fooled with politics. Practically nobody in Kiowa City knew that he had written a book called *The Great Betrayal.*

Nobody, that is, except the man who, for a brief time, was Tobias' partner in wheat, Cameron Perkins, a man from Illinois who had gone East to college, who had pretensions to gentility and culture, but who had wound up, like Tobias, in Kansas. It was just at the end of the bad season that broke up their partnership that I found Mr. Perkins knew *The Great Betrayal.* When I came into the room that evening, I sensed immediately the rancor in the air, and Mr. Perkins, whose manners were usually a little excessive, gave a most sullen reply to my greeting and did not immediately rise from his chair. Then a moment later he did get up, mutter something about having to leave, and start toward the door.

That day I had been dusting the bookshelves and had not finished replacing the books, some of which were yet stacked on a chair near the door. Now one of the books apparently caught Mr. Perkins' eye, for he stopped and picked it up. It was *The Great Betrayal.*

He swung round to Tobias. "Yes," he said, with the air of putting a clincher in, "you used to be able to write such a book. Yeah, because you were rich. Yeah, when a man's rich he can talk about the Idea and sneer at trying to get a dollar and get ahead. Oh, yeah, I knew your kind, back when I was in Harvard College, too, just in case you forget I was, and your kind were all full of fine ideas."

He was literally shaking in a gust of rage, the hand holding the book shaking as with palsy. "Thingism! Thingism, indeed!" he said when his voice came back. "Yes, your father was rich, but my father" —he flung the book to the floor, "my father was dirt poor and was putting his eyes out stitching on leather to make harness in a hole the size of a closet, out in Illinois, and he was forty-odd years old and getting ready to die of consumption, and would have if the wagons going west hadn't taken a short cut through home, when they put a bridge in, and he made a little money and started a factory, and made some more money, and yeah, yeah, that's Thingism, not to die of consumption, to have a little luck and get ahead and feed your family and send your son back to Harvard College because everybody said I was smart—oh, yes, I was so smart—I was a smart little snot—and look at me now!"

The wrath had suddenly faded into something worse, much worse, into a beseeching, naked anguish as he stared at Tobias, discovering in that moment the envy and hatred he had hid from himself under emulation, under the imitated manner, the imitated dress, the imitated learning, the imitated aspiration, staring at Tobias as the representative of all those high-headed and indifferent ones, at poor Tobias, who was, after all, a failure, too.

So Cameron Perkins left us there in the poor room, by the light of a single oil lamp to combat the night, the winter, the chill of heart, coming up over the enormous prairie, and he went out to his success, for having stumbled on his hidden truth he could now have his success. He would be a Senator, great black hat, graying locks worn long in the Western fashion, a stitched leather belt, an incorruptible fighter against the "interests," against the "Street," against "those Moguls of the East who would convert our human hand into a machine, and our soul into a cipher of their bookkeeping."

He went out our door to his as yet unrevealed destiny, and Tobias stared after him for a moment, then quietly sat down in the chair by the table. For a moment he did not look at me, as though he could not bring himself to do so. Then he looked at me, and with the same air of forcing himself, spoke to me. "I suppose," he said, "he is right. It is a foolish book."

I said nothing, glancing sidewise at the book over there on the floor, the cover now askew from Cameron Perkins' violence.

"Yes," Tobias said, and rose, with the smile of twisted irony which was almost exaltation growing on his face. "Yes, Mr. Perkins is a true philosopher. He has found reality. It is Dough. It is the Buck. It is the Dollar."

I went over and picked up the book, not looking back at Tobias, and replaced it on the stack on the chair by the shelves. I did not do what I might have done. I might have gone to Tobias and taken his hand and said: *Whatever truth was in that book is in you now, Tobias, and I would live it with you.*

But I didn't.

So we lived on as best we could, moving once more, to Halesburg, Kansas, failing westward, you might say, scrimping and saving, wondering how life might have been different, feeling the bones begin to creak, not recognizing the face in the morning mirror, or recognizing it all too well and not being able to remember another face. And then I saw the story in the newspaper, the story about the death of Seth Parton.

Seth was important enough, and rich enough, to be a story when he died. He lived in Chicago, he had a great mansion, he had made a fortune in the wheat market, the bucket shop, a slashing cold-eyed speculator, "Parton the Plunger," the paper said. He had branched out into railroads, into banks, he had an empire, to use the phrase of the time, and no friends. He lived alone in the great mansion, childless, with his wife. His wife was, he had often said, his inspiration. If she had been a man, he had once told a reporter, she could have taken it away from Mr. Astor. The papers now quoted that. The widow, the sole heir, was living in strict seclusion in the mansion, with a few old servants.

And I had a vision of Miss Idell at the end of a big table, in a dark manorial room, Miss Idell enormously fat, that glorious peach-bloom skin over a bosom bulging out of silks and satins, bare arms big as hams and white as milk, white wrists fat as sausages and dripping diamond bracelets like glittering ice, the small fingers lost in the white fatness of hands, hands reaching out to drive a silver spoon, big as a spade, into a mountain of peach cobbler and whipped cream, mouth open already in the moon-face of fatness, from which two beautiful blue eyes were fixed, with maniacal intentness, on the approaching load of juice-dripping delight.

Yes, her leg-spreading days and nights were over, I thought with a dry, twisting pleasure, which was like pain.

They were over, no doubt, but there had not been, I was to discover, any pleasure of peach-cobbler and whipped cream to take their place. For when, something over a year later, I saw a picture of Miss Idell, she was thin as a match-stick, gaunt-faced, flat-chested, swathed in black, not a jewel showing, not even a cameo.

*She is old, she is so old,* something in me cried out, desperately. I remembered that she was a lot older than I, older than Seth, too. Then I became aware that I had not ever reckoned on time doing work on her. She had always stood in the shadow of my mind untouched, the blooming pink and whiteness, the softness of flesh like fruit sweet in its skin, the gay twitch of the rounded haunch when she had slapped it to define herself, at last, to me, the parted lips, the blowsy, immortal avidity.

But now, as I saw in the photograph, not the blowsy goddess of deep beds, but the gaunt woman swathed in black, I felt only an infinite deprivation and sadness. I simply wanted to cry. It was as though I had forgiven her something.

With mysterious tears in my eyes, I went on to read the story in the paper. Mrs. Parton had announced that all plans were now complete for the founding of the Seth Parton School of Theology. Her husband, she was quoted, had once studied for the ministry, but the tragedy of war had changed his life, and she knew that it would be his wish, as it was hers, that what worldly goods Divine Providence had seen fit to bestow upon them should be devoted to the study of the ways and the glorification of the works of that Providence. The story concluded by saying that Mrs. Parton had long been known for her rigorous piety.

So that was it. I thought of the two of them, Seth and Miss Idell, alone, childless, locked in their great, dark house, locked in their wealth, locked in the big bed in the dark, each locked in some remorseless, unfulfillable demand of the other, locked in the self, and I wondered which one had finally risen one night, leaving the other asleep like a used garment, risen and gone out, after the mumbling of paps, the slickness of flesh, the sharpness of fingernails, the wrenching of bodies, and wandered the halls and rooms of that dark house by the northern lake, thinking: *after the bed-breaking the age of peach-cobbler and whipped cream, after the bed-breaking the age of brandy and cigar, but is that all, is that all?*

Well, whoever it was that had first risen to wander the dark house, it was a joke on Miss Idell. Long ago, planning to take Seth Parton as her bed-breaker, she had prayed with him in gay cynicism. But in the end she had knelt with him by the side of the bed, to pray in earnest, and there had been no peach-cobbler and whipped cream, after all. I felt my mouth twist a little, in appreciation of that joke.

But maybe there had been, if not peach-cobbler, then peace.

And I felt myself cry out in myself, saying: *oh, it's not fair, it's not fair, she had my father, she had Seth, oh, it's not fair she should have peace, too!*

What peace of forgiveness I had felt on seeing the picture of her gone old and gaunt, had disappeared. I could hate her again, for her peace.

But that hate did not last long. It died, or sank down in some dark cubby of my being, and I was engrossed again in the struggle and satisfaction of ordinary days. I worked in the house. I saw my daughter marry and move to California. I did my duty by Tobias, night and day, and kept the peace, and in the afternoon when he comes back from his office he will smell of alcohol and will greet me with "Well a-day, my sweeting!" and kiss me on the cheek. My sweeting, my coney, my dilly—some name like that remembered from his reading of the old poets, now spoken with a tinge of histrionic emotion in the tone, but in the tone, too, some stain, tiny but spreading, of the poison of sad self-satire.

Or he will say nothing, will kiss me on the cheek, and when he kisses me, I will wonder if I am a ghost to him, if he sees through me like mist, as though I were only a kind of mist in his eyes, as when you are on the verge of weeping and things blur, and he sees beyond me, through me like the mist of unshed weeping, to the chair, the table, the vase of artificial flowers, and all the appurtenances of this spot to which the years have conducted.

Then, having kissed me, he will pass on toward the pantry, and I shall stand rigid, waiting for the clink of a glass. I shall not be able to go into the dark pantry and draw his head down to my bosom and say darling, darling, darling, till he can believe my voice and heart, and believe that there is no success and no failure, just the sweet possibility of being, of defining ourselves as ourselves, together beyond loneliness in some charity deeper than what is love because it is the dark depth of the fountain from which love leaps but as the flashing spray.

But no, it was not possible. We had failed westward. We were failing ageward. Well, we were not alone. We were in Halesburg, Kansas. Others had come there, too.

Early one afternoon, in the spring of 1888, I walked down the Main Street of Halesburg. It was only May, but heat was shimmering up from the dust in the street, from the corrugated iron awnings in front of the stores, and far off yonder, from the pale wheat that stretches in all directions out of town. At this season, under the shimmer, there is the sweet color of distance that wheat gets just as the green is going and the palest gold begins.

When I turned the corner off Main Street into Vermont Street (the cross streets in Halesburg are named for the New England states, but the town is so small that half the time we forget the names), I saw the figure there crouching on the sidewalk, right before me. It was the figure of an old Negro man, huddled down on the boards of the walk, just around the corner of Mr. Hobson's harness shop, where he could get some shade and, I presume, still solicit a passerby on Main Street.

I gave a start of surprise. For one thing I had almost stumbled on him. For another, he was a stranger, and members of that race were rare enough with us in Halesburg, a few families in town with sober and menial occupations, a few farmhands, once buffalo-skinners or spike-drivers, flotsam left from the dwindling of the heroic flood westward, and of course, Old Uncle Slop, who gathered the town garbage in old lard cans hauled in a cart with a blind mule, who lived in a tin shack of old lard cans beaten flat, out on the edge of the prairie, who reeked most horribly of cheap whiskey and his profession of scavenger. He had a peg-leg, his real one, he claimed without inspiring belief, having been shot off by a Rebel cannonball.

But this crouching man was a stranger, as I realized at the first instant. He was crouching on his hams with arms forward over the hunched-up knees and the head bowed forward to rest there in a posture of the last weariness and despair. The grizzled old head, with the kinks scruffed away here and there to reveal a patch of seamed scalp, appeared nothing more than an object, a thing, something dropped in indifference. In that instant I saw, too, how the shirt was tattered, and I saw on the half-exposed shoulders and upper back the neat herringbone pattern of old welts and scars on the gray-black flesh.

The man then lifted up his head, and I saw the face, the face wrinkled and marred with time and violence, the blood-shot, blinking eyes, yellow-filmed, and the ruinous cavity of the mouth when he stretched out a hand and said: "Please—Mistiss."

Even at that instant my brain was making denial of the identity of the creature. No, he was larger than this. No, there must be a thousand old Negroes left with scars on the shoulders. No, there is no resemblance in the face. No, he would never beg, would never say, "Mistiss," he would die first. No, he is dead already, dead in Louisiana, all those years ago.

But the assertion was there, deeper than denial, manifesting itself in the very denial, and as yet, only in the denial, and in the clutch of nausea in my stomach, and all the while my hand was fumbling in my reticule, fumbling desperately as though by thrusting into that gray-palmed, twisted, clawlike old hand whatever bits of metal or stained paper I had, I could buy something, absolution, oblivion, knowledge, meaning, identity. I found the coins and one bill, all I had left. I put them into the hand and fled.

I was fleeing from that creature who was, I was sure, Lieutenant Oliver Cromwell Jones, who was Rau-Ru.

Whatever those bushwhackers had done to him, whatever that scream from the ruin of the Boyd house had meant, here he was, pursuing me all those miles and years, like an old hound sniffing devotedly on that cold and fading scent, here at last worn out by the trail, and that weakness was more terrible than any last mustering of strength for vengeance for my old betrayal, my old crying out in that ravaged room, could have possibly been.

I got home as fast as I could. I stood in the deserted house, and fixed my gaze beseechingly on each common, life-worn and time-stained item, appealing to the commonness, the daylight, the dullness to deliver me. I thought of my husband down at his office, in the middle of just another afternoon in Halesburg. I thought of my daughter off in California. I thought of my son and the little hump —no, it would be a trough now—on the edge of the prairie, miles away at another town. Something like a wave broke over me, a physical, suffocating mass, green like a wave, shot through with light and dark, whirling me over, and I knew it was the past.

I stood in the middle of the floor, and that flood overwhelmed me, and I said the word *nigger* out loud, several times.

You know, I had not thought about that for years. I simply hadn't.


The next day I did not go downtown. I pretended some illness. I half planned to continue that stratagem. I could give Tobias a list of groceries each morning and the grocery could make delivery, for a small extra charge. Or Tobias could bring a parcel home. No, I couldn't make him do that—not with his face the way it always was when he had to walk down the street carrying a sack of groceries, his face stiff and averted.

But I went downtown myself the next day. I had to. I had to know if that creature would be there, crouching in his rags and scars, stretching forth his hand to me in whatever mission of terror it was that had brought him here.

It was awful, thinking each day as I approached the corner that today, certainly, he would look up and know me. I began to feel that he was withholding the confrontation just to torture me. I would approach, clutching the half-dollar, the dollar bill, ready to give him my bribe, my propitiation. Then I would flee, go home, stand in the heat-throbbing house, where the roof quivered under the fist of the Kansas sun, and I would say aloud, "I can't stand it, I simply can't!"

Nobody can bear to stand and wait for that instant when all their life is going to lift up the head and recognize them.

Nobody could stand it, I said. Something just had to happen, I said.

Something did happen. One evening as Tobias and I sat at our supper—bacon sandwiches and a salad of lettuce with bacon grease sprinkled on it and a little sugar and vinegar, a light supper, it was so hot even at sunset—he all at once looked up out of his silence and said, "You know, something funny happened today."

It had been so long since he had said such a thing to me, had begun to tell me some little event of the day, that I really couldn't believe my ears.

"I got ten dollars out of it, though," he said.

I said nothing.

"Yeah," he said, "all of ten dollars."

"Ten dollars is ten dollars," I said.

"It is precisely that," he said. He took a bite of the sandwich, a niggling bite, chewed the morsel. "Damn this heat," he said, and flicked his napkin at a fly that was cruising about his head.

"It's hot, all right," I said.

When he began to tell me, I had forgotten how the whole thing had started, how something funny had happened that day.

"A detective came to see me today," he said.

"A detective?"

"Pinkerton's," he said, "that's the big agency, one of their men. You'd never guess who it's about."

"No," I said, "I don't reckon I could."

"Well," he said, leaning back, with some trace of animation, some hint of the story-teller's art in his purposeful delay, "well—it's Uncle Slop."

"What's he done?" I asked.

"Detectives do other things than run down criminals, didn't you know that?" he demanded impatiently.

"Yes," I said, "I guess I knew that."

"Well, it's not anything Old Slop has done," Tobias said, "unless you can jail him for being the most shiftless and foul-smelling old coon the All-Father ever let live. Yes"—and he leaned at me—"did he ever come back and finish carrying off that trash from the cellar?"

"No," I said.

"Well, why did you pay him?" he demanded, fretfully. "You paid him fifty cents, didn't you? Do you think money grows on trees?"

I looked down at the plate. I thought I was going to cry.

"Yes," he was saying, "you have to pay that violet-scented son of Ethiope and then get down on your knees and beg him. It was for this we bled and died. Hooray for William Lloyd Garrison, Harriet Beecher Stowe, Abe Lincoln and me."

I simply couldn't bear to look up. So I just waited until he spoke again.

"I thought you wanted to hear about the detective," he said.

"I do," I said, and tried to brighten, "I really do—it's just this heat."

"Well," he said, "this detective came to me. He wanted to ask questions, what I knew about Old Slop. By the way, did you know his name was Lounberry?"

"No, I didn't know it."

"Well, I guess nobody else does. But it is this way, a man named Lounberry back in Chicago, and from the way the detective talks he must be pretty well fixed even if he is a colored man, is trying to trace down his father. He has spent a pile of money already, the detective says, and it looks like Uncle Slop may retire off the garbage wagon."

"That's interesting," I said, and tried to mean it.

"Well," he said, sourly, "interesting or not, that may leave an opening in the business world in Halesburg for some bright young man who wants to come West and grow up with the country."

There was nothing I could say to that. I could just sit there and feel some last green sprig of my soul wither inside me.

"Bleeding Kansas," he said.

Then: "Bloody Kansas."

He rose abruptly from his chair, said that he had to go work, got as far as the door and looked back. "It was a good supper, Manty," he said, and managed a smile.

"Thank you," I said, and wondered when he would come back to the pantry.

No, that wasn't what happened about Rau-Ru, but it was the building up to it. And the next two or three weeks went on as before. I was drawn out of the house each day, every day except Sunday, for I knew he wouldn't be there on Sundays. I didn't even wonder where he was on Sundays, any more than I wondered where he was at nights. Maybe he went under a stone, like a toad, maybe dissolved into air and darkness, and with dawn solidified again from that realm of unreality and dream to become again, for the sunlit hours, the sad, tyrannous fact on the street corner.

Then one day, it was a Monday, he wasn't there. I couldn't believe my eyes, and the absence filled me with a new panic. I had domesticated the fear of his presence, but this was new. This was a trick, the last trick to torture me.

Tobias came home. He sat down to his dinner. Then he said, again, how something funny had happened that day, saying: "You know that old colored man that's been hanging around town. You know, sort of begging?"

My heart stopped. Well, this was it. I had been right. It was a trick. All at once I was sure that that old man knew all, else why hadn't he been on the street corner, he had found out who I was, and that detective, he must have had some hand in it, else why had he sought out Tobias, and who was he working for, who were they who were after me, was Rau-Ru working for them, or was the detective working for Rau-Ru? It was all a crazy flight through my head, and I knew it was crazy. But I couldn't help it, and I knew —I just knew—that the old colored man had been to Tobias. He would start on Tobias now, and day by day the revelation would be made, and each day I would have to wonder what had come that day, until the last day.

"You have seen him around, haven't you?" Tobias demanded.

I said, yes, I had seen him.

"Well, he's dead," he said.

I suppose that my first reaction was the predictable one. I suppose that I felt relief, freedom from those months of apprehension, bribery, propitiation. The death of Rau-Ru had set me free.

But if that was the first reaction, it did not last long. It lasted so little that in my memory it is overwhelmed by the second, a sense of loss, ah, this was the last trick, the trick to torture me forever, for now I would never know!

Know what?

That was the worst of all, not even to know the question whose answer I would now never know: to have to live a question and not know even what the question is.

Tobias' voice was going on. That afternoon he had had a letter, he was saying, from Chicago, from a lawyer, asking him to get the signature of Harry Lounberry on certain documents having to do with a claim for back pension for, as Tobias said, about a million years.

"And a million dollars, by this time," Tobias said. "Just think, that old toot sorting garbage all these years and a fortune stacking up for him."

"I suppose he thought pensions were just something for white people," I heard my voice saying, mechanically.

"Maybe," Tobias said, "but this lawyer—he's got a big letterhead on his stationery, expensive paper, too, from a big firm, about ten names on it, yes, it's a firm made up of what are vulgarly known as big guns, real successes—well, this lawyer says that the signature is probably a formality, that the government records have been carefully investigated, that Mr. Joshua Lounberry, his client, is now convinced of the paternal relationship, has in his possession a medal for gallantry in action won by his father at Chickamauga, and the papers with it, made out to one Harry Lounberry, and left him by his mother—he doesn't remember his father, it looks like, if he ever saw him—well, anyway it looks like Uncle Slop not only gets the million dollars in pension, he gets a rich son, into the bargain. Good-bye, garbage."

He fell into an attitude of brooding. Then he lifted his head, and said: "And the son, Mr. Joshua Lounberry, gentleman of color and, no doubt, culture, he gets a hero in the family. But he better scrub him down."

"But Rau-Ru—" I began, then in panic, choked myself off.

"What did you say?" Tobias demanded, coming out of his meditation.

"I just sort of strangled," I said. "I was about to ask where that old Negro beggar came in?"

"I got off the story," Tobias said. "I just got to thinking about Uncle Slop, rags-to-riches, garbage barrels to bliss. Horatio Alger will have to take a back seat now."

"What about the old colored man?" I asked.

"Well," he said, "so I got the letter and went out to the shack Uncle Slop lives in. You never saw such a place. I mean, you never smelled such a place. You can't breathe, it is so awful, but I took a deep breath and held it. I said to myself that beggars can't be choosers, that Mr. Tobias Sears, attorney, of Halesburg, Kansas, owes $73.48 to the Straight Goods Grocery, and that if I survived the present experience I would see that it cost Mr. Joshua Lounberry a real fee, if he was such a damned rich colored man. So I went in."

He stopped, seemed about to sink into himself again.

"What about the old man?" I said.

"I went on in," he said. "It was pretty dark in there, and I could have used a machete to chop through the flies, and there was a noise like a buzz saw hitting a beech knot. All the flies of Kansas were gathered in plenary session. When my hearing had grown accustomed, I detected another sound. It turned out to be snoring. Uncle Slop was on his cot, totally intoxicated. At least, there was some circumstantial evidence to that effect that might stand up in court. An empty bottle was on his chest."

"But the old man?" I said.

"Oh, the old man," Tobias said. "Oh, yes, he was on the pallet in the corner. He was dead."

So that was where he had stayed at night, I thought, not under the stone like the toad, not dissolved into dark and air, like a dream.

"He must have died in the night," Tobias was saying, "but Old Slop did not know it. He had drunk himself to sleep the night before, it would seem—there was another bottle by the cot—and in the morning he must simply have reached for number-two soldier, not even saying good morning to his guest. So I had to break the news to him, as nearest and dearest of the deceased.

"Oh, yes," Tobias continued, after he had lingered on his little irony, "I had a busy day. I got the coroner to take the remains, I got

Slop sobered up, only to find that he cannot sign his name, so I got his mark truly made and witnessed, and got the papers back in the mails. With statement for services rendered.

"But it will not quite pay the grocery bill," Tobias said. "The traffic, I fear, will not quite bear that."

"What will they do with him?" I asked.

"Send a chariot of fire," Tobias said, "send a band of angels, translate him without death's bitterness direct to Chicago."

I heard him finish the sentence, then I said: "I don't mean Uncle Slop. I mean the old man."

"Oh, him," he said. "He—it—is down at the Bended Head Undertaking Parlor. But he—it—will not be undertaken. There is not need to undertake anything that has been long in Uncle Slop's society. It is pickled already. It will rest there tonight on a slab and on the morrow, in a box of classic pine, will be carried to the Potter's Field."

Tobias drank the last of his coffee, and set the cup down. "Potter's Field," he said, "but you know that old bugger came near paying for his own funeral. They found $26.32 on him."

He got up from the table.

"Yes," he said, "that must have been his take on the corner of Main Street and Vermont. It is a better corner than I had imagined. Perhaps," he said with an air of gallant gaiety, "I shall buy myself a tin cup and negotiate a concession for the same location."

He formally excused himself, and left the room. I sat there and reflected that I had at least paid for, or almost paid for, the funeral of Lieutenant Oliver Cromwell Jones, who was Rau-Ru.

The next night Tobias said that they had carted off the old booger early so as not to interfere with the day's work.

I asked if they had used the hearse.

"I said carted," Tobias said, "and I speak advisedly. I spoke, you might say, with benefit of counsel."

It was the middle of the next afternoon before I left the house again. I did not go downtown. I followed side streets out to the southwestern edge of town, where on a slight rise of ground, the cemetery was. There were a couple of stone gate-posts, each surmounted by a decomposing angel, and for some fifty feet on each side of the posts ran an iron fence, and beyond were the graves that Halesburg had been able to accumulate in the few years since the railroad had sloughed it off here on the way west. Over yonder, down the slope you could see the rails glistening westward.

It was like all those prairie cemeteries, bare ground, the humps and troughs, the parsimonious pieces of marble, brought from so far away, grit-scoured now in the prairie wind, the wooden slabs sun-cracked and grit-pitted, marking the bereavements of poverty, marble and wood both irrelevant under the enormousness of sky. I went on through the cemetery, toward the back, where the rise broke southward.

It was there, all right, the little new ridge of sun-baked earth patted tidily into shape by a professional spade. That professional tidiness of the spade was, however, the only tribute. Unless the stob stuck askew at the western end of the hump, with a scrap of paper tacked on it, was a tribute, too, to the humanity of the occasion. The paper said, in a pencil scribble: *Old man, colored, no name.*

I stood there a minute or two, looking down at the grave. Well, there it was, and I had seen it, for whatever reason I had had to see it: to prove to myself, perhaps, that it was dead, was under the earth, that I was free. But I kept on standing there, nagged somehow. Perhaps if I could drive a stake down six feet into the earth, through the old black heart, then I would be safe, then it could never rise and come again, then I would be free.

I looked around, all quarters of the compass, the glitter of the rails westward, the town yonder eastward, lost in the prairie and sky. I felt distance spinning away from me in all directions, fleeing me, drawing the very air away so that I would be in a vacuum and could not breathe. I took a gasp of breath, like a fish.

Over yonder, a little way, I saw the wreck of an old wheelbarrow, the wheel broken off, abandoned. I went to it, sat on it a few minutes, then dragged it nearer the grave, and sat down again.

He was dead, but I was not free.

*Free from what,* I thought, *from what?*

I did not know, but I did know that nobody had ever set me free. Nobody, not even my own father, leaving me to be snatched from his grave-side. Not Seth in the snowy woods. Not horrible old Mr. Marmaduke, who had waited in the dark outside the attic door, suffering in the deprived memory of his life, and who had given me a dollar the next day. Not Hamish Bond—oh, I could hate him for kindness!—giving me a scrap of paper in the end, offering me love in the end, but in the last end looking down from the cotton bale, in the light of the pine flares, looking me straight in the eye, to say what he did say, and jump. Not Tobias, in the blue and brass of the the liberator, who somehow had fled me, fled the very moment when I thought I might feel free, fleeing the moment of my truth. Not Rau-Ru, to whom I had fled but who had elected hate not love, and then, in the Boyd house had elected his own death instead of me, but who had been repudiated by death and sent to pursue me down all the years—to die here at last and in his death confirm that I should never be free.

I hated them all. No, that was not quite true. I was too weak, too spent, for hate.

I looked down at the hump of earth. I looked across the cemetery, and saw the roofs of the town, the railroad coal-chute and water tower, yellow, needing paint. I turned my head and looked over the prairie. I thought of other towns lost on the prairie. I thought of towns beyond, towns lost back in Kentucky, Louisiana, Ohio, Massachusetts, all the places I had seen and not seen, and I was about to burst into tears as I thought of people in those places, people going about their business, doing the best they could, living and dying together, and I thought how that was the averageness I had sought, the sweet commonness of life, the waking from the nightmare.

But if they were good, if they were good, I cried out, why hadn't they set me free?

And then, with perfect clarity, I saw the people I had known, the people who had not set me free—my father, all of them—and they were crouching there on the sun-baked earth, a little distance off, and they lifted their hands toward me in some humble beseeching. And then it wasn't only they, it was other people, too, how many I don't know, thousands, millions, black and white, crowding the prairie beyond, people so ghostly you saw right through them, but they were looking at me, and they held out their hands.

I blinked my eyes and they were gone, just the sun-dazzle of distance.

Well, I couldn't help them. Nobody had helped me. Nobody had set me free.

*Nobody can set you free,* I thought.

That thought was too awful to stay in my mind.

But the next thought was worse. It was so much worse that even when it was in my mind it was just a big, dark shape, a kind of dark overpoweringness that I couldn't bear to put words to, like the thought of dying.

But the words came: *except yourself.*

This was more awful than the thought of dying. It was more awful because it was the thought of living. *Except yourself, except yourself:* and that thought meant that I had to live and know that I was not the little Manty—oh, poor, dear, sweet little Manty—who had suffered and to whom things happened, to whom all the world had happened, with all its sweet injustice. Oh, no, that thought, by implying a will in me, implied that I had been involved in the very cause of the world, and whatever had happened corresponded in some crazy way with what was in me, and even if I didn't cause it, it somehow conformed to my will, and then somehow it could be said that I did cause it, and if it had not been for me then nothing would ever have happened as it happened, Hamish Bond would never have plunged from his cotton bale, Rau-Ru would never have waited in the ruined house while Jimmee pleaded with him to leave, Tobias would never have become the sad, sardonic slave of bottle and bitterness, the betrayer of women, and the thought of my involvement in all things was awful.

I huddled there on the ruined wheelbarrow, in the blazing sun of August in Kansas, and I shivered. I shivered because I felt that somebody had snatched me naked.

My lips were whispering the words: *except yourself.*

Then I thought that it doesn't do you any good to know a fact if you don't know how to go about doing anything about the fact. Then I remembered that occasion, years ago, when I had confessed my identity to Tobias, and how, suddenly, I had been freed into the fullness of joy. True, that joy had not endured, but it had come for its little space. With that reflection I felt a leap of the heart, of hope. I stood up abruptly from the wheelbarrow.

That was it. I would go home, and tonight after supper I would tell Tobias the truth, after all the lies. My blood fired up at the thought.

*The truth:* I thought in my excitement.

But then I thought: *what truth?*

I might try to tell Tobias something, and he would look down at me and see the woman who had lived in his house and lain down by his side for nearly a quarter of a century, and no fact I could tell would mean anything.

Suppose I said to him: "Look—I went to Rau-Ru!"

And he would stare at me, faintly puzzled, and say: "Rau-Ru—what's Rau-Ru?"

Oh, what was Rau-Ru?

I looked down at the grave at my feet now, and knew that Rau-Ru, whatever he had been or was, was not here. It was not the grave of Rau-Ru. No, just another old colored man, nameless, with scars on his back from the old times of terror.

It had only been the scars I recognized. But I had never seen the scars of Rau-Ru's back. I had asked to see them, yes, but he had struck me across the mouth. I had only dreamed the scars, and this wasn't Rau-Ru, simply an image I had called up, as it were, out of the darkness of time, to fulfill some need I had now, in my age, in Halesburg, Kansas.

Oh, did you always need your old nightmares? Did you need them to hide something? To hide what? To hide the common light of day? To hide, I knew with an ebbing of the heart, my sad humanness.

I looked across the prairie, vacant now, and thought how people had their own humanness, and therefore had to have their nightmares, and the world had its nightmare, and history had its nightmare, but people put things out of the mind and went on living.

It was getting on in the afternoon. I moved out of the cemetery and off toward town, and home. I had never felt so old. But I felt quiet, too. Well, that was something, to be quiet at last.

But before I left I had leaned over and torn the scrap of paper off the stob at the grave-head, and let it go, and the wind had taken it off across the prairie.

Tobias did not get home at the usual time. It was dark when he did.

"Well," he announced, calling from the dark hall, some glint of excitement in his voice, "well, this is the day!"

I thought: *He is drunk. He has now begun to drink himself really drunk.*

He came to the door. He was stripped to the waist. One eye was bruised.

So I said: "What's the matter?"

"Nothing's the matter," he said, "it's just I have been off drinking with a strange nigger."

I didn't say a word. I just turned my back on him and went stiff all over.

But he grabbed me by the shoulder, and swung me around, and said, "Hey!" and kissed me right on the mouth, whiskey smell and all.

Before I could jerk away, he said, "Take it easy, I wasn't just drinking with a strange nigger for fun, I was making money, I was bringing much business to Halesburg, I was—"

"You are drunk," I said, and sat down in the rocking chair by the table.

He reached into his pocket. "I wasn't too drunk to make this," he said, and flung a bill into my lap. "Open it," he said, "it will thaw the stoniest heart."

I opened it. It was a bill for $100.

"With that," he said, "you can pay the Straight Goods Grocery."

I flung the bill to the table. "You're drunk," I said.

"I am not drunk," he said. "I affirm it, but I also affirm that a man has to drink something if he is going to help give Uncle Slop a bath."

I was about to say something, but that preposterousness simply stopped me.

"Yes," he said, "and I am not half-naked because I am drunk either. I left my coat, shirt, tie, and undershirt on the back porch, because they smell slightly of Uncle Slop and his domicile. Perhaps I do, too. Do I smell bad, my darling, my dearest chuck?"

"You have a black eye," I said.

"It is a badge of honor," he said, "and I flaunt it. I will come to that in time, after the bath of Uncle Slop. No, I'll start at the beginning. The bath is the climax."

I was looking at the carpet.

"Don't you want to hear about it?" he asked.

"Naturally," I said, not looking up. "When your husband comes home drunk and half-naked and with an eye bruised from a public brawl, it is only natural to have some curiosity."

"Speaking of baths," he said, "is there any hot water in the range? Couldn't you fix me a bath?"

"Fix it yourself," I said.

"Sure," he said, with utmost cheerfulness, a tone that I hadn't heard in all the years, and it made me look up. He was smiling down at me, and he didn't look drunk, not really, just gay in a peculiar way.

To my surprise I stood up and said, "No, I'll fix it." I said it grudgingly, perhaps, with some sense of being put upon, perhaps, but I said it.

"That's my good little Manty," he said, and tried to kiss me on top of the head.

"Don't call me that," I said in sudden bitterness, and jerked back. But I went on to fix the bath.

"Come sit by the tub," he called, "and I'll tell you all about it."

Early in the afternoon, shortly after the arrival of the afternoon train from the East, a strange man had come to Tobias' office, colored, dignified beyond the apparent thirty-odd years, soberly dressed, wearing a panama hat. It was Mr. Joshua Lounberry, and he had come for his father. He had, he said, taken a double room at the local hotel, Biggers Hotel, would bring his father there for the night, and take the morning train out.

"Which proved," Tobias said, "that Mr. Lounberry did not know Mr. Biggers.

"But," Tobias continued thoughtfully, lolling back, rubbing soap on his chest, "he knew him better than I calculated at first, for when I tried to hint at how things were he interrupted me and said, 'I think I understand you, Mr. Sears. When I asked for a room I noticed some hesitancy on the part of the clerk and so I laid a twenty-dollar bill on the desk, and the clerk looked over at a big old man— a large old gentleman—with a red mustache, and that gentleman gave a sort of a nod.

"'And the place they put me in, a kind of a storeroom, is of such an order that they may not mind admitting my poor father. They can send up some kind of tub and hot water for his bath, and I shall buy new clothes for him. We can go in the back way.'

"But he only had part of the score," Tobias said. "I almost told him that the back way and the front way are the same thing in a town like Halesburg, everybody knows who goes in and out, even of the windows, and if Uncle Slop got inside that hotel I should be surprised. Furthermore, I almost told him that once Mr. Biggers found out what was going on, he would have other grounds for disgruntlement, for it being he owns that tract of land where Uncle Slop's shack is, and Uncle Slop pays him a dollar a week for the last thousand years, Mr. Biggers will take the whole project as a conspiracy against his solvency. And him owning half the county. So I asked him if Mr. Biggers knew what was afoot, and if he had made arrangements with Mr. Biggers, and he said, no, in such matters he had sometimes found it expedient to confront interested parties with a *fait accompli.*"

Tobias applied more soap. "It is strange," he said, "to hear a colored man in Halesburg using French. It doesn't seem so strange while you're with him," he added, "it's just so strange when you think about it." Then, with more soap, he said: "Mr. Lounberry must be a very well off son of Ethiope."

"Did he get his father?" I asked.

"Yes," Tobias said, "and the funny thing, it was the father who was skittish. It was almost as though it was the son who smelled like downwind from the hog pen. Old Slop was sitting outside the shack when we rode up. We had rented a rig in town, I forgot to say, and we rode up and Uncle Slop was mending some harness for the garbage wagon.

"We stopped about thirty feet off, and I indicated the father to the son.

"I must say I had had some morbid curiosity about what the expression was going to be on the face of Sonny-boy when he saw Poppa. But when I said, 'There he is, Mr. Lounberry,' he just took one long look, then turned to me. 'You know,' he said, just as quietly and confidentially as if I had been the friend of his youth, and privy to all secrets, 'you know, Mr. Sears, I have waited a long time for this moment. That is my father, and I have sought him for years to do him honor.'

"Perhaps it was *my* face that was a little surprised," Tobias said, "for he said then, 'You see, Mr. Sears, I am a believing man, and I would try to live what I believe.'

"With that, he got out of the rig and walked over to Old Slop. He took him by the hand, and called him Father, and kissed him on the forehead. The detective must have already explained something to Old Slop, and I had to when I got the signatures—or marks, rather —on the pension papers, but this now was not hearsay, this was the real thing.

"I thought it was going to be Uncle Slop who would faint. But he pulled himself together. He sidled off a little, and looked at his new relative with dire suspicion, then sort of wiped the kiss off his forehead. But Mr. Lounberry, Jr., finally got him settled back down on the nail-keg by the door, where the aroma was juiciest and the flies most prosperous, and Mr. Lounberry, Jr., settled on an old cracker box, fanning himself with his panama hat and they talked it out. That fanning was Mr. Lounberry, Jr.'s only concession to human frailty and the smell.

"I was waiting in the surrey, and finally they came over together, and climbed in the back, and I drove them to town, creating, no doubt, a reasonable amount of humorous comment on Main Street as a Jehu to coons! I will not maintain that I was above a certain embarrassment."

I thought how his face must have been stiff and distant above the leers of Main Street, the same thing as when he had to carry a parcel, but worse.

So much worse that by the time they got to the hotel, something must have been really piling up inside him, waiting for provocation. They got to the hotel, followed by several of the town loafers and some loose boys. Tobias went into the hotel to speak to Mr. Biggers, knowing Mr. Biggers the way you know anybody in a town like Halesburg, and having done a little legal work for him. Mr. Biggers came out, apparently quite full of himself as usual, quite "Big-Mouth Biggers," but even so he might have been persuaded to let the back stair be used if there hadn't been that gallery of spectators waiting.

So he began to bluster. He said that Uncle Slop owed him some back rent. At that Mr. Lounberry, Jr., took out his wallet, asked how much, Mr. Biggers said five dollars, Uncle Slop said two, Mr. Lounberry, Jr., gave the five. Then when the question of the back stairs was raised again very respectfully by Mr. Lounberry, Jr., Mr. Biggers got offensive in his language.

Mr. Lounberry remained quite calm, and according to Tobias it was this calmness that kept Mr. Biggers going. He had to make a dent. But the only dent, when it came, was worse than no dent. Mr. Lounberry simply said, as calm as could be, that since the accommodations did not suit his needs, would Mr. Biggers please have his bag sent down. Mr. Biggers said for him to get it himself, which Mr. Lounberry declined to do, saying he did not feel he could with self-respect go into the establishment. Mr. Biggers said it could rot in there then, and Mr. Lounberry said that legal action might recover the property.

It must have been the phrase *legal action* that started Mr. Biggers on Tobias. He swung to him, and demanded had he put this coon up to such talk. Tobias said, no, but it struck him that the man might have his valise, he had paid his bill in advance, and twice as much as was normal, plus a twenty-dollar bribe.

"Bribe!" Mr. Biggers yelled, and asked did Tobias believe that. He dared him to take a nigger's word against his.

Tobias said he believed Mr. Lounberry's word. He called him Mr. Lounberry.

"You know," he said to me, telling it, "I was just stepping into it. Everything was simply drawing me on. I didn't want to get mixed up in it, but I simply couldn't help myself."

Anyway, Mr. Biggers said it didn't matter what Tobias believed; he was just a no-good lawyer—he intended to take his business away from him, anyway—and a drunkard to boot.

"Well," Tobias said to me, quietly, "that was it. You are in Halesburg and you have to live with people like that. You even have to hope to get a little of their business, to scratch along. But I didn't think, not the way I had been thinking for years. So I just said it."

Then he fell silent. Then he turned to me. "Get me some more hot water, please, Manty."

I got it, and poured it in.

"What did you say?" I asked, feeling the question portentous, fearful of the answer.

"To tell the truth," Tobias said, "I guess I was sort of surprised at first. I guess I must have gaped. Then I saw the colored man looking at me. It was a look that said, plain as day: *you, too.*

So I was one who had to take it, too.

So I just burst out. I heard my voice, and it was talking. I was calm, and I heard my voice off there, and I enjoyed hearing it.

"What did you say?" I asked.

"I said I believed what Mr. Lounberry said. I said that Mr. Biggers should feel honored to have Uncle Slop in the house, for I knew it to be a fact that Uncle Slop, even if he did haul garbage, had been honored by the Government of the United States for gallantry in battle at a time when, to my certain knowledge, and to the certain knowledge of the entire town, Mr. Biggers had been a bounty-jumper in Indiana, jumping west to avoid gunpowder, and if the town agreed to keep silent it was because he was rich, just as they had agreed to keep silent on the fact that he had got his start with brothels along the railroad a hundred miles east. Well"—and Tobias touched his eye—"it was about then he hit me. I was surprised he had waited so long."

I waited, while Tobias thought a minute.

Then he said, "I tried to hit him back. I did hit him, as a matter of fact, but it probably didn't jolt him much." He stopped a second, then went on: "Yeah, two old fellows swapping punches. Maybe we ought to have kicked and clawed a little bit, instead. It might have been more effective."

"What happened?"

"Oh, they grabbed us and pulled us apart," he said, "and maybe it was just as well. But you know, I hadn't even had a drink all day, but suddenly I felt like a million dollars.

"Well, things just sort of petered out then. The valise got thrown out the back window in the alley. Then in a very loud voice I told Mr. Lounberry to throw a quarter for a tip in the alley in the spot where the valise hit, that the clerk could come get it after dark. If Mr. Biggers hadn't beat him to it. And somebody laughed at that, so I felt even better.

"Then I went over and swore out a warrant for assault against Mr. Biggers, not that it'll do much good, but it'll cost him a little money to hire a lawyer, then I took my client and his aged father to my office and broke the seal on a bottle of whiskey and we drank some, then I put the bottle in my pocket, and we improved retail business in Halesburg. We bought a tub. We bought towels and soap and a scrub-brush and eau de Cologne. We bought clothes for the aged father, a pair of shoes—even if we only needed the left one—red necktie, silk handkerchief, every damned thing. We bought out the town. We had a procession of kids with us, and Uncle Slop would sit in the rig out front while we went in and bought things. We'd put that batch in the rig and go to another store, and Slop would follow with the rig.

"Then Mr. Lounberry and I climbed in, he in front with Father, me in back with the plunder, and we went home. We went home and boiled out Father. It took quite a time, heating water up in an old iron pot, and one dousing would not do. But we cleaned up Father. We certainly did, and we finished off with eau de Cologne. We had also finished the red-eye by then. So I came on home. And I can't unkink somehow, I feel so steamed up."

I got up and stood by the tub.

"Do you think I am a drunkard?" Tobias asked me.

I pretended not to hear him. "I'll go fix some supper," I said.

"Do you think I am a drunkard?" he asked again.

I looked down at him, and saw the middle-aged man lying back in the big tin tub, soapy water over him except for sharp knees and bony chest, and saw the face, white and scrubbed and, somehow, young, looking up at me with its question. I thought, all at once, of that afternoon, how I had seen the thousands of ghostly faces on the prairie, forms and faces thin as air and light through them, but all looking at me and beseeching me.

"I don't think you are a drunkard, Tobias," I said, "but I have been afraid that you might become one."

"I guess I had better dress," he said, after a moment, and dripping and cranky, his body glistening in the light of the tin lamp of the bathroom, he rose from the tub.

I went to the kitchen, lighted a lamp, and began to get something ready for supper. I didn't really know what I felt, it was so strange. I tried in my mind to see what had happened. Maybe it would finish us off in Halesburg. Well, we would go somewhere else, somewhere down the railroad, on west.

But I couldn't feel desperate or bad even about that. Maybe tomorrow I would, but not now. I just felt a little tired, and somehow, quiet.

I thought of Tobias in the livery-stable rig driving down Main Street toward the Biggers Hotel, toward the blow-up of our life here, his face stiff above the leers of the street corner. Poor Tobias, all these years nursing his hurt and deprivation—no, he couldn't even bear to carry a sack of groceries—and now a Jehu to coons.

But even that might not have made him blow up, not even the abuse of Mr. Biggers—he might have wanly laughed that off, a friendly joke. But that colored man had looked pityingly at him, with pitying, fraternal recognition: *you have to take it, too.*

And that was too much, after all the years downward, to be brother to a coon.

Yes, Tobias had been, long ago, the liberator, the bearer of freedom, and had risked his very life in heroism. But that was different, he had not been involved in that commonality of weakness and rejection, he had merely leaned down from his height, had inclined his white hieratic head that glimmered like a statue.

But this was different, and I smiled wryly in my mind: the hurt vanity of defeat, now in the last attempt to deny kinship with the coon, had struck out to defend the coon.

Brother to coons, after all, by accident not design, but I don't suppose it matters how it came about, just so it came, just so Tobias, himself somehow suddenly gay and free and young again, had ridden off in triumph through the town, looting like a conqueror, loading the chariot, riding off to the ritual in the gloaming, the winking fire, the steaming tub, the bottle passing gravely from hand to hand, mouth to mouth, the application of suds, the scrubbing of the scaly, smelly old black hide, the dousing with eau de Cologne, the honoring of Father, the redeeming of the past and all the vanity of heroism.

I sat down, all at once, by the kitchen table. My knees had simply given out under me. I laid my head on the edge of the table. I thought of my father, how he had betrayed me and how I hated him. I thought of Old Slop, how he had abandoned his son, going West, to freedom, to success, to gather garbage. And then I saw a picture of him sitting in a fine room in Chicago, in fine clothes, a red necktie hanging under his black, wizened face, being honored. And I suffered a dry, gnawing envy of Mr. Lounberry, who could honor his father.

I envied Mr. Lounberry, not merely because he could honor his father, but because he could honor the father who had rejected him. Yes, that was the thing to envy. With that I felt some relaxing in my soul. Maybe that could be learned, if I tried. Maybe Mr. Lounberry could teach me, if I tried.

Then, all at once, like catching the glint of a piece of thistledown drifting in high sunlight, I knew that my father had loved me. I knew it, as though my desire to honor him had brought me the knowledge. I heard again how Miss Idell had said it to me, but now it was different, now I believed her, and I knew what she would have told me, that day, had I permitted it.

She would have told me that it was, in a funny, sad, confused way, his very love for me which made my father leave me to be seized at his grave-side. He had not been able to make the papers out, or the will, that would declare me less than what he had led me to believe I was, his true and beloved child; he was afraid to hurt me, was seeking, hopefully, some way to send me North, keep me North, see me established in a land far away, and he had not believed that he would die, soon, at least, certainly not in the bed of love and pleasure. No, he hadn't betrayed me. Perhaps lying even in that bed of love and pleasure, after the striving and satisfaction, his mind had come back to me, and looking up at the ceiling, that yellow hair loose over his arm, he had told Miss Idell what was in his heart.

Yes, he would have had to tell somebody, and she had been, as she put it, nice to him.

I kept my head on the edge of the table, and my eyes closed. I had to get used to things. I couldn't move yet. I had to let so much of the old years slip away. Maybe they wouldn't slip. But I had to wait.

Then Tobias came in the door, and I got my head up just in time. He was pretty hungry, he said. So we ate. We ate without talking, then Tobias leaned back and said, "Oh, I forgot to tell you one thing about my client. He is an inventor. He was a teacher in some school for Negroes down South. He invented something. That's how he got his start. We got pretty chummy this afternoon, and he told me all about himself."

"Yes," I said distantly, still wrapped in my own feelings.

"You'd never guess what he invented."

"No, I couldn't."

"A new kind of hair-curler," Tobias said.

"Oh," I said, "you mean to take out the—" and I caught myself hesitating on the word *kinks*, thinking somewhere in the deep of my mind of my own crisp hair, then wondering how many times in my life I must have hesitated on that word, on my secret, then aware, all at once, that somehow I didn't have to hesitate any more, I could just say it. And so I said it, starting over: "You mean to take the kinks out?"

"No," he said, "to put 'em in. It is a curler to put kinks in white folks' hair. That's what Mr. Lounberry—he's really Dr. Lounberry—said, and I thought he would die laughing. Of course, we were sort of on the bottle, by then."

Tobias got up. "That's what I always said," he said, "just settle on some simple thing everybody needs and then go invent it. Get in on the ground floor. Grow up with the country."

At those old phrases, my heart contracted, and I looked up at him for the twist of sad, self-satire on his face. But it wasn't there. He was grinning.

eard him on the back porch, prob-
d clothes. I rose and went to his

inkwell. I laid the two pens ready.

l washing the dishes, I heard him
ng room, and without lighting the
stand my feeling. I was tired, I
quiet, but it wasn't the kind of
on leaving the grave of the name-
not Lieutenant Oliver Cromwell

tness, sweet with a steady hope,

he study. He came to the door.
for?" he asked.

k tonight. I'm too steamed up,
and school is let out."
hands on my shoulders.

oonlight night. Do you want to

ecause my chest was just filling
vful and too beautiful.
ck," he was saying. "You don't
Manty?"
"don't ever call me poor little

ou don't think it's too late, do

tried to, but maybe it wasn't
s chest, and the tears running
ll the old shadows of our lives
me on the back while he said

# $\mathcal{V}$OICES OF THE $\mathcal{S}$OUTH

Erskine Caldwell, *Poor Fool*

Fred Chappell, *The Gaudy Place*

Ellen Douglas, *The Rock Cried Out*

George Garrett, *Do, Lord, Remember Me*

Willie Morris, *The Last of the Southern Girls*

Lee Smith, *The Last Day the Dogbushes Bloomed*

Elizabeth Spencer, *The Voice at the Back Door*

Peter Taylor, *The Widows of Thornton*

Robert Penn Warren, *Band of Angels*

Joan Williams, *The Morning and the Evening*